The thing about Erick Holmberg's marvelously original, intricately plotted, and brave debut novel, Regna Born, is this: once you start it, you won't be able to put it down. A compulsively readable, surprising book, Holmberg has created an everyman in Gabriel Kelly, who just happens to be a sorcerer on his way up—or down if he can't figure out the riddle at the heart of a murder. Regna Born is also a book that defies classification, a hybrid of genres that are more than the sum of their parts—at the core is a gay urban fantasy, full of magic and mystery and spectacle and a love story as old and familiar as storytelling itself. I adore this book, and so will you.

David Samuel Levinson, author of *Tell Me How This Ends Well*

REGNA BORN

The Regna Sagas, Book One

Erick Holmberg

A NineStar Press Publication
www.ninestarpress.com

Regna Born

Content Warning:

This book contains depictions of historical Southern US slavery.

To John Minnock, a dear friend, singer, and composer, gone too soon.

Chapter One

adept / ˈæd.ɛpt/, /əˈdɛpt/

noun

1. The colloquial name of the human subspecies Homo sapiens psychica, born with enhanced senses, strength, and varying degrees of telepathy and telekinesis.

—National Intelligence Strategy White Paper: Top Secret (TS): Release of this document will cause severe damage to the security of the United States—Adept Assets

THE RICH GREEN jungle could be the Garden of Eden. Too bad it's just as full of snakes.

The journey was an endless cascade of rickety bridges and muddy craters, making travel in Myanmar dangerous, especially in remote areas. And this is the most remote of the remote areas.

Armies of mosquitoes cluster in clouds so thick they absorb the sunshine like miniature black holes. They stalk Gabriel in synchronized precision yet ignore the miners because the smorgasbord his unique blood presents is too enticing. A symphony of exotic birds and mournful crickets serenade predators and prey alike.

Which one is he?

He blocks the relentless sun with his hand and grins, recalling a quote from Rudyard Kipling: *Only mad dogs and Englishmen go out in the midday sun.* His Londoner father would be a shocking lobster color by now.

Gabriel's sense of smell, enhanced by the wolf bond, struggles to decipher the onslaught of sensations in the heart of the jungle. Rich chocolate from the wild orchids and the subtle honey of cherry blossoms suffuse the thick, humid air. The scent of metal and oil from the jaws of the mine conspire to wipe this sweet fragrance from the face of the earth.

As he draws nearer, the clamor of machinery drowns out the jungle's orchestra. The air pressure drops, and the siren song of gemstones laden with ley energy rushes to Gabriel's head. The tug grows stronger, threatening to pull him into the ground. He closes his mind because he can't risk getting ley drunk. Finally, he emerges into a stadium-sized pit of ravaged earth.

A guard carrying an ancient rifle and a scowl stands under a crooked sign written in English. "Welcome to Ruby Land," it proclaims in blood-red letters set against a white background. The mine is new, but the sign's battered lettering silently flakes away.

Tall and taciturn, the foreman's question-mark posture proves he lives in a world not made for the different. Eyes that refuse to meet

Gabriel's dart about looking for a safe harbor but find none.

"They'll meet you at the shrine." The foreman jerks his head to the north. "This way."

He grunts past the guard and leads them down a narrow, rocky path. They walk in silence, broken only by Gabriel's dog, Zuko, sneezing from the dust kicked up in the foreman's wake. Zuko's massive paws carry his lean one hundred pounds silently behind Gabriel, his snow-white coat oddly untouched by the dust and mud. Despite his size, Zuko's floppy ears and Snoopy-like face put everyone at ease. But if he were to bare all the gleaming white teeth Gabriel dutifully brushes each day, no one would be at ease.

Gabriel wipes sweat away from his eyes and takes in his surroundings. "Has anyone else been here?"

"No," comes the quick reply. "You're the first."

Gabriel smiles when he detects no lie in the foreman's answer.

Flowers cover the Buddhist shrine where he'll meet the latest warlord laying claim to this profitable hole in the earth. He's led to an open vestibule with a bird's-eye view of the vast countryside. If they have a bird's-eye view of the countryside, who has a bird's-eye view of them?

"Wait here," the foreman says. "It won't be long."

The distant rumble of a convoy snaps the foreman's head to attention. He reaches for his gun, and beads of sweat break out on his forehead. For a long moment, his ragged breathing joins the rhapsodizing birds and crickets.

"It's them," Gabriel says, smashing a mosquito against his forearm. Without a word of goodbye, the foreman turns and scurries away.

Deep in the outback, Gabriel expects a ragtag group fighting for independence, but a high-tech armada of bulletproof glass and modern weaponry barrels into view. They drive and park in that careless way that says they drive and park however they please. *Like cops*, and a shiver runs up his spine. In the middle of the caravan, the doors of a black four-door SUV open in synchronized precision, and the occupants, dressed all in black, march toward him with ramrod-straight posture.

Two men and one woman carry Kalashnikov rifles in the low-ready position and surround an older man in a protective cocoon. Behind them, two men carry a large wooden trunk. Their stance indicates a threat, so Gabriel sweeps the area. This highly trained squadron can't be mercenaries because they radiate military precision. Their conspicuous lack of uniforms means that whatever happens here will vanish without a trace.

When the man in the center enters the shrine, he makes eye contact with a slight tilt of his head. He's wiry and vascular in a way only triathletes and career military are. His gray hair is cut regulation short, and his teeth are shark white.

Gabriel wishes he didn't sweat so easily. He gingerly perches on the small wooden chair the leader offers him. Given his size, it feels as if he's stolen it from a six-year-old. *Please, don't let the fragile thing collapse.* A rickety table adorned with a single bright yellow flower sits in the center.

The leader sits opposite him, reminding Gabriel of a king on a throne. At his nod, two of the soldiers open the trunk, revealing the freshly unearthed rubies Gabriel's crossed the world to buy. Their jagged red edges tell the story of a violent ejection from the earth. Gabriel feels the urge to whisper them an apology.

"May I see one?" Gabriel's Burmese is tinged with a British accent. He wants to throw them off their game, which appears to work when the four exchange furtive glances. He opens his mind to one of the soldiers and touches the language skills part of his brain. As long as Gabriel is within close proximity of the man, he'll be able to speak Burmese.

The leader smiles. "Do you have the money?"

Another soldier, the one with a nervous eye twitch, grips her gun and stares at Gabriel. He picks up an image of her killing him and taking his money. In her grisly fantasy, she's applauded by her superiors and promoted. Gabriel watches the bloody scene replay in her mind, a movie trailer stuck on repeat.

A thrumming sound vibrates deep in Zuko's chest, and the leader's honor guard steps back. A grave warning emerges from the lizard part of their brains. *Run*, it says. An apex predator is on the hunt. The crickets and birds swallow their songs, and their symphony abruptly stops. Every leaf in the teeming forest stills, and the air goes silent.

The leader meets Zuko's gaze and doesn't look away.

Gabriel chuckles. "He's just irritable about not getting his usual food." At Gabriel's small gesture, Zuko submerges his face in his huge front paws. The crickets are the first to resume their song, and the birds quickly harmonize.

Gabriel gathers his adept talent when a childhood memory forces its way to the surface. Flashes of a blaring siren in the rearview and the taste of his mother's terror fills him. She turns on the interior lights reflexively, despite the sun gleaming off her gold Moroccan bracelets, and calms his fears with a deft touch on his mind. The cop lumbers toward their Mercedes; he's huge in a way that says pro wrestler gone to pot. Mirrored sunglasses can't hide the coiled violence that lies behind them. Steroids practically seep out of his pores.

The bare skin of his mother's delicate brown hands, glued at ten and two o'clock on the steering wheel, glistens in the sunlight. A twelve-year-old Gabriel withers at the onslaught of the cop's glare.

"Get out of—" The policeman stands back and smiles. "—next time, be more careful when entering the rotary, ma'am."

When they're back on the road, Gabriel asks, "I'll be able to do that one day, right?"

His mother hides the uncertainty in her mind, but she can't hide it in her face.

Gabriel shakes off the memory and returns to the stifling humidity of the jungle.

"Calm down."

Gabriel sends the thought into the woman's mind with as much authority as he can muster. The young soldier's head briefly leans back, and her eyes search for the leader, but her superior's eyes never leave Gabriel.

Have I just agitated her and made things worse?

Zuko's lips pull back from his teeth, and the soldier raises her gun. But then her iron grip relaxes, and the gun drops to her waist. Gabriel swallows hard and takes a deep breath while Zuko continues sitting with his ears perked.

"Hard United States currency as agreed," Gabriel says, pitching his voice at a volume he prays is commanding. "You know my reputation. I didn't come all this way to chat."

The leader nods and spares Zuko a long glance. The tiniest smile breaks the pronounced lines around his mouth.

"Come," he says in English and pats his legs with his hands. Anxious for canine attention, he reaches his arms out, almost in longing, but Zuko doesn't move. He doesn't even blink. The leader utters a number, still looking at the impassive dog. Gabriel lets it hang unanswered in the air as they sit and listen to the jungle's song.

"That number is much bigger than the trunk," Gabriel says, batting away a cloud of mosquitoes. In the empty silence, he sweeps his gaze over all four and rests his eyes on the rubies.

The plain-clothed military commander frowns, and his gaze narrows. He gestures toward the trunk and beckons Gabriel forward. Gabriel expected some kind of safe designed to look like luggage, but it's a common wooden chest such as found in a million attics.

Who are they that they're so unconcerned with basic security?

Gabriel plunges his hand inside, almost to the bottom, and withdraws a ruby. He scrapes it on the small table and examines it. If it leaves behind any red residue, it's fake. Feeling every eye on him, Gabriel studies the trail the stone leaves behind while the leader tips forward in his chair, holding his breath. Next, Gabriel removes a loupe from his pocket and examines the ruby. It's beautiful in all its imperfections, as with the best people. After a beat, Gabriel nods his assent, and the leader exhales.

One of the soldiers snaps his head to the right, catching Gabriel's attention.

"Where's the sniper?" The question rings so loudly in the soldier's mind it drills into Gabriel's temple.

A sniper? But why?

There's little defense against a sniper, and Gabriel wishes he'd left Zuko home. Holding the ley-rich ruby in his broad, thick-fingered hands, he siphons its energy to bolster his power and find the gunman.

"It's true. He's an intelligence asset." Now, it's the leader's thoughts that grind against Gabriel's psyche.

But I'm not. Did they sense me reading their minds? Who are they? Are they House Pyu?

Gabriel pulls out another rock and scrapes it across the table. Again, it leaves behind no residue, and the color is good. Some are excellent. He stands and grips the handles of the chest and lifts. It easily weighs four hundred pounds. For thirty seconds or so, he shakes the trunk. He wants to avoid these men robbing him by selling glass intermingled with genuine stones. This act doubles as a show of physical strength meant to intimidate his negotiators, who stare wide-eyed. Gabriel towers above them. He hasn't missed many meals. In point-of-fact, he's missed none. When Gabriel says his favorite foods are pasta and steak, no one is surprised.

He smiles. "Just making sure the weight is what I'd expect from rubies direct from the mine."

Placing the trunk back down on the floor, he states a number. It's higher than he'd typically pay because he wants to leave with all his internal organs where he expects them. A stabbing pain pulses in his temple, and he catches other soldier's thoughts.

"Aung gave the kill order."

I've been set up. Gabriel sees an image of himself bleeding from a bullet wound to the head coming from several of the soldiers. Then he hears the sniper's thought.

"Terminate."

Gabriel hones in on the assassin and plants an idea in his head.

"The target brought his own sniper. If I terminate him, I'm dead."

He repeats.

"The target brought his own sniper. If I terminate him, I'm dead."

He pushes the idea, sprinkled with fear, into the sniper's mind while siphoning all the ley energy from the ruby. The gunman's finger snaps away from the trigger.

It worked.

Gabriel lacks the power to communicate across the world, but in case they do kill him, he sends a thought out anyway, like tossing a message in a bottle off the Titanic: *Sorry, Joe. I thought this was a routine buying trip.*

Hear me, Joe. Don't let our last words be, "See you soon."

In the space between seconds, he hears it.

"Or you could kill them all," a voice says.

What?

Time stills, and Gabriel becomes one with every thought of the surrounding soldiers. Their emotions become notes on a keyboard he can play. Reaching for the sniper, Gabriel finds his heart as if it's beating in his hand—a tiny bird he can crush with a thought. Power shoots through Gabriel, and the shock of it stuns him. The power departs as quickly as it came, leaving Gabriel breathless.

The leader stands, his face ashen, and the sniper engages the safety. Gabriel's lunch threatens to exit the same way it entered, but when he exhales, it settles.

"General Aung," Gabriel says, seizing the moment, "I'm increasing my offer to apologize for my dog's inexcusable behavior."

Gabriel bows and continues in a low tone, "I think you'll agree it's more than fair."

Fear flickers across the leader's face in less than the blink of an eye. But Gabriel's eyes never leave the man with whom he's negotiating, and he hears the general's frantic voice in his head.

"He knows my name. We were set up."

You were set up?

The general nods in agreement and offers his hand to close the deal in the western style. It's a significant token of respect after Gabriel's bow. The young officer's disappointment smashes into him with hurricane force.

No promotion for you today.

Zuko prances to Gabriel's rented Jeep and patiently awaits admittance. As he drives out of the Mogok Stone Tract, wooden chest safely in the trunk, heart still pounding, Gabriel's cell phone comes into range. He looks at the display with Zuko's smiling snout, and his day improves. It's Joe.

"Where are you? I've been blowing up your phone."

"Did you hear my call?" Gabriel asks, though he knows it's impossible. Joe is an asset of House Angeles. They pay witches a princely sum to ward Joe's mind against intrusions because it holds their secrets. *But what if he did get my message in a bottle? What if love born out of desperation found a way?*

"What call?" Joe asks.

"Oh, okay." Gabriel shrugs. "Don't you remember? I'm in Burma." His knuckles turn white as the Jeep dips into another crater—Zuko still reclining serenely in the front seat. "I'm on a buying trip. My mobile has been a paperweight. Why? What's wrong?"

"Maybe nothing. Maybe everything."

"Is it Peter?" Gabriel asks. "Did you tell him?"

"Oh, not yet, but I will. I did it, Gabriel. I mapped your genome. I mapped Zuko's first, giving me the clues I needed. And I think I can infuse precious stones with what you call 'ley energy.' I mailed you a sample yesterday."

"What?" Gabriel exclaims. "I'm chuffed to bits"—Gabriel can't help channeling his British father—"I always knew you'd change the world."

"I'm excited but scared. Will your uncle protect me?"

"From what?"

"I'm announcing a new psychic human subspecies tomorrow. You won't be a secret anymore."

"What? Did the Angeles House patriarch approve you going public? We can do it?"

"I can't wait for the Angeles. Humanity needs this, Gabriel. Yes, it'll be a shock, but the cures and therapies we can create with the immunities in adept blood will be incredible."

"A *shock*? Joe, we can't defy House Angeles."

"What's the earliest I can see you?"

"I'll be out of the jungle and on the highway in about an hour. If I'm lucky, ah, tomorrow morning. I'll leave Rangoon ASAP." Gabriel hears Joe's mobile beep with an incoming call.

"Oh, no," Joe says. "It's Peter, and I have to tell him."

Chapter Two

ADEPT HOUSES

Adept society is governed by Houses. A House is comprised of the ruling families in a territory, which is equivalent to a country. These families, the most genetically powerful adepts, elect a matriarch or patriarch to lead. We know the CIA recruits from House Caddos. House Caddos rules over Texas, Arkansas, and Louisiana.

—National Intelligence Strategy White Paper: Top Secret (TS): Release of this document will cause severe damage to the security of the United States—Adept Assets

JOE HEARS HIS husband gasp when he opens their front door. The sound echoes off the granite floors in a foyer so large his father's trailer would fit inside. A painting covers one wall. It's by an artist whom his mother-in-law says every couple should own but whose name always escapes him.

"It's good to see you at the piano," Joe says.

"Why are you home so early? The last time you left work early, I had appendicitis. What's wrong? Did your trainer cancel? Is the gym closed?" Peter smirks and turns over his sheet music.

"I should've performed that surgery myself. Your doctor was an idiot. I'm making some coffee. Do you want any?"

"No, thanks," Peter replies.

Their massive living room covers at least seven hundred square feet, filled with modern furniture and art, also selected by Peter's mother. An interior designer staged the room, and an art consultant chose the art. Joe suspects his mother-in-law bought all the staged furniture when the apartment was for sale. It would explain a lot.

In the gleaming marble kitchen, Joe grinds his Peruvian beans for exactly six seconds. When the distilled water gets to 200 degrees Fahrenheit, he patiently pours it over the coffee grounds and observes the bloom. Joe sets his watch timer for four minutes to allow the coffee to steep. When it is ready, he'll go in there and get it done.

"Hey, Peter," he yells from the kitchen. "Play 'Giant Steps.'"

"Isn't that what I played the night you proposed?"

"That's the one."

Joe looks at the French press, knowing he has three more minutes to depress the plunger. He smiles, recalling Peter's concert two years ago when his deft fingers created an ephemeral art that ensnared him. Peter became the center of Joe's universe that night when everything made sense. Peter's music made him feel something, something lost. Joe's smile fades into oblivion. Peter's playing picks up speed, and he hears a flaw. Whether it's art, data, or love, there is always a flaw. Only math is perfect. Joe pushes the plunger down and pours himself a cup. So armed, he enters the living room.

"No need to adjust your posture," Peter says with a smile. "It's always perfect."

"Old habits die hard."

Joe sits and crosses and recrosses his legs. He gestures to Peter to leave the piano and sit opposite him on the couch. "I'll get right to the point."

"Okay." Peter's left eye twitches, and he bites his lower lip.

"This isn't easy to say, but our marriage isn't working. Don't you agree?"

"What?" Peter whispers.

"We haven't been communicating, and let's face it, we're avoiding each other."

"You've been avoiding me," Peter says. "Why? Are you giving up on us?"

"Admit it. You've seen this coming. Our relationship is dead, and I'm just burying it. You're angry all the time. Don't you ask yourself why?"

"Angry? I'm not angry. I love you."

Joe straightens unnecessarily and frowns. "I'm not good for you."

"You *are* good for me. You're—" Peter utters a guttural sound, seeming to rise from the depths of his being. It's low and dark and takes on a fury all its own, like his best concerts.

"I'm not, Peter."

"You are. What happened? Where is this coming from? I mean, whatever it is, we can fix it. We can work on it."

"No, we need to move on."

"Why not work on it?" Peter says, staring up at the ceiling. His eyes are a crimson red. "You're always working. It's what you do."

"We want different things."

"I want you to let me love you."

"I'm sorry," Joe says, his eyes darting away. "But this is for the best."

"The best?"

"I want us to be friends."

"Friends? You don't have friends." Peter's brow furrows, and he meets Joe's eyes. "Have you thought this all the way through?"

"Yes." The answer comes without hesitation, and Joe's voice doesn't crack or waver. He reaches up and gently massages his forehead with one hand.

"Are you seeing someone?"

"How does that matter?"

"Nothing matters," Peter says with a sigh. "Of course, you're not just seeing someone. You're seeing Gabriel. You're leaving me for your ex."

"He has nothing to do with this."

Peter chokes out a hollow laugh. "He has something to do with whatever it is you're planning. You've been calling him a lot. You're going to publish that paper, aren't you? You're going to betray Barbara and me. Well done. Are you going to credit her? Why are you talking to Gabriel and not Barbara? I won't let you do this."

"What did I say about you being angry all the time?" Joe raises an eyebrow and attempts a smile to lighten the mood, however briefly. "Barbara Bates doesn't need help from you or me or anyone, I imagine."

"I've heard you mention all your keywords—'peer review, grant money, and data.' You don't want me around for that? You don't want me around when you steal Barbara's prize?"

"What about your prize?" Joe counters.

"You know full well the music industry has turned its back on me, just like you."

Joe exhales and crosses his arms. "My publishing doesn't have any bearing on our future."

"Doesn't it?" When no reply comes, Peter lowers his voice in an apparent attempt to appear calm. "I believe that loving someone means putting them first, so if this is what you want, I have to think of you and not me. But if there's a chance we can get through this, we should take it. Give it a few months. Maybe we can get a therapist or—"

"There isn't a chance." Joe leans back in the armchair, relaxing for the first time, and sips his coffee. "I didn't let it steep long enough, or maybe the water wasn't ready." He stares at the cup. "Oh, I know what I forgot. I'll have to make a new batch."

"Is that what you're focused on? Your coffee?"

"I'm focused on the future, as you should be." Joe puts his cup on the side table and gives it a disgusted push.

"You don't have a future," Peter says.

The comment hangs suspended in the air. Joe says nothing in reply but frowns, and they sit in a stony silence.

"I'm sorry," Peter says. "I didn't mean that. You've been distant, but I love you, Joe, so much. Couples have come through worse than this. So can we."

"We can't."

"You mean you won't."

"Peter, don't—"

"Don't worry. I won't make a scene." Peter takes one shuddering breath. "I have a question, though. What happened to your love for me?"

Peter folds his arms across his chest. "You complain that when families hear a loved one will die, they can't accept it. Facts are facts, you always say. They don't stop being facts if they're difficult, and isn't this a death? If you're going to break my heart, then do it right. You do everything right."

Joe flinches, and the temporary loss of control wrenches his gut. "My love for you hasn't changed. We're going in opposite directions, and it's best we let each other go."

"At least you can't look me in the eye when you lie to me," Peter says. "I'm going to P-town tomorrow." One lone tear streaks down his cheek.

"Okay. Take all the time you need."

"Of all the men I could've picked." Peter grabs his sheet music, "Forever Mine," tears it up, and drops it on the floor on the way out.

*

THE SUN STREAMS into Barbara's corner office, lasering between the narrow slats of the blinds. She rejected the offer of expensive custom roller shades because the previous occupant, whom she forced out of the company, chose these blinds, and she didn't want to appear elitist by replacing them.

Barbara built a bar behind her desk where most people expect a bookcase because she wants to send the message *expect the unexpected.* Her diplomas hang off to the side, where her interior designer said people will look last. She wants to exude power—men respect that—but she doesn't want men to think she's smarter than they are—men hate that. She only hangs one doctorate, but she has two.

Her office is one of the largest on the executive floor and closest to the CEO.

Barbara has her blunt-cut hair expertly dyed every four weeks. Her preferred color is a shade lighter than what it was in her youth. Her sister would enjoy that if she were still alive because her hair was also this color. It was her sister's only beauty.

Barbara absentmindedly toys with the pearls around her neck while listening to her director of sales explain how their competition will undercut them. The sun's light frames her subordinate's face, giving him a beatific aura. Appearances, she well knows, can be deceiving. Henry may be droll and humorless, but he's competent, and the sooner she answers all the pedantic questions swimming in his head, the sooner she can get back to something interesting.

"If Liz Ingot publishes her paper on transient receptor theory," Henry drones on, "and the results of her novel series, then the writing is on the wall for Ingenux and Kalentum, two of our most profitable drugs. It will force us to lower prices. Where are we with drug discovery?"

Barbara ignores the question. She wishes she could ignore Henry as easily. Why does he need these meetings? Can't he make these decisions himself?

"Call Enrique and tell him to spike Liz's paper for another year," she says, "or we'll choke off his suppliers. By the fourth quarter, we'll have gone to market with Incenson, and we'll slash our prices for Ingenux and Kalentum as a humanitarian gesture. The patents are up in three years anyway. Make sure you give our PR agency a heads-up. We'll want to milk that for all it's worth."

Henry Stockton makes a show of taking careful notes. He looks up and raises his pen to make a point but reconsiders when Barbara's intercom blares.

"One second. It's Carol," she says.

"The last time Carol buzzed me, it was my sister telling me my dad died."

"My family is already dead," Barbara says. The truth of her words rubs salt in a wound that's never healed. Most of her family is dead for reasons lost to time, and those who are still alive are dead to her. Not all family is related by blood, some are chosen, and her chosen family was her husband, John, and Joe. John died of myocardial infarction after ten years of blissful marriage. Something so easy to detect and repair, yet one of the most heralded physician-scientists in the world missed it. Joe Martin, who left her employ to become the chief scientific officer of a rival lab, is the last of her family. Barbara isn't someone to begrudge anyone their ambitions.

She depresses the intercom button with a powerful thrust of her pencil. Carol, their administrative assistant, doesn't quite live up to the highly efficient multi-tasking admin trope, but she is a superb gatekeeper. If someone moved her to interrupt a meeting with the director of sales, something must be seriously wrong.

"Barbara, I hate to bother you, but there is a Peter Brandon at the security desk asking to see you. He says it's an emergency."

"Peter is downstairs?" Barbara casually opens her Birkin bag and withdraws her cell phone. There are half a dozen texts from Peter. "Send him up. I'll meet him at the elevator."

"I hope everything is okay," Henry says.

"I'll have Carol put you back on my calendar as soon as possible."

"No problem," Henry replies.

While standing by the elevator, Barbara considers all the things that could warrant an unannounced visit to her office, and she can only come up with one. Her heart pounds in her chest, and her breathing grows tighter and tighter. When the elevator doors open, she takes a step back.

Peter's hair, which is meticulously cut to look as though it isn't styled, is unkempt. His sunken eyes have a hollow look that say he's lost something precious.

Barbara turns away. "Peter," she says softly, out of breath.

"He stabbed me in the back, and you're next," Peter says.

"Let's talk in my office."

They walk in silence, ignoring the casual stares at the stranger who isn't there on any business related to Jeebom Pharmaceuticals.

"Sit," Barbara says. "And start from the beginning."

"He's divorcing me."

"Divorce?" Barbara is stunned. Not so much because she's distraught over the news but because of Joe's admission of failure. Surely, when she speaks with Joe about it later, it won't be his fault, but then again, nothing is ever his fault. "I'm sorry, Peter. That's awful and completely unexpected. What do you mean 'I'm next'?"

"Your upstart protege is going to publish."

Barbara sits for a long moment, then, "What—what exactly is he going to publish?"

"You know—" The venom Peter puts into the word, *know,* snatches her breath. "—I'm not a scientist, but I can tell when he's going to publish something big. The phone calls have increased to his staff. He's talking to the journals, and he usually tells me about what he's doing, except for this time. This time, he's closed-mouthed, and he's getting rid of me. I've heard your name in his conversations. I think he's going to publish your work. So, get ready because it's the Ides of March."

"I'm sure—"

"Sure of what?" Peter interjects. "That he's going to give you credit? A nice little blurb at the end of his Nobel Prize–winning paper?" Peter gurgles a mirthless laugh, and Barbara sinks further into her chair.

"You know it's what he wants."

"How can you be sure?"

"I'm not. I do know he's embarking on a whole new chapter. Whatever he's going to do, it's big and won't include me."

"Has he been talking to Gabriel?" Barbara studies Peter's face and watches it crack.

"Yes. They're sleeping together. Aren't they?"

"When will this announcement happen?"

"Soon. I don't know when, but soon. I hope you take him down a peg, but you know what? I don't care. I'm going to the Provincetown house. Thank God we decided not to rent it this season. I'm going to P-town for the summer to write music. Then, I'm selling the apartment and moving to New York in the fall. I don't want to risk walking by him on the street."

"I remember when I fished his dissertation out of the slush pile and saw myself in his work and his intellectual skill. I don't want to offend you, Peter, but I still love and respect Joe. I'm sorry about your marriage, but I can't see him betraying me or his professional ethics."

A flurry of suits walks rapidly past Barbara's office, casting curious glances through the window.

Peter scoffs. "Betrayal? Funny, I suspected Joe's personal trainer. So stupid of me to think of that cliché, running off with the personal trainer like some Bravo TV housewife." Standing, Peter says, "I wanted to touch base with you. You were always fair to Joe, and you don't deserve whatever stunt he and Gabriel are planning. I'll let you get back to work."

"Let me walk you to the elevator," Barbara says, forcing a smile.

When she returns to her office, she locks the door and flips the blinds closed. At her desk, she picks up her cell phone. Barbara stares at the burner for several more minutes, knowing that when she makes this call, there is no turning back.

She finds two pieces of paper with seemingly unrelated numbers, places them side by side, and inputs them into the cell. She expects the call to go to voicemail. She'll probably get the return call between 2:00 and 5:00 a.m., she thinks ruefully.

"Using the burner already?"

"Oh," Barbara says, slow to hide her surprise. "You're there. Peter Brandon just made an unannounced visit to my office."

"So? Who's that?"

"He had news to share. Joe Martin asked him for a divorce."

"So? You called to tell me this?"

Barbara sighs and slumps into the executive chair, designed to make her look powerful, and hopes it will help her *feel* powerful.

"Peter thinks he's mapped it, and he'll publish. You were right to follow Gabriel, but you government types follow everyone."

"Martin knows the rules about talking to the *dall* about adept business, even if the *dall* is his husband. I don't believe it. It's a trick."

"Dall?" Barbara asks.

"Human."

"Oh, adept slang, is it? It's interesting that you think it's a trick, but I don't agree. It's a guess on Peter's part but an educated one. He knows his husband."

The silence on the other end has Barbara wondering if their connection has broken.

"How do you wish to proceed?" they ask finally.

"How did you find me?" Barbara asks. "Why would the Pyu House of Southeast Asia express an interest in us?"

"Every House is interested in your research, and it was Gabriel

Kelly who led us to you and to Joseph Martin. Your friendship raised eyebrows."

"Did it now?"

"There's more to him than meets the eye."

"To Gabriel?" Barbara asks, her voice rising in disbelief.

"Yes, he should be back in Boston soon. He's in flight from Rangoon as we speak."

When no further information comes, she continues. "Joe may have mapped the adept genome, but he doesn't know all that it means, and he wouldn't steal all the credit." Barbara takes a deep breath and lets it out. "If Peter is right, I can sort it out."

"Bring us the genetic data."

"Make me CEO with a five-year contract, and I'll need a substantial signing bonus, of course."

Barbara waits, and another long pause follows.

"Agreed," comes the answer finally. "We'll be in touch." The call abruptly ends.

Chapter Three

THE MATHER RATING SYSTEM

The Mather Rating, sometimes called "Adaptation Variance," measures the degree of power an adept possesses. Adepts named it after its creator Cotton Mather, a 17th-century adept minister and author. The system includes the following adept ranks.

1. Incepto (Beginner)

2. Media (Intermediate)

3. Periti (Skilled)

4. Provectus (Proficient)

5. Regna (Monarch)

> The achievement of Regna, which is also a title of respect, is extraordinarily rare, and the Regna power has never been fully categorized.
>
> —National Intelligence Strategy White Paper: Top Secret (TS): Release of this document will cause severe damage to the security of the United States—Adept Assets

SOMETHING DARK IS happening on his walk to Joe's. Immersed in his headphones, Gabriel almost misses it, but there it is, a faint telepathic distress call in the back of his mind. The desperate plea comes in fits and starts and stays stubbornly out of reach. It's giving him a headache.

"No, this is silly," he admonishes himself. "I must be imagining this." He's never been able to pick up on someone's thoughts who wasn't nearby. Gabriel stops and looks around but senses nothing. He focuses on the distress call and, again, finds nothing, yet the menace lingers. His imagination must be running wild. The Burma trip yesterday was stressful, and this must be the aftereffects, or jet lag.

Nothing is menacing about the Seaport, Boston's newest neighborhood. The wide, newly paved streets reek of full city coffers. Identical oak trees dot the pristine brick sidewalks, and multicolored tulips adorn every corner. A sailboat in the port makes its slow but steady progress, swaying gently in the breeze. Gabriel relaxes as he breathes in the cool sea air. He strolls over Seaport's harbor bridge, in lockstep with Zuko, eager to see Joe.

The bright morning is in stark contrast to his dark mood. Something is desperately wrong despite the normalcy of harried office workers with their caramel lattes and humming EV's.

Zuko takes up half the sidewalk, yet the bernedoodle, part Bernese Mountain dog, part standard poodle, can look like a stuffed animal. Sometimes, when they lounge on a park bench, Zuko will sit statue-still, so still that passersby will stop to check if he's real.

In response, Zuko will playfully bark, his tail thumping the bench, guaranteeing a tsunami of attention.

Now, looking up at Gabriel with soulful brown eyes, Zuko emits the tiniest whine, but to Gabriel's ears, it's a blaring trumpet. He massages Zuko's head and pulls him in close; his tail wags, and the pain disappears.

After a few more blocks, the two pause. Gabriel may not be able to read an obscure thought across the country or hurtle a boulder, but Zuko did choose to bond with him and no one else. There hasn't been a wolf bond in the family for over three hundred years.

"Zuko, buddy, help me. I know you feel it too."

Touching Zuko calms Gabriel. The dog's serenity helps him reach out to the ley line. Zuko, like all animals, lives close to nature, so he easily taps into the field. With newfound energy, he searches for the source. Gabriel wishes he had an infused jewel to aid him, but he sent all the rubies to auction. Remembering what his ley energy teacher taught him, he recites, "Be like a teapot, a raging boil inside, but calm and unchanged on the outside."

The power is invigorating. He can hold more than most because of Zuko. The gentle giant of a dog shoulders much of the burden of the explosive energy. The power builds until it begs for release. Gabriel harnesses the tempest and opens his awareness. Voices and images flood his mind. He's the epicenter of thousands of thoughts throughout Seaport. He listens for the entreaty he felt in the corner of his consciousness, but it's like looking for a needle in a haystack. If only he could recapture what happened to him in Burma, where he hummed with adept power.

When Gabriel communes with Zuko, he gets a sense of that time before the first word of history was written. When wolves and man took those first tentative steps toward each other in kinship. Gabriel knew what man gained—a deadly hunting partner and a valuable ally against enemies. But what did the wolf hope to gain? Love and extended family are the only answers. Knowing man got the better part of the bargain, he leans down and kisses Zuko on the top of his head, and the dog smiles in return.

A minute later, Gabriel's search comes up empty. Or almost empty because he can't shake that he felt something familiar. With nothing but a sense of failure and misgiving, they resume their walk. Gabriel takes a moment to connect to the grid, a psychic bulletin board for adepts, but he hears nothing. There is no cry for help, only local routine chatter about an adept wedding between two great Houses in Europe.

As they approach Joe's building, Zuko slows his gait and whines. For a moment, he refuses to take another step. The grim warning constricts their chests. Gabriel awkwardly gulps as his heart gallops, and he forces himself to breathe. That foreboding of someone desperately in trouble moves from the back to the front of his awareness. This dire fear will blossom into panic if he doesn't master it. Maybe Zuko is afraid of something, and it's leaking into Gabriel? Why is he tuning into random thoughts and feelings now? And why only those full of dread?

There's a small gym in Joe's building but he rarely uses it. The only free time he and Gabriel spent together was a quick workout and always at Joe's fully equipped gym, where Joe worked with a personal trainer. Still, Gabriel can't help but spare a glance to see if Joe is squeezing in some morning cardio.

The doors to Joe's state-of-the-art green apartment building swoop open automatically. Besides the gym, which offers yoga classes, the building is equipped with solar panels, bike racks and dog walkers; it even recycles and posts the mail. There is also a solar-heated pool. It's so like Joe, finding a way to live in luxury yet still lay claim to a low-carbon footprint.

Gabriel takes in a nervous breath and rakes his hands through his dense tidal wave of curly black hair.

He and Zuko approach a stout young woman behind the security desk. Her uniform is a dark gray and unusually crisp, as far as his experience with people working doors to apartment buildings goes. She has long, straight black hair and dark brown eyes.

"Hi, I'm here to see Joe Martin, apartment 11C." Gabriel greets her smiling warmly, maybe even a tad ingratiatingly. It pays to be on good terms with the door person. He usually gets great results from this smile.

"And you are?"

"Gabriel Kelly."

Upon hearing his name, her well-done nails start stabbing the keyboard in a loud display of acrylic-on-acrylic violence. Tap-tap, tap-tap. Gabriel gets a few bars of Taylor Swift, marshmallows, Chanel no. 5, and pink unicorn pillows from her.

"I don't see you in our records," she says. "Is he expecting you?"

"Yes, he's expecting me."

She says nothing in reply but turns toward Zuko. Her face breaks out into a broad smile, and she gets up from her chair, which barely increases her height. "He's so beautiful," she whispers as if Zuko will overhear. "Or is it a she?"

"A he."

She studies Zuko for a moment. "He's one of the biggest dogs I've ever seen! What kind is he?"

"He's half poodle, half Bernese Mountain dog. Can you let Mr. Martin know I'm here, please?"

"Is he friendly? Can I pet him?"

And with that, before Gabriel can reply, Zuko, tail high and posture perfect, leans into his mother's poodle heritage and prances to her side. With her first tentative touch, his tail picks up even more speed.

"Oh, he's so sweet. His fur is so soft. It's like marshmallow." Her hands disappear into the mass that is Zuko's thick coat, massaging him. Her voice morphs into that high-pitched tone reserved solely for pets and preverbal children. "He's just a big polar bear. Yes, he is!"

After a pointed glare from Gabriel, she tears herself away to focus on calling Joe's apartment. She lifts the receiver, and pain scrambles Gabriel's brain.

"I'll buzzz—" Her voice garbles and slowly fades to a whisper. "—Doctorrr—"

The mind-numbing pain comes in a fury, ripping the inside of Gabriel's chest. He desperately looks for a bullet wound, but there's nothing. He takes a breath, expecting it to be his last. Why is there no wound, no blood? Zuko lifts his head and howls, his anguish ricocheting into Gabriel.

The floor beneath Gabriel's feet seems to vanish, and he falls to his knees. Memories of Joe flash before him, and then Gabriel hears Joe: *"Is that you, Gabriel? Something is wrong. I feel—"*

Searing panic rips from behind his eyes and down through his body. A cry explodes, shooting forcefully out of him. There is no containing it. His vocal cords tear and burn in his throat.

"Joe, are you okay?" Gabriel knows he isn't, but the thought spills out anyway.

Gabriel has forged a psychic connection between them, but how can that be? Joe's panic floods into him in a rush. The Angeles paid the witches to prevent anyone from reading Joe's mind. Gabriel has to sever the block. It's like drinking from a fire hose. Regret and sadness overwhelm him in a torrent. Joe's emotions combine with his to create a complicated morass. The cruel weight of disappointment bears down on Gabriel.

"I'll get to you. Hang on."

Gabriel struggles to his feet and turns to the door person. He reads her nameplate and says, "Chen, call 9-1-1." He collapses again. As Gabriel struggles to stand he calls out to Joe again.

"Joe. Joe. Get up."

Gabriel knows Joe has fallen upstairs in his apartment because their connection caused him to do so.

"What? Are you okay?" Chen asks, rushing to Gabriel's side.

Gabriel feels Joe in the corner of consciousness, but he's so distant now.

"I'm in trouble, and, Gabriel, I—"

Medical data rushes into Gabriel's head. It may as well be Egyptian hieroglyphs. Panic overcomes him. He wants to run, to flee for his life. But, no, it's not his panic. It's Joe's. Gabriel reaches out to Joe with all his might. In reply, he gets only *"the data"* and the image of a door with "2-L" printed on the outside. The vision burns the back of his eyes.

And then he hears it in Joe's mind. An echo of himself struggling to be heard. The desperate thought he sent to Joe when he thought Aung would kill him is here inside Joe.

He heard me. He heard me.

"Sorry, Joe. I thought it was a routine buying trip."

Gabriel savors the memory and reaches out to assure Joe everything will be okay. His desperate thought connected with Joe. Against all odds Joe heard him. Then, the richness of the memory fades to black, and all light dims. Where once there was a tapestry of knowledge and a connection, there is only a void. Joe's soul, once present, is irrevocably snatched away. There was so much left to do, so much left unsaid. At Joe's most dire hour, when he needed him most, Gabriel wasn't there. He was too late. He failed, but somehow, he got around the witch ward and Joe heard him.

At least we had that.

Chen darts out from behind her desk and drops down to help Gabriel. Zuko is licking his face and nudging him. Finally, Gabriel looks up at her and whispers.

"Joe is dead."

Chapter Four

ADEPT VILLAGES

Adepts who live outside of their territory congregate in neighborhoods, for example, a part of Los Angeles called "Little Salem."

—National Intelligence Strategy White Paper: Top Secret (TS): Release of this document will cause severe damage to the security of the United States—Adept Assets

THE SALEM HOUSE rules over what is informally called the "News," or New York, New Jersey, and the New England area. Salem is the oldest House in the Americas. It rose to power when Boston was the second largest English-speaking city in the world.

Anisa Aboud Walker, the 250-year-old Regna protector of the

Salem House stops breathing. Her beloved great-great-grandson's psychic scream ricochets in her mind, an ice pick in brain. It alerts all in its path, sending ripples of pain across the grid. She refocuses on the reports in front of her about a strange street drug called "J" currently ravaging adepts. But whatever Patriarch Meyer of the Angeles House is up to with the new medication, Jubilee, will have to wait. It is now the second most important thing in her day.

When Anisa was younger, about seventy but still appearing to be a woman in her thirties, all that gave her age away were her eyes. There was a trace of weariness in them. Now, her eyes match the rest of her. They look suspiciously out into the world with all the bitter experience of several human lifespans. Her dark skin is creased, and she says every line has a story.

Anisa concentrates on Gabriel and finds him unconscious across town. Zuko's mournful cries echo within her, making it difficult to hear Gabriel's thoughts. She tunes Zuko out and tries to hone in on Gabriel. But a loud bark pierces the silence, and once again, there is Zuko, Gabriel's personal Cerberus. Anisa smiles in her trance-like state and sends her reassurances.

"I'm here to help, Zuko. You know me."

Zuko withdraws, allowing Anisa entry into Gabriel's mind. Only the rarest adepts can link to an animal via the wolf bond. Through her link to Gabriel, she sends her respect and admiration to Zuko.

Russell Walker, patriarch of the Salem House, interrupts her. *"Regna Anisa! Do you—"*

"Yes, Russell. Dr. Martin is dead, and Gabriel has broadcast it on the grid." Anisa allows him to feel her disappointment at the edge of her mind. *"Why was he there?"*

She senses Russell choosing his thoughts carefully. *"We sift through voluminous amounts of intelligence, Regna. It's a challenge to separate the wheat from the chaff."*

"Because Gabriel broadcast Martin's death on the grid and our own poor judgment, other adept governments have as much wheat as we, and in our capital, no less. And the crows will know."

Anisa pauses and focuses on Gabriel. *"He has recovered from the shock of his friend's death, and now his abilities are struggling to protect him from further shocks. He is adapting."*

"Thank goodness for that," Russell sends back to Anisa. *"But we need to keep this secret."*

"Thank goodness?"

"That he's sane and functioning. It's enough for now."

"Others heard his cry, and they will come. Best we be prepared."

"Does Gabriel know where the Angeles' data are?" Russell asks.

"He does not."

Anisa pauses again as if in deep thought. *"Wait. Something is happening."*

"What is it?"

"Find that data." Anisa shuts Russell out of her mind and turns her attention to her great-great-grandson.

*

PATRICK MEYER, PATRIARCH of House Angeles, lurches up in bed so quickly he pulls a muscle. When he moans in pain, it's not from the torn muscle but from a searing ache behind his eyes.

"Martin," he screams into the void of his bedroom. A sliding door in the sleek glass wall is open, allowing in a gentle breeze. The flickering lights of LA twinkle below as if the night sky were turned upside down. The urban glow perfectly frames Meyer's cat, Blue, who precipitously lounges on a deck railing overlooking the cliffs without a care in the world.

I hope I teeter on the edge as deftly as you. Meyer struggles to steady his breathing until his heart stops thumping. A return to normalcy will take a while.

He grabs for his cell phone, fumbling it, and it skitters across the mahogany floor. When he reaches out, it flies into his hand. Meyer sits upright and initiates a call, which is answered halfway into the second ring.

"Mr. Meyer, it's—"

"Five a.m. here and 8:oo a.m. in Boston. I own a watch." The words fire out of his mouth. "I want all of Martin's data on my laptop now."

"What? Joe Martin? But why? We looked at his progress and—"

Meyer speaks slowly and deliberately. "I will be the judge of his progress." He takes in an aggravated breath. "I want my data, and if one byte is missing— Oh, and by the way, Martin is dead." Meyer hits the end call button. One big disadvantage to cell phones is they rob you of the satisfaction of slamming down the receiver. "Moron," he mutters.

Next, he mentally focuses on the Angeles inquisitor.

"Patriarch!" she responds immediately. Her usual disciplined thoughts are frayed. It's his fault; he let some of his panic seep through. It's too late now. He'll lean into it.

"There's a baby Regna in the making."

"A new Regna? It will shift the balance of power."

"Listen to me! The last thing the world needs is a new Regna, especially a House Salem Regna. Understand? Meet me at the jet in an hour and bring the twins. We're going to Boston."

*

THE HIGH PRIESTESS of the Ironbay Coven, Ravynne Quinn, spreads the *New York Times* across the table. She prefers the feel of newsprint with her morning tea. The iPad her son gave her is a poor substitute for a physical newspaper.

The sun streams through the open windows. During winter, there were few opportunities to feel its warmth. She relishes this spring morning and longs for an uneventful day. Deciding her tea has steeped enough, she begins to pour. The fluffy rolls with her favorite plum jam are especially inviting. Her legendary willowy figure is starting to thicken, but she no longer cares.

Ravynne's eyes fly to the bedroom door as energy from the protective threshold ward sends pinpricks through her body. The warning isn't a grave one, but someone hurriedly approaches. Staff rarely come to her living quarters this early in the morning. The rapid cadence of bare knuckles against wood smells of panic, and the frantic shouts of her security staff do little to assuage her fear.

"Yes, come in." Her deep raspy voice crackles but it's steady.

"High Priestess." The aide bows slightly and meets her eyes for a brief second. "It's fortunate that you're up."

Her hair is already stiffly styled to perfection. The thick black bouffant frames her head like a protective helmet. Despite her daughter's admonition that she looks like someone in a 1940s movie poster, Ravynne maintains the bouffant. It's her signature, as is her penchant for Chanel suits.

"The Angeles paid for a powerful protection spell around the mind of one of their dall assets. It's been broken."

"What?"

"The dall asset was sending his thoughts out, and they circumvented the ward."

"That's never happened. Who were they sending to?" The high priestess is careful that her sculpted eyebrows betray only the slightest irritation.

"We've been informed by the Angeles adepts that Gabriel Kelly, great-great-grandson of Regna Anisa Aboud Walker, in a moment of emotional distress, mentally broadcast his pain on their grid. He experienced a death. We believe he may have increased in rank."

"He adapted? Which rank was he?"

"A low to mid-level Media."

Ravynne utters a dismissive "Hmm" in reply. "I don't trust Meyer. He'd love to use us against the Salem House. What else did they say?"

"The Angeles are coming."

"They are?" Her eyes widen in surprise, and she leans back in her chair. "That's a drastic step. Russell will be displeased. Find out everything we can about that dall asset. I want a full report."

Her secretary wanders into the room, all ears. She allows it. What she does not allow is any emotion to appear on her face. Ravynne Quinn knows all too well the consequences of Anisa Aboud Walker's adaptation to Regna. Witches remember it as the "great cataclysm." Any spawn of Anisa moving up the adept food chain is sure to cause Ravynne's people alarm, but she will show none of it. She will not be Meyer's piece on the board. She is a player.

"What happened? Why the trauma?" she asks her assistant.

"Gabriel felt the death as it happened. He loved this thrall of the adepts. Dr. Joseph Martin."

Ravynne nods. "Something that draws the attention of the Angeles patriarch is something we need to understand. Give me everything we know about Gabriel Walker, and after you've done that, learn more. I need to know all there is about the little princeling."

"Gabriel Kelly, High Priestess."

"Yes, yes, whatever, Gabriel Kelly," Ravynne says waving her hand. "No refund on the dead asset. Even though our spell was broken, no one read his mind. And one more thing. Get my children out of bed." She rifles through her desk, pulling out random items. "Where are my cigarettes?"

"But, High Priestess, are you sure? You said—"

"Get them."

Chapter Five

MIND POSSESSION

The ability to control another person's thoughts and actions is reserved solely for Regnas. The Agency is confirming if the Chinese have a Regna-level adept asset in the United States. It could explain the behavior of several of our agents.

—National Intelligence Strategy White Paper: Top Secret (TS): Release of this document will cause severe damage to the security of the United States—Adept Assets

"ARE YOU OKAY?"

A voice penetrates the dense fog, a doggedly persistent voice. "Can you hear me?"

Zuko licks his face and nudges him. When that doesn't yield the desired response, repeated paw pats on his head and shoulders follow.

"Can you hear me?" Even louder now. "Can you hear me?"

Gabriel forces his eyes open to a blurry Chen looking down on him. *Poor thing. She looks terrified.*

Another voice. A voice not entirely Gabriel's says, *"Get up."* It has gone years without speaking, and this is the second time in two days. Despite hearing a voice inside his head, Gabriel doesn't think he's insane, but would an insane person think they're insane?

Gabriel takes the voice's advice and picks himself up off the lobby floor. He seethes in agony, every brain cell screaming in protest. A millennial couple with their collectible sneakers and bike helmets stops to stare blatantly. Anger rises inside him, but he can't be bothered with them now. His head throbs in complaint while Zuko growls in stereo because Gabriel hears it in his mind as well as his ears.

"Did you say Dr. Martin is dead?" Chen says.

"No," Gabriel replies. "Of course not."

"Really? Because you—"

Gabriel locks eyes with Chen and deploys his telekinesis. He needs minimal energy, but it demands a high degree of precision. Adepts are masters at reading facial expressions because they feel the emotion and then read it on the other's face. With enough experience, an adept can detect a lie when the words and expressions diverge even minutely. Now, sophisticated machines can do the same thing. Marketing will discard a sneaker design when the computer reads disgust on a face, even if the test subject in the focus group blandly says, "The design is okay."

With a surgical mental projection, Gabriel pushes Chen's facial muscles into an expression of confidence and admiration. This sends a signal to her brain to trust him. He thinks of it as a small wave he plans to ride into her subconscious. He ignores the pain and focuses his concentration. Gabriel places an unsteady hand on Zuko, and his headache recedes. He plants the idea that she must go back to work and that Joe Martin is alive in his apartment. He drives it home delicately but forcefully.

Chen returns to her desk and taps her keyboard.

"Gabriel! Gabriel."

His parents call out to him, their presence resounding in his brain. Did they feel it too? Did they sense the same onslaught of emotion from Joe's death through him?

Their message comes to him, not in words but as a panicked call to action and an emotional entreaty to return home. He sends them back his assurances.

"I'm fine. I'm okay."

"You broadcasted on the grid, not privately. The whole adept community heard you. Who's dead?"

"I did? Mom, Dad, get out of my head. Joe is dead."

"What? Gabriel, you should—"

He pushes them out and closes his mind. Grief burns through his body, leaving no cell unscarred. His throat constricts, and he starts to dry heave. Gabriel desperately wants to be mistaken, to believe he somehow overreacted, but he knows the truth. Joe is gone. Someone stole the future.

Taking a deep breath, he pushes the elevator button. The gravity of what's happened descends on him in a fury—and something precious hollows out inside him and vanishes. Anger, despair, and anguish intertwine to replace it, a bitter weight settling in the pit of his stomach. On the ride to the eleventh floor, his tears stubbornly refuse to fall. They cling to the corners of his eyes and sting his skin. He wipes them away and pushes that sick feeling down. Joe still needs him. There will be time to mourn later.

The elevator ding breaks Gabriel's mood. Entering the hall, he reaches out with his mind, and the bond with Zuko heightens his other five senses. He reaches down to stroke Zuko's head for comfort, but the dog's head hangs too low.

Zuko and Gabriel walk toward Joe's apartment door in synchronized steps. Zuko's nose twitches as he categorizes every scent. He learns every story others have left in their wake, taking in every detail. Who walked this way, when, what have they eaten? What fragrance did they wear? In this way, Zuko, like all dogs, can read the past.

The hallway feels as if it will swallow Gabriel whole. He stiffens and stares into it—the blue carpet with its modern paisley design, the art deco lighting sconces emitting a soft, subtle glow. Gabriel lays his hand on Zuko's head and reaches for the ley line, akin to a surfer riding a wave. He must understand when to tap in and out or suffer a crash. Gabriel finds the line, drawing power into himself.

Now, with their senses heightened, they scan the area for threats. Two girls in an adjacent apartment lounge in separate rooms. Sharon is worried about her medical boards, her stress palpable, a thick, cloying feel. Alice debates going on vacation with friends. Will they all pay their fair share? She wears a floral perfume, a gift from her mother. A couple down the hall relax together. One of them is having an affair. These are not the thoughts Gabriel needs to hear.

Zuko moves in front of Gabriel, slowing his pace, then silently approaches Joe's door in a stalking stance. He growls as Gabriel probes with all his awareness. Yet Gabriel finds nothing. He detects no living thing. Why is Zuko growling? Zuko pauses, stopping Gabriel's advance, and growls again. But this time, it comes from deep in his chest, the low, ominous sound full of menace. It's particularly frightening because Zuko is such a gentle soul. His warning is too powerful to ignore, but no one is there inside. Still, Gabriel gulps; the last time Zuko sounded like this, he was almost killed.

Gabriel links with Zuko's canine skill to smell emotions and detects it, a mix of rage and fear. The acrid scent assaults him, and Gabriel jumps in alarm.

Zuko barks with such force his front paws bounce off the floor. Gabriel imagines the entire building is awake now, and fear rains down on him. He thinks, between the two of them, if one of them is wrong about what is in that apartment, it's probably him.

With a shaking hand, Gabriel turns the doorknob. It's locked. He mentally feels for the deadbolt, and with a slight motion of his hand, the door unlatches. There is no creaking sound with these pneumatic doors, only a tiny whoosh as it swings open. How can he be afraid of what he'll find and know precisely what he'll find?

To describe the corner duplex apartment as expansive would not do it justice. The foyer seems endless, and is that an original Keith Haring? The painting must be Peter's. Gabriel steps slowly through the foyer, casting a million tentacles, probing for any sign of life, but there's nothing. He takes a big breath to slow his racing pulse. There's no threat, only a body, Joe's body.

Oh, Joe. Why? How could this happen? Gabriel stares at his lifeless body.

Zuko leaps over the couch in one wolflike bound. He doesn't bark but roars a paralyzing siren that stops Gabriel in his tracks. He hears someone scream. Zuko smelled them and broke their veil against Gabriel's probing mind.

Adepts are here. The intruder strikes him with a powerful kinetic blast. Zuko yelps in agony, and Gabriel stifles a cry, falling to his knees, Zuko's pain rebounding in his body. Gabriel gasps for breath, but he can't breathe. He sputters to get his lungs working only to see two figures walk through an open portal and escape.

Zuko limps over to Gabriel and licks his face. Gabriel pulls him in for a clumsy hug, and they stagger over to Joe's body. His eyes are open. It gives him a macabre, off-putting look. Not thinking about the sanctity of crime scenes, Gabriel reaches out to shut them, but Joe's once sparkling blue eyes refuse to close. So much for all those poignant scenes in TV and movies. Another trope dispelled by unyielding reality.

Zuko sniffs the body and whines, and then, despite his distress, the dog busily examines the room.

Gabriel stands motionless, his face gray. "At least one of us isn't paralyzed."

He closes his eyes and takes a deep breath. Folding space to open a portal leaves a trail. There were adepts here, and they teleported away. Anger now fuels his focus. Gabriel looks for a disturbance, recalling how his teacher described it as the ripples a stone makes in a quiet pond. Something obvious yet easy to miss. It's a temporary effect, so he must find it immediately before it fades away. His physicist father, who has an answer for everything, describes it as a stream of subatomic particles.

Gabriel taps a ley line again. There's a limit to how much of this pressure he can take. It fills his head, and the pain becomes excruciating. Finally, he starts to see colors, kaleidoscopic, swirling faster and faster. What did his teachers say? He should've paid more attention, but he does remember to be still.

Gabriel leans on his bond with Zuko, and his nausea recedes. Patterns start to emerge as if a puzzle suddenly comes together, and then, as quickly as he finds it, it vanishes. He wasn't strong enough to hold it.

It's gone. He failed. Whoever killed Joe is laughing somewhere. Free to go on with their lives. Gabriel sits on the floor and puts his face in his hands. Crying now would be a selfish indulgence, but why not? There is nothing left to do. For what will he cry first? Will he cry for Joe, or will he cry over his failure?

"Woof!"

"Zuko? What?"

Zuko trots to a spot in the room and stares. He sits and lifts his paw. "Woof!" He turns his head to Gabriel. They lock eyes for a moment, and then he turns back to the spot that captures his attention. Gabriel steps over to Zuko and slumps down beside him on the floor, and they stare at the spot together. Then, he chastises himself because it's so obvious. Why was this so hard to see?

It's a window. It's the address he needs. Countless times, his physicist father tried to explain how atoms come together and that an adept with telekinesis powerful enough can manipulate them and open a wormhole. It's so clear now that Gabriel can see what's on the other side. He can practically smell where the cowards scurried off to. He commits it to memory and gets up off the floor, but exhaustion overtakes him, and pain wracks his brain. Gabriel can't keep the portal open, let alone walk through it. How can he walk through a portal? He's only a Media. He's never had that talent. And then he feels it. A nagging sense that he's always been wrong about that.

"You're welcome," the voice says. *"And yes, you've always been wrong about that."*

"Gabriel."

He snaps his head up and sweeps over his surroundings. When his great-great-grandmother, the Regna, speaks telepathically, it's as if he's an audience of one in a symphonic hall. She may as well be standing beside him. Zuko gazes at him, his soulful eyes wide. Her voice is bright and comes with a trace of her sub-Saharan accent.

"*Bibi,*" he replies with trepidation. She sounds younger. Has she been there this whole time? Is she the voice? *"Did Mom and Dad call you?"*

"No, but you did. I felt what happened. I know you do not understand what occurred."

"Understand? Joe's dead. What is there to understand?"

Anisa pauses. Gabriel can feel her gathering her patience.

"Your friend was thinking about you in the moments before his death. He reached out with all his might when he transitioned. You were connected and unprepared for the psychic feedback."

"We were connected?"

With that thought, Anisa gives Gabriel a small glimpse into her past experiences, her loved ones being ripped away throughout her 250 years, and he shudders. He glimpses the death of her husband, a famous African American abolitionist and Uncle Russell's great-grandfather. Gabriel descends from one of her earlier relationships with an affluent, politically connected British doctor during the Revolutionary War.

He can't imagine going through something like this again, but his Bibi experienced this and much worse. Her husband, who was as real in his time as Gabriel is now, with all the same hopes and dreams for the future, died in 1830. That was when he and Anisa built their Louisbourg Square home. He died so young for an adept. What exactly happened? Whatever it was, it wasn't a natural death. A part of Gabriel is thankful she spared him that knowledge.

"You are stronger than you know," Anisa says, but it's more than words. It's a feeling.

"Run," the voice says.

Run? From Anisa? She's the Salem protector.

"What does it matter? Joe is dead." Gabriel says the unsayable.

"Yes, he is." Anisa's voice is clear and in surround sound.

The words "dead" and "Joe" coexisting in the same sentence is strange and unnatural.

"Your anguish will continue to be felt by many over the grid. I should have trained you better, prepared you better. These prosperous times have made us complacent, and even my memory can be short."

Zuko barks a warning.

"Gabriel." The tone in Anisa's voice stops him cold.

"Yes, I can feel them," he says. *"Four cops, almost here."*

"I am coming. I will deal with the constables."

"No," Gabriel answers. *"This is an upscale building. There will be more. And besides, too many people saw me, and who knows what technology tracked me. Someone must've alerted the police. Can you hear it? They're responding to an anonymous tip. No, I must handle this. Ask Uncle Russell to send an attorney. I'll need one."*

Gabriel lets out a ragged breath. "Let's do this," he whispers.

A framed photograph sits on a side table, taken by him years ago. He had no idea Joe valued it. He took it at the summer house of Joe's mentor, Barbara. Joe and Barbara are smiling over her homemade crab cakes and glasses of chardonnay. Joe's eyes are admiring, and Zuko lounges at his feet. Zuko's eyes are as affixed to Barbara as Gabriel's camera lens. How will he break this news to her?

Reaching out to his great-great-grandmother, he senses her presence but nothing else as she shuts down any hint of her emotions. That's okay. He understands all too well his family's reaction to the police despite all their wealth and connections. They're emotions he suspects other Regnas are wholly unfamiliar with, along with fear and dread.

"Why are the cops taking so long?" Gabriel wonders, their frenetic thoughts parading in his head like drunken party guests.

"Boston Police! Do not move!"

He winces upon hearing the command.

"On your knees; put your hands behind your head!"

Zuko growls, drawing the attention of the officers.

"Zuko, place!" Gabriel orders, and Zuko hops on the couch and curls into a ball.

"Shut up!" the policeman orders.

The demand echoes in Gabriel's brain. It's so loud; the cop's fear and aggression is a sticky hot thing Gabriel can't shake.

One of the other officers snickers. "Look at the cute dog."

"Cuff him and secure the scene."

"I'll call it in," another pitiless voice calls out.

A policeman approaches and shines a military grade flashlight in his face.

"I found him like this," Gabriel says to the blinding white light.

"I don't care," the light replies.

"You have the right to remain silent." And the light handcuffs him.

Chapter Six

CHINESE POLITBURO

The Politburo of the Chinese Communist Party comprises the twenty-five ruling adept families of China.

—National Intelligence Strategy White Paper: Top Secret (TS): Release of this document will cause severe damage to the scurity of the United States—Adept Assets

"YOU'RE HOME EARLY," Lawrence says while slicing and dicing a medley of vegetables. "I didn't expect you until a bit later."

"I can say the same about you," Janice Rizzo replies as she plants a kiss on his cheek and expertly disengages the intricate French hairpins that maintain her blonde tresses in a vertical state of repose. When her hair comes tumbling down, it's the signal the workday has ended.

Her husband smiles and reluctantly withdraws his playfully proffered cheek. He's seven years older than his wife at forty, with thinning hair, a close-cropped beard, and the thickening yet still solidly built physique of his athletic college days. To many, he doesn't look as if he has a PhD in mathematics, but he does. He'll often ask, what does a math PhD look like?

"I had a lunch meeting with a pharmaceutical company at the Mandarin and decided to work from home the rest of the day," he says. "What's your excuse? Not that I'm complaining."

Rizzo puts her arm around his waist and surveys the variety of knives and vegetables strewn across the island. "I just wrapped up that slasher case and schooled the FBI, so I think I can spare an early afternoon with the most handsome man in Boston. Come to think of it—" She observes the finely cut vegetables. "Your knife skills are suspiciously good."

"And who would this handsome man in Boston be?" He waves his kitchen knife. "I hope the good people of our fair city can keep from killing one another for at least one more night. I've been meaning to try this recipe."

"What are we making?" Rizzo asks, with an emphasis on the "we."

"We are making roasted vegetables, garlic mashed potatoes, and lamb chops."

"Lamb? That's Sebastian's favorite leftovers." Upon hearing his name, their cat saunters into the kitchen and rubs up against Rizzo's leg.

When they married, they promised to always have dinner together. They were able to keep that promise for about eighteen months. When Rizzo became a full detective, one of the youngest in the department, that promise would slip more often than not, but they make every effort to maintain this quality time.

"What can I do?" Rizzo asks.

"You can sit and converse with your husband and put this spice rub on the chops."

"Let me at it."

"We're invited to dinner at Mark's and Michael's on Saturday." Lawrence holds his breath and raises his eyebrows. Rizzo nods a quick yes and shrugs.

"Oh, come on," Lawrence says. "They love you."

"And I love them, but the last time, Michael went on and on about what a student of human psychology I must be as if I somehow know what evil lurks in the hearts of men. If he keeps it up, I'll have to tell him that people are predictable and seldom disappoint when you think the worst. Scratch that. Make that 'never disappoint.' Detecting can be me-thodical and plodding. There are very few surprises in this line of work."

Lawrence laughs. "Yes, and Mark thinks everything is CSI."

In the middle of applying the spice rub, Rizzo's cell phone both rings and vibrates in her purse.

Lawrence stops his chopping. "I knew it was too good to be true."

Rizzo frowns and looks at the flashing display. Her husband is right. It is too good to be true.

*

THE SEAPORT NEIGHBORHOOD of Boston sprang up practically overnight. Where mud lots and abandoned buildings once stood, sleek office towers, bustling bistros, and luxury condos now occupy the area.

This luxury condo building is unique not only because it's a mur-der scene, but because it's green. Not green in the color way, but in the environmentally conscious way. Solar panels decorate the roof, and high-speed electric chargers dot the parking area for the resident's vehicles. From what Detective Rizzo can tell on the drive in, the remarkably nondiverse neighborhood has plenty of electric cars.

Several police units dot the side of the road. So far, there are no news vans. That's good. The news crews haven't gotten word yet. A dead body or suspicious death in any well-to-do neighborhood will draw their attention, and Rizzo doesn't like attention, especially from the press.

"Right here is good," Rizzo tells the Lyft driver. She checks her watch and flips back her long blonde hair. It's still early, so maybe she can call this a day and be back in time for dinner? Murder is one of the few things that can preempt dinner.

A sullen, uniformed officer mans the security desk. He likely lost the bet to decide who got this particular duty. Rizzo flashes her badge, and he immediately stands. "The scene is on the eleventh floor," he says.

When the elevator doors open, Rizzo sees cops all along the hallway. The hive of activity tells her this isn't a normal dead body. When affluent Bostonians meet untimely ends, the BPD becomes unusually thorough. She steps inside the apartment and looks for the officer in charge. Rizzo muses that her living room would fit in this foyer, and what is that ugly painting? She closes her eyes, and the incessant buzz of voices reminds her of a bar.

This apartment has the same smell of corruption that her father's had in New York. By age nine, she was old enough to understand something was wrong with his consultancy work for the Kremlin. Also suspicious were his detailed knowledge of sophisticated weaponry, the art he didn't care for by artists he didn't know, the wine he purchased solely by price, and her mother's reluctance to discuss what he did for a living not only to her but to anyone. He was covering up a smell in the same clumsy way he dyed his hair. His acute disapproval of her joining law enforcement after Stanford drove her headlong into police work. This apartment, as perfect as it is, has the same smell.

"Ah, there you are, Detective," a voice calls out from the cacophony. "I was told by Commander McEntee to answer any questions you might have and to brief you on the case."

"McEntee? What's his involvement? And who are you?"

"Officer Esteban Herrera, ma'am. I'm the one who called you. Commander McEntee assigned me to assist you."

"Officer Esteban Herrera," Rizzo says, not bothering to stop what she's doing. "Answer my questions in the order in which they appear."

The junior officer's smile fades, and his back straightens. "Ah, Commander McEntee's involvement? I don't know, ma'am."

Rizzo turns to walk away, and Herrera follows with his head low. "Let's start with who's dead, time of death, and are we sure this is a homicide because if it isn't, I'm going home. My husband is making lamb chops."

Officer Herrera nods, retrieves his notebook, and flips it open. "The deceased is Dr. Joseph Martin, a geneticist. He's the chief scientific officer at Covian Pharmaceuticals. We were alerted by an anonymous tip, but when we arrived at the scene, a man was already here. He's in custody waiting for you."

He pauses and looks up from his notes. Rizzo gives him a blank stare. "Oh! Right, ah, 8:00 a.m. The deceased was poisoned. It could be accidental or suicide, but the medical examiner deemed it suspicious enough to call us. Homicide assessment hasn't turned in their report yet."

Rizzo shakes her head. "Just once, could the captain give me a cut-and-dried case." She walks until she finds the white taped outline of the body. Frowning, she bends down to examine the floor. "It's wet." Looking around, she says, "I can see from the surrounding photos he was married. Where is the bereaved spouse?"

This time, Officer Herrera is ready. "We won't know until all the forensic reports come back along with the results of the autopsy, but the ME thinks the coffee he was drinking killed him. He was holding a cup when he died. Forensics collected what they could of the spilled liquid and confiscated all the coffee beans in the house, along with the water filters and the carafe he used."

"Carafe?" Rizzo asks.

"It had a plunger in it." The junior officer's voice cracks in the face of Rizzo's scrutiny.

"You mean a French press? That makes sense. I haven't been here long, but I've seen enough to say that he doesn't strike me as the instant coffee type. But if that's the case, how do we know coffee was the delivery mechanism, and he wasn't poisoned some other way?"

Herrera hesitates, and his face loses color.

"I'm not expecting you to answer that, Officer Herrera. It's a rhetorical question."

"Yes, ma'am. The deceased is married to a Peter Brandon. He's a musician. When I reached him an hour ago, he was in Provincetown, where they have a house. He's been there since yesterday and coming back tomorrow."

"Does he—?"

"Yes, the captain wants you to meet the spouse," Herrera answers. He steps back a bit, half expecting an outburst. Instead, Rizzo sighs.

"It's the worst part of the job, Herrera. Meeting the family." She collects herself and stands to her full height, "Was he alone?"

Herrera looks down at his notes. "We don't know, but the only dirty dishes were his."

"Who did you say was found at the scene? You said there was an anonymous tip? I'll go see him now at the station."

Herrera flips through his notebook again. "Yes, an anonymous call about a strange man outside the victim's apartment. His name is Gabriel Kelly."

Chapter Seven

ADEPT LIFE EXPECTANCY

The United Nations estimates a global average life expectancy of 72.6 years for Homo sapiens.

Homo sapiens psychica, primarily referred to as adepts, live an estimated 168.9 years. Notably, a small subset of adepts in the Regna rank can live 250 years or more.

—National Intelligence Strategy White Paper: Top Secret (TS): Release of this document will cause severe damage to the security of the United States—Adept Assets

HANDCUFFS BITE INTO his wrists, and he rests his chin on his knees. Gabriel's only thoughts are for Zuko and Joe. Would they leave Zuko in

Joe's apartment or take him somewhere? An image of Zuko pacing and panting replays over and over in his head. Reaching out to Zuko, all he can sense from his loyal friend is anxiety. Gabriel leans his head on the police car window, willing his eyes to remain open. He concentrates on connecting with Zuko to comfort him. His effort results in stony silence.

Finally, the Boston Police Department headquarters comes into view. He's ushered into a small windowless room painted a dull orange. If they built this room for intimidation, it's working. The sign on the door says IR8. What's IR? Maybe Interrogation Room? Gabriel assumes someone is watching him on the other side of the black glass window. He opens himself to look when a wave of exhaustion sweeps over him. Despite the effort, no one is there; so much for that trope. After Joe's lifeless eyes refused to close, Gabriel knows he'll have a collection of false tropes before this is over.

After a few seconds, he reaches for his cell phone. "Oh right." The police seized all his belongings.

With elbows on the table and his face in his hands, he glares at the clock on the wall. Engulfed in the deafening silence, Gabriel tries to imagine the second hand making a sound. *Tick, tick, tick.* Indifferent to his presence, it continues its baleful journey around the clock face. It travels in the same lonely silence that surrounds him. He reflects on all the guilty and innocent who once occupied this same space. What has befallen the innocent? Did they find justice? He knew many did not.

After what seems like hours but was only ten minutes, according to the soundless clock, two men and one woman in uniform enter the viewing room. Gabriel is no longer unobserved in IR8.

He probes their minds despite the energy it costs. No hostility in them; that's good, but something isn't normal. Something has made them nervous.

The policewoman leaves the room and wordlessly enters IR8. She's carrying a rotary phone with a long wire trailing behind it. A rotary phone? She deposits the relic on the Formica desk with a thud.

"You're not under arrest, only detained. You're allowed a phone as a courtesy." She stands back and crosses her arms. "Make it fast," she shouts. "We don't have all day."

Gabriel racks his brain for how many phone numbers he knows by heart. He remembers precious few it turns out. He knows Uncle Russell's number, but he's already here, although Gabriel's not supposed to know that. Maybe he should call his uncle and cement the ruse? But why? He's not under that kind of suspicion. He could contact Barbara at Jeebom because it's early enough that she'll still be at work. She'll know what to do. She's a respected doctor, and she loved Joe. They always had that in common. If Joe's colleague comes to Gabriel's aid and vouches for him, that must mean something, right?

Gabriel's friendship with Barbara is an unlikely one that began when he met Joe. Barbara was mentoring Joe when he and Gabriel started dating and it seemed natural that Barbara should mentor Gabriel as well. Her staggering intellect and maternal manner were helpful in his gaining confidence. She convinced Gabriel to open the jewelry store to sell the gems that he, as she described it, had a preternatural way of ferreting out. It gave him a base of operations and gave his parents greater assurance in his future. Barbara was right; it kept them from thinking him a complete failure. When Joe broke off the relationship, it was Barbara whom Gabriel leaned on, and she was always there. Much to his surprise, they didn't grow apart after the breakup; they grew closer.

"Dial 9!" the policewoman commands.

"Ah, okay," Gabriel stammers.

The phone rings and rings, and just before it goes to voicemail, he hears Barbara's soothing voice.

"Barbara."

"Hello? Gabriel?"

The worried concern hits him, and he wants so much to hug her.

"Why aren't you calling or texting me on my cell?" she continues. "And why are you at the Boston Police Department?"

He studies the Formica desk. "Barbara, I'll be quick. There's no easy way to say this. Joe is dead, and I found him collapsed on the floor in his apartment."

There's a brief pause on the other line, and then she gasps. It's more of a rattle with jerky intakes of breath. "What? Was it a heart attack? Oh my God."

"They haven't told me anything, but I don't think his death was, ah, natural. Um, I wanted you to know first. Would you call my uncle? He's an attorney. Russell Walker."

"Why were you going to see Joe?" Barbara asks. "You can tell me. I'm able to help. Were you guys—?"

"Yeah, ah, now isn't a good time."

"What did he say? What did he want?"

The policewoman taps her watch impatiently and scowls.

"Barbara—Uncle Russell," Gabriel whispers.

"Oh, Jesus, you're under arrest, aren't you?"

"Technically, I'm being detained."

"What's his number?" Barbara's smooth tone is gone, replaced with her all-business voice. This must be the laboratory-Barbara Joe used to talk about.

Gabriel quickly gives her Russell's cell number.

"You know I'm not a dog person," Barbara says. "But knowing you,

Zuko was with you. How is he?"

"Thanks for asking. They took him to a shelter. I'll get him as soon as I'm out of here, believe me."

"That's some good news. Has anyone from the government spoken to you? The NIS, specifically?"

"The NIS? No. Why?"

"Joe had, ah, government contracts."

"Look, Barbara, I'm out of time. Make the call please."

The policewoman walks over and beckons for the phone. She grabs it and slams the receiver on the cradle and walks out. After another five minutes, two more men join Gabriel's silent observers, one of them his uncle. Gabriel is relieved he came himself instead of sending an attorney from the firm.

If Russell opens up to him, Gabriel will do the same. A "don't worry, we've got this" feeling washes over him. Gabriel takes a deep breath and relaxes slightly. Russell graduated third in his class at Yale Law School. As patriarch of the Salem House, Russell relies on those skills, and Gabriel knows he'll need all of them now. It's Russell's job to know what to do. Gabriel leans back in his chair and closes his eyes.

The police talk amongst themselves. Too drained, Gabriel can't summon the energy to follow along. A man he fell in love with and failed to help is dead. Zuko is out there somewhere alone and frightened, and again, Gabriel can't help. He's useless.

Finally, the policewoman is the first to exit the viewing room. It won't be long now.

A tall woman with blonde hair worn up flings open the door to the fluorescently lit IR8. Gabriel's uncle follows her and gives Gabriel a conspiratorial wink. The woman roughly jerks back her chair—the grating clanking sound breaks the silence—and takes a seat. In her left hand, she holds a file.

"They have a file already?" Gabriel projects into Russell's mind.

Her swagger must come from having mastered a lethal self-defense discipline, or so Gabriel assumes. She looks deadly. Her cream-colored suit hangs loosely on her body.

In contrast, Russell is dressed in a superbly tailored navy-blue suit that looks as if it were made for him because it was. Gabriel appreciates this because even though it's well past midnight, his uncle arrives dressed for the boardroom. Russell flashes a bright smile that barely creases his smooth skin. His bald head, a polished obsidian dome, sets off his neat close-cropped beard. He wears all his ties knotted with a perfect dimple. This one, a bright power yellow, is no different. His tortoiseshell glasses are an affectation since all adepts have twenty-twenty vision at a minimum.

Sometimes, Gabriel fears how his life will change when the dall start to notice that he doesn't age. "I have good genes" and "I'm young for my age" can only explain so much. Will he reinvent as well as Russell? Will he retain that same sense of purpose? Gabriel looks at Russell as he is now and can barely imagine the trailblazing World War II fighter pilot he once was.

The police detective twitches and taps her foot. The emotion emanating from her shocks Gabriel into wakefulness.

Well, that's interesting.

"Mr. Kelly. I'm Detective Rizzo. I'll be the lead investigator in the death of Dr. Joseph Martin. You're not under arrest." After a brief pause, she concludes her sentence with, "At this time."

Russell takes a seat beside Gabriel, while Detective Rizzo flips a switch on the table and says, "This is Detective Janice Rizzo with attorney Russell Walker and suspect Gabriel Kelly. I am recording this interview on June third."

Gabriel can tell Russell will continue to speak by his small intake of breath, and he doesn't need telepathy to know to keep quiet.

"If my client isn't under arrest," Russell says, "we'll be leaving unless you have probable cause to detain us."

"Counselor, he found the body!" Rizzo shoots back. "I think that entitles me to ask a few questions."

Gabriel senses her bristling at Russell's presence. And not because of his status, although that bothers her; she resents any hint of special treatment. What troubles Rizzo more is how Russell is here, how he knew so soon. She suspects a mole in the department. Gabriel chastises himself for reading too many mysteries into the situation. He can't peruse her mind here.

"Questions, yes," Russell continues. "But if you're going to be combative, perhaps the presence of the district attorney will prove helpful?"

"At this hour?"

"Yes, Detective, at this hour."

Rizzo says nothing in reply and directs her gaze back to Gabriel. She takes in a deep breath and exhales through her nose. He wishes he could project into her to back off, although he doesn't think Rizzo would be susceptible to his middling powers of suggestion.

"What is your relationship to the deceased?" Rizzo asks, meeting his eyes.

"Ah, we're friends," Gabriel replies.

"You were friends?" she repeats. At first, Gabriel thought she was going to follow that up, but instead she asks, "How did you meet Dr. Martin?"

"At a dinner party of Peter's. He introduced us, and Joe and I hit it off. After we broke up, Joe started dating Peter and end up marrying him." Gabriel laughs nervously.

Rizzo is unmoved and looks into Gabriel's eyes as she says, "Peter? He married Joe, yet you walk into his home while he is away. That sounds complicated."

There is no question posed, but Gabriel is just about to speak when Russell nods a "no." Gabriel stops and remains silent.

"How did you meet Peter?" Rizzo asks.

"At a concert. I approached him afterward to discuss his music, and we became friends."

"Was there any attraction between the two of you?"

"Me and Peter? No."

"How did Joe meet Peter?"

"The same way I did, I think. At a concert. Peter is very talented."

Rizzo looks at him, giving off a fleeting sense that she is about to push. The thought of projecting into her mind is tempting him, but Russell bursts inside Gabriel's mind:

"Don't use your abilities on the dall inside the station. It's part of our treaty with the witches. I say this not as your uncle but as your patriarch."

"What was the state of Peter and Joe's marriage?"

Gabriel winces at the question. "Not good. Joe told me he wanted out a while ago." His voice speeds up, but he catches himself and slows his cadence. "They were a good couple, for a time."

Rizzo makes a note. She will revisit this line of inquiry, Gabriel thinks, as a knot forms in the pit of his stomach. For a human, she looks as if she knows exactly what he's thinking. Her gaze is disconcertingly perceptive.

"Mr. Kelly, why did you go to Dr. Martin's home?"

"We had plans." Gabriel says it quickly, maybe too quickly. He breathes deeply, not wanting to appear flustered. He forces himself to appear calm, and then his uncle intrudes upon his thoughts again—

"I'm here because the entire family believes you're innocent. Be yourself."

Gabriel revels in the reassurance, and he relaxes just a little. The projection from his uncle was startlingly clear. He seems to be getting stronger with age, and he's already achieved a Provectus rank.

"Joe said he needed me."

Rizzo's surprise at his statement comes out of her pores, like pin-pricks on his body, but he reads nothing on her face. Not even a tremor.

"What about his husband?" Rizzo asks, again looking directly into Gabriel's eyes. "Why did he need you?"

"He, ah, said he needed some help with, ah, something to do with his work."

"Really?" Rizzo arches an eyebrow. "How are you in a position to aid the chief scientific officer of one of the major pharmaceutical firms in the world?"

The smooth ebony skin of Russell's face, which has thus far resisted any evidence of aging, creases in annoyance. Gabriel looks away, avoiding his gaze.

"My family firm is a large stakeholder in Covian."

"How large?"

"We're a top ten stockholder."

"I see," Rizzo says, her eyes blank. "How would that help Dr. Martin?"

"I don't know. What I do know is that he wanted to give the impression that a top ten stockholder had his back."

"Give an impression to whom?"

"I don't know."

"What exactly did you see in the home, Mr. Kelly?" Rizzo shifts in her seat, changing tactics. "No detail is too small or inconsequential."

"I saw—" Gabriel senses the longing in his uncle to hug him, despite his concerns about Joe. The pain in his gut threatens to escape out of his throat, but Gabriel pushes it down.

"I saw Joe, collapsed in the middle of the floor. He was holding a coffee cup when he fell. I could smell the coffee; it was spilled all over the floor. I screamed his name and felt for a pulse but—"

"Why didn't you call it in?"

"It all happened so fast. I would've, but the police showed up so quickly. Who did call?"

"There were adepts there?" Russell sees this in Gabriel's mind. His exclamation surges into Gabriel's psyche as if yelled at the top of his lungs, and Gabriel has little defense.

Rizzo squints as she taps her badge. "I ask the questions, Mr. Kelly, not you."

"No need to be argumentative, Detective," Russell says. "My nephew doesn't make it a habit of being interviewed by the police." He turns to Gabriel. "Just answer the questions, nothing more, nothing less.

Rizzo regards Gabriel with a dark expression for several seconds. "How did you get in the home? Do you have a key or the code?"

"It was open. Joe left it open."

Rizzo's expression is unreadable, but Gabriel knows she doesn't believe him.

"And I saw—"

Without thinking, he reaches for Zuko with his hand, expecting him to be seated at his side, and with his mind. To Gabriel's surprise, he receives the call. Zuko's reply is anxious and insistent.

"Come."

Gabriel has never been able to hear a call from such a distance before.

Russell connects with him. *"It's routine police procedure to take an arrestee's pet to the local shelter. We can retrieve him first thing in the morning. Gabe, I'm sorry about Joe. I can feel your pain. It's a complex sense of loss and guilt. Why is that?"*

"No one at the apartment complex remembers you, Mr. Kelly. Not the receptionist who signed you in nor other residents coming and going. Despite the fact that you were accompanied by a pony-sized show dog." Rizzo pulls out an 8 by 10 CCTV photo of Zuko and Gabriel and lays it on the table. "That's odd, don't you think?"

Gabriel shrugs. "He's not a show dog."

Rizzo's eyes narrow. "Answer the question."

"Folks have a lot on their minds. I'm not memorable."

Rizzo inhales deeply, not hiding her exasperation. "You're six foot one, 240 pounds, and you walk around with a pony off-leash, and you're not memorable?"

Gabriel says nothing. He's curious to see if, in her mind, she finishes her sentence with "And you're Black," but his uncle's withering glare occupies all his concentration. In truth, people are often confused when they see ethnically ambiguous Gabriel. In different lighting, he's a dark-skinned Italian or a light-skinned Black man or Latinx. He gets Puerto Rican a lot.

Expressionless, Rizzo returns the photo to the folder. "What did Dr. Martin say about wanting out exactly?" she demands while pinching the bridge of her nose.

The policewoman reenters the room, and Rizzo's sculpted eyebrows leap in alarm. She motions for Rizzo to join her in a corner as Russell smiles in satisfaction. Gabriel is too tired and sad to probe

Russell's mind, but he can guess that the district attorney has heeded Russell's call, and the interview is ending.

"Mr. Kelly," Rizzo says with fierce eyes. "You may go. I know it's a cliché, but inform this office if you plan on leaving town, and don't leave town." She hands a business card to Gabriel and Russell.

"Thank you," Gabriel says, taking it and reflexively reaching for his wallet, which, of course, isn't there. "Although I do have a business trip planned to Sri Lanka. You see, I'm in the gem business and—"

"We may need to revisit that!" Russell interrupts. "Regardless, Detective, I'll inform you well in advance of my client's movements. Oh, and one more thing. Express my regrets to the district attorney and Commander McEntee. I can't stay to say hello. My nephew needs to get home."

Rizzo says nothing in reply as she abruptly turns and exits. The clacking of her heels echoes down the hall.

"Uncle Russell, thanks for coming. I know that would've been much worse without you."

"It would've," Russell says. "Follow me out of the station, and don't speak to anyone. Don't look at anyone. We'll talk in the car."

Finally, with Russell behind the wheel, Gabriel begins to feel himself again. The fatigue takes hold, though, and his eyes weigh tons.

"You reached Zuko across too great a distance for a Media to manage."

"Yeah, I found him. He's okay."

"Impressive," Russell replies.

Gabriel rests his head and closes his eyes.

"The Angeles House asked for permission to enter our territory and investigate the circumstances surrounding Joe Martin's theft of their intellectual property. I granted it."

Gabriel snaps his eyes open. "Wait, what did you say?"

"And," Russell continues, taking a moment to look directly into Gabriel's eyes, "they specifically asked to speak to you."

Chapter Eight

LUPUS VINCULUM

The Lupus vinculum, sometimes called the wolf bond, is the psychic bond between an adept and a canine. The domestication of dogs began when the first wolf heard the call of an adept and wandered into a human encampment. The bond would prove helpful as wolves warned humans, namely Cro-Magnons, of predators and aided them in hunting.

This bond gave Homo sapiens the evolutionary edge they needed to wipe out the other human species on the planet. We believe that the witch myth of an animal familiar is the Lupus vinculum misunderstood.

—National Intelligence Strategy White Paper: Top Secret

> (TS): Release of this document will cause severe damage
> to the security of the United States—Adept Assets

WHEN THEY PULL up to the Louisbourg Square townhouse, Gabriel's mother is waiting by the door. She pulls him into a hard embrace, and after a long moment, she reaches for Russell and says, "We're in the library."

In the center of the great room, with its floor-to-ceiling books, lies a handwoven Moroccan rug, a gift from House Amazigh. Regna Anisa Aboud Walker sits in a massive high-backed chair. The stark contrast of his great-great-grandmother's aging body with the youthful power that occupied it a few hours ago weighs heavily on Gabriel. Her wizened figure is frail and stiff. She wears her hair, now streaked with gray, pulled back into a bun and clipped with decorative combs. As a child, Gabriel thought they were weapons she could employ in his defense. She always seemed poised to reach behind her head, grab a comb, and fight off any would-be attackers.

Her dress is colorful and free-flowing. More than once, Gabriel has caught her using telekinesis to enhance its billowing effect. He wonders if others notice or if it's their secret.

Beside her sits Gabriel's father, Adair, a physics professor. His reddish-blond hair is disheveled, and his midriff begs for release from his suit jacket. Despite his mother's best efforts, he refuses to wear any of the new jackets her personal shopper hangs in his closet.

He's getting heavier and not just because of the weight of his expectations, Gabriel thinks.

Adair's family suffered losses during the witch trials in the old world. For him, the wounds are still fresh. Adepts pass down emotions, memories, joy, and pain in the same way as the dall pass down jewelry. His father rises to hug him, and Gabriel revels in his embrace. He didn't know how much he needed it until he was fully submerged.

In her quiet yet authoritative voice, Regna Anisa intones, "Be seated." Unlike the clear voice that rang out in his head at Joe's apartment, her physical voice crackles, reminding him of an old radio transmission. "I need to explain to Gabriel what exactly happened."

Gabriel looks into her eyes and is reassured. Still, he can't help thinking that he's missing out on a crucial piece of information—one that everyone else in the room already possesses.

"What you went through at your friend's moment of the death was not just experienced by you. You projected onto the grid by instinct; so many adepts also heard his last cry. I am sure it did not go unnoticed by the witch community. Your pain and shock spread trauma throughout the grid. You were unprepared, and your mind rebelled. Trauma, remember, kindles our abilities. I am sorry."

Gabriel nods. "It knocked me to the ground. It was tragic and terrifying. Joe must've felt that same terror."

He's stating the obvious, but he wants his family to bear witness. He wants them to respect what Joe was to him and understand his loss. He opens himself, and comfort washes over him from Anisa and his parents. Anisa's projection is nuanced and laced with experiences similar to his own. They always were much alike.

Anisa motions to speak, and everyone turns to face her. Her gaze settles on her great-great-grandson. "We all sensed what you lived through in the moments after your friend's death. What did you perceive before it?"

Gabriel regards her wide-eyed. "Yes, yes, I forgot in all the commotion, but it was awful. I had this nagging sense something was wrong.

It was oppressive—that I or someone else was in danger. I—"

Gabriel pauses and inhales. "Of course, that was Joe's fear. But I was so far away. I've never been able to do that before. To pick up thoughts from the dall at a distance like that. It explains why I didn't hear a plea for help on the grid. I never imagined I could pick up thoughts from the dall without deliberately trying."

"Gabriel," Russell says, his deep voice monotone. "Tell us about the attack by the Provectus-level adept. They opened a portal and fled."

"Yes, at Joe's, near where I found him dead. There were two, but only one attacked."

"You didn't recognize either of them?"

"No. They hit me with a powerful telekinetic blast. They killed Joe. What are we going to do about it?" Gabriel's voice is thin. He looks down at the floor and chews his lip.

Russell tilts his head to the side as if to get a better perspective of Gabriel's question. "Joseph Martin was studying us. What do you know about it?"

"I—" Gabriel pauses to gather his thoughts.

"Open your mind," Russell demands.

Gabriel gasps. "What? No, I—"

"Yes."

Everyone, except Russell, turns to Anisa, Regna of the Salem House. Her soft utterance reverberates in the room. Gabriel's parents frantically project to Anisa to reconsider, but she rebuffs them. Russell may be the elected patriarch of the Salem House, but Anisa is the matriarch of this family and maybe the most powerful adept in the world. Adepts grow stronger with age and who is older than she?

Anisa's hooded brown eyes settle on Gabriel. "Open your mind. Open it to what you know about the doctor's interest in us and your part in it."

"What do you know about Joe and his work?"

"Impertinent." Anisa's eyes widen, but otherwise, she is motion-less. "While I respect your anguish, you broadcast onto the grid because you could not contain your grief over a scientist who treated us like lab rats. Now cooperate."

Gabriel looks away, and he submits. For the first time in his adult life, he will share thoughts with someone involuntarily. Russell's intrusion is a dull knife cutting across his psyche, leaving behind a trail of pain and humiliation.

Russell leans back in his seat after his effort and frowns. "He's in love with Dr. Martin. Such a stinging loss—he's full of heartache. There's guilt too. Martin reached out to him for help. He was trying to tell him about his data. That's all for now. He is rebelling."

"What's this about lab rats?" Gabriel asks.

Russell glances at Gabriel, and then turns away to address Anisa. "Gabriel opened a portal. True, he did it with his bonded dog, but he did it. That's a rapid adaptation." Russell turns back to Gabriel. "Did you pass out?"

"Gabriel felt the scientist from a great distance," Anisa says. "He successfully read a portal address. I came into my abilities as a child when under great stress. As it often happens to us, cruel circumstances are the crucible of our abilities."

Russell rises out of his chair and locks eyes with Gabriel. "Do you know where Martin keeps his work?"

"No, I don't know. Um, his lab, maybe?"

"And where is that?"

"I'd visit him at the lab sometimes. He works for Covian now, in Cambridge, but he used to work for Jeebom."

"Explain," Anisa says, her attention focused on Russell.

"There are a variety of governments and pharmaceutical firms striving to be the first to exploit our genetic secrets. Two of the major ones are Covian and Jeebom Pharmaceuticals. Covian is owned by the Angeles House, and it's where Martin worked. The Angeles are unhappy at the loss of their dall asset and their missing data, so I've granted them leave to conduct subtle inquiries in our territory."

Gabriel bristles and glares at Russell, but he says nothing and nods his acquiescence.

"The other," Russell continues, "is Jeebom, owned by the Koli House in Mumbai, India. The Koli are a powerful House. They control Western India and the economic powerhouse that is Mumbai. They're not fools. They'll be expecting something."

Turning his gaze back to Gabriel, Russell asks, "Can you get us in? We need to find the data."

"I'm going to follow those adepts," Gabriel says. "If we find them, we find the killer and the data."

"And if you find them, you'll do what?" Russell responds. "No, I'll send a qualified agent."

"No one is more qualified than me to find Joe's killer."

Russell smiles a thin smile. "Who else knows that Martin cracked our genetic code?"

"I don't know," Gabriel replies. "But of course, you don't care about Joe, only his work. I don't know why I'm surprised. He was afraid and asked me for protection. What a fool I was. I'm going after them. I owe it to Joe."

Gabriel's mother utters a high-pitched "No." It comes out more as a squeak, but Gabriel's father puts his hand on hers and shakes his head.

"I don't approve," Russell says, "but if you're going, I won't stand in your way. Turn the tracking on your phone off." Russell seems un-moved by Gabriel's psychic sharing of his grief. "The dall police are monitoring your movements."

Gabriel stands with a forceful show of energy and straightens his shoulders.

"Ready?" Russell asks.

"I'm ready," Gabriel answers without any hint of hesitancy.

"Take this." Gabriel's mother removes her wedding ring and hands it to him.

"Mom, no."

"Take it. It has ley energy. You might need it without Zuko."

"But Mom…"

"Bring it back to me," she says and moves to stand beside her husband.

"Gabriel."

Anisa calls out to him, but she's done something else. She's linked all their minds. This is an extraordinary step rarely done. Now, all will communicate in more than words to avoid confusion.

"Bring us the data. The killers will follow," his father says.

Gabriel nods and calls on the energy of the ley line. It surges through him, but he senses nothing. He winces at the effort. Defeated, he says, "It's not like before. I can't do it. I need Zuko."

"When you are trying to—" Anisa stops and turns to Adair. He interrupts her telepathically, a bold move, and she nods for him to take the floor.

"Thank you, Regna," he says and approaches his son. "Have you ever heard of the double-slit experiment?"

"No, I haven't, Dad." Gabriel's voice is barely audible, his exasperation there for all to see.

"The double-slit experiment," his father explains in his professorial voice, "is when you shoot an electron, it should go through the left or the right hole. Yet, occasionally, it goes through both simultaneously, and we don't know how or why. These particles can be in two places at once. That's what you can do, but on a grander scale, and I'm in awe of your talent. I'm in awe of you. I have never been prouder."

His father's eyes glisten, and he hugs Gabriel.

Now that he's increased in rank, he's worthy of his father's love, but what if after the crisis passes his power fades back to Media? He might cry if he's not careful. But, tossing that thought aside, he lets the tears come. This is no time for stoicism. They all know what's in his heart because of the connection. Let them see it on his face.

Gabriel takes a deep breath and dries his face with the palm of his hand. "Dad, thanks, you better sit down."

"Go open a wormhole, son."

"Sorry for saying you could never understand me because I'm—because you do."

Gabriel turns and draws on the ley line. Energy and pain fill his body in equal measure. He sees his father's encouraging look even as he fades away.

A memory in Joe's living room comes to him. Gabriel grabs hold of it and doesn't let go. The colors and shapes that make up the "address," as Anisa described it, come into view. The puzzle solves itself at lightning speed. A door opens and closes in his mind. It's more akin to a garage door. It opens again, but this time, Gabriel wills it to remain open. Sunlight scorches his face, and car horns erupt all around him. In the distance, he hears the forlorn call of a cuckoo bird, and the smell of salted fish fills the air of the library.

A frisson of fear creeps up Gabriel's spine and threatens to suffocate him. So what? It's normal to be afraid, and he steps through the portal, unmoored from time and space.

Chapter Nine

ADEPT GOVERNMENT

A matriarch or a patriarch, elected by a council, governs adept society. There are seven council seats, the number having significance to adepts, three of them hereditary and four elected. This is a holdover of the influence held by the most genetically gifted families.

Marriages are often strictly arranged to maintain powerful bloodlines. The United States has ten adept Houses, and Canada has two.

—National Intelligence Strategy White Paper: Top Secret (TS): Release of this document will cause severe damage to the security of the United States—Adept Assets

GABRIEL COLLAPSES. THE energy drain from the teleport sucks the air from his lungs. He drags himself up and over to the window. He's been here once before to buy jewels, but the reason for the instant recognition is the memories he inherited from his father. Adair worked for the British government in Mumbai between the world wars, and his memories wash over Gabriel in a flood. Gabriel never knew his father lived here before today. The imprinting leaves behind his father's connection to this city he loved. Nothing else can explain this joy. Melancholy also tugs at the corner of Gabriel's mind because his father loved a woman here. It didn't work out.

Shards of light bathe the room, causing Gabriel to squint and cup his hands over his eyes. Sunshine in Mumbai is rare this time of year; his father's knowledge tells him to spare a moment to appreciate it. The bright corner office has an oversized mahogany desk, oddly paired with a modern ergonomic chair. The high ceilings imbue the office with the air of a courtroom. Whoever occupies this office loves plants, Gabriel thinks. It's a jungle in here.

The intricate maze of downtown traffic flows with a rhythm all its own, and the smoky air tints the landscape with a reddish hue. The color lends a romantic aura, but Gabriel knows there is nothing romantic about it. The air quality is abysmally low today. The neon sky may be beautiful, but it's deadly.

"He showed him all the kingdoms of the world," he mutters.

Gabriel withdraws his phone and takes photos of every document on the ornate desk. He doesn't pause or look up from his task. As he snaps the photos, he wonders about the adept inquisitor investigating him. Law enforcement officials are largely unknown in adept society. By the time you figure out who they are, it's usually too late. His uncle as much as said that the Angeles suspect Gabriel of murdering Joe and taking their data. Would his uncle steal the data and give him up as a sacrificial pawn? No, how could he even think that?

Still, someone will burn for this. Burning is the ultimate punishment. Two Regnas, the most powerful of all adepts, would be required to complete the task—severing the part of the brain responsible for adept abilities. It's the ultimate maiming reserved for capital crimes. Gabriel can't remember a burning in his lifetime. He shivers and pushes the thought away. Gabriel reads the name on the nameplate: Shreyas Anand. Who are you, Shreyas Anand?

Gabriel's heart sinks when he sees a memo written to Anand from Barbara. He knows she's racing Joe to crack the adept genetic code, so how much does she know about him really?

Gabriel senses someone outside the room, not an adept—a dall man coming to care for the plants.

Obscuring someone's mind to make them not see you is an advanced skill. It involves isolating their senses only around you, convincing them to ignore what they hear, see, and smell. Gabriel decides not to push his abilities and hides under the great mahogany desk.

A young man enters the office, humming to himself. He's thinking about his parents pressuring him to get married. Maybe it's time, he thinks. Perhaps it is time to leave behind Bollywood dreams and work in the family business. A brief glimpse of the young man driving a pest extermination truck appears. It would please his parents. Maybe he will meet the girl his father wants him to marry. One more audition and finish up the improv class, he thinks, then I'll call Dad, but what about my girlfriend?

Gabriel smiles. The man's thoughts are an open book.

The gardener makes his way across the office until he's behind the grand desk, looming over the plants. He prunes one of them, overflowing and reaching for the sun in the floor-to-ceiling window. One of the pruned leaves lands on Gabriel's head. The man reaches down, plucks the leaf out of Gabriel's hair, and tosses it in the wastebasket. For a moment, it seems to Gabriel as if he looked directly into his eyes. The gardener's warm breath gusts onto his face as Gabriel spots a strand of his hair in the basket next to the leaf. Finally, the man gathers his things and leaves.

Gabriel takes a deep, relaxing breath. Good luck with the marriage, dude, he thinks. Confident in what he was able to achieve, Gabriel decides to venture outside the office to see what else he can discover before returning home. He passes employees busy working in the spacious open-floor room, but everyone ignores him. Cubicle after cubicle, for almost as far as the eye can see, it's an office farm. Gabriel smiles again. What if he imagines sewing machines instead of laptops across this sea of desks? This could be a scene out of a Dickens novel. What would happen if he stood in the middle of the room and held up a sign that said, "Union"? Would the office workers swarm?

Gabriel moves silently through the halls, a ghost, completely unnoticed. *Just like high school.* The bold, confident Jeebom letterhead is prominently displayed throughout the floor.

Gabriel reaches in his wallet and performs the pantomime for the benefit of the CCTV cameras that are surely documenting his visit. He can hide himself from people's perceptions but not from mechanical cameras. He touches his wallet to the door sensor and mentally calls for the open-close mechanism, and the door silently clicks open.

In the elevator, he notes the music "Don't Get Around Much Anymore" by Duke Ellington. This version is with Louis Armstrong. He chuckles. *I was ten time zones away twenty minutes ago.*

Once outside in the bright afternoon sunshine, Gabriel takes stock of his surroundings. The sun is oppressive, but the streets are slick. It's at least 90 degrees, or in India, 32 degrees Celsius and oppressively humid.

The world goes dark.

He's pushed into a clammy void, and he screams, but in this emptiness, there is no sound. Time slows, and the air thickens. Gabriel remembers his sister pushing him into the deep end of the pool when he was five, knowing he couldn't swim. He feels that same terror now. Except this time, he never hits the water. He falls without end, twisting and turning. Where is the pain coming from? Nausea and despair cut into his psyche and intermingle in a macabre dance.

Hitting the water with a deadening thud, he tries to make sense of the attack. There is no light, and he doesn't know which way is up. The freezing water morphs into quicksand, and Gabriel tries to breathe, but he can't command his lungs. Isn't that an instinct? The pain comes again in wave after wave of searing agony. A certainty comes that he's going to die. He accepts his death in a Mumbai alley and hopes his mother can claim his body. *Will she find me here? Will my body be unclaimed halfway around the world?*

Gabriel feels Zuko reaching out to him and the pain subsides. A memory of his sister and mother coming to see Zuko as a puppy comforts him. They both marvel at the bond between man and dog. His father's pride is thick in the air because he's projecting to everyone in the room. A warm feeling of security and love surrounds him. He sees Zuko at twelve pounds, curious, yet never far from his side.

"*Get up,*" the fragmented voice says.

"I'm trying." He sucks in a breath.

A car full of malice is coming. Smelling their sweat-dampened hair, Gabriel revels in his new talent to detect them, but with the psychic connection, his smile is wiped away.

"How dare he."

"Crush him like a bug."

"Listen to the Salem scream."

Gabriel's stomach twists, the truth of it strong in his bones. They will make him scream.

The leader of the Koli calls out with all his telepathic power.

"Regna Kotak, help us. The Salem spy will get away."

Suddenly, Gabriel's thoughts are frozen, and he can't move. It's as if time stands still, and he's floating in space, connected to the Koli Regna by a giant umbilical cord. He tries to hide his dread at the prospect of failure as the men come to kill him or worse. He learns the driver's name is Uday and that he was just admitted as a junior inquisitor. Fear wells up inside Gabriel; he's about to be sick. He's as helpless as a fly in the Regna's web.

"I hear your request for aid deputy inquisitor, and it is denied. You have failed under Article 3 of the Regna Charter to present evidence that this incursion is on behalf of a foreign government. I will hear your petition again without prejudice if you return with sufficient proof. The Salem encroachment will be taken up at the Assembly, but it does not meet the standard of a Regna-level response."

"But they're spying."

"Yes," Regna Kotak says. *"This adept is spying, but you have failed to meet your burden that it is on behalf of the Salem government. Request denied."*

With that, the Koli Regna seems to say hello, but to whom? Was it to Gabriel? And then it's over. The psychic TV is turned off, and he's in control of his body again.

The dragon lets me go, but a pack of wolves is coming.

The assault comes again, but Gabriel is ready. The memory of Zuko as a puppy in the great room of his home anchors him. The now-familiar paroxysm of color comes into focus. What was so confusing now makes sense. The portal is opening, he thinks, full of pride.

Gabriel cries out, both hands cradling his head. He loses control of the portal, and it snaps shut, siphoning his energy away. He lurches forward with no control of his limbs because he's zooming along the highway. Trees and buildings flip by. No, he's not in a speeding car. Someone driving a car is coming to kill him. The assassin devours the road, block after block, in a continual blur.

I can compel that man to drive over a cliff. Isn't that what they deserve? To be wrapped around a pole and left for dead? What will the Koli Regna do then?

Gabriel followed someone here but found nothing that would rise to the level of adept or witch protection. *So, what are they protecting?* Gabriel's heart pounds in his chest, and the panic rises, a bile in his throat, but there's anger too. The rising power in his body has a voice but sits sullenly in a corner. He must calm himself.

"Open the portal," the voice says. *"Or let me out, and I'll handle it because you can't."*

I can't, Gabriel agrees. I'm here for Joe and to find answers. Joe wasn't perfect. He was distant and loved his work before all else, but he didn't deserve to die. He deserved the protection he asked for and I couldn't give. *I should die.*

Gabriel reaches into his pocket and grips his mother's ring to draw on its stored ley energy. He gets flashes of the rugged Cornwall coast, the sandy beaches, and the Druid power in the trees. The setting of the ring was crafted by his father's cousin, something Gabriel never knew, but he knows it now. He knows it like his own name. Gabriel hears an echo of his father talking to his Cornish cousin.

"I love her, Cadan. Make a setting for this."

Even in the memory, the energy in his father's hand shocks Gabriel when he hands over the diamond. The ring, as if guarding its treasure, releases a modest amount of ley energy into Gabriel's body. It flows into every capillary, singing its alarm. The certainty of his father's desire to marry his mother centers Gabriel, and he hopes to feel the same one day as space folds and light dims and his portal opens. Gabriel steps through into Louisbourg Square.

Screams of Koli anger, loud and piercing, slam into him. It's a needle to the ear, and then it's over.

"It's okay. It's okay. I'm back. I'm back."

"But it's not okay," the voice says from the furthest corner in him.

Chapter Ten

ADEPT RANKS

When we complete mapping the adept genome, our next goal should be to understand the mechanism that determines the extent of an adept's power. When we achieve that, we need to develop therapies to turn those genes off.

—Confidential Memorandum, Covian Pharmaceuticals

DETECTIVE JANICE RIZZO sits in the ornate lobby of the Green Acres condominium trust, commonly referred to as "the Green." She's waiting for the arrival of Joe Martin's husband, the widower Peter Brandon. She read the forensic reports of the coffee beans and water filtration system. They are clear of any poison. Some in the department want to declare this a suicide, but Rizzo knows it's murder.

A man of medium height in disheveled yet expensive clothes comes striding out of the parking garage elevator pulling a two-wheeled carry-on. He has sandy-brown hair, already thinning, and his eyes are sunken. One would expect sadness at a time like this, but Rizzo is often confronted with anger from family members who suffered the violent loss of a loved one as if she could've prevented it somehow. In her experience, anger is the easiest emotion.

The victim's husband is shorter than she expected and average-looking. His light jacket, although hopelessly rumpled, reeks of money. He greets her with a mad rush of words, but she catches the crucial part. "I want to see him."

"Ah, Mr. Brandon, I don't know exactly where the body is, but I'll make some calls and get back to you today."

"What do you mean you don't know where the body is? You lost him?"

That didn't take long, Rizzo thinks ruefully. Brandon's eyes flash hot and then cast downward. He slowly brings the heels of his hands to his eyes and rubs, trying to hold back tears or at least making a show of it.

"Mr. Brandon, the remains are with the medical examiner. As soon as the body is released—"

"What? I didn't approve an autopsy."

"Sir," Rizzo says, keeping her voice steady. "It was a court-ordered autopsy. It's routine when the death is deemed suspicious. As soon as the ME has completed her work, the body will be remanded to you."

As often as Rizzo has uttered this same sentence, it always lands differently, and it always sounds awkward. Where once there was a husband, now there is only property. These details drive the reality of not only a death but a murder home. She's watched the grief process unfold countless times.

Brandon utters a small gasp and speaks in a barely perceptible whisper. "Okay." He turns and heads for the elevator.

"Mr. Brandon!" Rizzo approaches him until they're face-to-face because she doesn't want anyone to overhear. Rizzo finds his haunted gaze has an innocent, almost naive nature. "I'm taking you to the station. It's where the interview will take place."

Brandon shakes his head. "But if I can't see him, then I at least want to see where—" Brandon gulps in a breath as if he just came close to drowning. "—where he died. All the officer on the phone said was that they couldn't determine how Joe passed. He said homicide would investigate. Can you at least tell me what happened? Where it happened?"

That familiar pang twists in her gut. It churns and begs Rizzo to put her arms around him, to comfort him, but all she can say is, "We can continue our conversation in your home."

"Thank you, and how did you even know he died? Was he late for something at Covian? He's always late for something."

Rizzo waits for the elevator doors to close. "We received an anonymous call about a man breaking into the apartment."

"What? So, he was murdered?"

"Mr. Brandon, Dr. Martin knew the man. They had plans to meet. He was worried when Dr. Martin didn't respond."

Brandon's head slowly turns in Rizzo's direction, his face a block of ice. She tenses, expecting a reaction. Brandon has been out of town for only a day, and already, his husband has a man in the home—a man who is concerned because he claims they have plans to meet.

"Who was with him?" he asks.

Rizzo's response is interrupted by the elevator chime announcing their arrival on the eleventh floor. At the same time, she feels her cell phone vibrate.

"Mr. Brandon—"

"Call me Peter. We'll get to know each other extremely well, right?"

"Yes, um, Peter. While this might not be an official crime scene, we must treat it as such until we know for sure. Put on these gloves, and don't touch anything unless expressly told to by me. Follow my lead—no need to open the door. I have a key. Stand aside."

Rizzo flashes her badge at the officer standing vigil at the apartment door. She takes this opportunity to open her purse to glance at her cell phone and sees there's a text from Herrera.

Preliminary results of the autopsy are consistent with poisoning. Forensics confirms they found sodium fluoroacetate in the coffee. Later in the day, we'll have confirmation that it was the cause of death.

Whatever sodium fluoroacetate is, Rizzo thinks. The following text from Junior Officer Herrera is the Wikipedia page of sodium fluoroacetate. It's a deadly, colorless salt. She smiles and thinks he might end up being a passable detective.

The apartment door opens easily, which is unusual for Rizzo. She constantly has to shove her sticky door open in her one-hundred-twenty-year-old Back Bay brownstone. Rizzo and Peter walk inside. The only sound is the wheels of Peter's luggage on the polished marble floor. True to his word, Peter doesn't make himself at home but remains by Rizzo's side.

"Oh! God—" he gasps.

Peter stops midstride at the tape outlining the body. His hand flies to his mouth, and he tries without success not to cry out. He shivers, and for a moment, Rizzo thinks his knees might give way, but they hold.

"And he died yesterday morning?" Peter asks, his voice small and fragile.

"Yes, I came into some news about Mr. Martin's death—"

"*Dr.* Martin!" Peter interjects.

"Yes, Dr. Martin. Your husband likely didn't die by natural causes or by accident. We found poison in his coffee. He either killed himself, or someone murdered him."

Peter's face creases in disbelief, and he blinks. His eyes grow more and more bloodshot by the minute. "He would never kill himself. Joe thought he was God's gift to the world, and he always, I mean *always*, made his coffee himself. He was a perfectionist, but when it came to his coffee, he was even more particular. The few times I made it for him, to his exacting water temperature standards—coffee ground at just the right consistency, just the right amount, steeped for just the right amount of time—the highest praise I ever got was, 'It's adequate.'"

"He took his coffee seriously, did he?" That explains the Peruvian coffee beans.

"That's an understatement. According to Joe, there was only one person who could make coffee to his liking."

"And who was that?" Rizzo asks with her notebook at the ready.

"The one who taught him. Gabriel Kelly."

"He taught your husband how to make coffee?"

"Yes, I have him to blame for rough grinds and impossibly meticulous water-to-coffee ratios."

"How do you know Gabriel Kelly?"

Peter's face creases in distaste. "We were friends. He came to my show once. I ended up introducing him to Joe, and they hit it off. After Joe and Gabriel broke up, I started dating Joe, and we married."

"Mr. Brandon—Peter—" Rizzo hesitates a long moment. It has the desired effect of focusing Peter's attention. "It was Gabriel Kelly who found Joe collapsed on the floor."

"What? He was with Gabriel?" Peter staggers back and sits down in a rush. "I thought I was being crazy. Well, I'm not crazy. I was wrong about a lot of things."

"Do you believe Mr. Kelly and your husband were having an affair?"

Peter gently massages his forehead. "I don't know. I don't know. I'm confused."

Rizzo pauses, hoping for more information, but nothing comes. "Did your husband have any enemies?"

"Wait," Peter says. "Yes, of course they were."

"Having an affair?"

Peter expels a breath. "It's so obvious now, but it's too late."

Peter's cheek twitches, creating a small dent near his eye. He reaches up to scratch his earlobe. Some might see the cheek twitching as a tell, and some would interpret touching his earlobe as the physiological response to lying. The body restricts blood flow in the extremities first, and when lying, people will unconsciously scratch their nose, or earlobe.

"And as for enemies," Peter continues, raising his voice. "There's no shortage in that department. My husband was a brilliant scientist, but he walked over plenty of other brilliant scientists to get where he is." Peter pauses for a moment and frowns. "Where he was. He didn't get many happy holidays cards."

Rizzo looks at Peter with her hand poised to take notes, and he gets the hint.

"I don't know their names," he says. "They were beneath Joe's notice. I'm sure you won't have to dig very hard to find out who they are."

"Is it fair to say that your husband was disliked by his colleagues?"

Peter smiles ruefully. "Yes, and he welcomed it. Except for his mentor, Barbara Bates. She loved him."

Rizzo raises an eyebrow. "Usually, in the case of a homicide, the victim knows full well who would have a motive to kill them. Think about this, Peter, and give it some serious thought. Did he mention anything untoward lately? Did he say anything unusual?"

Peter regards Rizzo with narrowed eyes, but his gaze soon drops to the floor. "That's all I think about. That's all I've thought about since I got the call. Did he say anything I should've picked up on? Did he want to hurt himself? Would someone want to hurt him? I don't know. All he said was he was expecting a Nobel Prize. My husband didn't lack confidence."

"A Nobel Prize? For what?"

"He was a geneticist," Peter replies. "He believed that a human subspecies exists with enhanced immunity, slow aging, amongst other things, and he was going to map their genome and find the genetic marker to identify them."

"Really? And he had evidence of this?"

"Yes. He was going to publish his paper with all his supporting data sets and blood samples. He was going to expose the community. He had to, to bring lifesaving drugs to the world. Mapping their genome was the achievement of a lifetime, he said. Or it's what I pieced together."

"Expose them? They're secret?"

"Have you heard of anyone like them?" Peter snaps.

"No," Rizzo replies without a ripple of irritation on her face. "Tell me about them."

"I don't know much, but Joe believed their genetics imbued them with special abilities such as telepathy and telekinesis. They're governed by Houses that rule over territories. The Salem rule over the

Northeastern United States. Boston is the Salem capital. Joe worked for the Angeles House, and they rule over Southern California. They have a class structure based on how powerful they are. They give themselves ranks like they're in the army. Joe complained that he needed higher ranking adepts—the term for the enhanced humans—to study. I gathered that Gabriel, despite his family pedigree, is low ranked."

"Joe told you this?"

"Of course not. I read it on his computer when he failed to lock it and listened when he thought I wasn't listening. I loved him but never trusted him, and he kept handwritten notes. He was brilliant, but he never fully grasped computers."

"Handwritten notes? Show me."

Peter beckons Rizzo, and she follows him into Joe's office.

"He keeps his notes in the top drawer. Joe locks it, but there's a spare key under the lamp. Do you want to move it?"

Rizzo nods and snaps on a pair of thin plastic nitrile gloves to move the lamp. She picks up the key and opens the drawer to retrieve three manila folders. Rizzo opens one, revealing neat, dense, and uniform handwriting. She scans the page, and upon seeing the word "adept," she closes the folder.

"Any more like this?"

"No," Peter replies.

Rizzo motions with her hand to direct Peter back into the living room, and they retake their seats.

"You believe he was able to scientifically prove what you told me before his death?" Rizzo asks, taking the folders.

"His murder. Yes."

Rizzo pauses to write in her notebook and flips through its pages. "Is it fair to say you believe Mr. Martin wouldn't take his own life?"

Peter rubs the back of his neck and looks around the room. "No, not unless he realized his life's work was amounting to nothing. Maybe he'd take that hard. The thing is, his work wasn't amounting to nothing. It was amounting to everything."

"And how were things between you?" Rizzo asks.

Peter's eyes blink, and then they flash again, hot. Rizzo's stomach starts to churn, but she keeps her face impassive. Peter looks confused. He must still be in shock, Rizzo thinks.

"They've been better. I was in P-town when he died because we had a fight."

"What was the fight about?"

Peter's shoulders sag, and his face goes slack. "He said I wasn't working hard enough on my music. My reviews are mediocre, and I embarrass him."

"What kind of music?" Rizzo notes he makes no mention of the divorce Gabriel Kelly brought up. Typical. Always tell the side piece you're getting divorced.

"I'm a jazz pianist and composer."

Rizzo looks over at the piano. The grand living room is full of light, and it sets off the jet-black instrument in an extraordinary way. No matter where she looks in the room, the piano inextricably draws her eye back. The nook it occupies is at once a public and yet private space.

"That's where the magic happens," Peter says, his eyes fierce yet downcast.

"Was your husband behaving differently leading up to his death? Was his routine upended?"

Rizzo can see the grief running through Peter's body. The way it makes him shudder at odd times and fills his dull eyes with pain. Grief is a virus that infects the loved ones of the murdered and the guilty.

"Nothing that he did during the day. He worked all the time. At the office day and night, and when he wasn't in the office, he was on the phone with colleagues and executives all over the world. I noticed he was talking about publishing something big. Lancet catnip he called it."

"Lancet catnip?"

"It's a fancy medical journal. Hey, can I go to the kitchen for a drink?"

Rizzo smiles and wonders why a man of wealth doesn't say, "May I."

"No, I'm sorry. We should conduct the rest of the interview at the station now that you've seen where Dr. Martin succumbed. I can accompany you while you collect some clothes and personal items as, unfortunately, you'll have to make other living arrangements for a few days."

Peter breathes in and utters a loud sigh. "Okay, I understand. Can we do the rest of the interview tomorrow? I'm tired, and I haven't slept after getting the news."

"Yes, of course. Tell me where you'll be. I'll have a car pick you up tomorrow morning. Do you know where you're going?"

"I'll go to a hotel. The W."

"Would you like a lift?" Rizzo asks as she puts her notebook back into her purse.

"No, thanks. When can I get back into my apartment?"

"As soon as we've collected all the evidence we need. A few more days."

Peter nods, and Rizzo watches him exit the apartment. She says goodbye to the officer guarding the door and double-checks to ensure it's securely locked.

Chapter Eleven

TELEPATHIC CLOAKING

Telepathic cloaking is the ability of an adept to mask their presence from other adepts. We believe that Russian adepts have developed the ability to cloak other less powerful adepts. Even an adept of low rank can wreak havoc on an installation if they're admitted on the assumption that they're fully human.

—National Intelligence Strategy White Paper: Top Secret (TS): Release of this document will cause severe damage to the security of the United States—Adept Assets

GABRIEL CLOSES HIS mind as tight as a drum, but mental tendrils still reach out to him as he and Zuko enter his jewelry store. He just rescued

Zuko from the shelter, and his loyal companion is in no mood to be separated again. It's here that he sells gems without ley energy to the dall. Presently, there are two adept couples in the shop and two dall. His friend and employee, Margot, is helping the adepts, although she has no clue what they are.

Murder is good for business, Gabriel observes. Broadcasting on the grid has attracted rubberneckers. Let them take a good look, but that's all they'll get. He's here to talk to Margot about the new rubies from Burma and to meet his witch friend, Sellers. Running the shop is Margot's domain. He's the ley-gem hunter.

Margot greets Gabriel with a sly smile unnoticed by even her adept customers. Like his mother, she has light copper skin, and she keeps her hair in a glorious crown of tightly knit intricate braids. Lately, she's been wearing them up in a modern take on a beehive. She's sporting a vintage ivory Dior skirt circa 1955, paired with a sleeveless navy cashmere top, sensible pearls, and boots.

Margot's fashion sense is one of many reasons Gabriel adores her. Watching Margot is like experiencing a live-action Fred Astaire movie from the 1930s. No matter the occasion, s road, as she takes he always seems as if she's about to laugh, her head coquettishly tilted, holding a martini. With the possible exception of the classic movie channel, Gabriel hasn't found such carefree elegance anywhere else.

After about an hour of helping out in the shop, Gabriel catches sight of a man peering in the window and then back at his phone. The visitor must ultimately determine he's in the right place, and the store bell chirps his arrival.

Immediately, Gabriel can tell this customer is different. He opens his mind to get a sense of his rank. The man's energy signature shimmers as he walks. A witch, an adept, something else? No, he's an adept and a powerful one. Whoever he is, he's not bothering to cloak himself. Another gawker? His face is all strong angles and sharp edges. The smooth, polished skin is so meticulously cared for; it reminds Gabriel of the most delicate smokey quartz. His bone-straight hair, although already thinning, has a bright shine. The man cuts an impressive figure with broad shoulders and average height. He wears a charcoal suit with an open French-cuffed shirt, and cufflinks show off two brilliant rubies. Gabriel gives him points for the rubies.

This visitor is South Asian, Gabriel guesses, perhaps from the Indian subcontinent. He studies Gabriel with an inviting, open expression. In contrast, his thoughts are entirely closed off, which usually means one of three things: an adept, a witch, or a traumatized dall. His lean and muscular physique writhes beneath the designer suit. *He's definitely an adept. I follow adepts to Mumbai, and now Mumbai adepts follow me to Boston.*

Adepts are almost always lean and naturally fit. Gabriel is a fine example of the "almost" as he sports an extra thirty, he likes to believe, well-proportioned pounds. Even Gabriel's high metabolism can't burn off his abiding love of pastry, pasta, and potatoes. His deadly "p's," he calls them.

"Hello, I'm looking for Ms. Davis or Mr. Kelly," the well-dressed man inquires with just the right amount of job interview eye contact.

Zuko makes the monumental effort to leave his sunny window seat where his adoring street traffic fans can admire him, and saunters over to sit beside Gabriel. The usually lackadaisical bernedoodle is fully alert and statue still. Gabriel reaches down to touch the top of Zuko's head and gently strokes him. Every muscle in Zuko's body is pulsing. But why?

Is this who you smelled in Joe's apartment, buddy? Is that what you're trying to say?

Gabriel reaches out his hand while trying to hide his trepidation. "I'm Gabriel. Mr. Kelly is my father." A bold move to touch an adept and risk an unintended exchange of thoughts, but he can't show fear, and if this adept did kill Joe, now would be the time to find out. As a registered Media, no one would expect Gabriel has the power to open a portal.

The young man's eyes widen in surprise when they clasp hands. The energy signature is unmistakable as a bolt of electricity shoots through him as if he's being supercharged. Gabriel's fingers burn and tingle from the contact. The warmth of the visitor's smile, along with the tingle, compels Gabriel to grin in return. He's disarming, this powerful Provectus, which makes him all the more dangerous. Perhaps this was the cause of Zuko's apprehension? Meeting another adept is a rare occurrence. Meeting an unannounced Provectus is rarer still. Gabriel makes a mental note to play the lottery.

"Welcome," he says.

"My name is Ankit," the visitor replies. "It's a pleasure to meet you and thank you for the welcome. I wasn't expecting this."

Wasn't expecting what? My less-than-perfect physique? Are you that confused I'm an adept? Are you looking at my thirty-six-inch waist?

It's the rare adept who carries extra weight, just as it's rare for an adept not to possess perfect vision and robust health. The same genetic gifts that bestow perfect sight bequeath all manner of physical vitality. Gabriel knows all too well he's an embarrassment. He doesn't need reminding from a stranger.

Is it conceit that he probably knows who I am and who my great-great-grandmother and uncle are? And what is my energy signature after the last couple of days?

Gabriel manages to maintain his composure. No, not all adepts know each other, but he's the great-great-grandson of a Regna, and his uncle is patriarch of the northeast. Perhaps this adept's surprise is because he's a recent transplant to Boston? Gabriel can't know for sure. For now, he'll keep his suspicions to himself.

"Pleasure meeting you, Ankit."

"Mr. Kelly," Ankit says with a polite nod. "Are you a Brit?"

"Ah, please," Gabriel says, waving him off, "call me Gabriel. And I'm not. I imprinted on my Cornish dad."

"That's a rare, amazing thing, imprinting. You and your dad must get along."

Gabriel says nothing in response.

Ankit says, "Right, right. Gabriel, I'm here to express interest in being your store manager. I passed out from the Boston University MBA program, and I—"

"Passed out?" Gabriel interjects.

"Oh. Sorry. It's an Indian expression. It means I graduated."

"So, you're here for a job?"

"Yes, sir. You are hiring, right?"

"We are," Gabriel says. "We recently discussed hiring someone, so word has gotten out quickly. My name may be on the door, but you'll have to impress Margot as well." Gabriel gestures toward her. "I know you're an adept. Can you tell me more about yourself and your background?"

"I've just graduated with an MBA from Boston University," Ankit says, perhaps a bit too earnestly. "I spent many unproductive years before BU wondering what I would do and what my purpose is. At my parents' insistence, I got my MBA. Now it's time to do something I care about and worry about pleasing my parents later."

"I know something about family pressure," Gabriel replies, and just when he's about to ask another question, Ankit opens his mind. His thoughts waft into Gabriel. They're complicated. With Gabriel's brief glimpse into Ankit's psyche, all those complex emotions wash over him. The truth of Ankit's words envelops Gabriel as Ankit's need to please his mother fills Gabriel's heart.

For an instant, Gabriel wants to call her and talk up every accomplishment Ankit ever achieved. Gabriel can almost touch the rich vein of respect flowing through Ankit for his father, but underneath that, he tastes the bitter ichor of fear. The fear Ankit has of his father constricts Gabriel's chest and then it's gone, almost as if Gabriel imagined it. Ankit shuts off the silent exchange.

It forces Gabriel to think of his own father. Margot describes him as the whitest man she's ever met, and she has a point. Would his father ever fully understand who and what Gabriel is? Probably not. And yet for all their issues, he never felt fear.

The fear is real. Or is it? Gabriel can't help but like Ankit, but isn't that what a well-trained Provectus does? They spin and weave emotions as easily as yarn. Gabriel assesses Ankit and knows he's here for far more than a job.

"And," Ankit says. "I would prefer to work with an adept. The dall can be exhausting."

"Yes, they can," Gabriel says, steadying his hand, which is still shaking from Ankit's fear. "Did you register with the Salem consulate?"

"I did." And Ankit opens his mind again. But this time, he's more careful, so Gabriel can only read the truth in Ankit's words. Gabriel gets nothing else from him.

Adepts can shield their thoughts from each other, but few can lie to another adept, making their teenage years particularly difficult. A few adepts can train themselves to lie to other adepts, but the time and talent required is the equivalent of learning to play Rachmaninoff. Going to all that effort to lie raises suspicions. Some can cleverly choose their words to achieve a meaning not found in the actual text of their speech. They're the ones to avoid. An adept can only get away with a lie if they completely close off their thoughts, but that means communicating like the dall, and what's the point of that?

"I'm ready to do something on my own. This is an interest that, until now, I've never dared to pursue. Your search for rough gems, to be the first to find a new mine, well, that's exciting. I heard you came back from Asia two days ago with a rich cache of ley-filled rubies. I know that's not the job at hand, finding and selling gems, that's yours, but to work here and learn would be something, a golden opportunity. You are the preeminent seller of ley-rich gems." Ankit makes a show of looking around the shop. "None are here, so you must have your adept shop else-where."

Adepts do know what to say, Gabriel muses to himself. Still, he's confident he'd pick up a lie. Gabriel decides to ignore Ankit's fishing expedition for now. Who did he tell about the Burma trip? Oh, right. He put the auction on the grid.

"Your accent is perfect. Did you grow up in the US?"

"Yes, Manhattan Beach in Los Angeles. During my teenage years, my father accepted a promotion that took us to LA."

"You were raised partly in California," Gabriel says. "I can understand coming here for school, but to voluntarily live through our winters?"

A glint of humor lights up Ankit's rich brown eyes. "Yes, I do know what you mean. My parents' shock at the winter weather was hilarious. We're from Mumbai, but these rubies"—he brandishes his cufflinks—

"are from Bangalore." Ankit pauses and continues more somberly. "I feel I need to be here in America to accomplish my goals."

"Ah, Bengaluru, the garden city," Gabriel says, showing off a bit. "They have a ton of ley energy, those cufflinks of yours."

"Yes!" Ankit replies. "You know Bengaluru?"

"Not well, but I do love that part of India. Are those rubies from Karur?"

Ankit lifts his forearm to better study the gems in the cufflinks. "They're a gift from my maternal grandmother, so maybe they are."

"Since you're from Mumbai, you're House Koli, right?"

"I am Koli, yes."

But are you a Koli killer?

"And" Gabriel says, hesitating. "I get the sense you're a Provectus. Aren't your talents better used elsewhere?"

"Aren't you a Provectus?"

"Ah, no, much to my parents' chagrin."

"Really? You're not a Provectus?"

"No. Anyway, you'll have to interview with Margot. She's dall, not adept, and I'll be keeping an eye—"

At a sudden cracking sound, Gabriel and Ankit turn to the shop door as a towering figure kicks it open.

Chapter Twelve

WITCH POPULATION

We estimate the witch population to be significantly smaller than the adepts. While adepts have managed to take control of several governments, there are no known societies where witches impact policy.

—National Intelligence Strategy White Paper: Top Secret (TS): Release of this document will cause severe damage to the security of the United States—Adept Assets

A SLENDER COLOSSUS in a flowing baker's apron fills the store entrance. One vertical arm holds a tray, and the other flung the door open. One size twelve foot, at the end of a very long leg, holds it open.

"Stand aside, mortals, stand aside. You're about to be graced with the finest croquembouche in this and every universe! For the peasants amongst you—and that would be all of you—that's pastry."

Enter Sellers, Gabriel's childhood friend, maker of wickedly good strawberry scones, and proprietor of Journey's End Bakery. Sellers always draws attention. It is, as he has often lamented, his burden to bear. As a younger man, he tried to tone it down, but as he's grown older, Sellers has come to realize it's an exercise in futility. His creamy alabaster skin sets off jet-black hair, which Gabriel suspects he dyes. This crowning glory adds another three inches to his prodigious height. As tall as he is, he never shies away from heels. Sellers trained as an actor, so he can't help but sound like Anthony Hopkins despite being from the Boston suburbs. He is also a witch, a literal cauldron-stirring witch, as Gabriel likes to say. Sellers's famous croquembouche pastry is as tall as Zuko and an all-time favorite of Gabriel's.

Sellers catches Gabriel's eye and surreptitiously mouths, *What's wrong?*

"Sellers!" Gabriel exclaims. "You brought croquembouche!" He has to look up to meet the eyes of only one person in his life, and it's his best friend. "Later," he whispers.

Sellers winks in reply and says with a flourish, "Indeed! Gather around and partake of the food of the gods via my blessed oven." He sets the dessert down on a counter and turns toward Zuko. "And for you, dear Zuko—stalwart guardian of Charles Street and all that is good—for you, I've baked the most delicious treat of all." Sellers gingerly places the biscuit in Zuko's mouth, and he gratefully accepts it and trots off.

"Margot!" Sellers exclaims while opening his arms wide and rushing in for a hug. She is the only person Sellers willingly hugs.

"You're a dream," she says. "What have you done now?"

"I know, I know. It's difficult to take in so much talent and delicious goodness all at once, but do try."

"I'll do my best." Margot plants a well-placed kiss on Sellers's cheek, then turns to Gabriel. "A white girl came in looking for you. Her name is Keira, and she bought a diamond tennis bracelet. Do you know her?"

"Oh? I don't know any Keira." Gabriel considers a moment. "Marg, come on over. This is Ankit. He's here about the store manager position."

"I didn't know we posted already," Margot says as if deep in thought. "Thanks for coming. It's your lucky day. We get to talk over choux pastry puffs."

Sellers lean in and whispers to Gabriel, "Who's the adept snack?"

"You can tell he's an adept that quickly?"

"Really?" Sellers raises his aquiline nose. "What do you take me for? Adept power radiates off him."

Gabriel nods in agreement. "It does. He's a Koli Provectus." Gabriel glances around the store. "Did you cast the sound spell so no one can overhear us?"

"Indeed, I did," Sellers replies and puffs out his chest. "What do you take me for? I also cast an obfuscation spell, so we'll be ignored for a few minutes or, at least, very difficult to notice. I bet you missed that! Please tell me you missed that. Still, it hurts my pride that your handsome friend has noticed my clandestine spell-casting. And what's a Koli? You can't expect me to keep up with your Byzantine politics."

"The Koli House is the great adept clan of western India," Gabriel says, afraid he might sound like his lecturer father.

Sellers speaks slowly and deliberately until he's barely audible. "I can feel his mind pushing up against the protective spell that shields my thoughts, but he camouflages it. He's subtle or trying to be." Sellers tilts his head. "I can't believe that cutie isn't all over the—what do you call it?—the matrix by now."

Gabriel rolls his eyes. "It's the grid. It's called the grid."

Sellers never calls it the same thing twice. Last time, it was the adept Amber alert.

"Well," Sellers says, half laughing, "I do love a man of mystery." He waves his hands around the store to impress Gabriel with his handiwork, proving no one notices them.

"You're a scary good witch."

"Correction." Sellers raises a finger. "I'm a scary, amazing witch. So amazing, our high priestess called me to the conclave." Sellers takes a slight bow. "Please, hold your applause."

"The witch conclave?" Gabriel says with some alarm. "That's quite an honor, but seriously, is that good or bad?"

Sellers take a deep breath. "That remains to be seen."

In the Americas, before witches and adepts struck their fragile armistice, they fought one another. They warred over prominent dall humans to wield influence, and they fought for control over industries, land, and wealth. Anisa was part of the last war in the 1800s. Gabriel often wondered if that was how she lost her husband, but she never speaks of it, at least not with him. For now, the cold war between witches and adepts is at no risk of thawing.

Both species have long memories. The unlikely friendship between Sellers and Gabriel, while not openly discouraged, was never encouraged either. It was years before they were allowed into each other's homes. They learned early not to share too much information about their witch or adept sides or risk ostracism. It was unspoken yet obvious.

They became friends at a private school favored by the wealthy families of Boston's Beacon Hill. Gabriel was the husky kid dressed in fine yet old-fashioned clothes. Exceptionally long-lived beings like adepts have difficulty adapting to new fashions.

The sad outfit invited vitriol from his elementary school peers, who gawked and guffawed. Gabriel swallowed his feelings. He would eat those feelings later.

Sellers was quick to come to his verbal defense. He said that while Gabriel may talk funny, he was under his protection. At recess, Sellers demonstrated that he was just as capable coming to Gabriel's physical as well as verbal defense. Years later, Gabriel learned that Sellers having three older brothers with pugilistic reputations helped to buttress his courage.

Gabriel crosses his arms. "I'm going to hire him."

"What?" Sellers exclaims, jerking back his head. "Already?"

"I think he's a spy."

"Okay," Sellers says, all the mirth gone from his voice. "What must be discussed under the power of a spell and in the middle of my hectic workday? My scones are flying off the shelves. Why the cloak and dagger intrigue?"

Gabriel looks around, not to ascertain if it's safe to proceed but to avoid the unavoidable. As of this moment, Joe is still alive to Sellers. In a way, Gabriel is about to kill Joe all over again.

"Joe is dead. He was murdered."

Sellers blinks, and his brows furrow. "What? Sweet Hecate."

Although Sellers thought little of Joe, Gabriel imagined more of a reaction.

"I found him yesterday, at his home, dead on the floor. The cops came, and I spent hours in the police station before my uncle fished me out."

"The patriarch himself? What were you doing at Joe's?"

Gabriel was braced for this moment. "We've been talking. I was on the way to his apartment to see him."

"Oh, no. You wouldn't—"

There's a pause, and Gabriel looks away from Sellers.

"Your taste in men sucks," Sellers says. "You know that, right? I'm sorry he's dead, but he only loved himself, his work, and the gym. I concede that I might've gotten the order wrong."

"Don't throw a wobbly," Gabriel says.

"Speak American," Sellers retorts.

Gabriel forces a weak smile, leans in toward his friend, and whispers, "I need help. I need to catch who did this. And by the way, he asked his husband for a divorce."

Sellers winces but says nothing.

Gabriel continues. "I learned that even before he died, Joe was nervous. I felt what I now know was him reaching out to me, but I didn't know what it was at the time. I've never been able to sense someone at such a distance. When I got to his lobby, I felt him die."

Sellers grips Gabriel's hand, and Gabriel instinctively clasps it. "What? Oh, no. I'm sorry, Gabe. You know I never cared for Joe, but I never judged your relationship, such as it was, with a dall. When you met, Joe's mind was warded. He was an adept asset. You adepts can't help but manipulate the dall, though it's often subconscious—emotionally nudging them this way or that to trust or admire you. But at least your feelings were honest because of that warding. Do you think you might have imagined him reaching out to you?"

All adepts know that everyone carries with them the aura of another life, the paths not taken that linger in the soul, the half-remembered secrets half-open but never discussed. Because of the witch ward around Joe, his mind was blessedly blank. Gabriel and Joe were like any dall or adept couple, they could know only what they observed or cared to share. So, it was a shock when Joe touched Gabriel's mind.

"I know it's hard to believe, but he reached out to me, Sell. I felt him burn out like a candle. One second, he was there, and—" Gabriel looks at Sellers, who smiles warmly for him to continue. "When I entered his apartment, I was attacked by an adept or maybe two, and they teleported away."

"They attacked you? Are you all right?" Sellers's hands clench into fists, power congealing around them.

"I'm fine. Zuko and I are tough."

"The bastards attacked Zuko? Oh hell no."

"We're fine," Gabriel repeats. "But this isn't over. I'm going to find them. I'm going to track them down, and I'm asking for your help."

"Of course. I'm yours. But what does this have to do with the snack?" Sellers nods toward Ankit, who is in the middle of an animated conversation with Margot.

"Yes, 'the snack.' The adepts teleporting away like that yesterday is a rare skill. Only a small percentage of adepts can do that—and then in walks a Provectus adept asking for a job, a job that we barely discussed advertising. I'm betting he scanned Margot."

"That little—" Despite his powerful obfuscation spell, Sellers looks around to ensure his raised voice didn't pierce the veil.

"Hold on," Gabriel says. "I need to get this out. I was able to see where the adepts fled to because teleporting leaves a trace. They went to Mumbai, the Koli capital, and I followed them there." Sellers's eyes widen in shock, but he remains silent. "Ankit is from Mumbai. Do you know what else is in Mumbai?"

"No, what?" Sellers asks, leaning forward.

"Jeebom Pharmaceuticals' headquarters. Joe's old job. They

weren't happy with him leaving. They threatened to sue him, something about intellectual property, but they never did. His current employer, Covian Pharmaceuticals, worked something out. Joe managed quite the backdoor deal."

Sellers nods. "Sounds like Joe. So you think Ankit's a spy. If he is, he's inept."

"Yeah, I don't think the adepts expected me to be able to follow them to Mumbai. I certainly didn't expect it. What's happening to me—it's like when a mother lifts up a car to save her child, except sometimes with adepts, it sticks. We call it adapting. I might be rising in rank."

"Good. I won't have to worry about being seen with you, then." Sellers turns toward Ankit. "He's not cute anymore."

Gabriel smiles. "No?"

"Maybe a little," Sellers says with a sly grin. "So, you think he was in Joe's place? He killed him?"

Gabriel shakes his head. "That's the thing. That's where my sleuthing falls apart. Why would he be at Joe's? It doesn't make sense. Nothing makes sense right now. Remember Barbara?"

"Vaguely. She was a friend of you and Joe."

"Yes. That's right. She was Joe's mentor. I spoke to her, and she brought up Joe's research. She asked if I found it. Why would she do that?"

"Because she wants it. So, you need to get it. It's either at his job or on his home computer or maybe a flash drive somewhere. Unless he hid it, the cops have it locked up in their evidence locker. What can I do to help?"

"I need a particular spell."

Sellers leans into Gabriel's ear. "Come to the bakery tomorrow. I'll get my cauldron out."

A courier enters the shop so quickly the door's usually pleasant jingle turns into an alarming rattle. He heads straight to the desk and sets down a package. Margot approaches him, and he says, "Is Gabriel Kelly here? I have a package that needs his signature."

"Can you drop the obfuscation spell?" Gabriel asks.

Sellers snaps his fingers. "I'm going to head out. I'll see you at the bakery."

Gabriel walks over to the courier and Margot. "I'm Gabriel," he says.

"Then this is for you." The courier looks relieved. "Sign here."

The door chimes make the same unsettling rattle at the courier's hasty exit. Gabriel stares transfixed at the package. He's unable to move.

Margot says, "Are you going to open it?"

"Yeah, sure," Gabriel says softly. He checks the shop and sees that Ankit has left, so he opens the package. Inside is a plain box. Gabriel has an idea what's in it because the ley energy is so thick he can almost touch it. The energy tells Gabriel that whatever is inside, adepts will pay a fortune for it.

When he opens the box, Margot gasps so loudly customers turn their heads. A five-carat diamond glimmers in his hand.

"It's spectacular," Margot exclaims. "Where did it come from?"

"It's a gift from Joe." His voice cracks.

Margot reaches out and squeezes Gabriel's shoulder. He takes a deep breath and leans into her.

Gabriel remembers his first gift to Joe. Joe said once in passing that he loved his prep school sweatshirt. Joe was proud because he attended school on a scholarship and was eventually accepted by his legacy peers. He wore that sweatshirt until it was a tattered rag. Gabriel called the school and bought him a new one. Joe said it was the most precious gift he ever received. That look in Joe's eyes after opening the gift was the first time Gabriel dared hope that Joe might love him. That was before their breakup and before Joe's marriage. Back when there was a chance. Now, he looks at Joe's last gift to him and maybe the last thing he ever did, and there is no chance.

"There's a card," Margot whispers. "Do you want me to leave?"

Gabriel doesn't reply but opens the card wide enough for Margot to see. It reads, *Gabriel, keep this close. It's the gateway to my heart.*

"That's beautiful," Margot says.

"In the mail." Gabriel shakes his head. "It's typical of Joe. He was so good at face-to-face confrontations but so bad at face-to-face expressions of love."

"Men." Margot kisses him on the cheek and leaves him staring at the card.

Chapter Thirteen

WITCHES

It is the position of this Agency that those who define themselves as witches are genetic cousins to those who identify as adept. Most witches inherit their power from a strong female witch. The energy is connected to the earth in ways still under study.

—National Intelligence Strategy White Paper: Top Secret (TS): Release of this document will cause severe damage to the security of the United States—Adept Assets

SELLERS'S BAKERY IS a wall of sound at the height of the brunch rush. Employees power walk to and fro while the kitchen staff bark orders. There are fifteen tables, and satisfied customers occupy every one of them. Gabriel approaches the counter, examines the menu, and lets out a baleful sigh.

Joe's voice rings out in his head. *"You have to work just as hard outside the gym as you do inside."* Gabriel pushes the memory aside. If he eats a strawberry scone, that's fine under the circumstances.

"I'll send it down to the main kitchen, Gabe," Bethany says. Turning her attention to Zuko, Bethany beams, and Zuko knows where his next treat is coming from.

"You're the best dog?" Bethany says, her hands a blur over the register, but she manages to find time to ruffle Zuko's coiffed head. Bernedoodles have hair, not fur, and they don't shed, which is the sole reason Sellers allows him inside the bakery. But everyone knows that's a pretense, and Sellers would let him in anyway.

"Treats," Bethany says, winking at Zuko.

That was all he needed to gingerly weave between the crowded tables to the back of the bakery.

Bethany murmurs, "Just love that pony of a dog."

Someone grabs Gabriel's arm. He turns and says in surprise, "Jaime?"

His face is unshaven and haggard. His bright blue eyes lurk behind heavy bags. Gabriel gets a flood of emotions from the sudden physical contact. A longing for the drug J, self-hate, and embarrassment. So much comes at him because Jaime can't contain his thoughts, so Gabriel throws up a wall.

"Gabriel? Hi."

"Are you okay?" Gabriel asks.

Zuko turns and barks, and it's not playful. The casual din of the bakery stops for a brief second, and every eye turns.

Jaime doesn't wait for a reply. He turns and walks out. The scene was over as soon as it began. A confused and startled Gabriel glances back toward Zuko. He shrugs at Bethany and follows the eager pup downstairs.

The fabled kitchen encompasses the entire basement floor of the building. Sellers bakes all his food here. From this location, he sends his baked goods out to local restaurants and his two other venues, one in the Back Bay, and the other in the South End.

His frequent unannounced visits strike fear in the hearts of apprentice bakers. One had a panic attack and stopped breathing when Sellers held up his tarts and drily commented, "Why the histrionics? The base isn't soggy. Nicely dry, flaky crust. Now, if that weren't the case, then it might be appropriate to stop breathing altogether, but seeing as you're a passable baker, you may continue. Breathing and baking."

After a moment, Sellers adds, "Someone give him a paper bag."

Sellers holds court in the oversized kitchen, his hair a spiky ebony tower, as his voice fills the room.

"I ask you. Is this a golden brown? It's not golden. It's not sun-kissed. It's the color of—"

Upon seeing Zuko enter the kitchen, Sellers pauses and reconsiders. "Well, you know what it is. Bake a new batch," he orders and throws the baked confection, container and all, in the trash.

In two strides of his long legs Sellers goes to the foot of the stairs and looks up. "Zuko! Gabriel! I don't know which one of you is more handsome. I thought it might be you when I saw extra jam and a strawberry scone on the same order."

"Hi, Sellers," Gabriel says, face downcast. "May I hide out here for a while?"

"But of course, dear sir. I freely offer sanctuary from jealous lovers, bill collectors, and the law. Anton," Sellers calls out. "Do me a solid and make some of that Darjeeling orange pekoe tea. We have a Brit in the house."

Sellers's gaze turns serious. He points to corners in the kitchen and, with a sweep of his arms, recites:

Seal the room,

Quiet as a tomb.

See no more,

We ignore.

"Thanks," Gabriel says, suddenly feeling tired. The lack of sleep is taking its toll. "I'm knackered. You know I love your style, Sell, but did you watch every *Bewitched* episode?"

"Darling, I wasn't the one dating a tiresome mortal like you and Samantha. How did you stand the boredom? But to answer your question, yes, I did watch every episode. And, of course, you love my style; everyone loves my style. I have too much style. Do you need some? I can spare it."

Gabriel can only wanly smile at Sellers in return. Their usual repartee will have to wait.

"Are you okay?" Sellers asks, his eyes softening.

"Not really," Gabriel says quietly.

Tears begin to well in Gabriel's eyes. He gulps in a big breath of air and chokes it out. A dishwasher ducks behind him and grabs a towel, oblivious to their presence.

Sellers grips Gabriel's hand. "Oh, honey, how many times have I snot cried in front of you?"

Gabriel gurgles a laugh despite himself. "A few," he replies, just above a whisper.

"More than a few. I'm a champion snot crier." Sellers looks around the room, quickly locating his quarry. "I know what'll make you feel better. A delicious sandwich on my mind-bending ciabatta, toasted only for you—anyone else I'd throw out—with prosciutto, fontina, and extra fig jam. Goodness knows eating makes you feel better. It's why I love you."

"God Sell, I can't believe I just laughed, even if it's just a little. I was convinced I'd never laugh again. You're so good for me. You are magic."

Zuko maneuvers in between them, laying his head against Gabriel's knee.

"Aww," Sellers says. "He knows how to make an entrance. I do admire that. So, tell me, how may I be of service to the scion of the noble Salem House?"

Gabriel grabs a stool and sits, and Sellers joins him. "We adepts, we're mind readers, yes, but if another adept knows you're trying to read their mind, we can fool you, we can twist our thoughts, make you think you're reading our mind when you're not. You're getting a false narrative we're feeding you."

Sellers nods. "So, you can't just say to an adept—read my mind?"

Gabriel nods back. "It's difficult to lie in a mental connection. I can't do it, but a few talented adepts can. Think of it as the adept version of not being able to use a lie detector test in court."

"I see," Sellers says.

"We adepts can do many extraordinary things. If I knew who was guilty, I might be able to compel them to confess even though I'm only Media—although I may have moved up a notch since—"

Sellers smiles crookedly. "You want a spell."

"I want a spell that compels the truth. Can you do it?" The hope in Gabriel's voice hangs in the air.

Sellers considers and gets up off his stool. He walks around the high table and looks Gabriel in the eye. "Then you must believe you know who did it, that they're in your life."

Gabriel shrugs. "I don't know. All I know is that someone called the cops on me right after the murder. Joe was only dead a few minutes. So maybe I was just a convenient fall guy, but I want to be prepared."

"It would impact everyone, not just the murderer. You'd have to know who to ask."

Gabriel brightens. "I can do that."

"It all depends on you. We have to focus on your intention, pour all your need to know the truth into it. Tell me. Why do you need to know?"

Gabriel squints his eyes, and his chin muscles twitch. Zuko's lips curl back, and he growls.

"Whoa! Zuko!" Sellers jumps back. "Your mental connection with Zuko still surprises me. I think it's hilarious that adepts have familiars, and witches don't."

Gabriel laughs. "Yeah, we always thought the whole familiar thing came from adept-to-dog communication. The dall always confuse witches and adepts."

"That explains a lot." Sellers looks at them both with wide eyes. "It would be natural for humans to do that. They get so much wrong in their legends. I haven't seen a single pointy hat in my entire life."

Gabriel rubs Zuko's tummy. "We're good at keeping secrets, aren't we?"

Sellers smiles wryly. "We kill to keep them."

A long moment goes by when they say nothing. They sit in silence and stroke Zuko, who smiles and wags his considerable tail.

Finally, Gabriel speaks. "I want to know who killed Joe because I loved him, and I want to face this threat, this killer, and make them accountable. I put Joe onto adepts. In a way, I got him killed. And I must figure out where the data are. Sell. If I don't get it back, I think Anisa might burn me? Exile me. Thank goodness I have Uncle Russell in my corner."

Gabriel casts his head down, and Zuko slumps onto the floor with a resounding plop.

Sellers stands to full height. "Wait right here. Watch the birds out the window or something. I'll be right back." As Sellers exits the bubble, he breaks the spell, and one of the startled bakers exclaims in surprise.

"Jeez, I didn't see you guys come back in!"

"That's because you're so focused on your work, right, Anton?" Sellers says.

A few moments later, he returns with a rolling pin, some measuring cups, and a baking sheet.

Gabriel nods. "I appreciate what you're trying to do, Sell, but I need magic. Not that your strawberry scones aren't magic, but—"

Sellers raises his finger as if he's about to wag it. He takes a moment's pause.

"We don't talk about our gifts because that's what they teach us, right?" he says finally. "We're so powerful and yet so afraid. Aren't we? My spirit first came to me when I was nine years old. I was in the kitchen baking with my grandmother while my three older brothers played football in the backyard. She'd just finished preparing the dough, and I remember her letting me roll it out with this same rolling pin, and whoosh! My spirit appeared, bigger than life. It went from my head to the ceiling. I remember it looked down at me and smiled. I jumped back, but I wasn't scared. My grandmother hollered in delight, and the whole family came running. My spirit had visited me for the first time. We bonded. Gabriel, I make my most powerful magic when I bake."

Zuko gets up and rubs against Sellers, making him smile.

"Thanks, Gabriel," Sellers says. "You know I hate hugging everyone except Margot. It's our thing, but for you, I make an exception."

Sellers wraps Gabriel in a hug and holds him close.

Gabriel reaches up and runs a hand through Sellers's hair. Gabriel did it without thinking, and just when he thought Sellers might scream bloody murder, Sell's hugs him tighter.

Gabriel slowly breaks away. "So funny," he says. "I wanted to hug you but didn't because you're not a hugger, but Zuko handled it for me and got the ball rolling. Hey, wait a minute— You hug Raul, the hairdresser down the—"

Sellers snaps, "Oh, do shut up." He moves to the kitchen counter and motions "come here" with a nod, and Gabriel joins him.

Sellers grows serious and turns to Gabriel. "We're going to make your favorite strawberry scones. And while we work the dough, while we prepare this dessert, think about Joe, think about finding the truth, think about justice for Joe. Pour your soul into it—the stronger the intention, the stronger the magic. You're the fuel to this fire."

Gabriel nods. "I can do that."

"And where you eat this scone—that's where the magic will ignite. It's where the magic will be the most powerful. Eat it in a place of power for you, where you're in command.

"Compulsion is subtle magic. It's old and will demand much of you to work. Focus on your goal and look your subject in the eye. Consuming it where you're strongest will give us our best chance of success."

"Okay, I understand," Gabriel says. "Where, though? My store? Margot runs it, and I'm rarely there. My house? That's belongs to Anisa. Maybe where I cut gems?"

"I don't know. Maybe the store? Your name is on the shingle. It's where you're obeyed when push comes to shove." Sellers places a three-by-five card on the counter. "Let's read this together while we bake. Let's recite it. Words focus our minds. There's a reason we recite. Don't laugh, but *Bewitched* got this right."

"Okay," Gabriel says, determined.

"Now. You pour in the heavy whipping cream. Next, I'll put in the honey."

Gabriel pours in the cream. "I'm getting a clue as to why I love these so much."

Sellers chuckles and nods. "You don't want to know how the sausage is made. Now, let's recite together."

If you know who killed Joe,

Confess it now or be my foe

In this room, truth will prevail,

All your plans sure to fail

Suddenly, Gabriel feels a twinge in the back of his mind as if there's a thought he can't recall. A burst of energy runs through him as if he's on fire. And then he sees it, an image that seems composed entirely of smoke appears in the ceiling. The figure gazes at him and drifts away like fog in the wind.

"Was that a... What was that?" Gabriel asks in an undertone, trying to remain calm.

"You saw it? I'm the only one who's seen him so far. This must be a good sign or an ominous sign."

"A good sign?"

"It's a blessing. You saw the guardian spirit of my family. That's incredible; I thought only witches could see them. But look, we have to stay focused; the spell is in motion. Your emotion, your intensity is the fuel."

Gabriel nods and takes a deep breath. "Let's do this."

Gabriel watches Sellers's hands work the ingredients. "There's a touch of magic to how you do that," he says.

"Years of practice," says Sellers.

And they knead the dough and prepare the scones until, finally, they're out of the oven.

"Now remember," Sellers says, "the scones will work anywhere, but they'll be strongest where you have the most authority and weakest where you have the least. When you eat it, repeat the rhyme, and focus all your desire for the truth in every bite. You can already compel humans, but this will work on my kind and adepts. If you're up against a powerful adept or witch, you must focus with all your intensity."

Sellers carefully wraps the scones and hands them to Gabriel.

"I don't know what to say, Sell, except thank you. And by the way, I know every black-and-white episode of *Bewitched* by heart."

Sellers laughs with his heart and his eyes.

"Will you come with me to Covian tomorrow morning?" Gabriel asks.

"Anything for you. You know that. But why?"

"You said it yourself. If I want to know about this data that was so important to Joe. Let's go to his job and see what we can find out. I'm an adept, and you're a witch. How hard can it be?"

Chapter Fourteen

ADEPT LAW ENFORCEMENT

We know little of adept law enforcement. Most adept societies have Inquisitors. These are highly trained Provectus-level adepts. They enforce laws against the inappropriate use of mind control, suggestion, theft, and other crimes. They are responsible for finding the rare cases when an adept is born to non-adept parents. It's widely believed they steal these children from their parents, but no documented cases have emerged.

—National Intelligence Strategy White Paper: Top Secret (TS): Release of this document will cause severe damage to the security of the United States—Adept Assets

SELLERS SITS IN the waiting room and eyes the young witch taking fraught messages with some envy. It's a coveted internship to work in the office of the high priestess. He applied for a similar job when he was younger, but his family, while prominent, was not quite prominent enough. Sellers doesn't know why he's been summoned to the high seat, but he can guess it has to do with his friendship with Gabriel and the death of Joe Martin.

The High Priestess Ravynne Quinn inherited the seat of the White Raven from her childless aunt forty-five years ago. Her husband, a low-born Mexican witch, was a child prodigy and quickly mastered three of the four elements, making him uncommonly powerful. Ravynne knew that marriage would elevate his family to extraordinary new heights in Mexico City, and it did, but it also won her valuable new allies. That was all Sellers knew, and that information came from his father who was bitter and prone to conspiracy theories.

The seat of the White Raven presides over eastern Canada and the eastern United States. Only the far-flung covens of the Crone seat in Paris, the Tshawe seat in Cape Town, and the Dragon seat in Nanjing rival it. Oceans are good at keeping the peace, his father says.

"High Priestess," her intercom chirps. "Your four o'clock is here."

"Send him in," a voice says through the ancient intercom.

Sellers learned long ago to own his height. He walks with squared shoulders and faces the seated Ravynne Quinn from a respectable distance. "High Priestess," he says, bowing deeply. "How may I be of service to the White Raven?"

Her black bouffant is teased to perfection. It sets off the huge pearl earrings and matching necklace. Sellers wishes she would stand so he could see the tweed Chanel suit in all its glory.

Ravynne Quinn snaps her fingers. "Seal." A protective ward falls around them—a steel cage. No listening or recording device can detect them now.

Only one word to ignite the spell. Sellers stifles a shudder. Her voice is low and raspy. How many times has she been mistaken for a man on the phone? Sellers stands at attention and waits to be addressed.

"You're a delight," Ravynne says, gesturing to him with a smile. "Your height is a reminder of what witches were before penicillin and pasteurized milk."

Sellers chuckles. "Thank you, High Priestess. Do you mind if I quote you?"

"Not at all." Ravynne takes a moment to appraise him. Her eyes move up and down with a blank expression betraying nothing. "Have a seat, and no titles today. Call me Ravynne."

Sellers takes a quick look around. Being in the inner sanctum of Ravynne Quinn is exciting yet terrifying. The old house creeks with activity. Footsteps pound the floorboards in rhythm with the blood throbbing in his temples. It lends the house an odd sense of being alive. Air freshener covering up a thin veneer of cigarette smoke lingers in the air.

He gingerly takes a seat opposite the oak desk of the high priestess, the experience so heady a part of him feels as if a joke is about to be played on him.

Her blood-red jewel draws Sellers's eye. An enormous stone adorns her ring finger, which bends slightly under its weight. The Eternal Flame, an impossibly rare red diamond, is laden with ancient ley energy. He shudders to think what power she can wield with it.

"Would you care for some tea?" Ravynne asks, gesturing to the elaborate tea set.

Sellers nods and pours a cup for the high priestess and one for himself.

"Do you know why you're here?" Ravynne asks. She says it in the same causal tone as offering the tea.

"I can guess." After a pause, Sellers says, "Ravynne."

"A man died two days ago while drinking his morning coffee. An ambitious mortal named—"

"Joe Martin." Sellers says it as matter-of-factly as he can, yet the tremor in his voice is unmistakable.

"No love lost?" she asks.

"None. He wasn't good for—"

"No, I suspect he wasn't," Ravynne interrupts. "Gabriel Kelly, your friend, appears to be quite upset about it. What an unusual friendship you have. The lion and tiger don't often frolic."

"Ah, yes, we met at school and remained good friends," Sellers says in a quiet voice.

"Tell me about your friend, Gabriel."

Sellers silently curses himself as heat rushes to his face. He must look like an embarrassed teen in front of the most powerful being on the planet. Why is she asking him? She has access to information he can't imagine. She must know.

"He's sweet, generous, and unswervingly loyal." Sellers says. "He's a good friend, and he didn't have anything to do with Joe's death. For stupid reasons, he loved him."

"Did Joe love him?"

"Joe only loved himself."

Ravynne rolls her eyes and smiles. "Lovers are rife with betrayal, death, and intrigue. An age-old story. Do you trust him? Even though he's an adept?"

"Ah, yes. But I haven't met many adepts, only his parents and sister. Once in middle school, I met the Regna."

"You met Anisa?"

"Yes. I remember her as being very serious."

"That's Anisa all right," Ravynne says with a smile. "You know, Sellers"—her smile fades and her voice drops an octave—"adepts are going to kill each other to get their hands on what this Dr. Martin was doing."

Sellers's eyes widen. "Kill?"

"Yes. What do you think is worth killing for?"

"A-ah, a few things."

"Go on. Tell me. I want to know."

"Love," he replies. "And to defend your family and coven."

"Love." Her eyes grow distant as if she's trying to recall an elusive concept. "Family and coven. A wise list."

"And what, High Priestess, are the adepts after? Why kill?"

"Oh, they kill for sport and many other depraved reasons, but this Dr. Martin was a threat to them. A threat they clumsily dispatched, but the danger he posed lives on through his work. Whoever dealt with him failed to capture that crucial piece."

"What is it? What was he doing?"

"Can't you guess?" Ravynne retorts. "Whatever freak accident of nature made them. Maybe with it, we can unmake them."

"I, I don't know," Sellers says, looking at the ceiling.

"You don't know what?"

"If, if I can help."

"Of course you can help. What do you want for your services? I'm not a tyrant."

"I don't want anything, but don't hurt Gabriel. Please."

"Ah, something you want does emerge and without any negotiation. Don't do that again. Always understand your worth. I'll do something exceedingly rare in your case. I'll ask a second time. I want to hear it from your own lips. What do you want?"

"Nothing, High Priestess. Ravynne."

The air in the room thickens, and Sellers's heart flutters. The high priestess of the Ironbay coven, the White Raven, is gathering power. She reaches down and pulls out a deck of tarot cards.

"Very well," she says. "If you won't speak, then you will shuffle." Ravynne Quinn hands him the deck.

"But High Pri—Ravynne, I don't want anything."

"Shuffle."

With shaking hands, Sellers takes the cards. They're heavily infused with her energy, and they burn his fingers. He returns the deck to Ravynne as quickly as he can manage.

She gently touches the edges of her stiff black hair and locks her blue eyes onto Sellers. She spreads the cards out across her desk face down and says, "Choose."

"But High—"

"Choose," she repeats, her mouth a thin line.

Sellers appraises the deck and picks a card furthest to the left and turns it over. His hand unconsciously stops halfway, so he forces himself to lay the card on the table with as much casual disregard as he can muster.

"Hmm," Ravynne says with a satisfied grin. "Can't say as I'm surprised."

Sellers stares at the card he used all his magic to avoid and takes a deep breath.

"This is within my power," she says, holding up the card depicting two intertwined lovers.

Sellers frowns as he sits, staring at the card.

"Despite what dall popular culture would have you believe, I can do it. I can even teach you. I sense you possess enough of our gift. Will you help me? Will you serve your coven? In exchange for this?" She caresses the tarot card.

Her power vibrates in the room. It's as if Sellers never felt witch power prior, and he hasn't, not at this level.

"Succeed," she exclaims, her blue eyes wide, "and I give you your heart's desire and your family a seat on the conclave. A seat in the unkindness, or as our southern brethren call it, 'the conspiracy.' Think of what you could do with this." Ravynne holds up the card. "If this comes to pass, you can protect him."

"I do protect him," Sellers says.

Ravynne Quin sits impassively and waits.

"Tomorrow," Sellers says, hesitating. "Gabriel and I go to Covian Pharmaceuticals."

"Covian? The jewel in House Angeles's crown." Ravynne smiles and leans back in her chair as her energy gradually seeps away. "To what end, exactly, do you enter Patrick's lair?"

Sellers's heartbeat slows, and he wipes sweat off his forehead. "To track down Joe's killer."

"I don't care who killed him. I want what the adepts want. I want his research. I want their secrets."

Sellers nods. "I understand."

"What is your plan?" Ravynne asks.

"Plan? Ah, we're going to look around in Joe's office."

"Your plan—and that's being generous—is to walk into the belly of the beast, maybe confuse a few minds, look around, and walk out? You realize Covian is House Angeles?"

Sellers hesitates, but when he opens his mouth to speak, Ravynne waves him off.

"Don't tell me, just keep me appraised. Take this notebook. Whatever you write in it will appear here." Ravynne holds up an identical notebook. "Keep that in your back pocket. Can you work a ball or a mirror?"

"Of course," Sellers says, unable to keep indignation out of his voice.

"Good. There's a small mirror on the last page of the notebook. Use that for face-to-face communication."

Sellers rises from his chair and bows.

"Oh, Sellers," Ravynne says. "Take this as a reminder." She hands him the tarot card depicting the two lovers, and he leaves, clutching it in his burning hand.

Chapter Fifteen

ADEPT POWER RATING

It's a common misconception that adepts are born into a rank and never change. Their powers can adapt to meet the threat when put under tremendous stress. Only one of the living known Regnas—the current Regna of the Northeast—was born to an Incepto and a Media.

—National Intelligence Strategy White Paper: Top Secret (TS): Release of this document will cause severe damage to the security of the United States—Adept Assets

ZUKO CURLS UP on the bed, snuggling close to Gabriel. He gently lays his hand on Zuko's stomach in the hope that the rhythmic rising and falling of the dog's breathing will lull him to sleep. Gabriel meditates to gain control of the growing energy in his body and to make sense out of the senseless. Murder permanently seared its memory into his consciousness. The pain will never soften or change with time as with other memories. Joe was part of Gabriel's psyche when he was ripped away. He'll always feel the ache—as if his love life isn't complicated enough.

Zuko utters a small cry in his sleep, and an escaping rabbit zooms by in the corner of Gabriel's eye. He smiles and takes a deep breath to still his thoughts when his eyes snap open and focus on his phone. A second later, it rings, and Barbara's photo appears.

Gabriel watches the call ring out and reflects on how grateful he is for their unlikely friendship. She was quick to embrace him at the lab. And it wasn't just any lab, it was Barbara's. She knew everything about her colleagues: their pets' names, relatives, even favorite foods which, on occasion, she prepared. Gabriel was sad to think of losing her when Joe broke up with him, but Barbara was quick to say that her love was her own, and if Joe wasn't for him, she still was. A thought that continues to warm him. During the time Joe worked for Barbara at Jeebom, everything in Gabriel's life was perfect, or so he thought. After Joe left for Covian, and they broke up, nothing was the same.

"Barbara, hi."

After several seconds of silence, Barbara finally says in a subdued voice, "How are you holding up?"

"I'm...ah..." Gabriel pauses, not because of any spike in emotional pain but because he hasn't asked himself how he's doing, and the simple question takes him by surprise. He'll deal with his feelings after he's secured Joe's legacy and found his killer. There's too much left to do before he can deal with the wreckage left behind by Joe's murder. "I'm doing as well as can be expected."

"How's Peter?"

The question is a punch in the gut. The complication of dating Joe only to see Peter marry him eighteen months later has prevented Gabriel from calling him. Shouldn't they talk though? What's important now is the love they shared for Joe. And yet, they can't seem to comfort each other. Did Peter kill Joe?

"I don't know. Everything has been happening so fast I haven't had the chance to call."

"You're both in shock," Barbara says. "So take your time. Do you know how it happened?"

Gabriel strokes Zuko's fluffy coat and lets the dog's serenity wash over him. The sadness dulls enough for him to speak.

"I don't know. I got to his place too late. He was already dead." With that, Zuko utters a pitiful whine. Why, Gabriel asks himself, is Zuko always more in touch with his emotions than I? His eyes surprise him, and he rubs a tear away.

"Oh, Gabriel. I'll be praying for you and Joe. You're going to be okay. What did the police say?"

Gabriel lets out a long breath. "The cops had a lot to say, but it was all questions. They had no answers. I don't even know how he died. The detective said I'd be hearing from her soon."

"Tell me again, when was the last time you spoke with Joe?"

"Oh, that was the day before it happened. We were going to meet that morning."

"What was his mood?" Barbara asks in her maternal tone. "What did he say?"

Gabriel pulls Zuko's snoozing body closer to him. "He sounded excited but apprehensive. I can't say he was scared. Well, maybe he was scared. I don't know. Maybe I'm reading more into it now. Why didn't I pay more attention?"

"You couldn't know this was going to happen. Did he say anything at all? About his work?"

"Hmm," Gabriel takes a moment more to gather himself. He ponders what to say. He vowed to stop saying too much. "He said he was divorcing Peter."

"Yes, I heard," Barbara says flatly.

Heard from whom?

"He called you before he died?" Gabriel asks.

Barbara lets out an exasperated breath. "Gabriel, if you've come into possession of his work, it's important that you give it to me."

"Give it to you?"

After a long, drawn-out pause, Barbara speaks slowly. "You understand better than anyone how Joe and I worked together. I understand Joe and his data. I fostered his career when no one else would. Who better than me to safeguard his work, our work, and see to it that it's used properly?"

Gabriel touches his head as vertigo comes over him. This talent upgrade feels like a hangover. He can't read her mind because she is a Koli asset. For the first time in his life, Gabriel has real power at his command, and it's thrilling. He's tempted to test the witch's ward around Barbara's mind.

"You love it, don't you?" the voice says. *"But you're afraid power corrupts. So, what if it does?"*

Gabriel reaches for the voice, but it eludes him. He catches a scent of fear, and it reminds him of Anisa. Five feet two inches of an adept colossus who parts every room she enters. It doesn't make sense.

"Who will use it?" Gabriel asks. "What exactly was he studying?"

If Joe didn't want any more secrets to remain in the world regarding adepts, it's best to start now.

"We're geneticists. We look for clues in our genes that can help us treat diseases."

That's skillful. It's the truth and yet a lie by omission. Very well, let the truth come out.

"You're studying us," Gabriel says. "You've been studying us all along. I'm starting to worry I've been used and my meeting Joe wasn't an accident."

"We study everything," Barbara replies.

"What do you know about me and my family?" Gabriel wishes now he was physically with Barbara. Most people are blind to the emotions of others, even though all they need is attention to detail. The crook of a smile or the sudden stiffness of a spine speaks volumes. There are a million tells. "Tell me. Tell me what you know, not what Joe may have known."

Barbara sighs. "I'll tell you everything if you promise to work with me to find the data and turn it over to me. It's rightfully mine. At least half of it is my work. I am its rightful heir if anyone is."

Again, not a single lie but not the whole truth either.

"Sorry," Gabriel says. "I want the whole truth first, and then we'll talk. I can't believe we're bargaining like this. There's a killer out there and all you talk about is Joe's data. Do I need to pay you a visit in person to get the truth?"

Not that it would work.

"Honey, listen to me. You could get hurt. Dangerous people want that data."

"Like you?" Gabriel waits for a reply, but none comes. Barbara won't lie today.

Gabriel takes a deep breath. Zuko is alert now as his eyes survey the room for threats. "Who wants the data, Barbara? Do you know who killed Joe?"

"Every government and pharmaceutical company in the world wants the data. Don't poke your nose in his death however much you want to, or the same thing could happen to you. I'm trying to help you as much as myself."

Every word was accurate, but Gabriel's no closer to the truth. He did learn that Barbara is not in possession of the data, and one thing is for sure. If every pharmaceutical company and government wants Joe's work, Covian is the perfect place to start.

Chapter Sixteen

SPORTS

The policy of the Agency is not to investigate adepts involved in professional sports. However, there was one high-profile case of a basketball player who came out of seemingly nowhere and began to lead his team to championships, despite being only five feet seven inches tall. An anonymous tip alerted us that this was an infraction of adept law. After a phone call to one of the deputy inquisitors known to us, the player announced his surprise retirement.

—National Intelligence Strategy White Paper: Top Secret (TS): Release of this document will cause severe damage to the security of the United States—Adept Assets

SELLERS PAYS WHAT he describes as "extortion" to park his Maserati Quattroporte in Covian Pharmaceutical's underground lot. Gabriel saw a spot on the street, but Sellers doesn't like leaving his baby exposed to the elements, even on a morning such as this, when the sun sparkles against the city's glass towers.

Kendall Square is at the intersection of the Massachusetts Institute of Technology and enough venture capital to buy and sell small nations. Startups and biotech companies occupy every corner. Twenty-somethings in five-hundred-dollar sneakers casually look at their phones as they stroll to work. Gabriel catches a stray thought: *They're lucky I go in at all.*

In the tallest and sleekest of the new towers, Gabriel and Sellers enter the elevator at garage level and press "L." When the silver doors open, they reveal a filmmaker's fever dream of heaven. Everything is white marble and clear glass. Even the maintenance crew wears white. Suspended in the center, a transparent spiral staircase floats with no visible means of support. Gabriel guesses it's decorative until he watches someone descend it.

"How do they do that without magic?" Sellers asks.

"It's amazing," Gabriel remarks, gazing up.

"Don't look up like that," Sellers says. "You make us seem like bloody tourists. Now remind me, what's the plan?"

"I ask in my most persuasive way that they take us to Joe's office, where we'll look for clues. Then we go to his apartment. And why is it that I imprinted on my British dad, but you're the one who says 'bloody'?"

"Because I hang out with you, and I have style," Sellers says, raising both hands. "Speaking of the English, did you eat a scone?"

"I did. I'm ready."

"You can't handle the truth," Sellers says with a grin.

They approach the reception desk occupied by two young women with blonde hair. One wears diamond earrings that hum with a trickle of ley energy. Her nametag reads, "Ellen." He leans in slightly to her.

"Hi, Ellen. We're here for you to take us to Dr. Martin's office."

To help his adept talent, Gabriel has picked up a few techniques such as name repetition and mimicking body language. People love the sound of their own name. Every good salesperson knows that instinctually.

Gabriel's power implants the memory that her manager asked her to do this. It's so effortless he must pull back lest he damage her mind. Her momentary look of confusion disappears, and certainty replaces it.

"Oh, of course," she says. "I remember. Come this way."

"Wait, Ellen," her colleague says, standing up. "We need their IDs to make visitor badges."

"Oh, of course, what's wrong with me?"

Now is not the time to encounter diligent employees. Gabriel probably could've handled the two of them, but he can't afford to experiment now. He and Sellers pose for their photos, and Ellen leads them through security.

"This feels like checkpoint Charlie," Sellers remarks.

"I'm uneasy, too, but I don't sense any minds on us," Gabriel replies.

"Dr. Martin was the highest-ranking executive in this location," Ellen says while leading them down the hall. "Our headquarters are in Los Angeles, in case you didn't know. Dr. Martin has his official office in the executive suites, but he spent most of his time in a small office off the lab. I know because I always found him there when I forwarded his calls."

"Thanks, Ellen," Gabriel says. "We'll go to his office off the lab first. Which floor is his official office on?"

"The fortieth. You'll need a card key."

Ellen turns the corner, slows her walk, and approaches two double doors. On one is the word "Laboratory," and the other, "2-L." Gabriel freezes and touches his forehead. He relives the trauma and recalls the two phrases Joe was able to send to him, the first one, "the data," and now he understands the second, "2-L." He glances at Sellers who sees his quiet panic.

"This is Dr. Martin's working office," she says, opening the door.

"Thanks, Ellen." Gabriel gives her a warm smile. "We'll take it from here."

He and Sellers enter the small office and look around. It isn't a church, but Gabriel senses the same sacredness of the lab that Joe felt as well as a part of his spirit. This is where he was happiest.

A lab demands respect, Joe said, because what emerges from it can literally be life changing. Tranquility seems to drift in the air. It wafts past Gabriel making him want to reach out and grab it. Whether real or imagined, is the only vestige of Joe that he can find. Gabriel takes a breath and realizes, too late, he's trying to smell him—maybe find some faded essence of the cologne he wore or the suit he chose. He walks to the closet, where a lone gray suit jacket hangs. *Good. Joe branched out and discovered gray.*

"Well?" Sellers asks. "You're the psychic. What do you think?"

"Let's check the computer." Gabriel starts to approach Joe's desk, then stops. "Wait," he exclaims. "Someone is here."

A woman with light-brown hair and a muscular, toned body appears before their eyes, sitting in Joe's chair.

"Sweet Hecate!" Sellers exclaims.

"I was going to let you two keystone cops keep looking around, but I was getting bored—glad you finally noticed. At first, I thought you were adepts, but then I thought, what kind of an adept would sign into security? The answer is two adept morons. The security guard at reception input your destination. Didn't you think someone visiting our recently murdered chief scientific officer would raise an alarm bell?"

The woman has her arms crossed with her feet up on the desk. Her teeth are pearly perfection, and she wears no jewelry. A fact that perturbs Gabriel. She does wear makeup that lends her a natural, wholesome look. It clashes with the murder in her eyes.

"Careful, Sel—" Gabriel was about to use Sellers's name but catches himself before giving more information away. "She's a Provectus if she's powerful enough to cloud both our minds."

"Very good. You get a gold star."

"Who are you?" Gabriel asks. "What's an adept doing in Joseph Martin's office?" He's surprised not to hear the same fear in his voice that pounds in his chest.

"You break into House Angeles, and you ask me who I am? Who are you? Not that I don't know." She removes her feet from the desk and stands.

"I'm Gabriel Kelly. Now your turn."

She looks up at Gabriel and then even further up at Sellers. It's a look that says, *I wouldn't spit on you if you were on fire.* "I'm Inquisitor Keira D'Cruz. I'm here with Patriarch Meyer."

Gabriel's eyes widen. "The Angeles patriarch is here?"

"He's here, and you're going to see him." Keira moves to the door, keeping her eyes on Gabriel or Sellers.

"Have we met?" Gabriel asks, not moving an inch. "Did we meet at Joe's apartment a few days ago? When you killed him? Did the

Angeles kill Joe after they got what they wanted? Where's his work? Where's the data?"

"Careful, thieving adept; you might make me angry. And I don't answer your questions. You answer mine."

Gabriel narrows his eyes. "I've been hearing that a lot lately, and I'm fresh out of patience. I'm not going anywhere with you. I'm going to my patriarch, Russell Walker. You're in Salem territory."

Keira lashes out, invading Gabriel's and Sellers's minds, trying to gain control of their nervous systems and thoughts. The room swerves as her strike against Sellers slides off him, and the energy explodes. Sellers explained to Gabriel when they were drunk in a bar. Witches can't guard their minds the same way as adepts can. They use a spell to redirect the invading adept into another nearby mind or back onto the attacker. Keira's command that Sellers obey her ricochets between her and Gabriel. It leaves them momentarily stunned, but she recovers and pins Sellers to the wall telekinetically. She prevents him from speaking or moving.

"What did you do?" she demands. "I've never felt that before."

What are high-ranking Angeles doing in Boston?

The room closes in on Gabriel, and he turns to face Keira. Her slight smile tells him his status as Anisa Aboud Walker's great-great-grandson and nephew to the patriarch will not protect him. *That look isn't sane.*

She flicks her finger, and Sellers flies across the office, screaming. His cries stop when his body collides with the concrete column in the corner. Sellers's body slumps to the floor, and Gabriel watches helplessly as crimson blossoms on his head.

"Delicious, isn't it?" Keira says. "The scent of blood." She gives Sellers a quick glance. "Is he dead? Maybe. You Salem are so fragile."

Gabriel clenches his fist and wills himself to remain impassive. Sensing his fear, Zuko appears in the corner of his mind. Zuko, whose emotions are so straightforward, but when it comes to his protective instincts, he becomes nuanced and complex. Zuko imparts to Gabriel that the two-legged are the most vicious and deadly of all living things, and Keira is the most dangerous of the two-legged. Do not show fear, Zuko warns. If you do, she'll strike, and we die. Give her cause to respect us. If a predator doesn't respect you, it will rip you open and walk away without a second thought. Then, Zuko calls out, but not to Gabriel—to something else.

"He's right, you know. Rip her heart out," the voice says.

"No," Gabriel replies. *"I'm not a killer."*

"Then be killed."

Keira flicks her finger a second time as if brushing away a gnat, and Gabriel flies into the wall. She doesn't slam him into the concrete column as she did with Sellers, so he remains conscious. Keira telekinetically lifts him, slithering his body up the wall. Panic spreads across Gabriel's face, and Keira nods with smug satisfaction.

"Go on," she says. "Take a few breaths. I'm feeling generous."

Gabriel gulps in air with wide eyes.

"I'll ask this once, and depending on your answer, you might live. Do you have the data?"

After a few seconds, when no answer comes, Keira shrugs. "You know what? I don't care if you know or not. I'll bring your dead body to my patriarch."

Blackness descends on him, along with it an overwhelming desire to slip into blissful sleep, but a thought stabs him. It's the realization that if he dies, so does Sellers. Willing the metronome beat of his heart to speed up, Keira's telekinetic fist squeezing his heart weakens, and

Keira's eyes flash in annoyance.

"The mouse struggles," she says.

The pain comes roaring back, and Gabriel feels his life force ebb. She's too strong. The box around his heart grows smaller and smaller, and in seconds, it will burst inside his chest. Where is his great-great-grandmother? Where is Anisa?

"She can't help you, and it's because you're wrong. This is House Angeles territory. Our HQ has embassy status. You may as well be in Beverly Hills, you idiot boy. And besides, you attacked us by spying. Not to mention the fact that the witches have warded this place to the gills. It costs us a fortune."

Keira puts more power into the squeeze. "Will you just die already."

Gabriel fights a desire to lie down when he gets a thought flash from Keira.

"The reward for killing a Regna. But I'm no Regna."

One last thing to do for Joe, he decides. Keira laughs in response, and blood gurgles up Gabriel's throat. He's too weak to even close his eyes. Trying to move his arms and legs is akin to discovering someone stole your car; what you thought you had is gone. Darkness descends on him, and it's good. But, what about Sellers?

I brought him here, and I must protect him.

Gabriel sucks in a breath and looks at Sellers, wounded on the floor.

He bled for me. I have to get him away.

Gabriel agrees with the voice, and when he does, power starts to flow through him. It flies with a life of its own from the deepest recesses of his mind, and he hears a shadow of himself say, *"Finally."*

Sellers recovers, and he chants in an odd rhythm.

Earth Ignore

Flee the floor

Keira cries out in frustration as gravity warps, and she falls upward, slamming into the ceiling.

"I'm not an adept. Now, who's a moron?" Sellers says.

As Keira tumbles down from the ceiling, Gabriel catches her telekinetically in midflight. Keira tries to speak, but Gabriel constricts her throat. Feeling her instinctual need to take a breath, he stops her lungs from working. Her eyes burn with hatred, but this time, her power is weak and brittle.

"Delicious, isn't it?" the voice says.

"You will answer my questions," Gabriel demands.

He summons his focus and thinks of Joe. He remembers him when they were happiest, remembers finding him in his apartment, lifeless. Then Gabriel looks directly into Keira's eyes and recites from memory.

If you know who killed Joe,

Confess it now or be my foe

In this room, truth will prevail

All your plans sure to fail.

Miles away, Zuko utters a powerful four-second howl in Gabriel's home library. Strange, unfamiliar energy envelops the room. It prickles the skin and raises the hair on his arms. To Gabriel, it's as warm as a tumbler of whiskey on its journey through the body. Sellers's magic ignites.

"Who killed Joe?" Gabriel asks her flatly, looking directly into her eyes. The effect on Keira is immediate. Her expression wavers, and her predatory defiance evaporates.

"You're aligned with crows?" she says. "You use magic on me?

Traitor!"

He enunciates each word slowly as if he's counting them off. "Who. Killed. Joe."

Keira's eyes narrow, and her face reddens. "I'll answer your dull questions. You should know the truth, and the truth is I don't know. But I think your shop boy Ankit did it." She gasps in a breath in a desperate heave as if she were being waterboarded. "Or your friend here."

"Ankit," Gabriel says, unsurprised, but his stomach contorts. "How?" Gabriel tries to act as if he already knows the answer. Keira looks nauseous and remains silent, but Gabriel knows her thoughts.

"It's not a lie to keep the truth to oneself."

He experiences a fraction of her nausea as if it's his own and watches as it overwhelms her resistance.

"Either Jeebom or someone at Covian got to Joe Martin first, or the crows did," Keira says, choking out the words. "Maybe your crow."

"The witches," Gabriel exclaims. "What do the witches have to do with this?"

Fleeting exhaustion washes over Gabriel. It's coming from Keira. The scone magic is wearing down her defenses. Sellers's magic connects them, compelling her to tell the truth.

She says tremulously, "How stupid are you? You think the witches have nothing to do with this? They want Martin's data. Imagine the leverage it would give them over us. I'm here to find the data, the gene sequence that identifies us at birth. To learn how many in the dall medical and academic communities know about us."

Keira's face loses its color, and she vomits on the floor.

"Your pet crow?" she says in defiance. "Is he the one responsible for your truth spell?"

"Temper, temper." Seller wags his finger at Keira.

"You want the truth?" she asks Gabriel as her lips curl. "Your witch friend here has the same mission as me. The high priestess wants that data as badly as us, and it's this crow's job to get it." She blurts it out with a hint of triumph. "He's my competition."

"Competition?" Sellers sniffs. "Doesn't look it from here."

"We'll be going now," Gabriel says, keeping his voice steady. A million thoughts of Joe pummel him, and he releases her. Keira falls five hard feet to the ground with a satisfying *crack,* and with his release of power, the voice battering his mind falls silent.

"Blimey! Run!" Gabriel exclaims.

Sellers turns and flings open the office door. A small crowd has gathered outside, but he and Gabriel hustle through it.

In the stairwell, Sellers huffs, "I got blood all over my Kiton shirt, and I'm sending you the bill. It's bad enough I'm not getting my parking ticket validated."

"Let's split up," Gabriel says. "I'll go to my shop, and you go to the bakery. We'll talk later."

Chapter Seventeen

SUBVERSIVE CELLS

"We have neutralized one well-financed, highly trained Russian adept network that was working to subvert the government of the United States."

—Confidential Department of Defense memo: #1647: Top Secret: (TS) Release of this document will cause severe damage to the security of the United States—March 2024

"MR. KELLY, CAN you spare a few moments?"

Without waiting for a reply, Detective Rizzo elbows her way into the shop. The spritely jingle of the door chime matches Rizzo's upbeat mood.

"I've been meaning to chat with you again." Rizzo looks around as if admiring the space. "Is anyone else here?"

Is that what she thought of their last meeting? Gabriel thinks. A chat? This meeting is a lucky break for Rizzo. He's in the store intermittently at best. Or is it a lucky break? *Am I under surveillance?*

"Ah, no, just us," he replies. "When I got here, I let Margo leave early with our new hire, Ankit. They've been working long hours. Let me lock up and close the store, and we'll talk in the back. If a customer sees us, I don't want them banging down the door."

"We can talk here," Rizzo says. "I don't want to interrupt your business."

"No, I'll lock up. I don't want any distractions."

I want to see what's going on in your head, Gabriel thinks as he leads Rizzo to the small backroom office. Alone in his sanctuary, free from the threat of disruption, he can fully concentrate on the detective.

Once inside, Gabriel glances down at his desk and sees Ankit's résumé that he never bothered to read and frowns. *Wait. What? Ankit Anand. His last name is Anand, as in Shreyas Anand, the president of Jeebom?*

Gabriel has never paid much attention to the retail side of his jewelry business. *This time, my lack of attention to detail will literally get me killed.*

He wants to crush the paper in his hands and scream, but he calmly turns the résumé over, smiles, and says, "Have a seat, Detective."

Gabriel gestures to a chair and waits for her to sit. His smile is more to put himself at ease than her. He hopes it disguises his anxiety and the surely audible pounding of his heart. Inquisitor or dall, his feelings about law enforcement are complicated and cops make him nervous. The silence in the room is unnerving. Not silence as in lack of sound, but instead, he hears very little of the usual chatter from Rizzo's mind.

Adepts can find each other in a crowd because of the inability to detect the other's thoughts. Rizzo isn't a blank slate, but very little is coming from her. She's remarkably disciplined. For a moment, Gabriel loses himself in admiration. If only he were more like her, how much happier his parents would be.

"You look shaken up," the detective says. "Are you getting any sleep?"

"I had a rough morning. It went sideways, and no, not much." Without meaning to, Gabriel casts his eyes downward. "I don't sleep well lately."

A sympathetic smile crosses Rizzo's face. Gabriel searches for something in her thoughts to match her expression and finds nothing. She must've had lots of practice to get it just right in her line of work. She can fake it at will. "That stands to reason," she says. "Finding a dead body is traumatic."

Gabriel nods slowly and makes a conscious effort not to bite his upper lip.

"Have you talked to someone?" Rizzo asks. "I can recommend a trauma specialist."

"Is this why you're here, Detective Rizzo? To discuss my mental health?" Rizzo's expression remains impassive, but she flushes, pressing him to add, "I-I'm sorry, Detective. I didn't mean to snap."

"When was the last time you saw Dr. Martin alive?"

Gabriel pauses to think, although he knows exactly when it was. "I ran into them in Brazil."

"'Them' being Dr. Martin and his husband, Peter Brandon. Is that right?"

"Yes."

"In Brazil?"

"Yes, I was in Brazil to buy emeralds, and Joe and Peter were on vacation."

"When was that exactly?" Rizzo asks. "And was that a coincidence?"

After a pause, probably much too long a pause, Gabriel answers, "It was about a week and a half ago. It was right before my trip to Burma."

"I see. And how long ago were you in Burma?"

"Ah, four days ago." Gabriel can't help but notice she's taking a long time jotting down notes. The scrape of her pen reverberates in the small room, and he wonders if it's because he avoided the coincidence question. When he thinks about it, avoiding the question is tantamount to an admission because it was no coincidence.

"Why did you let yourself into the apartment he shared with his husband? If he didn't reply to your text or call, why the urgency?"

The questions pummel his carefully constructed composure. He knew they'd be coming, but he couldn't evade them. "I told you. I felt something was wrong."

Rizzo blinks in rapid succession but keeps her face set in stone. "What drove you to go to the apartment and let yourself in? Why not wait for him to call you back?"

Blood rushes to his face now, and Gabriel takes a breath. "I told you. He didn't call me back when he said he would, and he always does. I knew something was off, and besides, we were supposed to meet. Joe isn't the type to—wasn't the type to miss a meeting."

Rizzo rapidly writes in her notebook again, barely glancing down at the page.

Subpoena phone records, he imagines her writing. He tries to probe her mind but only finds some stray thoughts about her weekend plans with her husband. He gets a vague sense of her wanting to prepare coq au vin. She focuses on the task at hand. Intense concentration is a wall.

"Were you in a romantic relationship with Dr. Martin during his marriage?"

Gabriel was about to blurt out a frantic *no* but thought better of it. "How does this matter?" he asks, when he knows it matters. "Why are you prying into my personal life? What does that have to do with why Joe is dead?"

This time, a flicker of emotion dents Rizzo's face. She looks up and stares at Gabriel for a moment and puts down her pen. "I recall mentioning to you, Mr. Kelly, that for the duration of this investigation, my job is to ask the questions and yours is to answer them. I will tell you this. Dr. Martin's personal life is pertinent. The more I understand him, the closer I get to what happened." She picks her pen up and leans back in her chair, ready to take notes.

"All right," Gabriel says. "I loved him. Is that romantic enough for you?"

"Did he love you?"

"I thought he did."

Rizzo's pen glides across her notebook and Gabriel's gut twists.

"How did he die?" His voice is thin and shaky. "May I ask that? Since you're still investigating, he must've been murdered."

Rizzo takes a deep breath, and the hard line of her jaw softens. "The cause of death was poisoning."

Gabriel shudders. "What? How did that happen?"

"We found poison in the beverage he was drinking. The poison attacked his organs, and they failed."

"Oh my God." Gabriel's face turns blisteringly hot. "The coffee."

Rizzo leans forward. "Mr. Kelly, every indication of Dr. Martin's state of mind leads us to believe someone took his life. We have to pursue a line of inquiry that someone purposely poisoned him."

A million thoughts assault Gabriel—one of them, how easy it would be for an adept, especially one of the upper ranks, to compel Joe to poison himself. He has to find who teleported out of Joe's home. He needs to be smart and make a plan.

"Is that a French press?" Rizzo asks, gesturing to a high shelf. "Do you use it here?"

"Yes, I often make coffee for Margot and me and the customers."

"No coffee maker for you, then?"

"No, I prefer the French press."

"Why is that?"

Gabriel smiles wanly. "At first, it was a way to make a connection with a customer, to prepare a cup by hand. But over time, I learned more and more, so now I prefer coffee I prepare myself. I can't imagine making it any other way."

"The same type of French press is at Joe Martin's house."

Gabriel frowns. "Yes, I know the one. I gave it to him. Barbara and I are both coffee snobs, and we turned Joe into one."

"You and Dr. Bates?"

"Yes, Barbara and I are both Bri—"

"You and Dr. Bates are both British?"

"No," Gabriel says. "I was born and raised here. I meant, my dad is British, and so is Babs. The Brits take their tea very seriously and their coffee somewhat seriously. Barbara has a lot to say about a proper cup of tea and a proper cup of coffee. She was Joe's mentor in lots of ways…"

"If you're not British, why the accent?" Rizzo asks, pen at the ready.

"I, ah, picked it up from my dad, and I lived in London as a toddler."

"I see." Rizzo jots down her notes. When she looks up, she asks, "Were you planning a life with Dr. Martin?"

"Oh." Gabriel feels as if he's been shaken from a stressful dream. "Okay, ah, yes. He told me he was divorcing Peter, and I believed him. When Joe makes up his considerable mind, it doesn't change."

"But in your case, it did change. You dated before his marriage and after your relationship ended, he married your friend, Peter Brandon. And then, you're in love and about to start a new life with Dr. Martin after the divorce, correct? His mind did change about you, didn't it? What could have done that, Mr. Kelly?"

Gabriel looks into Rizzo's eyes and mind for some inner meaning to that question but finds nothing but focus and keen attention. *She* would've noticed Ankit's last name immediately.

"You've been in love, haven't you, Detective Rizzo?" Gabriel tries to sound irritated at the question, to hide his shock. "Yes, right, you don't answer questions. Joe knew his marriage was a mistake from the start. For my part, I made mistakes in my relationship with Joe while we dated. I'm sure, looking back, he felt the same and wanted to try again. Haven't you made mistakes?"

"When you let yourself into the apartment, what did you see?"

Gabriel rolls his eyes to the ceiling. "I don't enjoy reliving this, but I understand that you have to keep asking. I remember seeing his body and the spilled coffee. I remember rushing to him and trying to see if he was still alive. When I learned he was truly gone, I tried to close his eyes, but they wouldn't close. I kept trying, but they stayed open, and it was awful."

Tears well up in his eyes, and he smears them with the palm of his hand. Rizzo's expression is unchanged. Gabriel's display of emotion, no matter how sincere, does nothing to dissuade her businesslike demeanor.

"The muscles in the eye contract, and it's not possible to close the eyes of a recently deceased person. That's only in the movies," Rizzo says. "Tell me about his work."

"His work?" Gabriel inhales deeply and tries to modulate his breathing. He doesn't want to sob in front of her. She wouldn't care in any case. "He was a geneticist. He developed drugs."

"There are several photographs of you and Dr. Barbara Bates, his director at Jeebom Pharmaceuticals, on Dr. Martin's phone. You all appear to be friendly outside of work. Tell me about your and Dr. Martin's relationship with Dr. Bates."

"Ah, Joe worked with Barbara," Gabriel says in a soft voice, glancing away from Rizzo.

"Are you friends?" Rizzo asks, her pen at the ready.

Gabriel probes her mind and hits a wall of intense concentration. All he gets from her is heightened anticipation of his answer and intense scrutiny of his every gesture and movement. She makes a show of taking notes, but Rizzo has excellent echoic memory. She recalls everything she hears. Gabriel knows this because he can almost feel his words etch into her memory.

"Yes, we're friends. Barbara is a joy, so full of surprises and interested in everything. She's also a doctor. They're both geneticists, working together in the same type of research developing lifesaving drugs. Although, they call them therapies."

"Tell me how you met Dr. Bates?" Rizzo's eyes grow sharp at the mention of another doctor, and she leans slightly forward. When she does this, despite his size, Gabriel feels as if Rizzo will swallow him.

"I met Barbara when I was in the lab visiting Joe. He was testing me and Zuko."

Rizzo raises an eyebrow. "Who is Zuko? And he was testing you? For what?"

Gabriel knows Rizzo is looking for the tiniest flicker in his face, so he tries to remain impassive, but he knows he fails; he's always saying or showing too much.

"He said he wanted some blood samples of me and my dog Zuko. I'm not sure why. Maybe some kind of study on why some people resemble their dogs?" Gabriel forces a smile, hoping to get Rizzo to laugh, but her face remains eerily unchanged.

"It was a study on adepts," she says, "and you're an adept. Or should I say, *Homo sapiens psychica?*"

Gabriel's heart falls into his stomach, and his jaw drops.

"Don't get any ideas about erasing my memory or tampering with my mind, assuming you can do that. My colleagues are in possession of written materials that will refresh my memory, and I will take such action against me poorly."

"What—what do you want?" Gabriel stammers.

"I want to know about adepts. Who governs you? What is the power structure? Where do you fit in, and who in the adept world has a motive to kill Dr. Martin? Motive is important because if Martin is to be believed, all adepts have means and opportunity."

"Ah," Gabriel hesitates. He avoids Rizzo's stare and studies the wall.

"Do you want to find the person or persons who killed Dr. Martin or not? Choose now."

Gabriel takes a breath and puts his face in his hands. "My uncle. He's the patriarch of House Salem. He governs us."

"What is a patriarch and what is House Salem?"

"There are five ruling families in our territory. A territory is the equivalent of an adept country. Ours is called Salem. It's New England, New York, and New Jersey. We have a council made up of the five families, and every seven years they elect a matriarch or a patriarch. My uncle is two years into his second term."

"You come from a powerful family. You must be powerful. Where do you fit in with House Salem?"

"My family is powerful. I'm somewhat of a disappointment. I'm only a Media."

"A Media?"

"We're evaluated around college age to access our level of power. There are five adept ranks. The least powerful is an Incepto. I'm the second rank. I'm a Media. My father is Periti, which is a respected rank. My mother is a Provectus, as is my uncle. They're adept royalty. My great-great-grandmother is a Regna. They're like gods."

"Your great-great-grandmother is alive?"

"Yes. Regnas live an extraordinarily long life."

"Why isn't she the matriarch?"

"Would you like a copy of our constitution? Perhaps sit in on a civics class?"

"You know my policy on questions, Mr. Kelly."

Gabriel looks away, takes a deep breath, and exhales through his nose.

"Our laws forbid it because it's too much power vested in one person. The Regna reports to the elected matriarch or patriarch."

"Your great-great-grandmother reports to her son or grandson?"

"Grandson, and it's complicated. It's better than the witches. The high priestess or priest is usually the most powerful."

"Witches?"

Gabriel's ragged breathing is the only sound in the room. He tries to slow his breathing, but realizes he can't. His small office closes in on him, and his chest constricts.

"Who governs the witches?"

"I'm saying too much. I need my uncle."

"Believe me when I tell you, Mr. Kelly, this is extraordinary, but I'm not interested in your trade secrets. My only concern is bringing those who brought about Joe Martin's death to justice. If you share that concern, then answer my questions."

Gabriel puts his face in his hands for several seconds.

"Her name is Ravynne Quinn. Beyond that I don't know anything."

"Who in the adept world wants Joe Martin dead?"

"His employers at Covian Pharma. That's House Angeles. They're rich and powerful. They control Southern California."

"They employed him to do what?"

"I think you know. To map our genome. To find the secret to our power. Joe did it, and he was going to release it with or without the Angeles approval. Mostly without."

"Who else?"

"House Koli. They're Joe's ex employers at Jeebom Pharma. They control Mumbai and all its wealth. They have a claim to Joe's research as they used to finance him."

"What is the nature of your relationship with Dr. Bates of Jeebom Pharmaceuticals?" Rizzo asks.

Gabriel was hoping to avoid this line of inquiry, that Rizzo would accept he met Barbara when he was with Joe and leave it at that. "We met at Joe's job, and we stayed friends."

At this, Rizzo says nothing but scribbles in her notebook.

Rizzo puts the cap back on the tip of her pen and closes her notebook, unmoved by Gabriel's show of emotion. "I must ask you to surrender your passport, Mr. Kelly, because I am making you a person of interest in the murder of Joe Martin. You see, in addition to his phone, we searched his personal computer, and there was an e-mail in a draft folder that said he was afraid of you, and you were not what you seemed to be, and I can see his point."

"Wait, what? I don't believe it," Gabriel cries.

"Be that as it may, Mr. Kelly," Rizzo says in her methodical deadpan. "The Boston Police Department isn't interested in your beliefs at this time. Perhaps in the near future, your state of mind will be of great interest to us. As of now, surrender your passport to headquarters as soon as possible, and by ASAP, I mean by tonight or tomorrow morning." Rizzo closes her notebook. "Thank you, Mr. Kelly, for seeing me on such short notice. I have no further questions. I'll see my way out."

"Cheers," Gabriel says, without meeting her eyes.

Rizzo leaves, and Gabriel waits for the cheerful ring of the store chime. It irritates him for the first time.

He picks up his phone and texts Russell because he can't face a mental communication. *My new employee is a Koli spy. His full name is Ankit Anand, and the dall police know all about us.*

Gabriel wonders what Russell will think of the fact he's a person of interest in the dall investigation and puts his face in his hands. The overwhelming emptiness of loss descends on him, and his stomach hollows out. He hopes Uncle Russell can keep him out of a dall jail because he knows that as suspects go, he's perfect.

Gabriel opens the small safe on his desk and withdraws the

diamond Joe sent. Surging in the stone like a bottled-up hurricane, ley energy swirls and sparkles in the facets. He hoped that the diamond held romantic significance, but the packed ley energy tells him Joe must've artificially infused it. *Maybe it's a prototype. One of his last acts was to send me this, but why?* The stone is worth about ten thousand dollars to the dall and about one million to an adept because the ley energy is potent and easily accessible.

Gabriel examines the diamond through the loupe and sees nothing but a good quality diamond. Confused and crushed, he puts it back in its box and returns the jewel to the safe.

Chapter Eighteen

ADEPT MENTAL HEALTH

Mental health is an issue in the adept community. The ability to read thoughts from those around them, if not properly mastered, will lead to insanity. What adepts do with those unfortunate enough to not master the skill is under investigation.

—National Intelligence Strategy White Paper: Top Secret (TS): Release of this document will cause severe damage to the security of the United States—Adept Assets

AFTER THE FRENCH witches representing the Crone Seat leave her sitting room, the high priestess's intercom chirps.

"I have Sellers Collinsworth here to see you. What should I do?"

"Sellers Collinsworth? Alive and free? Well, I'll be damned. Send him in and get me a bottle of that champagne the Crones are so proud of, and bring two glasses, plus Collinsworth."

"Yes, High Priestess."

Sellers is ushered into the plush office for a second time, but now he's accompanied not only by the high priestess's wealthy scion of an intern but by two young men. They appear out of nowhere. One carries a bucket of ice containing the champagne and the other a silver plate with two flute glasses.

"Shall I pour, High Priestess?" one of the young men asks.

"It's six o'clock somewhere," she says while rifling through her desk.

The young witch's hands shake, but he manages to open the bottle and pour without incident.

"That looks ugly, Sellers," Ravynne says, glaring at the wound on his head. "Don't overuse the pain spell."

Sellers gingerly touches his head. "I'll live."

"Which is a surprise," Ravynne says in a loud voice. "Oh, you do drink, don't you, Sellers? How rude of me. Young people are so health conscious these days."

"I can use a drink," Sellers says with a smile and carefully takes a seat. "Especially champagne."

"You have some sense. I would, too, if I walked out of the Angeles den."

Ravynne finds what she is looking for, ignites an electronic cigarette, and greedily inhales. "I'm trying to quit. Do you think these help?"

"I don't know, High Priestess. But it's good that you're trying to quit."

"Ravynne, please, we've been over this."

"Yes, of course." Sellers bows his head a bit. "Ravynne."

"Despite our robust constitutions, what passes for my healer says that sixty years of smoking two packs a day is catching up with me." She inhales a deep drag of the e-cigarette, her expression as if she's walked barefoot through the Sahara and, just at the edge of death, takes that first sip of delicious cool water. "Listen to those bubbles," she says with a smile.

"Listen?" Sellers says, taking his glass.

"Yes, the bubbles should be tiny and give off a high-pitched sound, and this bottle is singing." Ravynne admires her full glass and then takes a long sip. "Delicious—liquid joy. The Crones do make the best champagne."

"Ravynne." Sellers puts his glass down. "I'm here to report on what happened at Covian."

"Of course. If you're all business, then I'm all ears. I must say, I'm impressed you're not being ransomed," Ravynne says, leaning back in her chair.

"Ransomed?"

"Alive even. You walked into Patrick's lair with him in it, and you haven't been drawn and quartered. Wouldn't you love to be a fly on the wall in Patrick's office now?"

Sellers's blank look makes Ravynne laugh.

"Sorry, Sellers," she says, amused. "I'm not mocking you, but imagine if the Angeles or the Salem walked in here, nosed around my offices, and walked out. How do you think I would react?"

Now, the look on Sellers's face isn't blank, and he goes white.

"Yes, exactly," Ravynne says. "Now tell me everything." She takes a long vape as if it's oxygen and locks eyes with Sellers.

"Ah, Gabriel obscured the minds of some security guards at the front desk who took us to Joe's office. When we got there, an Angeles adept confronted us. Her name was Keira D'Cruz. She said she was—"

"The Angeles chief inquisitor," Ravynne says, interrupting. "She's the best and worst kind of killer. She's dead inside. Why is that ruthless bitch here?"

"Dead?"

"In order to kill well, you first must kill something inside yourself. The *geist*. If it ever lived in that one, she strangled it in its crib."

It's a devastating indictment. The geist, or the soul, is what witches use to draw power.

"She must've let you go, but why? What is Patrick up to?" Ravynne asks, more to herself than to Sellers, and then remembers he's still there. "Sellers, don't mind me; go on."

"She attacked us, and we fought back. I used a chaos spell on her, reversing gravity. She thought I was an adept, so she might've thought it was telekinesis. But when the adept attacked that part of my brain and nothing happened, maybe she caught on that I'm a witch?"

Ravynne takes another long vape and sips her champagne. "What happened next? The Angeles inquisitor is on the ceiling and annoyed. What next?"

"Things happened fast after that. Gabriel got her in some kind of hold, and she was choking in midair. He released her, and we ran."

"Extraordinary. You left her gasping on the floor and ran?"

"Yes, I regret that we didn't learn anything."

"Didn't learn anything? Are you thick? Meyer's pit bull is a Provectus of the second *daan*, which means Gabriel Aboud is a Provectus or maybe— My God."

"Gabriel Kelly," Sellers says softly, "a Regna?"

Ravynne lets out a loud breath. "Don't let him out of your sight.

Bind him to us, Sellers. Bring me something of his I can use."

Sellers stares straight ahead, stone-faced. "I can bind him. It must be me."

"You know what that bitch Anisa did to us?"

"I—I remember," Sellers says, looking down.

"Never forget and never again." Ravynne takes another long drag on her vape.

"Never again," Sellers replies.

"Bring me Gabriel's head."

*

THOUGH IT'S AN office on the executive floor, it's modest by Covian standards. Patrick Meyer, chairman of the board of Covian Pharmaceuticals and patriarch of the Angeles House, has never visited the Boston branch before, so his unannounced arrival left everyone scrambling for accommodations. Keira, his chief inquisitor, stands with her hands clasped behind her back in military style, not daring to take a seat until the Angeles patriarch acknowledges her presence. Moments tick by while he makes a show of finishing a paragraph he's doubtlessly read several times.

Meyer wears a black silk suit, and his haircut hugs his head in flawless geometric precision. He paints a picture of relaxed urbanity, but Keira sees the violence behind Meyer's eyes, a coiled tempest kicking its cage and itching to get out.

Without looking up or granting her permission to sit, Meyer asks, "Does the infant Regna live?"

Keira flinches. "He's stronger than we knew."

Meyer doesn't react but slowly moves the paper he was reading into a folder, opens a drawer, and files it. "Do you have my data?" He looks up to meet Keira's eyes, and again, she sees the beast lurking behind them.

"No, Patriarch."

"You stand there without my data while my enemy ransacks my offices and is enjoying lunch." Meyer steeples his fingers. "'Stronger than we knew'? I told you he's a Regna, or weren't you listening?"

"I'm sorry, Patriarch."

"We have a small window to find out what he knows and kill him before he comes into his powers, and now due to your bumbling, we've lost a golden opportunity."

"Patriarch Meyer—"

Meyer raises his hand, and Keira stops cold. "We're in Salem territory. Regna Anisa is watching everything we do. Every time we take a piss outside this building, she's in our heads. Still, our quarry does us a favor by wandering into our Boston headquarters, and what happens? He walks out under my inquisitor's nose, a Provectus of the second *daan*. You've made fools of us. The Salem laugh while you stand there looking stupid."

"A crow was with him," Keira says.

An involuntary tremor rolls across Meyer's face, and he stands. "What did you say?"

"He was with a crow, and it attacked me."

"An Ironbay witch defended Gabriel Kelly?" Without waiting for a reply or her permission, Meyer probes Keira's mind. She quickly submits and lets down every defense, allowing Meyer to rifle through her thoughts as if skimming the pages of a book. That's what Keira's mind is now, an open book. Every instinct tells her to throw the intruder out, but she stifles the nausea the invasion instills and waits for him to finish probing.

Satisfied, Meyer sniffs. "I see you believe that."

"He came looking for the data, so he must not have it," Keira says, doing her best to keep the defensiveness out of her voice.

"And you know this how?" Meyer snaps. "Enlighten me as to the inner workings of Gabriel Kelly and Russell Walker, if you please."

"It was a risk to come here. Why else would Kelly take that risk?"

"To find Martin's killer. The man he loved is dead, and you think his sole motivation is our data." Meyer sighs deeply and returns to his chair. He makes a show of sitting and takes a long moment to glare at the still-standing inquisitor.

"This is what I deserve for hiring a psychopath," Meyer says out loud, as if to himself. "Or, perhaps you're right. You're right, and Russell doesn't want me to suspect he has the keys to our genetic code, so he allows his lovesick nephew to be captured as a sacrificial lamb. What a surprise it must be for my enemy, the Salem patriarch, to have Kelly return home unscathed after besting my best-trained Provectus."

Keira's cheek spasms. "I'll right this wrong, Patriarch," she says, her chin finding refuge in her chest.

"If anything, it makes me suspect the Salem killed Martin for the data, and Russell is setting up his distant nephew on the wrong side of the family. Oh, how pained he'll be to reveal the sad truth of Kelly's betrayal."

"Gabriel Kelly couldn't have killed Martin. I saw his mind—"

"Of course he didn't kill Martin, you idiot. Russell killed Martin and stole our data. Once it's revealed the Salem are in possession of the data sequencing our genome, Kelly will have an accident. He's marked for death already. That's why he was allowed to enter our headquarters. No one would doubt Russell's sincerity if he had to sacrifice a Regna on the altar of justice."

"So if I killed him," Keira says. "It's what the Salem patriarch secretly wants?"

"You're not completely stupid."

"But Gabriel Kelly is a budding Regna. Why kill him or discredit him?"

"Haven't you been listening? Because he has our genetic map. He can find other Regnas and recruit and enlist them to the Salem. He can kill them in their sleep in other territories. He can learn how to breed them."

Meyer lets an uncomfortable silence envelop the room before he speaks again.

"You did one thing right, even if it was by accident. You unwittingly observed something useful when Kelly left you gasping for breath. His concentration was broken not by any talent or training of yours but by the cacophony of thoughts battering his brain. He's not sufficiently skilled enough to block so many thoughts from so far. His power exceeds his grasp, and we can use that. If, and I emphasize if, you have another opportunity to face Gabriel Kelly, pick up every stray thought you can from the dall, throw it at him, and he'll crumble. I want him dead. In this case, I'll give Russell what he wants."

"Yes, Patriarch," Keira says, thinking it best to say as little as possible.

"We brought Carlos and Pablo with us. They're two of our most powerful Provectus inquisitors next to you. Why weren't the twins with you?"

"They were deployed—"

"Your arrogance cost us." Meyer's voice echoes off the walls in a mad torrent. The beast looks directly at her now. Its cage begins to open, and she instinctually takes a step back.

"Tell no one about your encounter with the witch. If there is a witch-adept alliance in Salem territory, we should be the only House that knows about it. Now stop embarrassing yourself and get my property back."

Keira takes her cue and leaves with her eyes on the floor.

Chapter Nineteen

ADEPT POPULATION

Our best estimates are that adepts are one-tenth of one percent of the population. How exactly that breaks down into the five adept ranks is unknown.

—National Intelligence Strategy White Paper: Top Secret (TS): Release of this document will cause severe damage to the security of the United States—Adept Assets

ANGLED STRUTS AND random crystal chandeliers fill the lobby of Jeebom Pharmaceuticals. Where the lobby of Covian gives off a feeling of "trendy youth," Jeebom is "we've been here forever, and we're rich."

"Officer Herrera and Detective Rizzo to see Barbara Bates," Rizzo says to the security guard in the mausoleum that doubles as a lobby.

"Open the gate." Rizzo nods to the sliding glass doors that bar her way and flashes her badge.

A middle-aged employee in an ill-fitting suit glides past them. He withdraws his card key, walks through the sliding glass doors, and heads for the elevator without looking back.

"You're the police?" the security guard asks. She's a young African American woman with her hair in a tight bun. "I'll let her know you're here."

"I prefer you wouldn't," Rizzo says in a clipped tone. "It's a surprise. After you open the gate, ensure the elevator goes up to the executive floor."

The gates resemble subway turnstiles, but only the ones at the upper-income stops.

Herrera smiles at the security guard, and she meekly smiles back. "Now," he says, gesturing toward the gates and displaying his badge.

She pushes a button, and the sliding glass doors open.

"Thank you," Rizzo says. And they proceed into the elevator bank.

"How did it go with Kelly?" Herrera asks.

"He's holding back. How did it go checking out Peter Brandon's alibi?"

"Something is off about him. His car was charged three times. You don't need that many charges to drive the distances he claims."

"Don't let that go. He's hiding something, just like Kelly."

Looking up at the numbers flashing in the display, Herrera sees they're about to arrive at the executive floor. "I hope Barbara Bates is here?"

"Oh, padawan," Rizzo replies with a smile. "I put her under surveillance this morning. You don't want to walk into someone's office with all the authority of the Boston Police Department only to find that they're in the Bahamas bribing midlevel government bureaucrats with expensive meals and golf outings."

"Don't you hate that?" Herrera says. "Do you know how to get to her office?"

Rizzo glares at Herrera and then looks awkwardly straight ahead into the elevator's mirrored glass. "Of course."

The elevator opens into a bright lobby with a large painting, rich in blues and reds, taking up the whole wall, the effect like being in a museum. An impact that someone paid an interior designer a great deal of money to impart. Rizzo strides past it while flashing her badge to the receptionist, who is there only to arrange for town cars and catered lunches. She gets up to follow, but Rizzo turns to face her, badge still displayed.

"Police business. Sit down." She turns and continues with Herrera one pace behind. Soon, the senior staff's big, airy courtroom-like offices come into view.

"She should be the third office down, next to the CEO. And remember, you're the good cop," Rizzo says.

"I see you're not stretching yourself," Herrera says with a grin.

The door to the office is open, and Rizzo knocks lightly. "Dr. Bates. Detective Rizzo and Officer Herrera of the Boston Police Department. May we have a word?"

"How—?" Bates starts but quickly regains her composure. "Do you have an appointment? I don't see you on my calendar." She rearranges her hair, which is already perfect.

"No appointment, Dr. Bates. We're investigating the murder of your former colleague Joe Martin."

"Yes, of course. Come in." Bates's tone is commanding in an attempt to regain control of her office. "May I offer you something to drink?"

Rizzo gives an efficient "No" and takes a seat. She crosses her legs and withdraws her notebook in one fluid motion. Herrera sits in the chair, crosses his legs, thinks better of it, and uncrosses them. Rizzo places her purse on Barbara's desk and glares at it. Most female police detectives no longer keep their guns and handcuffs in purses but rather carry them on a belt, often custom-made for women's clothes. Rizzo's jacket opens to her side, revealing the service revolver at her waist, and Barbara's eyes shift from the purse to the gun.

Bates wears a navy suit with a discrete band of pearls around her neck with earrings to match. Her clavicle pokes through her skin in her lean frame, a point of pride for women of a certain age in certain circles. She picks her Birkin bag, valued at tens of thousands of dollars, up off the floor and opens it to withdraw a lozenge. She then leaves it on the corner of her large desk and, Herrera notes, spares Rizzo's modest bag a dismissive look. Leaning back in her custom-made, Danish-designed executive chair, she settles in for the conversation.

"I still can't believe it happened. I was just talking with Joe," Bates says. "It doesn't seem real."

"When was the last time you spoke with Dr. Martin?" asks Rizzo.

Bates makes a show of considering the question before answering. "He called me the day before he died."

There is a pause where Rizzo waits for Bates to mention what they discussed, and Bates waits for Rizzo to ask. Rizzo's eyes narrow. Herrera hides a smile, maintaining the standoff.

"And what did you discuss, Dr. Bates?" Rizzo asks, her pen at the ready.

"His latest research."

"Did he always discuss his research with the competition?"

"We work for competing companies, that's true." Bates's face turns grim. "But we're colleagues trying to make the world a better place, and it's in that spirit we spoke that day and in general."

"And what was the subject that you discussed?"

"It's hard to explain."

"Try me."

"It was highly technical and scientific in nature."

"Did it have anything to do with *Homo sapiens psychica*?"

Bates gasps involuntarily and looks at Rizzo as if weighing her options.

Herrera thinks, *Will she go for "don't be ridiculous" or "act casual"?*

Bates grinds her teeth, and her jaw muscles contract. "It did," she says as if she just mentioned it's going to rain. "What do you know about the theory of a human subspecies, Officer?"

So, it's casual.

"Detective," Rizzo says. "I usually don't answer questions, Dr. Bates, but I'll make an exception in this case. There is practically nothing online about this human subspecies. What is online comes off as crazed conspiracy theories, not sober scientific assessments. My information comes, in part, from the deceased's PhD dissertation, which isn't online, oddly. I have an old-fashioned hard copy. I understand that you hired Dr. Martin based on his dissertation. Is that correct?"

"How did you get it? The university sealed it."

"Did they? That's interesting. I'm not at liberty to reveal my sources, Dr. Bates."

"Look, Detective." Barbara enunciates the word to properly observe her rank as she leans forward in her stylized Danish chair. "I don't know what Peter told you, but I can guess. Joe's death has nothing to do with his work in human subspecies. Have you asked Peter what his alibi is?"

"His alibi? Are you saying that Peter Brandon should be our number-one suspect? On what basis—"

"No, I'm just—"

"Detective Rizzo—" murmurs Herrera, cutting off Bates mid-sentence and flashing her a wan smile.

"What?" says Rizzo, obviously annoyed.

"I don't think Dr. Bates is saying that, Detective Rizzo," Herrera says. "Are you, Dr. Bates? You expect us to look into every possible avenue, but from what you know about Dr. Martin, we'd be wasting our time." Herrera nods and smiles.

"Yes, exactly right," Bates exclaims, raising her voice for the first time. "I'm glad one of you knows what I'm trying to say."

"And what is that?" Rizzo asks. "Peter Brandon knows something he hasn't told us?"

"Peter is volatile. He was exciting to Joe because he's unpredictable. He was attracted to that. Peter is an artist and a romantic. He's everything Joe isn't—wasn't. That worked for them until it didn't."

"And?"

"And," Bates's curiously unlined forehead creases for a brief second and then preternaturally snaps back into frozen amber. "You're wasting your time looking for clues in the scientific community. Yes, indeed, Joe wasn't well-liked, but we're not murderers."

"Motive is a factor, yes, but I look for means and opportunity, Dr. Bates, not motive. Although, would you humor me? Who stands to gain by Dr. Martin's death? Not his husband, at least not financially. Wouldn't you personally gain, as well as Jeebom, by having your main competition suddenly disappear? Are you now the preeminent scientist in this field?"

"I always was," Bates says, her unlined forehead now shiny with sweat.

"Janice," Herrera says, turning to Rizzo. "We're here to ask questions, not to accuse anyone."

Bates appears slightly reassured. "We were competitors, but it went deeper. I loved him like a son." She gets up and opens a cabinet, revealing a mini kitchen, and pours herself sparkling water. She turns and walks to the front of her desk, within a foot of Rizzo and Herrera.

"The point I'm trying to make," Bates says, "is that I loved Joe, but more importantly, he loved me back. Joe was married to Peter, but he was in love with someone else. He didn't love Peter. I don't know why Joe married him, and now, we'll never know. I'll never know."

She drops her head and slowly continues back around her desk and sits down in that marvel of Danish engineering. "Peter harbors resentment. He's trying to bring attention to the research when our competitors can discredit it. He knew that was a constant worry of both me and Joe."

"Who is this someone else?" Rizzo asks.

"Oh, the sweetest man in the world. His name is Gabriel Kelly, and he's a dear friend. Although it was complicated with him too."

"Complicated? How so?"

"He was afraid."

"Afraid?" Rizzo doesn't bother to hide the alarm in her voice. "Was the relationship abusive?"

"No, no, nothing like that." Bates waves her hands. "Maybe it was the potential for it? Gabriel saw something that I don't." She loses her wistful look and throws her hands up. "Relationships."

"What did Dr. Martin say about Gabriel Kelly to make you think this?"

"He sent me an e-mail not long ago, and we didn't have a chance to discuss it." Bates puts her face in her hands and then runs her fingers through her once perfect hair.

"Send it to me," Rizzo says and hands Barbara her business card. "Now."

"Now? Yes, well I have to find it."

"We'll wait," Rizzo replies.

At last, Bates sends the e-mail and looks up from her computer, the lines in her forehead winning the battle to crease against the Botox.

"Received." Rizzo takes a long moment reviewing her notes, then asks, "Why would bringing attention to a scientific theory that two giant pharmaceuticals are pursuing discredit it?"

"Why?" Bates says, clearly showing restraint. "Because talking about a race of humans with superpowers invites ridicule without peer-reviewed data."

"Superpowers?" Rizzo asks.

"That's how our critics would characterize it. If we're right, millions of years of evolution have imbued certain humans with specific genetic markers for psychic ability."

"I see. What data do you have regarding these certain humans and what can you tell me about them?"

"That's a trade secret, Detective. I won't discuss that without Jeebom lawyers present."

"Understood," Rizzo says, writing in her notebook. "You won't discuss House Salem, House Angeles, or what interest the high priestess might have?"

"The high priestess? How do you...? Oh, I see. You're baiting me. Impressive, Detective Rizzo. I must say, you're not the usual cop on the beat. Which makes me suspect, neither are you, Officer Herrera. You make quite the team. Your skills are wasted. Most boardrooms couldn't keep up with you."

"Our skills aren't wasted. Who has the greatest motive to kill Dr. Martin? House Angeles? Are they infuriated at their research disappearing?"

"Yes, they certainly are, as are the Koli. Tell me, Detective. How do you know so much? Do you have the research? It's useless to you."

"We don't answer questions, Dr. Bates. We ask them. Who is the patriarch of House Angeles?"

"Patrick Meyer, chairman of Covian, but you knew that. Before you ask, I report to Shreyas Anand, patriarch of House Koli and chairman of Jeebom."

"What do you know about Ravynne Quinn, the high priestess, and what is her interest in this?"

"Witches hate adepts and the feeling is mutual. Of course, the Ironbay Coven wants the research. What an advantage it would give them over their ancient enemies. What did Joe know about witches?"

Rizzo smiles but not with her eyes. "That's all for now. We'll see our way out." She stands and Herrera quickly follows suit. "Do you have any plans to leave town in the near future, Dr. Bates?"

"None right now," Bates says, her eyes wide.

"Good." Rizzo closes her notebook with a thud. "See that you don't. We'll be in touch."

Chapter Twenty

PORTAL CREATION

By leveraging geometric triangulation, adepts can fix a location on the planet and open a portal to that spatial position. They can transport themselves and others at great distances instantly. This is a rare Provectus-level skill of great interest to the institute.

—National Intelligence Strategy White Paper: Top Secret (TS): Release of this document will cause severe damage to the security of the United States—Adept Assets

SOMETHING WET ASSAULTS his face, and short bursts of hot air pummel his eyes. Gabriel gasps and jerks awake. Zuko's internal clock is unerringly accurate.

Is it 7:00 a.m. already?

Gabriel groans while reaching for his phone and checks the time. It's 7:02.

Who needs an alarm clock?

He falls back in the bed and pulls the covers over his head. He jostles Zuko off his chest, who paws his face. Zuko gives his hand an urgent nudge, prompting Gabriel to shower him with belly rubs, and his tail thumps.

In the bathroom, Gabriel studies his face in the mirror. *Do I look different from the dall?* He scrutinizes every feature, slope, and curve. *What does a subspecies look like? Me, I guess.*

Rummaging through a drawer, he pulls out his passport. He wonders how many Anisa has with how many names. He looks through it, examining every stamp and every adventure. Now, Gabriel must give it all up, and his face flushes with anger.

Whoever is doing this to me, I'll find you. And when I find you. I'll hurt you. It's not like me, but I'll learn.

"Oh, it's like you."

The anger boils even as he ignores the voice. He'll use it to drive himself forward. After he's found Joe's killer and his research, he'll determine if he's insane or not.

Gabriel props himself up on the bed and opens Joe's Instagram page. He wonders how many social media accounts lie dormant because their hosts have died. Even with this image of Joe, his thick blond hair cut down to businesslike standards, it's like standing in front of a gravestone.

With the long life an adept, how long until my phone is so full of dead people it becomes a cemetery? The account takes on a whole different meaning with Joe gone. What was once light and airy is now heavy and painful.

Where would Joe hide something from mind readers? He had to hide the data without varying his routine. Gabriel prepares to search Joe's account, but for what?

To find his killer? To mourn him?

For the first time, Gabriel reads the comments on Joe's page. It's rife with thinly veiled flirtations splattered with emojis. He ignores the thirst traps from men because it's the data he wants, not some hookup. There must be a colleague on here somewhere. A scientist vainly trying to get attention perhaps? Gabriel goes through innumerable feeds and drowns in gym selfies. He scrolls and scrolls until his eyes get sore. For a man with no friends, Joe was extremely popular on social media. How many of these commenters know he's dead? Probably none of them. Well, maybe one.

Image after image of Joe floats by showing a handsome professional man in custom-made suits that hug every curve. There are images of him at a few high-end restaurants, but mostly, they're of Joe at all the right events. And then he sees it. A shot of Joe at Fire Island last summer. Gabriel remembers a business trip to New York City but not an excursion to Fire Island.

Joe grins at the camera in a stylish tank top. He's at an upscale house festooned in marble and glass. Gabriel wonders who owns it. Probably some software magnate who sold his company to eBay for hundreds of millions and is sorting himself out. Joe curated his posts to avoid alcohol, and that must've taken some effort here. An odd blur takes up the corner of the photo, barely noticeable. Someone is cropped out, but a bulging bicep survives a clumsy attempt to erase its owner. The arm is dark-skinned, the shoulder thick and rounded. Joe stands a good foot away from that boulder-esque shoulder, yet the way he leans in ever so slightly and the crook of his glance radiates affection. Gabriel can almost feel the warmth coming off the screen. It's how he always wanted Joe to look at him. Gabriel considers for a moment. Could it be?

He opens the browser to Joe's overpriced gym's website, and under the list of personal trainers, Gabriel sees a name: Akinola Adeoye. His dazzling smile makes Gabriel dizzy, and his eyes, the color of autumn leaves, are framed by a flawlessly symmetrical face. Gleaming black curls spiral out in a flawless halo, making Gabriel unconsciously touch his unruly locks.

Akinola is spotting a client, and his arms are the focus. Gabriel switches back to Instagram and searches for the personal trainer, and there he is, in all his glowing sweat and genetics that are a kiss from God. Gabriel huffs and searches back to last summer on Akinola's page, and there, from August, are photos from his weekend in Fire Island.

You did plan to start a new life, but not with me.

"You're a fool," the voice says.

Jazz music suddenly plays in the room. Gabriel has it programmed to click on every morning. He pauses and listens. It's the new John Minnock.

Gabriel decides to call Sellers as planned. He made a promise to Joe, but more importantly to himself, to see this through. Despite what inconvenient truths he might learn along the way or the taunting of some malevolent force.

"Anton! Anton! Use the shipment of diastatic malt powder!" Sellers pauses and pitches his voice lower. "Hi, one second." He yells again, "We need a darker crust!" and then more quietly, "Hey, I'm back. Sorry about that."

The bass in Sellers's voice sends a warm wave through Gabriel, and his pulse slows.

"I need help. Will you come with me to Mumbai?" Gabriel holds his breath, but Sellers doesn't hesitate.

"Mumbai? India? I've never been there, but sure, I'll go. Are you asking me so they don't succeed in killing you this time? I've got your back, but I only fly business class, and don't test me. I stay in five-star hotels only. When do we leave?"

"Today, two hours." Gabriel exhales, and Zuko sits in rapt attention.

"Two hours! It takes two hours to get to the airport. It'll take me hours to pack."

"Two hours. It's only a day trip, and we're not flying. I'm opening a portal."

"Shut the front door! You can do that?"

Gabriel smiles at the breathless response.

"Can you teleport anywhere?" Sellers asks, pitching his voice lower. "Can we go to Tahiti for the day next week? You see, there's this—"

Gabriel cuts Sellers off. "I can only teleport to where I've been already or where I've read the address. You have to be conservative. I don't want to teleport in the ocean or inside a door. But yeah, if I've been there before, we're safe, and we're going if you want. But when this is all over. Assuming I'm in one piece, we can go somewhere."

"Anton! You're in charge. I'm taking the rest of the day off."

"Poor Anton," Gabriel says with a chuckle.

"Why are we going to Mumbai? What do I bring? What time is it there?" Sellers's enthusiasm storms Gabriel's mind.

"Ankit is from Mumbai. The adepts in Joe's apartment fled to Mumbai, Barbara and Joe worked for Jeebom, and they're headquartered in Mumbai." Gabriel's voice grows tighter. "Ankit's father is the president of Jeebom and patriarch of the Koli."

"Let me guess," Sellers says. "They're in Mumbai."

"That's right."

"Wow. What about your uncle, the patriarch? Should we ask him?

Gabriel had been considering that all morning. "No. He'll discourage me from going. He'll say it's too dangerous, and maybe he's right, but I don't care. I told him about Ankit, and he hasn't called. If we run into him in Mumbai, I'll be sure to apologize. And Sellers, I can't lie, this is dangerous or could be. I'd understand, and I mean it, if you choose to stay home. It won't be weird between us. You mean—"

"Oh, do stop the dramatics. Of course I'm coming. You need talent. You need creative thinking. You need me."

"I do," Gabriel says softly. "I do."

"This is serious. What do I wear?"

"It's Mumbai in June, so hot, humid, and rainy."

"Ah," Sellers exclaims, "this calls for my HOKA One Ones."

"Okay, I'll bite. What's that? A spell? And whatever sorcery you whip up to keep your hair doing, well, what it does, mother nature will put it to the test in Mumbai."

"Dear sir," Sellers says as if insulted. "The fact that my hair prefers a vertical state of repose is completely up to it."

Gabriel lets his eyes roll, only because he's on the phone, and grins. "Of course, of course. Hey, do you mind coming with me to the police station first?"

"Why? You turning yourself in?"

Gabriel sighs. "No, Rizzo said they found something Joe was writing. It said there was something about me that was off, that I scared him. Rizzo is making me surrender my passport. I'm suspect numero uno."

"What?" Sellers asks, then pauses a moment. "Is there a numero dos?"

"I'm numero uno, dos, y tres," Gabriel says, his voice trailing off.

Sellers takes a deep breath. "That doesn't make sense. I knew Joe. He was an ass, but afraid of you? I don't think he was afraid of anything. All the fool him."

Gabriel had wrestled with the idea that Joe had grown apprehensive and fearful over the course of their relationship. Who could blame someone for having a fear of the unknown? Even Gabriel didn't know the full extent of Anisa's powers, and anyone who wasn't afraid of what she could do was a fool. Maybe Sellers is right. Steer clear of the dall.

Sellers takes a calming breath. "I know you're the nephew of the patriarch and the grandson of a Regna, but if word gets out more than it already has, Russell might have to take steps, perhaps banish you, maybe even make you dall. The witch's conclave is coming up, and you'll be high on the agenda."

"I know, I know." Gabriel's voice pitches higher. "I want off of the agenda. I want to find Joe's killer, hold them accountable, and understand why they did it. That's why we're going to Mumbai. And second is to find where he stashed his work, and I think I have a lead on that. But yeah, you're right, things may not go well for me unless something breaks, and that's an understatement."

"Gabe, remember, he might've been using you. No, I take that back. He *was* using you."

Gabriel's anger welled up, but it just as quickly evaporated. Death brings into focus what is and isn't important. All that matters now is justice for Joe.

"Maybe you're the real mind reader," Gabriel says. "Okay, I'll pick you up in an hour, and we'll go to the police station."

Sellers scoffs. "Pick me up? In your electric tin can? I think not.

What if I'm seen? No, I will pick you up in my Quattroporte. I love you, Gabriel. I'll risk my life for you. I'd die for you, but I have my limits. Under no circumstances will I wear plaid, sleep on sheets of 500 or less thread count, or be driven around town in that—" Sellers pauses. "Is it even on the road?"

Gabriel opens his closet and looks for something that would function in Mumbai and not embarrass Sellers. He would never allow anything to happen to him, although there is always that chance. Criticizing his car? The nerve. Making a mental note to bring it up again when this is all over, he chooses sandals, a pair of khaki shorts, and a vintage Rolling Stones tee shirt. Then, he reconsiders and exchanges them for a pair of white linen pants and a button-up navy blue short-sleeve shirt. Despite the expensive clothes, he still can't shake the unkempt look.

Sorry, Margot, you tried.

"Can that gas-guzzling tank make it across town without breaking down?" Gabriel asks.

Sellers takes a massive breath. "It's these brutal city roads. They haven't been paved in decades. You can't blame my automobile. It's a precision Italian machine."

Gabriel debates laying the clothes on the bed, but Zuko is lying across it. His head is up as he serenely takes in his surroundings, keeping a watchful eye on Gabriel. Suddenly, Zuko lifts his head higher and howls a long mournful sound. It startles Gabriel.

"Ha!" Sellers laughs. "Even Zuko prefers the Quattroporte."

Gabriel rushes to Zuko and strokes his head. He looks up at him with his deep brown eyes and howls again.

"Okay, fine, we'll take your car. See you soon, okay?"

"Do you have a lead on that data?"

"Yeah, maybe," Gabriel says.

"What is it?"

"We'll talk about it later, okay?"

"Sure," Sellers says, and he clicks off.

*

SELLERS OPENS HIS notebook and picks up a pen. His hands shake and a wave of nausea sends bile into his throat. He grimaces, flips to the last page, and scries into the mirror.

Chapter Twenty-One

CONJURATION

It's theorized that a Japanese Regna opened a portal and transferred an item of large mass and great significance to the Russian federation in 2012. We have no verification that any adept in North America possesses this ability.

—National Intelligence Strategy White Paper: Top Secret (TS): Release of this document will cause severe damage to the security of the United States—Adept Assets

"I CHANGED MY mind," Gabriel says. "I'm going to teleport into the police station. Can you ground me?"

"We're in my car. My beautiful Italian car that I don't want ruined."

"I'll try not to materialize in your transmission," Gabriel says. "Your precious car will be fine, and I need the practice."

"You sure you want to do this now?" Sellers asks. "Seriously, I don't want you materializing half inside a wall."

"I'll be okay, Sell. With your help. Do witches teleport?"

"Not by ourselves. A witch with a talent for teleportation spells can enchant one door to open into another door, but the entrance and exit don't change. It's fixed."

"Hmm, okay," Gabriel says. "Have you ever done it?"

"No, we charge big money for that. Out of my price range."

"This trip, assuming we survive it"—Gabriel winks—"is free."

They grasp hands. Gabriel looks Zuko in the eyes and touches his head. The dog leans against Gabriel's leg, snuggling into his head. They join together, and Gabriel can feel Zuko's beating heart, his lifeblood moving through his body. He values love and friendship to the exclusion of all else. His mind takes on the serenity of the dog's. It would take the average bondless adept hours of meditation to achieve this, but with Zuko, Gabriel assumes a centered state in minutes. All extraneous thoughts are gone. His mind empties of the pressures and demands of the day. He becomes, at least temporarily, the best version of himself.

His inner eye sees the bleak orange room where the BPD held him for questioning in what feels like a lifetime ago, but it's only been two days. Gabriel takes a breath as the rhythmic sounds of the busy police headquarters become audible. A stream of colors come together randomly at first, and then they suddenly make a wild kind of sense. He sees the chair in the room, and he sits. As he looks down at himself, he is in the interrogation chair, and Zuko is beside him. He's in that dreadful orange room. He focuses on the cameras, and with a burst of energy, they shatter.

Zuko and Gabriel rise as one and exit the door. They walk down the hall in the same direction Rizzo's high heels clacked off to on the day Joe died. An odd smell comes to him—a combination of takeout pizza, disinfectant, and the panicked soon-to-be incarcerated.

They pass one officer and then another. *"You don't see me,"* Gabriel suggests. *"You need to get where you're going."* Officer after officer passes them by. The last one, Maya, is concerned about the detective exam. *Good luck to you.* Gabriel rounds the corner only to see dozens of cops at their desks. This will be a challenge. He's worried that by making himself ignorable to so many people, he'll lose focus. Gabriel touches the top of Zuko's head and reaches for the ley line. He's careful, as drawing in the energy of a line can be like drinking from a fire hose. The first time Gabriel pulled on a line, he absorbed too much too soon and became violently ill. He can't afford mistakes now. The earth's energy fills him. He touches every mind in the room and calmly approaches the first cop he sees.

"Excuse me, which desk is Detective Rizzo's?"

The officer looks up, eyes narrowed. "And who are—"

Gabriel cuts her off with authority. "Officer, which desk is Detective Rizzo's?"

She glares back at him. A brief flash of anger creases her expression, but it evaporates, her expression now deadpan. "Two rows over. She has a large photo of her cat, Sebastian. He's a Russian Blue. You can't miss it."

Gabriel smiles. "Thank you. Forget I was here."

Gabriel strides over to Rizzo's desk. The officer was correct; he couldn't miss it with the photo of Sebastian. That is one adorable, chubby cat. If Gabriel had to guess, he would've thought that Rizzo had a dog, perhaps a German Shepherd, or maybe a pit bull. As it turns out, Rizzo is a cat person. Does that make any sense? Gabriel loves all animals—cats, dogs, goats, horses. Are there cat people and dog people?

He looks down at Zuko. "Would you like a feline little brother or sister?" The answer he gets back isn't a resounding "no," but it isn't a resounding "yes" either. This may take some negotiation.

Gabriel tears off a piece of paper from Rizzo's stationery. He admires it and thinks he should get some of his own, then he writes, "Sorry I missed you." He drops his passport on the desk. For good measure, he takes a photo of it. Technically, "sorry I missed you" is a lie, but Gabriel forgives himself for the transgression.

A velvet box sits on her desk, partially obscured by the cafeteria menu for the upcoming week. Gabriel opens it and finds inside a Boston Police Department Medal of Valor.

"I'm not surprised," he mutters. He closes it and carefully replaces the menu on top. Nothing on her desk seems noteworthy, not a memo or calendar. Gabriel reaches for her desk drawer, expecting it to be locked, but to his surprise it slides open. He looks through the folders, a couple titled Martin Murder #1 and Martin Murder #2. Wincing at the word "murder," he runs his fingers over Rizzo's neat block handwriting as if to convince himself it's real. He opens the first folder and reads.

"Understanding the Genetic Inheritance of *Homo Sapiens Psychica*: A Human Subspecies Genome Project."

This is Joe's PhD dissertation, and he wrote it about us. He theorized we existed long before we met.

Sellers's feelings about Joe had some merit. Or at least, more merit than Gabriel cared to admit. Included in the folder is Joe's autopsy report and interviews with his neighbors. Gladys Brady in 11B has lots to say, as usual. But Gabriel can't spend too much time here because, unbeknownst to Rizzo, the trail leads to Mumbai.

Gabriel turns to leave and looks for a private place to teleport. He spies the men's room. *Good as any.*

Officer Maya walks toward him again on her return trip. He lets his guard down slightly, allowing her to notice him. The sight of Gabriel and Zuko stops her in her tracks. Gabriel looks at her and says, "Good luck on the exam," Gabriel says to her. He imagines she'll assume he knows about the exam because he's a glamorous undercover detective.

He ducks into the men's room and opens a portal.

"Did you think you could just waltz in here?"

Gabriel's breath catches in his throat, and his heart hammers. He didn't see or feel anyone.

He turns to a gray-haired cleaning lady with a supply cart and wearing a simple smock. For a moment, Gabriel sees the older woman through Zuko's eyes as vibrant colors of red and orange pulsate around her. Contrary to conventional wisdom, dogs can see color, maybe not the full spectrum humans see, but they know color. The woman isn't old and gray, but young, raven-haired, and cloaked in pulsating energy. Zuko knows a witch when he sees one, and he lets Gabriel know.

Then it dawns on Gabriel. The witch designed this illusion for humans, both species, but not for dogs. Her hair begins to rise and separate as if submerged in water.

Zuko, seated at first, quickly decides he prefers to stand. He begins to stalk and bares his teeth. A low growl of warning echoes against the lavatory tile.

She smiles. "I just cleaned the floor."

"A witch," Gabriel says ruefully. He decides to try the earnest route. "Thank you. I'll be going—"

The gray cleaning lady looks at Zuko and casts her spell.

Eyes that see me

close them sleep

Your duty done

dream of the sun

Zuko flops down on the floor with a hollow thud. Gabriel staggers as if he'll faint, his head so heavy.

"Tired? We always knew there was something about you and that dog."

The cleaning lady, now a vibrant young woman with violet eyes, strides toward him, her hand waving. She sends Gabriel flying upward. He crashes through a false ceiling and collides with a very solid steel pipe. His ears ring in violent protest. His shoulder and hip erupt in a paroxysm of pain. A piercing banshee wail assaults his inner ear, and his vision blurs.

"You broke our ward," she says. "Our protection spells are expensive. We're paid by adepts like you to maintain wards. But the grandson of the adept Regna breaking a ward, a murderer breaking into police headquarters, now that should pay triple."

Gabriel struggles, but he has no wish to fall from the ceiling. A witch's ward here? Of course, witches would have warning spells in all key parts of the city.

"Wait until I tell the high—"

Pain erupts like a solar flare and burns through his body. Gabriel tries to move his shoulder and can't. Forcing himself to close his eyes, he stops fighting and breathes. He feels for the scone; it hums and crackles inside him. There is still some power left. The hair on his arms and neck rises, and colors race across the room. Colors that belong to him and colors that belong to an aggressive violet-eyed Ironbay witch.

If she weren't trying to do whatever it is she's trying to do, he might say to her that, with the right makeup, she'd look alarmingly like Elizabeth Taylor. Instead, he finds her colors and pushes his own into their path. When the two streams of energy merge, the scone stops humming, and he falls unceremoniously to the linoleum floor.

The wind goes out of Gabriel, and a muscle in his leg rips. Good thing adepts are strong. The witch recovers, and the air crackles with her burgeoning energy. Gabriel recoils in the face of such power. Then he hears a strangely familiar voice.

"You're not afraid of her. You're afraid of me."

Gabriel raises his feeble defenses when Zuko leaps a foot off the floor directly toward the witch, baring his teeth. Zuko's rarely seen canines, now fully exposed, flood the air with menace, and Zuko lifts his head in challenge and barks. Except it isn't a bark; it's a roar that stops time. It's a sound that rumbles and tears space apart.

Gabriel is frozen, and so is the witch. Her spell snaps off, its fire deprived of oxygen. Gabriel recovers and limps to Zuko, pain shooting through his body, and sends a mental command not to attack. The witch's fright hits him, and he swallows back the panic. That roar, the sound is numbing.

Zuko licks Gabriel's hand.

"Good boy," he says. Tapping a ley line fills Gabriel's body with energy. A fury swirls inside him, and energy seeps out of his mouth and nose in wisps of red smoke. At least, that's how his brain interprets the experience. The human body, a poor vessel, isn't up to the task of storing ley energy. Mother Nature stores her energy in gems, in hard rock, not fragile flesh.

Zuko also channels the ley energy, diverting some of it to Gabriel's injuries, knitting his shoulder together and strengthening the sprain in his leg. Gabriel opens a portal at their feet, and he and Zuko drop away. The witch glares at him, her expression mixed with fear and rage, mostly fear. He leaves her with a brief departing wave.

Chapter Twenty-Two

LUPUS VINCULUM

Of particular interest to the institute is if adepts can bond with something outside the Canidae family. We suspect the answer is yes but have no verification yet.

—National Intelligence Strategy White Paper: Top Secret (TS): Release of this document will cause severe damage to the security of the United States—Adept Assets

"YIKES!" SELLERS SCREAMS so loudly Gabriel thinks he feels the car shake. "Can't you give some warning when you teleport into a man's car? And you think witches are creepy?"

"A witch attacked me," Gabriel exclaims, trying to keep his voice down.

"A witch." Sellers's mouth becomes a thin line, barely moving a muscle. "Tell me everything, starting with what they looked like."

"She was beautiful. Violet or blue eyes—I got close enough to see them, and I hope I don't get that close again—when she crashed me down to the floor, then smashed me into the ceiling. She was dark-haired—"

"That's Camilla, the daughter of the high priestess," Sellers says, interrupting. "It sounds like her. Plus, to do that so quickly, it would have to be a powerful witch. It has to be her, but why?"

Gabriel considers. "I think I broke a ward, but I didn't do anything wrong."

Sellers tilts his head. "What did you do?"

"I made a cop trust me, and I compelled her to answer a question..." Gabriel trails off sheepishly. Of course, he understands he broke a ward, and Sellers probably knows that.

Sellers nods. "We'd want to know if adepts were interfering with police work, but still, why confront you? And it's not the first time you were in a police station."

"Russell warned me about manipulating the dall at the station, but we did communicate telepathically; we used our abilities."

"Yes. But you didn't use your powers on the dall. That triggers the ward. Why attack you though? To force you to the HP?"

"I think so. She practically accused me of killing Joe."

"Ah." Sellers puts his hand on his forehead. "The HP wants leverage with the adepts, both the News and the Angeles."

"The Angeles?"

"The HP would gladly extradite you to Los Angeles for the right price. She was supposed to capture you for a minor infraction and sell you to House Angeles."

"How much could she get?"

"I wouldn't make light of this," Sellers says, raising his voice slightly. "This will go straight to the HP, and from there, it's a short hop to your uncle, or worse, the Angeles and Koli."

Gabriel sighs deeply and nods. "Everything is a short hop if you know how to teleport." He takes a breath. "It's about 8:00 p.m. in Mumbai. Are you ready? And don't say you were born ready."

Sellers shrugs. "That goes without saying. What do we know about Ankit and Shreyas Anand?"

"They're from a prominent adept family. Very talented, very gifted, they were under the radar until Shreyas Anand was elected patriarch. He reinvented himself once that we know of. He is about one hundred years old. He's a doctor now and president at Jeebom. Before his life as a doctor, he was a politician in Mumbai and ran the family real estate business. They have extensive holdings in Australia and London. Because his father is an executive at Jeebom, we assume Ankit was after Joe's research. He'll be ready for us if I go back to the store."

"Okay. Ready?" Sellers asks.

"Yes. We'll appear in an alley. It's across from Anand's office building."

"An alley? Why not go directly to his house?"

"Because I've never been there, "Gabriel answers. "Remember, I can only teleport to places I've been or when I've seen the address."

"Well then, let's get to this alley," Sellers says with a grin.

"Okay, let's hold hands."

Gabriel closes his eyes and places his free hand on Zuko's head, reaching for the line. Zuko licks his hand as ley energy reveals the alley in a paroxysm of color. Gabriel takes a deep breath and steps forward into the breach.

*

"WELCOME TO INDIA," Gabriel says.

"Well done. I thought I'd be nauseous or tired."

"That's me. I feel like I ran around the block. Give me a minute."

Two stray dogs trot up to Gabriel and sit.

"Dogs love you," Sellers says.

"And I love them. You can expect lots of stray dogs and the occasional strolling cow." Gabriel leans down and gives them treats, which Zuko does not begrudge them.

"Where do these Anands live?"

"Malabar Hill, Altamount Road," Gabriel replies. His heart skips a beat. Soon, he might confront Joe's killers. He hails a cab, and it streaks across two lanes of traffic, horns shrieking an angry symphony, and skids to a halt.

Because Gabriel imprinted on his father, much to the shock and surprise of his mother, his memories of Mumbai are not all his own. His father lived here and loved here, so the colors, fragrances, and remembrances are shared with Gabriel. What Gabriel and his father love most are the magnificent colors. There is color everywhere. It's in the graffiti and the red brick and white stone. It's in the clothing that staid Bostonians never muster the courage to wear.

Sparkling palatial palaces sit in the clouds next to ancient stout buildings that seem to look askance at their new upstart neighbors. The sea air hugs Gabriel and Sellers in a damp embrace as they draw closer to Malabar Hill. The great bay beckons with a calm invitation for a swim. The bay is one of the reasons for the immense sums the residents of Malabar Hill pay to live here. The magnificent views of Back Bay are impossible for the rich to resist.

The air is humid like London, and the sky a bright reddish color just beginning to darken after a long day. Gabriel's is just beginning.

Gabriel hums to the omnipresent car horns, sweet melodies to his ears. He delights in the bustle and excitement of the metropolis. To him, the traffic exhilarates. Meanwhile, a vein pulses in Sellers's temple, and he clenches his teeth.

Gabriel grips Sellers's shoulder. "Traffic in India takes some getting used to."

Through gritted teeth Sellers only says, "This humidity is murder on my hair."

Their driver speeds off, leaving his cargo of one witch, an adept, and a loyal canine, standing on a corner. They face the front of an opulent residential tower about twenty stories high.

A Ganesha statue constructed in natural stone adorns the entrance. The great god, depicted with the head of an elephant, has a tiny mouse at his foot, representing the ego. It jumps out at Gabriel as he rings the bell. Gabriel's boss at his first job as a gemologist was Hindu. They enjoyed sharing stories from their religious traditions. The origin story of Ganesha touched Gabriel the most. He would go into this with an open mind and his ego in check.

"Witches protect this place," Sellers mutters softly. "The magic is thick. Past spells permeate the building, but nothing is warning me. Do you feel anything?"

Gabriel calms himself and reaches out with his mind. Imagining his friend helps him pick up how witches shape and manipulate energy. He finds something.

"Yes, I think I feel it. The most powerful energy ribbons run counterclockwise. It's a different color. It feels different from you. You're smooth, but this is prickly. You glow, and this—"

"I have to figure out how you do that," Sellers says. "You can tell the difference between my coven and the coven that crafted this—well done. How different covens shape spells is a deep mystery. It's been a source of study forever. I don't sense any hostility to us here, so let's go."

He opens the door to the building, and Gabriel walks through it. A doorman posted behind a large wooden desk doesn't bother to look up. He wears his thick mane of gray hair brushed back from his head, and deep wrinkles etch the skin around his eyes. He's relaxed, leisurely reading a newspaper. He stands out in his colorful uniform, and it imbues him with an air of unthreatening calm authority. Suddenly, he stands ramrod straight and raises his hand for them to stop. Before Gabriel can speak, Sellers moves before him and addresses the guardian of these gilded glass apartment boxes.

"Good evening. We're here to see Shreyas Anand. I'm Sellers Collinsworth of the Ironbay coven, and this is Gabriel Kelly of the Salem House."

A shadow of consternation takes over the guardian's expression. He collects himself, slowly picks up the phone, and dials. All the while, he never takes his eyes off them.

Sellers leans into Gabriel and whispers, "He's a witch."

As surprised as he is at Sellers's news, Gabriel's face remains stoic, and he looks straight ahead.

"There's very little energy emanating from him," Sellers says softly. "He's a minor witch."

The doorman, whose name tag reads "Ramesh," gently hangs up the phone. Eyeing Sellers with undisguised suspicion and a hint of surprise, he says, "Mr. Anand will see you."

He leads them into an elevator, where he produces a key seemingly from nowhere and uses it to activate the penthouse button. Then, he stiffly bows and exits, and the elevator begins its rapid ascent to the twentieth floor.

Sellers lifts his hand as a mime would, feeling for an invisible wall. "This moving box is powerfully warded. I daresay someone who meant Anand harm would be unable to enter. The witch downstairs didn't cast this ward. It's an elegant piece of work and demands a considerable amount of energy to maintain. Quite impressive."

"Well, we'll be sure to compliment Anand on his taste in witch associates."

"Don't use the magic of the scone here," Sellers whispers. "You'll become violently ill."

The elevator opens to Anand greeting them as if he's personally guarding the elegantly appointed apartment. By his side stands a plain, well-dressed woman in a traditional blue-and-silver sari. A white marble kitchen gleams behind her left shoulder. Gabriel guesses it's used mainly by caterers, if it's used at all.

Anand looks startlingly like Ankit, only shorter. He wears a flowing white oversized linen shirt with jeans and sandals. The scowl on his face indicates that he isn't accustomed to accepting unannounced guests. He gives Gabriel the "puzzled" look but doesn't mention his parentage. For all his adept talent, Anand can't seem to contain these tells; they emanate from his pores. His consternation tickles the edges of Gabriel's mind and speaks volumes.

Gabriel touches Zuko's head and connects with him. Through Zuko, he smells respect with a touch of fear. The Anands must be afraid of Sellers, Gabriel thinks. Adepts are always fearful of witches. *I can't possibly scare them.*

"Welcome to my home," Anand slightly nods. "This is my wife, Deepa. You are known to me. Hello, Gabriel."

For a long moment, Anand offers Sellers only a steely hooded-eyed gaze, then says, "But you, sir. I admit, other than the fact that you are a witch, you have me at a disadvantage. What is your name?"

"I am Sellers Collinsworth of the Ironbay Coven. My compliments on the ward. It's powerful and well-struck."

"Thank you, Mr. Collinsworth. It was expensive. Was it worth it?"

"Please, call me Sellers. Since we all made it to your apartment in one piece, I trust you know we come as friends."

"Friends?" Anand says, almost to himself.

In a louder, more conversational tone, his wife enters the conversation. "Are we in the presence of the *Lupus vinculum*?"

"You are." Gabriel strokes Zuko's unmoving head without bending down.

"There are only one hundred documented cases of the *Lupus vinculum* in the subcontinent. To see one in my home is a rare experience indeed," Anand says, admiring Zuko.

"May I approach the dog?" Mrs. Anand asks.

Before Gabriel can reply, Zuko takes one step forward but then backs up and remains glued to his spot, statue still.

"Remarkable!" she says, slowly approaching Zuko and offering her hand to smell. He doesn't move. She raises her hand to pet Zuko's head, but he withdraws further.

"What is his name?" Mrs. Anand asks.

"Zuko."

"What is his real name?"

Gabriel smiles and tilts his head, hopes it doesn't look too canine. "You know something about the bond. His name can't be put into words. It's more of a feeling. Something like, 'a watchful eye, a soldier and a friend, a still lake surrounded by lush grass full of game, protector of the pack on a clear day or in the midst of a storm.' That's about as close as one can get verbally."

Mrs. Anand nods and bows slightly to Zuko.

A chill runs down Gabriel's spine that comes from a grave warning from Zuko. His deep brown eyes, filled with suspicion, swoop from Gabriel to Mrs. Anand.

"The weather has cleared," Mrs. Anand says without taking her eyes off the dog. "Please, let's sit on the veranda and admire the bay. I'll gather some refreshments." She motions to a far corner as her husband leads them through the apartment.

"Your plants are beautiful, Mr. Anand," Sellers says. He stops to touch a leaf. "What is this? It's so unique."

"That's my favorite. It's a variegated Monstera Albo Borsingiana. It's fully rooted, and these are half-moons."

"Gorgeous," Sellers says.

The high sheen of the buffed marble floor reflects every ounce of light. A long, narrow couch weaves its modern asymmetrical way along a wall adorned with what appears to be an original Jackson Pollack. Two Francis Newton Souza works pridefully float on the opposite wall in their gilded frames.

One advantage of owning a penthouse apartment is the skylights dotting the ceiling. Gabriel glances up and admires the retractable blinds. In the foreground of the room, two large French doors open onto an expansive deck overlooking the Arabian Sea. The unobstructed view allows in the cool night air. It's a world away from the alley near Anand's office. The couple must entertain here frequently because there is more than enough room for it. Zuko sniffs the sea air, wide-eyed and alert. They sit near the edge of the deck, overlooking the water.

"Mr. Anand, I love the view. It's beautiful," Sellers says, gazing at the lights flickering off the bay.

"Yes, it is beautiful this evening," Anand says as his wife returns, pushing a serving cart with a bottle of wine and some pasta and rice dishes.

"I hope you enjoy this. It's an Indian sparkling wine. My husband and I are quite taken with it."

Gabriel eagerly grabs a plate and does his best to serve himself a small portion, but he fails.

Anand picks up the sparkling wine as if it's light as a feather. He twists the bottom of the bottle, and the cork releases with a tiny *pfft*. He tips a glass at a forty-five-degree angle and pours.

"If you're here, you've seen through our son. What do you want? I want my data. Let's start there."

Chapter Twenty-Three

WARRING ADEPT FAMILIES

The rivalry between the patriarchs of Northern and Southern California is an open secret. We've been able to leverage this to our advantage. We request resources to investigate the great Asian Houses.

—National Intelligence Strategy White Paper: Top Secret (TS): Release of this document will cause severe damage to the security of the United States—Adept Assets

"YOUR DATA?" GABRIEL asks.

"You teleported into my office and stole corporate secrets," Anand says. "You're a registered Media. That's a lie. Is it routine for the Salem House to lie about rankings?"

Zuko jumps to attention and stands in front of Gabriel, his eyes alert and head high. Gabriel gently strokes his head, and he reluctantly sits.

"I'm not here to explain myself to spies," Gabriel says. "Or worse, murderers. I'm here to find out what happened to Joe and what Ankit was doing at Joe's apartment. Why did he run?"

Gabriel doesn't know if it was Ankit, but who else could it be? It's worth the gamble. The prickly touch of both Anands brushes against his mind. They do it gently and probe for weaknesses. He can't afford any breach of his defenses.

"Did Ankit kill Joe?" Gabriel presses. The sullen silence in the room is deafening. Gabriel is rooted in place, not daring to move. Anand sits in the quiet, showing no discomfort, but Gabriel senses his internal calculation.

"No, my son went to see Martin to discuss his work. He died while they were conversing."

If only I could use the scone on you. Gabriel knows why they want Joe's work even though Ankit Anand isn't a scientist. Adepts will kill for scientific knowledge of how their powers work. *No, that's not quite right. Anand will kill to keep it for himself.*

"Who was with him? I saw two adepts," Gabriel asks.

Anand leans back and sips his sparkling wine. Gabriel brushes up against his mind and finds a cold fortress. "You want to know who killed Joseph Martin?" Anand asks. "I want his data. He stole patented work belonging to Jeebom Pharmaceuticals."

Gabriel bristles at Joe being called a thief, but he's not here to defend Joe's reputation.

"What exactly did Joe steal?" Gabriel asks.

"Eleven billion rupees of research and development, my goodwill, and a chance to save the world. If the dall get ahold of this work, they'll use it to ferret us out, conscript us, enslave us, and kill us. We're powerful, but we're few."

There is no hint of hyperbole in Anand's tone or demeanor. Gabriel guesses that Anand means adepts might go to war over the data. The thought chills him.

"What will you do if you find it?"

"Rejoice," Anand replies.

"Aren't you going to ask me, Patriarch Anand, what I'll do when I find it?"

Anand's face shows only a slight tremor.

"I have choices," Gabriel says. "One of them includes Patrick Meyer of the Angeles and head of Covian." Gabriel learned Meyer was Chairman of Covian from Google. He makes a promise to himself to pay more attention to adept politics.

Anand's poker face folds. "What do you want?" His voice moves higher now and deadly sharp.

"Your son was skulking around Joe's apartment after he died. You know more than you're telling. Give me something I can use. Help me, and I'll help you."

Gabriel realizes too late that he raised his voice. His uncle never raises his voice.

"I'll speak to my son," Anand replies.

Gabriel and Zuko rise to their feet in one synchronized rapid motion, and Anand flinches. His defenses slip, and his fear washes over Gabriel in a tidal wave. The expensive witchcraft permeating Anand's home protects him, but for a flickering moment, his fear of Zuko, his doubt that the witch protection might not extend to dogs, slips. *Perhaps the ward doesn't? Maybe Anand should be afraid? Has Zuko been growing more aggressive?* Gabriel narrows his eyes as he looks at Anand. *Let him be frightened.* He opens his mind just a little. Something tells him Anand's mercenary magic couldn't hold Gabriel forever. Let him feel that.

"We're not here to hurt anyone, Patriarch Anand," Gabriel says. "We want the truth."

Sellers approaches Gabriel and touches his shoulder. It appears to be a calming deescalating gesture, friendly and supportive. But Gabriel took it for what it was, an admonishment, and the two resume sitting.

"My son is distraught by what happened. Martin's death is not in our interests."

Zuko gets up, walks around Gabriel's chair, and sits. *We have to work on your poker face.* Gabriel strokes Zuko's head.

"I want that data, which is why I sent Ankit to your store. The data will emerge, and when it does, I want it because it's rightfully ours. I will commit resources to solving Joe Martin's death if we need to trade."

"A trade?" Gabriel's stomach twists and flips. "You'd trade the data for a murderer?"

Gabriel opens his mouth to speak again, but when Sellers's hand rests on his forearm, he changes his mind. He accepts Sellers's warning. It gives him time to gaze off into the distance, and he scrutinizes the moody bay. Gabriel envisions ironclad walls around his mind and his emotions under control.

"With all your scientists," he says, "all your adept and witch talent, it was a dall doctor who unlocked our genetic secrets. That took you by surprise, didn't it?"

Now, it is Anand's turn to remain expressionless. Still, despite his best efforts, his tone betrays his frustration. "You have a high opinion of Dr. Martin. For all his gifts, he did not accomplish that work alone, if indeed he did at all. Regardless, that intellectual property belongs to us."

"What if Joe were someone you loved?" Sellers asks.

Anand smiles ruefully. "You sound like my wife." He runs a hand through his still-dark hair and takes a breath. Gabriel notices that Anand deliberately avoids his wife's glare. He can't say what he's about to say and look at her.

"Martin's death was a tragedy for everyone here, for the world, for different reasons, but yes, a tragedy. His legacy is at risk of being lost. That is another tragedy. We must forestall it."

"If you find Joe's research and, along the way, discover the killer, will you expose the murderer?" Gabriel asks.

The only answer is a growing silence that continues to lengthen uncomfortably. It fills the stagnant night air with a dull menace. Finally, Zuko breaks the bleak mood. He shoots to his feet, startling the humans in attendance. Zuko knows Anand's answer is "no." Finally, Anand speaks.

"Perhaps. It depends."

"Depends on what?" Gabriel asks, his voice sharp.

"Our self-interest."

"I'll keep that in mind. We'll be going now."

Another silence hangs in the air, but this time it's Mrs. Anand who breaks it.

"I hope, Mr. Kelly, we can see each other again under better cir-cum-stances." Mrs. Anand extends her hand and smiles sincerely, a welcome sight.

Gabriel has an impulse to hug her but suppresses it, though her sadness and disappointment fill the room. Gabriel takes her warm, dry hand. It's soft and fragile in his meaty grip. Her subtle floral perfume is heartening and causes him to smile back. Her touch, even though their mental defenses are high, emits a sense of calm. But who knows what kind of witchcraft is going on in this house or how outclassed his adept talents are?

"Thank you, Mrs. Anand. Your hospitality was wonderful. I, too, hope we meet again under better circumstances."

"Before we go, I have one last question for the patriarch," Gabriel continues, and all eyes turn to him.

"Certainly," Anand says.

"What do you know about the drug Jubilee? It comes from Covian and targets us, right?"

Anand's eyes squint and turn downcast. He takes a deep breath and exhales through his nose. "Some adepts have great difficulty screening out thoughts. They pick up the dreams of others and incorporate them into their own, losing where they end and others begin. Life for some of us can be torturous. My company, Jeebom, and Covian are working to develop a drug for adepts. We want a drug to block our abilities and—"

Sellers cuts him off. "Or enhance them?"

Anand turns to Sellers, makes eye contact with him, and continues. "Our attempts, so far, have failed. We're still in development, but Covian found that their drug, while it's a superb antidepressant for the dall, blocks our powers for a time, yes. Still, it also has an intense hallucinogenic effect, and then the crash comes and the craving. Covian can alter their drug chemically without much effort, and presto, you have the drug Jubilee or *J*."

"That explains a lot," Gabriel says.

"Do not let that drug loose in your community. It has serious addictive properties, and withdrawal can be life-threatening."

"Does Meyer know about this?" Gabriel asks.

"Of course, he does." Anand's words are clipped and sharp. "He pokes and prods us for power and profit. He doesn't care if the drug destroys us. He cares that the drug makes money. He'll sell the disease and the cure."

"We say goodbye like my parents—long and drawn out. Thank you both again, Mr. and Mrs. Anand, for seeing us. We'll be going."

"Where are you off to?" Mrs. Anand asks.

"Sellers is quite the gourmet," Gabriel says. "But since you were kind enough to feed us, I'd like to show him Marine Drive along the bay. He can look out onto the Arabian Sea as we drive. It's beautiful lit up at night. Don't you agree?"

"A wise choice," Mrs. Anand says. "I know it can be a tourist trap, but my husband and I still take the occasional drive to enjoy the view. Take our private elevator to the lobby, and Ramesh will drive you."

"Thank you, good lady," Sellers says with a smile and one of his signature, well-practiced bows."

Gabriel and Sellers enter the elevator with Zuko close behind. Gabriel is about to offer a small wave, but when the door is a fraction of an inch from closing, Sellers screams. Gabriel reaches out, but a telekinetic force thrusts Sellers and Gabriel backward. The elevator doors click shut, and the portal activates, sucking them into space.

Chapter Twenty-Four

CAMOUFLAGE

The ability to make themselves ignorable, or to give themselves a different physical appearance, is a skill available to a powerful Periti or a Provectus. The more powerful the adept, the more people they can deceive at one time. It's the recommendation of this committee to fund further study in this area to determine our agent's limits.

—National Intelligence Strategy White Paper: Top Secret (TS): Release of this document will cause severe damage to the security of the United States—Adept Assets

GABRIEL'S SHOULDER WRENCHES out of its socket with a dull *crack*. He chokes back the pain, but an ugly sound escapes his mouth. It tells him that despite his exponential leap in power since Joe died, he's still profoundly mortal.

Sellers, meanwhile, lands gracefully on his feet. "Don't move," he says. "I mean it."

As if he could move. Gabriel waits for his eyes to adjust to the gloom while he breathes in the stale air. Zuko trots about the room, examining every corner.

"What happened? Where are we?" Gabriel asks, struggling to sit up. "You seem to know."

"That elevator was a witch portal," Sellers says, running his hand across the wall as he edges along it. He looks at Gabriel as if he's doing complex math in his head. "I sensed the spell, but too late. Anand sent us here. Wherever 'here' is."

Now that Gabriel's eyes have adjusted, he sees a dimly lit room with a bed, a table, two chairs, and a bathroom. The carpet is threadbare. The chairs are torn, and the walls are an eye-piercing yellow.

"That color breaks the Geneva Conventions," Sellers says, seeming to read Gabriel's mind. He looks up and points at cameras in a far corner. "This is a prison. Careful what you say."

Gabriel limps to the door, places his hand on the doorknob, and twists. It's locked. He invokes his telekinesis to move the deadbolt, and searing pain stabs his forehead. Zuko howls while Gabriel rushes to the bathroom and empties his lunch.

"You okay?" Sellers says outside the door.

Rage boils up alongside Gabriel's nausea, a rage that has a voice. The same voice that told him to get up after Joe was murdered. He looks in the mirror and sees a trace of the voice's smile. Gabriel gasps and steps back.

"I'm okay," he calls out. "What was that? Do you know?" Gabriel exits the bathroom, and Zuko nudges his hand, demanding attention.

"This room," Sellers says, "is infused with energy. There must be a team of witches—at least four, representing the four cardinal directions—pooling their power. We're up against not only their power but the stored energy they've poured into this place over time."

Sellers's gazes upward at the cameras. They buzz toward him in acknowledgment and open their malevolent metallic eyelids. Sellers makes an obscene gesture in response.

Gabriel whispers, "Can you get us out?"

"Let's see what they've got." Sellers breathes in and out and approaches the door.

Prison lock

Heed my knock

And unblock

Let us walk

Sellers buckles over and coughs. When he turns to face Gabriel, all his color has drained away. Then, Sellers reaches for something in his back pocket.

"Is it still there?" Gabriel asks. "Whatever it is. I'd be afraid you lost your wallet, but you never seem to bring it."

"Very funny," Sellers replies with a wan smile. "It's just a notebook."

"It's a magic notebook. How did I miss the colors and energy swirling around it? And the magic isn't yours."

Gabriel leans toward Sellers, eager to see more.

"You're getting too good at this," Sellers says, turning to block Gabriel's view. "I can't fault your impeccable timing. If you're choosing now to start overachieving, I highly recommend it, given our current circumstances." Sellers gestures about the room.

Gabriel winks at Sellers in response.

"I'll do my best." Gabriel reaches out, searching for a line, and gets nothing but the barest trickle. He frowns. "We're a long way from a line."

"Which means," Sellers replies, his voice thin, "if we break out, we're far from a populated area."

"Very good, very good," a tinny voice says. "Why would anyone build a prison on a ley line?"

Sellers and Gabriel regard each other grimly and then lift their eyes to the camera.

"Anand, what do you want?" Gabriel demands through gritted teeth, his gaze menacing.

"I want my data. Give me actionable information, and I'll ransom you to Russell, and you live. If you refuse and attempt to escape, your stay will be painful, and you will disappear."

Gabriel says nothing but offers his middle finger to the electronic eye.

"What he said," Sellers mutters with a mirthless grin. "You'll kill us anyway."

"My patriarch won't stand for this," Gabriel says.

"Your uncle won't risk a House war over you. Someone in his branch of the family, yes, but not you. You're talking in that ridiculous British accent, so you must've imprinted on your father's side. The powerless side. No, Russell will let you rot." The electronic eye's red light winks out.

"Figures. I'm friends with the poor relations," Sellers says.

They stare at each other for a long moment as Zuko explores their prison.

"We have to work together," Gabriel says.

"Dr. King would be so proud," Sellers replies, his lips quirking up on one side of his mouth. "Adepts and witches working together."

They sit cross-legged next to each other on the threadbare rug, eschewing the bed or the chairs.

Gabriel speaks first. "What are we up against?"

Sellers takes a deep breath and examines the carpet as if he'll find something valuable hiding in some tiny crevice. "Anand's witches magically sealed this room from all sight and sound. I can feel the illusion spell around it. You could give a map to someone, and they'd never find us. Hostile magic flows through the studs of this place, reinforced over the years. Witches have harnessed the pain and terror of those imprisoned here before us and used it to reinforce wood and frame. There are teams of trained witches and adepts focusing on us, countering everything we do with all that stored power. With every escape attempt, expect the pain we feel to increase. This house will learn about us. It will learn how best to hurt us. It's what they've built this room to do."

Zuko sits and stares unblinkingly at Sellers, who smiles in return.

"What are you thinking?" Sellers asks. "I've seen that look before. You have an idea."

"When I tapped a line in the earth, I felt a huge store of ley energy in your boot. Am I crazy?"

"You're not crazy," Sellers says. "That's my athame." He withdraws a small ceremonial knife with an enormous blue sapphire embossed in the hilt.

Gabriel pitches his voice in a low even tone. "I'm touched you took it. I hope you didn't steal that for me. What if your father finds out?"

"Excuse me? I have every right to our athame and all its power. When I invoke it, with one nick of this knife—if it's my will—the victim will die, among other nasty things."

"But you're the youngest," Gabriel says.

Sellers snaps his head to attention. "I'm the youngest in years but not magic. Our family's guardian spirit came to me first, before my brothers. I am the most highly favored of my generation. This athame is mine by right. I carry with me not just my magical power but a portion of every other owner's before me."

Sellers is silent for a moment, and his usual mirthful demeanor evaporates. "I wish to introduce you to the athame. You will be the first nonwitch to be initiated."

Gabriel staggers back a step.

Sellers smiles. "That I know about. I propose a binding. It brings you under our protection, and if we need you, you'll feel it. You won't be able to ignore the call. It'll be like an itch that you have to scratch. This isn't trivial. It's a big step, but it will help us combine our powers and escape." Sellers locks eyes with Gabriel.

"But we have laws against that. What would I owe you?" Gabriel asks.

"You would be obligated to come to my aid. That compulsion would be strong, but truthfully, since a loyalty oath binds me to the HP, you, too, would feel a tug if she called, but it would be much weaker."

Sellers steps back and straightens his shirt. "You saw my guiding spirit. That means something. You mean something—to me."

Gabriel grasps Sellers's hand.

"This is breaking a rule," Sellers continues, "maybe even an adept law. Probably a law. Definitely a law."

Gabriel brings his forefinger to his lips and makes a gentle *shh* sound. He wraps his hand behind Sellers's neck and pulls him in until their foreheads lightly touch. "How is it possible you smell so good? Is it magic?"

"Since we're being totally honest," Sellers whispers. "Once, in middle school, I caught my mother enchanting the soap my brothers and I use. I think she still does it." Sellers puts his hands behind Gabriel's head and presses their foreheads together even tighter. "You should grow your hair out. It's not as beautiful as mine, of course, but it's beautiful."

Gabriel laughs. "How can you make jokes at a time like this? And no one's hair is more beautiful than yours. Mine is wild and unruly. You'd hate it."

"I'd love it the same way I love your wild and unruly side, which, if it wants to come out, now would be a good time. And why do *you* smell so good? What's your excuse?"

"I'll tell you after we get out of this." Gabriel grips Sellers's shoulders, breaks their embrace and puts him at arm's length. Their eyes do what their bodies can't. They hold each other tight. "Now, how do we do this?" Gabriel whispers.

"I'll need some blood. Just a little. No need to be alarmed. We're not vampires." Sellers gives him a lopsided grin. "Just a drop."

"Okay. I'm ready."

Sellers nods. "Hold out your dominant hand." He takes Gabriel's outstretched left hand, palm up.

"There's magic in your touch. I first felt it at the bakery," Gabriel says.

"You did? Probably when we were kneading the dough. Food magic is life. It's a special magic."

It's more than that.

With the slightest touch, the ceremonial knife draws blood. It travels up the blade and melts into the sapphire. The gem lights up in a brilliant blue, and in a burst of color and sound, a face emerges out of the sapphire in a billowing cloud. It looks down on them and drifts away.

Sellers holds the athame high above his head and recites.

Come what may

Obey the call

Bind us athame

None will fall

The jewel in the athame hilt pulsates in bursts of azure until, finally, it's just another ten-carat sapphire.

"May I hold it?" Gabriel asks, but Sellers has already turned the hilt for him to take. Gabriel laughs. "You're the mind reader now?" He grips the handle, and immediately, energy pulses inside him.

"Move with it," Sellers says.

Gabriel raises the athame; its balance is perfect. It moves in concert with his heartbeat. "Amazing. That sapphire at the hilt is fantastic. It's full of ley energy. I mean, crazy full. Where did it come from?"

Sellers tilts his head at Gabriel. "Hmm, I don't know."

"Thank you."

"You're my brother, as much as, if not more than, those uncultured cretins who share my DNA. And about that, when this is over, can you ask Barbara to run DNA tests? I have my doubts about two of them."

Gabriel smiles and shakes his head.

"You did see my guardian spirit, right?" Sellers asks in a hushed tone.

"I did. It was brief, and it drifted off. I don't remember the face."

"Wow, what a gift. I think that's why you can feel magic because he let you see him. I'll have to ask him about it."

"Ask him about it?"

"I'll tell you this much," Sellers says, losing his usual insouciance. "The spirit chooses us, often within a family. It follows the generations.

The spirit lives in my head; he occupies a space. I can sense him, his thoughts. Sometimes he influences me, but we maintain boundaries. In return for letting him live in me, with my emotions, see through my eyes, he gives me magic. My brother's magic comes from me. If the spirit leaves me, my generation is powerless."

"That's amazing, Sell. I never knew that."

"Yes, few do. You deserve to know because I have to wonder if you carry it."

"Me?"

"That's usually what it means when you see them."

"It— What?" Gabriel massages his forehead. "A spirit in my head? No, I'd know."

Sellers shrugs. "A question for another time. For now, let's break out of here."

Chapter Twenty-Five

REGNA ASSEMBLY

Little is known about the governing body of Regnas. We don't know how often they meet, where they meet, and when they have taken steps to enforce their laws. We do know from a reliable source in the House of Braganza in Brazil that Ellery Misk has been burned. It appears that without his adept abilities, his fortune is rapidly dwindling.

—National Intelligence Strategy White Paper: Top Secret (TS): Release of this document will cause severe damage to the security of the United States—Adept Assets

GABRIEL STRUGGLES TO slow his racing heartbeat. He reaches for Zuko and soaks in the dog's dispassionate review of the facts.

This is not a new den. We're surrounded by predators. Stay alert, attack swiftly and without mercy.

He looks at the mixed-breed dog with his pouty eyes and recently groomed coat and doesn't doubt Zuko's resolve.

Your job is to be a loving dog, mine is to give you a good life and protect you from harm, not the other way around.

Turning toward Sellers, Gabriel says, "Let's open ourselves up to each other. Drop the spells around your mind so we can better combine our powers to escape. If we fail separately, we can succeed together."

Sellers's mouth drops, and Gabriel sees the naked fear, the paralyzing thought of every secret laid bare, and every insecurity open to each other. He doesn't need telepathy to see that. Gabriel pulls Sellers in close, and their eyes lock.

"Imagine everything you want to keep private and create a safe place for it in your mind. This works both ways, so I'll create a curtain that you can't look behind. If you look for it, and maybe even if you don't, you'll come across my curtain. Don't open it. You'll be able to open it when you're inside my mind, but please don't."

All adepts know everyone keeps some things secret, even from the people they love and trust most. Adepts learn from an early age to keep the darkest parts of themselves to themselves.

"I respect your boundaries. You can trust me," Gabriel says. He expects a smart aleck reply or an allusion to the curtain in *The Wizard of Oz*, but something else comes out of Sellers's mouth.

"I would never," he replies tremulously.

"So, what does it look like? Your safe space?" Gabriel asks. "So I know what to avoid."

"I don't know. A place where I'm an only child?"

"Mine is a curtain because, in a family of mind readers, it's our signal to keep out."

"I shared a room with a brother," Sellers says. "Privacy is a foreign concept."

"Where did you keep special things as a kid? And don't say 'a safe deposit box.'"

The corner of Sellers's mouth quirks. "A chest at the foot of my bed."

"Okay. Imagine that."

"A locked chest," Sellers says, nodding. "And I imagine all my secrets in there? And they'll be safe?"

"Yes. They'll be safe."

"Okay. What's the plan again?"

"I'll enter your mind, find your locus of power, then combine it with mine. I don't know if anything will happen, but it's worth trying."

Sellers nods.

"One by one," Gabriel says, "place what you don't want me to know in the chest, lock it, and sit on it."

Sellers reaches for Ravynne's notebook in his pocket, pulls it out, and lays it on the floor. He closes his eyes, and for five minutes, they sit in silence. "Okay," he says finally. "Ready."

Gabriel looks up at the camera and then back at Sellers. "Let's do this."

He takes both Sellers's hands in his and opens his awareness. Gradually, he sees ribbons of magical energy. They're the same colors he saw at Anand's building.

"Yes," Sellers says. "Oh, what a freaky feeling. I think of what to say, but then I hear my thought in my head. It's like two recordings playing at once, but one is a second behind."

"You don't have to talk out loud. Just think it. It's easy once you get the hang of it." Gabriel projects this to Sellers as the space between their minds recedes. He reaches for Sellers, pulling his psyche in for a bear hug, observing the colors of the opposing coven until he's sure he and Sellers see the same thing.

"This gives me a queasy feeling," Sellers's thoughts flow into Gabriel. *"Are we sharing the same pair of eyes?"*

This time, Gabriel doesn't speak. He sends an assurance to Sellers that everything is working. Then, Gabriel perceives himself as Sellers did in the second grade. *"Is that what I looked like?"*

"Yup."

Gabriel witnesses the moment Sellers first met his guardian spirit as he baked with his grandmother. It's like watching a home movie. He can almost hear the clacking of the reel as the memory and the images unwind: Sellers's first kiss, his intensive witch training, and finally, his locked chest. Strength mixed with shame emanates from it. Odd, Gabriel thinks, but the complexity of people never fails to amaze him.

He turns away and focuses on the colors in the room. They swirl in a mad kaleidoscope. He reaches for Sellers and his magic. Sellers represents it as an oven, burning hot and delicious smells. Gabriel puts his hands over the stove and takes in the racing colors around the room. Time slows until he sees a witch in meditation and an adept watching him with the electronic eye. Their jailers are on the job.

Gabriel squeezes Sellers's hand and starts to recite. He's only one word in when Sellers joins him, and they chant in unison.

North, south, east, west, break

Unmake this prison mistake

The adepts and witches unleash their full power, but Gabriel and

Sellers take it and flush it back into the magical psychic pipeline. The witches gasp, and the adepts scream. Sellers is up first and rushes to the door, but it remains sealed. Gabriel unleashes a telekinetic blast, and the door shimmers and shakes, but it holds. When he thinks it might shatter, a pressure grows in his head so intense he thinks it might explode. He retreats and erects defenses around his mind.

Searing pain burns Gabriel's mind and doesn't let up. Pain courses through the house's floorboards. It draws power from the land. He takes the pain meant for Zuko and screams. It mingles with Sellers's cries in a twisted chorus.

Sellers catches his breath and vomits. "So, so close," he sputters. "It almost worked. But Gabe, they're not holding back. Next time, they might kill us."

"Yes. And because it almost worked, I doubt they'll ever let us go. At least we bloodied their noses."

"But we held back. Didn't you feel it? Why?"

"You know why," Gabriel snaps. "You're hiding something, and it's blocking your power. This isn't 'I cheated on my physics test when my dad is a physics teacher, and the guilt is weighing on me.' It's something bigger. You don't trust me, but how can that be? Because you're a witch, and I'm an adept? Because our stupid communities are enemies? If we keep holding back, we'll never tap our full power. What is it, Sell?"

"You're one to talk," Sellers murmurs. He looks at Gabriel and then at the ceiling and slumps his shoulders. "I do trust you. It's me that I don't trust *with* you. Every witch knows that to master real power, we must master ourselves in unflinching honesty. But you'll never look at me the same way again. If you see—"

"Stop, Sell," Gabriel interrupts. "Listen. When the dall describe someone, they mention stuff like ethnicity—oh he's Black or white, sex, sexual preference, class, vocation, nationality, religion. But adepts see deeper than all that. We know that's all artifice. Those are all add-ons. We strip that all away to see a person for what they truly are. I love you here and now, and I'll love you after the chest is open. Okay?"

"Not sure I believe that, but we're running out of options. If you end up hating me, at least you'll be alive."

Gabriel reaches out his hands to Sellers, and he takes them. It's intimate, holding hands and gazing into each other's eyes. Sellers's porcelain skin glows, and his gray eyes shine, and it's too much. It's too soon after Joe.

Not to be left out, Zuko burrows his head between them and nestles it on Sellers's lap.

Gabriel pushes his thoughts down. "Open your mind, Sell. I won't reject you. Merge."

Sellers breathes out squeezing Gabriel's hand. "I think I can sense Zuko, but more than physically. I hear what he hears. That's my connection with you, isn't it? Zuko perceives me as a smell and a protective presence. '*This dog knows me well.*'"

"*Yeah, he does.*" Gabriel half smiles.

"*Where are you?*" Sellers asks. "*I can't find you. You're complicated. Ha, I didn't see that coming.*"

"*Reach out for me. I'm home in the library. It's safe here, and Zuko is sleeping. Where are you?*"

"*I'm back in Miami Beach. Do you remember that vacation? That first night at the restaurant overlooking the ocean. Zuko loved the salt air. We're on the deck having oysters and beer.*"

"*I remember, and he did love it,*" Gabriel replies as Zuko and Sellers shake their heads in unison. "*I can join you there. It's a memory of the three of us, so we can all meet.*"

Gabriel and Zuko sit down, joining Sellers at the outdoor table overlooking the ocean, and Gabriel continues. *"This scene is a blend of our two memories, and we mostly agree. The waiter, though, wasn't wearing shorts."*

"I can see your curtain." Sellers ignores the shorts comment. *"Can you see my trunk?"*

"Yes. I expected it to be more, I don't know, ornate."

"I love you."

"I know you do. I love you too."

"I don't think you do." Sellers flings open the trunk.

Gabriel expects a Pandora's box, exploding with secrets, but instead, a sense of peace comes over him, and Zuko's tail wags.

Gabriel sees himself through Sellers's eyes on that friendless first day of school. It's as if he can reach out and touch his seven-year-old self. He sees their long walks around the schoolyard, talking while other kids play. He sees Sellers helping him pick out clothes for his first date. All these memories and a million more flood him, warming his heart. And Gabriel knows as surely as he knows his name that Sellers is deeply, irrevocably in love with him. He missed it. Wrapped up in himself and his shallow pursuits, he missed it. And it's no wonder. Joe was brilliant but distant. Sellers is everything Joe isn't. Wasn't. Memories rain down on Gabriel, and the signs of Sellers's love—no not signs, *actions*—fill his mind. Sellers being there when Joe broke up with him to marry Peter, making his birthday some kind of holiday, and sharing his magic. A witch sharing magic with an adept. What a daring risk, and it rolled off Sellers's back as if it were nothing.

This sharing leaves no room for doubt. Gabriel sees the best version of himself through Sellers. Can he be that person? Does he want to be that person?

"You are that person," Sellers assures him.

Yes, I want to be him, Gabriel muses to himself, hiding the thought. *Why am I hiding? Even here. Even now. I'm a coward.*

A woman with ebony hair and an eerily unlined face comes into view. The thought of her makes Sellers choke and his heart race. She's the high priestess—mistress of the most powerful coven in the Americas. Her tarot cards teem with her power across an old oak desk. She asks Sellers to choose, and the card he picks is "the lovers." She offers him Gabriel as if he's a prize steer in return for Joe's data, the secret to adept power and the ability to turn it off.

"I accept, High Priestess," he says.

Love is complicated, she explains. It's different for each person because love isn't one emotion. It's many emotions combined into one. It's the one flower a person picks out of the bushel.

"How well do you know him?" she asks. "Well enough to bring me the personal symbols I need to ensnare his senses? To make him love you?"

Sellers nods yes, and Gabriel feels the struggle inside him. Sellers hasn't decided what to do.

"Betrayal," Gabriel thinks, knowing Sellers can hear. *"That is your truth. She offers me to you like a Stepford husband. What next? Your coven burns my entire family? That's why you initiated me into it, not to protect me, but to control me? That's why you have that notebook isn't it? To spy on me for the high priestess. To neuter me or auction me off, and I thought—"*

Sellers pulls back the curtain, and Gabriel turns away, but there no avoiding what he's hidden. The locus of Sellers's magical power is represented as a household oven, and he expects something similar to represent his power. But what the weakest of Anisa Aboud's line hides, even from himself, isn't tiny. It's a raging waterfall that stretches to infinity. The crescendo of the crashing water assaults his ears. Sellers covers his with his hands until Gabriel tells him the obvious. The sound isn't real. It's a trick of the brain, and just like that, they're enveloped in eerie silence.

Fear reaches up from Gabriel's insides and grips his heart. He imagines other adepts asking why he was given such power—a race car—when he's unable to drive it. Gabriel knows he's weak, not in power, but in mind. His power will corrupt him as thoroughly as it ennobled his great-great-grandmother and turned her into a towering figure. As she became bigger with each increase in rank, he'll become smaller and pettier until, finally, he's ejected from adept society and forced to wander the world alone. That, he now understands, is what he's hiding.

Sellers delves deeper into Gabriel's mind and sees the voice's smile in their prison's bathroom. Gabriel is both repulsed and thrilled by it. The smile makes Sellers shudder. Who is Gabriel? What is he? An image appears of a child's room in ruins, the ceiling caved in and the windows in pieces. The horror on the faces of Gabriel's parents makes Sellers recoil.

Gabriel flees to a corner of his mind, but Sellers reaches out.

"Stop. You can't run. Or maybe you can. Who knows what you can do? But, Gabriel, witches are like adepts in that we believe everyone has a core. Maybe it's a soul, but we think of it as a seed. It never changes, no matter how old we get or what we experience. You're a good person, Gabe. Trust yourself. Trust me."

"Trust you? With that notebook you've been hiding?"

Sellers gestures to the giant waterfall. *"This explains a lot. You're fearsome. Let's not kid ourselves; it's you, and I love you, smile and all. You know that, just as you know about the notebook. You know I don't want the data. The HP will have to do it without me. I've always known that, but I was weak too. I wasn't strong enough to confront her. Love means letting you make your own choice. Love makes us strong, not weak. I'll defend you from the HP. I'll die, or worse, suffer ostracism before I let her have you."*

The truth washes over Gabriel: Sellers's acceptance of not just Gabriel's power but also that part of him that wants to use it to set himself above others. The part of him that would crush Shreyas Anand and sleep like a baby. He pulls Sellers close and gently kisses him. Just their lips touch. Gabriel slowly breaks the kiss, and they look up as one, seeing through the other's eyes when the top of the waterfall comes into focus.

"Are you ready?" Gabriel asks.

Chapter Twenty-Six

THE FIRST ADEPT

The prevailing theory is that an adept wolf drawn to a human's thoughts was the first to initiate contact. Other wolves followed, nurturing the adept talent in humans, thus cementing our evolutionary advantage over other species. Most notably the Cro-Magnons.

—National Intelligence Strategy White Paper: Top Secret (TS): Release of this document will cause severe damage to the security of the United States—Adept Assets

WITH A TILT of Sellers's head, the athame flies from his boot into Gabriel's hand. He places the blade on his arm and cuts. Blood runs up and past the blade and is absorbed by the jewel. The gem fills their prison in an azure luminescence.

Zuko yelps and licks his paw. Gabriel sees him sitting beside Sellers in the Miami Beach restaurant enjoying the outdoor dining. Gabriel can tell that he expects Sellers to slip him a piece of steak.

The early evening sun blazes orange. Gabriel senses the sound of the ocean waves calming Sellers's heartbeat as he takes a sip of his beer.

"You cut your arm," Sellers says. *"How did you know that all potent magic demands a sacrifice?"*

"You told me," Gabriel replies.

"I didn't have to though. Did I?" Sellers hadn't expected an answer.

"We're sharing all our thoughts now. Can you see it? Can you feel it?"

"Yes. Your power, it's deafening. I don't blame you for being afraid of it, of yourself. I understand."

Sellers's fear floods Gabriel, and it chokes off their connection. For a moment, Sellers's thoughts grow dim, and Gabriel's confidence drains away. Then Sellers's presence returns and grows stronger until his fear is a distant shadow.

"Gabe, your pain, it's yours. Embrace it, and let it be a part of you, and invite it in. The more you fight it, the more it's going to hurt. Embrace the pain. Embrace the voice. You're beautiful in all your imperfections."

The afternoon is warm, and the dinner rush hasn't started. The smell of a grill comes from somewhere, and Gabriel's stomach grumbles.

"You know, we can't stay in our memories forever." He holds out his hand for Sellers to grasp.

Sellers smiles in reply. *"No, we can't, but thanks for the extra minute."*

Sellers reaches across the table, grabs Gabriel's dinner knife, and slices a smooth line across his own arm. Gabriel knows that outside their memory, back in their prison, he gripped his athame, not a dinner knife. At first, Gabriel thought nothing would happen until a rich crimson river blooms on Sellers's arm. The blood disappears, and Gabriel's power roars. He marvels at the knife as it turns a shimmering cobalt blue. The sapphire in the athame's hilt burns with the seminal brilliance of a lighthouse during a storm. The evening sun in their shared memory shines now like midday, and they shield their eyes.

Sellers nods at Gabriel. *"It's time for the real world."*

All three rise as one and walk out of the serene safety of the memory toward the deafening waterfall, the locus of Gabriel's power.

Maybe I die now...

Gabriel hears Sellers thought, and he shudders, takes Sellers's hand. Sellers knows his magic will manifest what's in his mind for good or ill. He clutches Gabriel's hand tightly in return.

"Gabriel, I hear the voice in your head, you know. If you can't embrace it, then the waterfall that you're trying so desperately to convince yourself isn't real will stop our lungs from working and drown us. I'm no doctor, but I'll bet my flour bill, which is outrageous, that our autopsies will say 'drowning.'"

The heat of Sellers's magic envelops Gabriel in a red glow, and he walks straight into the plunging waterfall, inviting death.

The frigid water swallows them whole.

"Don't let me die here, Sell."

Memories they skillfully avoided change course. Doubt, fear, and every bully's taunt conspires to kill them. Sellers breathes in, but his chest constricts in a vise. He tries again, and his mouth hangs open, his lungs do not move.

"This tempest, Gabe. This storm. It isn't coming from far away. This storm is you, and I love you."

As far as last words go, Gabriel hears Sellers think. *I could do worse.*

Gabriel's fleeting smile vanishes as Sellers walks in front of him.

He's so brave. Braver than I'll ever be.

Gabriel feels the sting of the waterfall on Sellers's skin as it parts and a path becomes visible. Sellers's knees buckle, but he recovers and remains upright. Sellers leads them into a soundless transparent igloo-like room with rushing water on all sides, trapping them. The water rages, and they both know they're in the eye of the hurricane. Gabriel turns to face Sellers, and the water swerves in his direction. Gabriel and the water truly are one, and Sellers gasps. The reddish glow of Sellers's magic bathes Gabriel as well as Zuko. Gabriel controls his power, at least for now.

What have we wrought?

Gabriel hears the thought echo in Sellers's mind.

Time heals all wounds they say, but time hasn't dulled this pain. It's sharpened to a razor's edge.

Gabriel reaches for the voice, and though it's too far in the back of his mind, he does speak to it. *"We will figure this out together."*

Sellers and Gabriel lock eyes, and they chant in unison. Zuko joins them, howling in low tones.

North, south, east, west, break

Unmake this prison mistake

Gabriel places his hand on the floor, and the orange-blue of Sellers's Ironbay coven starts to spread. Like an ink spot, it covers the floor until it crawls up the walls. It unmakes the years of work it took to infuse this prison with stored magical energy.

North, south, east, west, break

Unmake this prison mistake

The orange-blue of their coven takes the shape of a raven on the wall, and it flies.

The opposing witches chant, and Gabriel sees one in his mind with his adept power. The witch stares into a bowl of water, where he observes his fellow witches.

Sellers exclaims, *"He uses that as his crystal ball. It's his scrying device."*

"Water was a poor choice," Gabriel says as the water gushes up out of the bowl and into the witch's face, breaking the spell.

Four Provectus-level adepts attack Gabriel, but all that reaches him is their frustration, not their triumph.

"They can't find us," he says.

"No," Sellers replies, almost to himself as a slow smile crosses his face.

"But I can find them." Gabriel turns his gaze upward. The water, in a paroxysm of fury, rises until Sellers hears screaming in his mind.

"You broke the eastern water witch," Sellers exclaims and then demands, *"Give me that."* He takes the athame. *"We don't need to combine our powers for this. Take my hand."* Sellers strides boldly out of the chamber and toward the raging waterfall. The water parts and reveals a door. Zuko, trots to the door and sits patiently by the doorknob.

"Ready for the real world behind that door?" Gabriel asks. *"Ready to break the merge?"*

"I was born ready," Sellers says, standing taller.

Gabriel grips the knob and steps through the door, followed by Zuko and Sellers.

Back in their prison, they gasp for air and blink their eyes. Zuko for his part, is unbothered.

Sellers examines his arm. It bleeds from a deep four-inch gash. "I loved this shirt," he laments.

Sellers and Gabriel stand in place while Zuko races to the door of the prison. "No stalwart Zuko, the weakest spot in this sick illusion is here." Sellers strides to a far wall and plunges the athame into it. The wall splits open, and the room is bathed in sunlight. They tear at it until the fragile plywood gives way.

"The real world isn't what it's cracked up to be," Gabriel says.

They gaze at each other and their new, unfamiliar surroundings.

"This is a trailer," Sellers chokes out. "Tell no one of this."

"It's our secret, believe me," Gabriel says with a sly smile.

"My voice, it's—"

"Strangely unfamiliar?"

"Yes." Sellers nods. "And inefficient."

Zuko approaches the plastic front door and swats it with his paw. It swings open and raps against vinyl. He gingerly descends the cinderblock steps leading down to touch the dusty ground. Sellers and Gabriel follow.

"It looks like Mars," Gabriel says.

"Or worse, Utah."

"Can you call a Lyft?"

Sellers gives Gabriel a long-suffering look. "Witch talent comes from the four elements—fire, water, air, and earth. I'm fire, and you, my friend, are water, but any witch worth their salt knows something of all four."

Sellers bends down and places his hand on the ground.

Mother earth, heed my call

Where do our feet fall?

Sellers straightens. "We're in Western Australia."

"How do you know?"

Sellers's face turns contemplative, and he looks to the side. "Magic is energy. It's about finding new ways to move it. We sense the imprints people leave behind on the earth. They tell a story if you're willing to listen."

"How did you know you could walk out? How did you know?"

"Same way I know there's a photo in your wallet of you and your grandfather. Your father's father, the British druid. I just knew. I feel..."

"As if you have a hangover?"

"Yes." Sellers puts a hand to his forehead.

"It's common after a merging. You'll feel better soon."

"I hope so." Sellers grimaces.

"You're a fire witch. I got that from our joining. Can you be both a fire and water witch?"

"Yes," Sellers says. "We're forbidden to discuss this, but I think we crossed that bridge. It works much the same as your rankings. I've mastered fire, but I can work the other elements on minor levels. Some of us are masters of two disciplines. Two disciplines are a heady thing and make you a powerful witch. Three elements make you fearsome. Only the most powerful witch families have members that are masters of three. The high priestess is a master of four."

Gabriel pauses, then says, "Try to master water. I bet it will come easily."

Sellers tilts his head as a quizzical dog might. "Okay. I think it will."

"I can teleport us home," Gabriel says. "I used so much energy, but I'm not tired."

"The athame will let you use its stored ley—" Before Sellers can finish his sentence, Gabriel yells and holds his head.

"Gabriel, what is it?" Sellers exclaims. "Is it Anand?"

"No. It's worse. It's the Regna, and she's angry. She's calling me home. Are you ready to go?"

"I'm always ready."

Gabriel's power flows around him in waves, yet he's swimming this time, not drowning. He focuses on the backyard of his Louisburg Square townhouse and casually strolls through the portal with Zuko and Sellers.

The first thing Gabriel hears is the controlled calm of his great-great-grandmother's young, vibrant voice. According to the witches, there's a part inside us that does not age—the kernel of our soul. Gabriel understands now this is the true Anisa, the Anisa who will never age.

"Go to your room," she says to him, and it's not a request.

Gabriel turns to Sellers. "I can't thank you enough; we learned a lot today. Anand won't get away with what he did. I'll talk to you soon."

They hug and say their goodbyes, and Gabriel begins the long march to his room.

Chapter Twenty-Seven

POWER OF SUGGESTION

We believe that what adepts call "mind control" is, in fact, enhanced hypnosis. We request project 1074C to be fully funded.

—Department of State Memorandum: Top Secret: (TS) Release of this document will cause severe damage to the security of the United States—April 2024

THE DOOR BARELY shuts behind him when Anisa appears. On the way to his bedroom, he strained his awareness to its limits, searching for any sign of her. He sensed nothing. He'd play this adept game of hide and seek with his sister and friends growing up, and he was good at it, or so he thought. Without warning, she appears, an apparition, staring at him, silent and deathly still.

The combs in her bun regally frame the back of her small head. Her necklace isn't subtle. She wears a fifteen-carat cobalt-blue tanzanite that hums with stored ley energy. The giant blue gem comes from deep within Mount Kilimanjaro. It gleams about her, in a deep lapis glow. He instinctively grips the emerald around his neck, the modest ley energy gently thrumming against his fingers.

Anisa's flowing dress dances about the floor, betraying her agitation, yet all the while, she remains deathly still. Except Anisa is no cat, only betrayed by a twitching tail, she's one of the most powerful beings on the planet. Gabriel senses her exertion to remain on the ground, her simmering anger threatening to propel her aloft.

Still, the Regna says nothing, her small arms crossed. Gabriel knows what this means—*Why don't you start?*—and that this is no time to play games. He gathers his strength and lets down every mental defense; please, let his sister not be nearby, he begs the universe. He would call his great-great grandmother Bibi, but he understands she's not here in that capacity. She's here as the Regna of the Salem House.

"Regna, I gave my blood to the dall. I gave it to Joe."

"You gave it to House Angeles."

She is in his mind. It's akin to the classic scene in a crime movie when the villain ransacks the hero's room, and every book on the shelf is unceremoniously flipped open on the floor, its contents scoured. Every drawer in his head has been pulled free and upturned.

She opens her mouth to speak, and Gabriel braces himself.

"You don't know what the dall did to us. What the consequences are of breaking covenants with witches. Your father implored me to pass down my memories, but I said it wasn't necessary to burden you. This is a different time, I said. I was wrong. I must apologize to Adair, you impetuous boy."

Heat rushes to his face in a flash. He struggles to take a breath and mutters, "I broke the law."

"And what is the penalty?"

Anisa says nothing more, her question hangs in the air, the persistent last party guest who won't leave.

Gabriel breathes in deeply and, eyes downward, whispers, "Burning. The loss of my sight."

Now, she lets his answer hang in the air as if it needs to calcify.

"The young do foolish things in love. I am not so old I do not remember that, but let there be no further violations. Do you understand?"

"Yes, Regna Anisa," Gabriel stammers. "I understand."

"I felt your battle with the adepts and the witches. That is a rare alliance you have with Sellers. I foolishly made the assumption you battled the Angeles adepts earlier, but you have managed to engage in hostilities with yet another great House. You know that you are no longer Media. Yours is an enormous amount of energy. It drew my attention. I shudder to think what other great powers in the world noticed it because, noticed it, they have. Why have you not mentioned your increase in rank, and why so much power?"

Of course, she knows the answers by now. He understands she's giving him an opportunity.

"I have felt my abilities increasing—"

"And what of the increased responsibility?"

"I wasn't sure it was permanent," Gabriel sputters. "I thought it was because of Joe, brought on by grief, and because a killer is threatening me, or someone, something."

She sees the truth in this. He can't see it on her face because he can't read her physically or telepathically, but he's naked now, his mind an open book. Every emotion, every insecurity, petty lie, and secret are hers if she cares to look.

"You combined your abilities with a crow. Others will want this power. To understand it and you. You have drawn a target on your back, and by extension, the Salem House."

She regards him for a long moment.

Gabriel's heart beats faster until he thinks it might explode. His head feels light.

"What is the law about tampering with dall minds?" she asks, her voice unnervingly calm.

"Bibi, I—"

"Quiet! We have a treaty with the witches. We only manipulate the dall to protect ourselves, our secrets, or our interests."

She stares at him now, her eyes boring into him. "You broke the law to oppose the Angeles on your own. What were you thinking entering Covian Pharmaceuticals Headquarters? It is an embassy. It is Angeles territory."

"I didn't know it was the Angeles, and I didn't do anything for personal gain," Gabriel exclaims, grasping at straws.

Anisa frowns and ignores his plea. "You are a child with too much power and too little sense."

Gabriel's throat constricts. For a moment, he thinks it's Anisa, but it's fear.

"We will need to explain your actions." Anisa pauses and looks hard at Gabriel, examining his thoughts.

"The energy I used to escape Anand. It was so exhilarating. How much can I wield? What are my limits?" There! There it is in the back of his mind. A whispered admission. *"I can't wait to do it again."*

The voice is there as if it shouted from the rooftops.

Anisa approaches Gabriel, her hand outstretched. She will download memories into his brain like a flash drive. These are the memories his mother wanted him shielded from and the memories his father wanted him to shoulder. It's then that Gabriel is aware of Anisa's thought—a bitter wind on a cold February day. His white father had no right to ask this. Gabriel closes his eyes and opens his mind.

Chapter Twenty-Eight

MEMORY DOWNLOAD

We know that adepts can pass down lived memories from one generation to another. We suspect they're able to transfer other knowledge as well. For example, a lawyer can download knowledge of the law to his child.

—National Intelligence Strategy White Paper: Top Secret (TS): Release of this document will cause severe damage to the security of the United States—Adept Assets

GABRIEL BRACES FOR a flood of memories to sear his consciousness, but the impact never comes. Instead, he's still here, on his bed with Zuko. The banality of it makes him laugh. Anisa seems to have changed her mind; she's disappeared.

He's about to get up and disturb Zuko's slumber when an unmoored emotion comes without warning, and everything goes black. It disorients him as if a dream spilled over into wakefulness. He strains his eyes to focus, adjusting to a dim light. He's transported out of his bedroom and onto a plush field of rolling hills. How foolish to think Anisa would change her mind.

Somehow, Gabriel is in rural Georgia, not in a field but in a pasture. He knows this in the same way he knows the locals call it a pasture. Anisa's subtle presence remains on the outskirts of his consciousness, and the reason for his knowledge becomes apparent. He's in her memory. She is aware the locals call it a pasture because she was once one of the locals.

The scene slowly comes into view, all the varied shades of green in the wild grass. The fragrant smell of hydrangeas and flowering tobacco compete in the gentle breeze. In the distance, a golden eagle cries out. He'd love to catch a glimpse of the magnificent raptor, but it isn't in Anisa's memory. Watching birds, even eagles, was the last thing on her mind this day.

Despite the hot and humid air, goosebumps erupt on Gabriel's arms as he observes two men busily examining dueling pistols. Are they about to duel? They're quite gentlemanly about it. They even shake hands. He observes with bemusement as they calmly discuss how many paces to march before they try to kill each other. After debating ten, they decide on the customary twelve. A chortle escapes Gabriel. *They can agree on something.*

The men display their pistols one last time to prove they each have one bullet in the chamber. Despite the early dawn hour, the heat of the day has already begun. Accounts of the duel written years later will describe the weather as "extreme hot."

Gabriel looks around at the sparse crowd—a few attendants and some ghoulish spectators.

The youngest of the attendants addresses one of the duelers. "Congressman Gwinnett!" he calls out. Button Gwinnett was an influential political figure in revolutionary Georgia, one of the state's three signers of the Declaration of Independence—Gabriel then remembers that Anisa has a rare copy of Gwinnett's signature, only fifty of which remain in the world.

Gabriel studies Gwinnett carefully and notices someone standing behind him. There, in the corner with his party, is a little girl, diminutive, with shiny ebony skin set off by a moth-eaten white shift, her posture erect and her eyes ablaze. Gabriel has a flicker of recognition and, yes, a little fear. He focuses again, sure his eyes are playing tricks. There's no mistaking those eyes. It's his great-great-grandmother, Anisa. She's carrying water and towels, surely to administer to the white people's comfort.

The emotions and stray thoughts of Button Gwinnett's party swirl, stinging wasps, biting her and tormenting her all day, every day. These people are annoyed at the inconvenient recent death of Anisa's mother. *My great-great-great-grandmother.* Through his bond, deep in her memory, Gabriel sees Anisa's mother as Anisa did. He can almost reach out and touch her.

Where to put the girl? Gwinnett's attendant wonders. *Maybe sell her? She's small, weak, and useless, like her mother.*

Gwinnett's power is a palpable thing to Anisa. He's an adept. His plans are there for any adept such as her to read because he's positive there are no nearby adepts to read them.

Hate for General Lachlan McIntosh, the other duelist, pervades the air. Gwinnett's thoughts pollute Gabriel's mind. He'll send McIntosh a compulsion to shoot wild at the eleventh pace. He'll quickly dispatch his enemy. Upon his arrival back home, he'll sit down to the fine breakfast he ordered for his triumphant return.

They count off the steps, one, two, until at the eleventh pace, Anisa sends, with all her might, a mental assault on Gwinnett. She's a slip of a thing, an Incepto, who, up until that moment, only used her abilities to commune with her mother. A mother who shielded Anisa from the thoughts of the white people surrounding them, a full-time job that demanded all of her energy and focus, leaving none for herself. Her mother might've been a minor Media or a powerful Incepto.

The assault comes as a surprise to Gwinnett, and he adjusts instantly, but an instant was all that insignificant slip of a girl needed. McIntosh hits his mark. He shoots Gwinnett in the thigh. A scream rings out in Gwinnett's camp, and a whoop of triumph erupts in McIntosh's. Button Gwinnett returns home writhing in pain, barely able to think. Three days later, he'll be dead.

The callousness, the inhumanity of Anisa's early life, descends on Gabriel's preconceptions, laying waste to all of them. He dry heaves and breaks out into a cold sweat.

While Gwinnett's funeral occupies the family and staff, Anisa Aboud takes some bread and a block of cheese. She begins her journey north. Anisa is a Periti now, although she doesn't know it. Gabriel sees through Anisa's eyes as she walks on the side of a dirt road, taking in the birds and crickets and every living thing. She's alert to all that moves.

As she walks with a steady purpose, one foot in front of the other, she whispers, "You can't see me, you can't see me, you can't see me."

The dirt road fades. It morphs into a cloud until Gabriel is back in another field, this one in the center of Boston. And yet another memory takes shape. Oh no, he thinks, not another. He can't take another.

The grassy Boston Common looks much the same, except for the cows grazing. *When is this?* Gabriel marvels at the thought of cows grazing in the heart of Boston. He tries to slow his galloping heart, girding himself for whatever comes next, while he watches them languidly go about their day.

Gabriel turns and beholds a man, a stunningly handsome man, and such overwhelming love fills him. An undercurrent of admiration and respect flows through him. It colors his every thought. The man gazes into his eyes, and Gabriel goes serenely still. Except, it isn't his love filling him. It's Anisa's. Gabriel is looking at the man through Anisa's eyes and with her heart.

Before Gabriel stands Uncle Russell's great-grandfather, David Walker, born free, in a free state, and a dedicated abolitionist. There is much of Russell in him. They share the same flawless obsidian bald head. Perhaps that's why he's Anisa's favorite. Like Russell's, Walker's fiercely intelligent eyes miss nothing. They sweep up everything in their path.

Two other adepts accompany Anisa and David, a man and a woman with long black hair and pale skin that rarely sees the light of day. Are they brother and sister? The woman opens her mind to Anisa, and Anisa smiles. A friend.

Gabriel can't imagine Anisa having a friend. She is first among equals. A Regna, perhaps the first amongst Regnas. But she's not a Regna now, not yet.

Anisa wears her thick, black hair up and tied back. All through Gabriel's life, it was thin and steel gray. Her trademark combs are still there, securely fastened in the back. Gabriel drinks in her smooth, unlined face and commits this youthful version to memory. She appears to be about thirty years old now, although her eyes, even when smiling, are etched with worry.

Anisa screams a warning, and it reverberates through Gabriel to his core as every instinct, every muscle focuses on one goal: to run. He turns to check on David. He's safe, but Brenna, Anisa's friend, lies dead on the soft ground. Where once there existed a pulsing energy and a library of knowledge that taught Anisa and had yet more to teach, there is now nothing but a void. The most powerful of their party is dead. Gabriel recalls his great-great-grandmother imparting that African proverb: *When an old man dies, a library burns.*

Anisa doesn't stop to think or feel. She lashes out wildly, but Zander White, the high priest of the Ironbay coven, counters her. His eyes still glow with the power he unleashed, his placid face unmoved by the adept lives he's taken. In that moment of anger, of lashing out, David Walker, the first husband and second love of Anisa Aboud, is struck dead. She strikes again, but again, the calm high priest defends himself and his witches. It's then that Anisa imagines the headquarters of the witch's coven in her mind's eye, there on an unassuming corner outside Harvard Square. The university looms over it in an almost protective way. Anisa focuses all her rage, and the stone house implodes. It crumbles in on itself, killing eighteen witches, including Rosina White, wife of the high priest. The witches, to this day, commemorate August 6, 1830, as the great cataclysm. The day Anisa Aboud Walker became a Regna.

The grief wrenches, and claws swirl in his gut, straining to get out, and Gabriel sobs. All he can think, is why, why?

"Why does anyone go to war?" Anisa's voice pierces the memory, then bursts like a child's soap bubble. "To gain wealth and status, or to preserve wealth and status. Maybe there are other reasons, but those were ours."

Anisa's voice has a terrifying gentleness. She takes a breath and continues.

"Your father has memories to share. We are not always the victims. Sometimes, we are the tyrants. Those memories are hard to stomach. We are at risk now of being controlled and conscripted by the government or the drug companies. Do you understand? We must keep our secrets."

Gabriel nods. "Yes, I should've stopped Joe."

Anisa says nothing but regards him for a long moment.

"Humans," she says, her eyes boring into him, "the dall, they were our stock in trade. They were our wealth. Through them, we controlled commerce in the Americas. After the war, we agreed on how to behave and share. We signed a treaty. We adepts control the management of money, the witches medicine. That's why our House has no holdings in biotechnology or pharmaceuticals in our territory. We agreed to stay out of each other's income streams and to share the wealth with our people. That was my idea. We cannot have rogue adepts running amuck, manipulating humans to make a dollar. That is why the Salem House ensures every adept has a guaranteed income. We must maintain our wealth, security, and the uneasy peace we have with the witches."

Anisa pauses, waiting for a reaction that is late in coming. "Gabriel?" she says.

Gabriel wipes his eyes and takes in a long, soothing breath. He looks at Anisa. Her face, at this moment, contains complex emotions he can't read. "It's not just that, Bibi."

"No?" Anisa says, bemused at the meek challenge.

"No," Gabriel flatly replies as if it's an obvious fact. "You can't bear the thought of the Sightless being forced into servitude because—"

"Yes," she says in a sharp voice that Gabriel knows all too well.

"You do see. Every person deserves agency. Every person has a right to chart their course, not have it diverted to suit our petty needs of the moment. We must not be victims or tyrants. We must be fair, equal citizens, living our lives and pursuing our bliss wherever that takes us. Of course, there can be exceptions."

Gabriel nods. Throughout her long life, she has never had the luxury to pursue that bliss; the burden of responsibility has always been hers. He knows not to press her on the exceptions.

He closes his eyes and remembers being with Anisa at seven years old, in the back of a wagon in 1777 Savannah, Georgia, on the way to a duel. It's dark, the sun hasn't risen yet, and she's so alone.

Chapter Twenty-Nine

BURNING

Burning is not the ultimate price an adept can pay. Indeed, losing their telepathic and telekinetic powers is a dreaded penalty. It is mind prison that they fear the most. A Regna can take a person's consciousness and entrap it in their mind. The adept spends the rest of their life trapped in their body, comatose.

—National Intelligence Strategy White Paper: Top Secret (TS): Release of this document will cause severe damage to the security of the United States—Adept Assets

GABRIEL'S DAY GETS off to a slow start after his sojourn into the past. Zuko, blithely unaware anything happened, takes his usual afternoon nap. Anisa must've severed their link for the duration of the sharing. What else can a Regna do? Gabriel has no wish to find out.

Zuko yips and twitches in a deep, far-off REM canine dreamland. An ability to quickly achieve restful, restorative sleep in mere moments, now that is a talent Gabriel can never borrow from the stalwart Zuko. Hopefully, in his dreams, Zuko can catch the black squirrel who taunts him from the environs of his oak tree.

Adept law forbids entering someone's mind while they sleep. It isn't just the invasion of privacy, but an adept can run the risk of getting lost in the vast subconscious. Getting caught up in a dream risks finding oneself in an unfathomable maze. Gabriel closes his eyes and touches Zuko. He connects with him to channel his serenity, and just as blessed calm washes over him, his phone rings. The landline number of the jewelry shop, Kelly's Stonework, lights up. Zuko lifts his head and glares at Gabriel.

Gabriel has been ignoring the shop. He braces himself before picking up the phone.

"Hey. It's me," he says.

"Gabriel!"

Zuko lurches upward to his feet. Before Margot can speak, her thoughts rush into Gabriel's brain with all the energy of an uninvited drunk friend. She's a five-minute walk away, but the rush of her thoughts pounds his brain. When this over, he'll have to be evaluated and assigned a new rank.

Margot's speech comes out in short bursts. "The police are here. They have a search warrant. Oh, Gabe," she says in a long sigh, "they're everywhere."

"Is Ankit there?" Gabriel blurts out, trying to keep any excitement out of his voice.

"No. I haven't seen him. Remind me to fire him."

"On my way."

Gabriel takes a deep breath to steady himself and focuses on Russell. He might need a lawyer at the shop. Nothing comes back; Russell is too far away.

"Fine!" Gabriel exclaims in frustration and sends a text. *Please come to the shop now! The police are searching the store. Is the house next?*

During the brief walk from Louisburg Square to the shop, Gabriel feels Ankit brushing against his consciousness. It's the adept version of knocking on the door.

"What do you want?"

"No one wanted to involve you," Ankit projects. He opens his mind to Gabriel, and his feeling is genuine.

"Yeah, well, Joe involved me, and I'm not done with your father."

Ankit projects nothing for a moment, and then, finally, *"Sorry about the cops, and what my father did was... Let's work together—"*

Work together?

Gabriel shuts Ankit out of his mind when he approaches the shop, Margot standing outside it. Any further discourse with Ankit will be in person. Zuko runs ahead to greet her, unable to contain his excitement. He looks up at her with his best "do you have a treat?" pose, expecting attention to rain down. When he gets nothing more than a tentative tap on the head, he snorts derisively and begins to pace.

As Gabriel stands in the street outside the shop with police cars double-parked, the air fills with the smell of malice, iron, and gas. Gabriel's head burns with a massive headache. But how can that be? That only happens if there is— A high pitched whining noise comes out of nowhere. Gabriel recognizes it as the sound an electric car makes when it accelerates. Gabriel leaps to the side as something heavy hits him on his right hip and knocks him to the ground. Margot's screaming and Zuko's barking crowds out every sound on Charles Street. An image of Zuko leaping toward him flashes in Gabriel's head.

A sound from overhead comes to him. "Gabriel are you okay? Are you conscious?"

The fear in Margot's voice shocks him back into reality. That and the coppery taste of blood in his mouth when his cheek made contact with the sidewalk. Gabriel shields his face from Zuko's tongue, but it still manages to coat his entire face. The gritty taste of concrete is bitter in his mouth.

"I'm okay," Gabriel croaks.

A uniformed police officer says, "Don't move. You might've broken something."

"Like what?" Gabriel asks. "The parking meter?"

The officer's face doesn't crack a smile. "Your hip, your back," she says.

"I'm fine."

"That didn't look like an accident. Is someone trying to hurt you? Do you have enemies the department should be aware of?"

"No. None."

An eyebrow arches, and her wavy ponytail sways beneath her black cap emblazoned with "Police" in bold capital letters. "I'm going to take a statement, and you should have those cuts and scrapes looked at. I've seen injuries like that get infected."

Gabriel gets up and brushes the dust and dirt off his clothes. There is some blood on his knees, which he wipes away with his hand with little success. She reaches into her back pocket and offers him a handkerchief.

"Thanks," Gabriel says and wipes his hands. He hesitates when he's about to return the bloodied handkerchief.

"You can keep that."

"I appreciate that. Look, Officer, I'm fine, and I have nothing more to say about that car. I didn't see a thing. I'll talk to Detective Rizzo about it. I'm here to see her."

"Rizzo?"

"Yes." Gabriel gestures to his shop. "She's expecting me."

"At least get checked out. You could have a head injury."

"I doubt it. I come from a family of notoriously hard heads."

"Who are your family? Where can I get my handkerchief back? Assuming you washed it and assuming you're single?"

Gabriel chuckles. "Police have to be bold, right?"

"Bold like Rizzo," the officer says. "It doesn't hurt."

"I promise to launder it Officer Martinez," Gabriel says, leaning in to read her badge.

"What are you, if you don't mind me asking?" the officer asks.

"What do you mean, 'what am I'?"

Is this cop an adept? Does she know I'm no longer a Media?

Then he sees the puzzled look and understands.

"I mean...what nationality are you? Puerto Rican, maybe? Like me?"

"No. And sorry, you've run out of guesses."

"He's just cranky." Margot grabs his arm and pulls him away from the officer. "Do you always have to wear shorts twelve months a year?" Margot whispers. "Your knees are a bloody mess. Come inside." Gabriel chuckles as Margot hustles him to the store. "And why are you laughing?"

"It's funny when the word 'bloody' is used literally."

The door to his store opens with a chime, and Rizzo's voice cuts through the air like a knife, stopping time.

"What happened?"

"He was hit by a car is what happened," Margot says.

Rizzo locks eyes with the officer. "Interview everyone on this block. Get as much information as you can on that car. Start with Margot." She waves another officer over. "Administer first aid to Mr. Kelly since he's refused medical treatment."

"I'm fine, Detective Rizzo," Gabriel says.

Rizzo looks him up and down. "I think you merit a bandage. Did someone try to do you harm, Mr. Kelly?"

"I—I don't know."

"Charles Street isn't known for high-speed chases or motorists losing control of their vehicles. Did you see anyone or anything?"

"No, I was standing in the street and the next thing I knew I was on the sidewalk."

"There is no sign of a concussion," Rizzo says staring into his eyes. "You were only stunned. You're lucky it wasn't much worse. Are you sure there isn't anything else?"

"What are you doing at my store?" Gabriel asks. "I'm going inside."

She knows I'm lying, but how? She's not an adept. On entering, the first thing Gabriel hears is the constant snapping of blue nitrile gloves echoing from every corner. The first thing he sees is an officer with his French press in a plastic bag and what seems to be his discarded coffee grounds in another.

"Rizzo, what's going on?" Gabriel demands. "Is that why you're here? Because of my coffee supplies?"

"That's Detective Rizzo, Mr. Kelly." She corrects him with the patience of a kindergarten teacher. "We must adhere to the social niceties, or we're just savages. Don't you agree? Where's your CCTV footage? I'll take it into custody."

Margot glances at Gabriel sheepishly.

"Is there a problem?" Rizzo asks.

"We, ah, don't have a CC camera," Gabriel says.

"No CC camera?" Rizzo says, her head snapping to attention. "Isn't that necessary to insure all this?" Rizzo sweeps her hands around the store, then places them on her hips, fists clenched.

Gabriel shrugs. "Our family trust owns the building. There's no one making me do it."

"No one?" Margot says, crossing her arms.

"You mean to tell me—" Rizzo pauses and raises her already highly arched brow. "—that none of this is insured?" She looks up and down about the shop. "You have no insurance?" She looks directly at Gabriel now, daring him to confirm what she's said.

"I've been meaning to get to that." How can he tell Margot and Rizzo that Sellers's magic is all the insurance he needs? Now he's sorry he didn't get insurance to pacify the dall. He promises himself that if he gets through this, he'll get some.

In reply, Rizzo shoots Gabriel an icy stare.

"Detective," Gabriel says in a smooth tone. "Why the coffee? You think I poisoned Joe?"

"The delivery mechanism was coffee. The cup he was drinking was heavily poisoned, but there were no traces of poison in the beans found at the house and no poison in the water supply or filters. We even checked the milk, despite the fact that Dr. Martin drank his coffee black."

"Of course he drank it black," Gabriel says in a muffled tone.

"Why do you say that, Mr. Kelly?"

"We both like our coffee the same way."

"Hm" is Rizzo's only reply.

"*Careful, Gabriel, don't say anything.*" Uncle Russell's words ring out in his head. In reply, Gabriel gives Russell the psychic equivalent of a push out the door.

Gabriel squares his shoulders and faces Rizzo.

"I hope you know that I didn't kill Joe. I don't have any motive. Why would I want him dead? Nothing makes sense."

Rizzo flips her notebook closed and places her pen behind her ear. "Where did that come from, Mr. Kelly? Guilty conscience? You're defensive. And just between us, I don't know why laypeople think that motive is the overriding factor. It must be the movies. People do all sorts of things for all sorts of reasons, and I'll never understand why. When conducting real police work outside the movies and TV, it means before motive, and you had the means. As for the motive, you were in love with a married man. Was Dr. Martin entertaining others beyond yourself in his extramarital emotional bonding?"

Gabriel tries to control his face but knows he failed. Of all the cops in the BPD, he had to get the smart one. He looked up how many homicides go unsolved, and it's about 40 percent. Most of the ones that are solved are obvious, and it isn't necessary to call in Hercule Poirot. Getting away with murder is, in fact, not that hard. In his heart of hearts, Gabriel thought that Rizzo, in all her stoic charm, would believe his ill-conceived outburst. After all, he is innocent. It stands to reason he has to be acting innocently.

Rizzo removes her pen from behind her ear and places the tip to her omnipresent notebook.

"If you're so innocent, Mr. Kelly, then tell me where you were this afternoon."

"I was, I—" Stammering doesn't suggest innocence, Gabriel thinks ruefully. "I was with my friend Sellers. He owns the bakery a few doors down. I needed a friend, and he took the afternoon off to be with me."

"Did you go to a restaurant? Did anyone see you?"

"No, we spent the day at his house in Brookline. He has a yard. Zuko likes it."

Russell appears at the door of the shop. He's suited up. It's been a long time since Gabriel has seen his uncle out of a suit. He'd have to fix that when this was all over, assuming he can keep himself out of jail. He motions for an officer to let Russell in, but she only glances at Rizzo for direction. Rizzo accedes with a nod, and when Russell enters, he gives the proceedings his best lawyerly gaze.

"That's all for now, Mr. Kelly, but don't stray too far." Rizzo closes her notebook and whispers to a plainclothes officer with her back to Gabriel.

"*Gabriel,*" Russell projects to him. "*Can you be quiet around the cops? And Anisa tells me you were in Mumbai consorting with witches and Indian adepts, who, by the way, have filed an official complaint against us.*"

"*For what? Kidnapping me?*"

"*They admit to detaining you. Did you share our secrets with the witches? Adept secrets?*"

"*I...*" Gabriel pauses because the truth of his uncle's words and the political gamesmanship he's about to be ensnared in scares him.

"*Regnas throughout the world felt what you did, as did some witches,*" Russell continues. "*The high priestess has requested a meeting. What you did, no one understands. What people don't understand, they fear. Some think you're the next Salem Regna. Are you? Do you realize what that means? Regnas despise competition.*"

Gabriel cuts off the contact. Russell's love, warnings, and grave disappointment overwhelm him. His fear of putting Sellers in danger is like chalk in his mouth.

"It wasn't like that—what I did with Sellers; it just happened," Gabriel protests.

"It didn't just happen. You wanted it to happen. You wanted—"

Gabriel's phone repeatedly buzzes. He looks at the text. It's anonymous.

GIVE US THE DATA YOU STOLE, OR WE'LL PSYCHICALLY PUSH THE POLICE TO ARREST YOU, AND YOU'LL BE BURNED.

Chapter Thirty

ADEPT PHYSIOLOGY

The average resting heartbeat of an adept is twenty-five beats per minute. This rate makes them cardio vascularly fitter than elite human athletes—the obvious caveat being that our sample size is small.

—National Intelligence Strategy White Paper: Top Secret (TS): Release of this document will cause severe damage to the security of the United States—Adept Assets

THE PREPAID CONVENIENCE store phone rattles to life in her purse. For a moment, she's grateful she doesn't have to explain to her husband that she has a burner. Barbara has been a widow for many years, but her husband still talks to her, a whisper in the dark. *When do the dead truly die? Perhaps when everyone that person has ever known is gone?* If that's the case, then her husband, John Samuel Bates, is still very much alive. She knows John would not approve of her having a burner phone or why she needs to answer it.

Barbara opens the phone and pays careful attention to the number. There is no point in answering a wrong number on a burner. A burner phone has one function, and that's to speak to the one person you'd rather not. Soon, with some luck and some justice, she won't have to do anything she doesn't want to do.

"Hello," she says, her voice sharp. This is no time to show weakness.

"Report," the voice says.

"You're so military," Barbara replies, trying to show some levity. She's felt precious little of it lately.

The person on the line takes a deep breath and says nothing.

Humorless despot. "I haven't found the data. I've searched Joe's apartment in Boston and home in Provincetown. I've exhausted all my contacts at Covian. I've tracked down every PhD student, research assistant, and the few people in his life who could pass as friends."

"What of House Koli? Do they suspect you?"

Barbara doesn't like the emphasis on the word "suspect." Coming from these people, it sends a chill down her spine. "Not yet. I plan on meeting Gabriel—and keep your eye on him. If I don't find it first, my money is on Gabriel."

"He's under surveillance as well as his crow. I know from firsthand experience he leans into being underestimated. The Salem have a secret Regna. What an idea. He could've crushed me and my team by accident. His power is undisciplined."

"I can't believe Gabriel is Regna, but you have evidence, not me. I didn't think he was capable of that kind of subterfuge."

"If you bring the data to us, we will protect you. You will become a Pyu asset, and the Koli and Angeles will be satisfied with the financial arrangement we will make. They won't have any choice. But this isn't about money for us. You will be renowned throughout the world as the discoverer of adepts and our healing power. I will stand with you as an adept representative of the Pyu."

"And what of the Salem?" Barbara asks.

"If you secure the data, Dr. Bates," General Aung says, "one way or another, then the Salem will not be a factor. The Salem, if Kelly gets to it first, will only have the genetic map, which they'll have no legal claim to keep. I knew he was the key when I sensed him reaching out to Martin at the Mogok Stone Tract, but a Regna? Our intelligence was that he was a spy, but Russell Walker was behind that. Clever of the Salem patriarch to plan to kill me with a rogue Regna. Had I pushed Gabriel harder, I'd be dead."

"What if something should happen to him?"

"As long as it happens after you've secured the data for the Pyu House, the world will be a safer place," General Aung says, and the line goes dead.

Barbara grips the burner tightly and pulls back her arm to throw it with all her strength against the wall. She reconsiders. The last phone she destroyed was a hassle to replace. Barbara puts the phone back in her purse and takes a Valium.

*

IN THE NOT-too-distant past, Anisa would sit cross-legged to commune with other Regnas. Now, before she contacts her Pyu, Koli, and Angeles peers, she pours herself a glass of sweet tea and luxuriates in her favorite chair. Her legs don't bend as they used to, and her back needs support.

Anisa's cat, Simon, leaps onto her lap. He has plenty of room in the wide luxurious chair. Eighteen years ago, she sensed Simon on the side of the road while driving through the Berkshires. She ordered the car to stop to retrieve the cat and to head for the nearest animal shelter, but instead, she and Simon ended up going home to Louisbourg Square together. A long life for Simon, Anisa thinks, as she recalls her daughter's cat, Sassafras. Her daughter and Sassafras died in the waning days of the Vietnam War. A long life for them both, she thinks, realizing that even the life of a long-lived Regna ends.

Anisa glances at her watch because she knows that when she connects with the other Regnas, their conversation will seem as though it's taken the same allotted time as any normal dall conversation, but the sharing of thoughts conveys information in nanoseconds. To this day, it amazes her.

At 7:00 p.m., Anisa reaches out into the void. She imagines herself seated in her library. The image of her that her fellow Regnas will see is how she sees herself. And Anisa isn't sure what that is exactly, but others used to tell her it's how she looked when she was in her midthirties. There is no one left now who remembers her then.

Anisa finds the other Regnas and meshes their minds together, a living conduit to freely pass their thoughts back and forth.

"I welcome Regna Kotak from the Koli House, Regna Chesa from the Pyu House, and Regna Chaz from the Angeles House," Anisa says. *"We have two subjects to discuss before we bring them to the Assembly."*

"Which would you prefer to address first, Anisa?" Chesa asks. *"This is your meeting."*

Regna Chesa appears in Anisa's mind to be a seventeen-year-old girl, but Anisa knows she's one-hundred and fifty and must look to be in her forties in real life. Ah, Anisa thinks, how we see ourselves is never how others perceive us.

"Hostilities," Anisa says, *"may break out between our Houses, and we must prevent this."*

"Easy for House Salem to say"—this from Regna Kotak—*"You have nothing to lose and everything to gain. We financed this work and were forced into a compromise to keep the peace."*

"No one forced your hand, Kotak," Regna Chaz of the Angeles says. *"Your House was paid handsomely. Besides, we're above politics, and this isn't the subject of this meeting. We're here to establish ground rules for our intervention."*

"Chaz is correct," Anisa says. *"My goal is to prevent any loss of adept life within Salem borders. I ask you all to speak to your people to negotiate. In particular, you, Chaz."*

"Your goal is to prevent loss of life, Anisa?" Chaz asks. *"A lofty goal since my patriarch has ordered his more ruthless inquisitor to Boston. Her moral compass is admittedly askew."*

"No one wants or can afford a House war," Regna Chesa says. *"The last one nearly ruined us. I, for one, want to learn more about the Regna who wasn't meant to be. The Regna you assured us, Anisa, would be kept at bay by the circuit breakers you installed. We all felt him break those barriers and crack the Koli prison like an eggshell. I vote we terminate him. He's a wildcard. When he was last in my territory, he was a Media, unworthy of notice, but now, who knows what damage he can do?"*

"You suspected because you prevented him from sensing the trained adept soldiers of your House when he was innocently buying

gems," Anisa says. "You practically forced him to adapt."

"No one innocently buys ley-rich gems," Chesa retorts.

"His fate is not up to us alone, Chesa," Regna Kotak says. "It's up to the Assembly. In the meantime, control the Pyu in Boston. We all know the Provectus, General Aung, is in the field."

"My grandson is not a Regna yet," Anisa says, "not fully. He is my responsibility and under my protection."

"Protection?" Chaz says. "After what he did to Keira, he doesn't need protection. It's unfair that the Salem now have a Regna on the board, however untrained."

"I agree," Kotak says. "I vote we muzzle him until the Assembly decides."

"I disagree," Chaz says. "You're angry, Kotak, because the infant Regna destroyed your prison. I was impressed with his grit and will vote to leave him be. The Angeles know how to handle unfair situations themselves."

"You vote this way, Chaz, because you believe the Angeles inquisitors can kill the upstart Regna? How? With the aid of the Ironbay Coven, perhaps? Would you leave Kelly in the field and risk a House war? The naked ambition of House Angeles is reckless."

"Technically, Anisa is right. He is not fully Regna until he accepts it. Anisa said she would work to prevent any loss of adept life," Regna Chesa says, "but what of the witches? My vote was for termination in part because of his unseemly union with the witches."

"The crows can defend themselves," Anisa says. "And if they can't, it's none of our concern. If an adept House takes offensive action in Salem territory, no Regna, save me, can intervene."

"If an adept House takes offensive action against House Salem, then you can intervene," Chaz says. "But no one is attempting regime *change or to challenge the authority of your government, Anisa. None that I can see."*

Unlike the mental images of Chesa and Kotak, who appear young and vital, Chaz seems old. Anisa associates House Angeles with California and youth-oriented Hollywood, but Chaz's appearance hints at a far older culture holding some sway in the Angeles House government. A culture that prizes age and experience doesn't fit with what she knows about Patriarch Meyer.

"Then our Houses remain on the brink of war," Anisa says. *"Let us agree on restraint."*

"Don't be so dramatic, Anisa," Chesa says. *"We Pyu know that the Houses Koli, Angeles, and Salem wish to maintain the status quo, but a new age is coming, no matter what happens in the next few days. House Pyu will practice restraint."*

"As will House Koli," Kotak says.

"I will speak to the patriarch," Chaz says. *"That's all I can promise."*

"I will state again. My grandson is under my protection. He's not to be culled."

"Until we meet at the Assembly, then," Chesa says.

"This meeting is concluded," Anisa says. She looks at her watch to see how much time has elapsed. It's 7:00 p.m. and ten seconds.

Chapter Thirty-One

MIND TRANSFERAL

According to Patriarch Ignacio of Northern Italy, an elderly Regna transferred his consciousness into a young Incepto in 1577. The European Regnas subsequently killed the Patriarch Ignacio, and the knowledge of consciousness transference died with him.

—National Intelligence Strategy White Paper: Top Secret (TS): Release of this document will cause severe damage to the security of the United States—Adept Assets

GABRIEL, SELLERS, AND Zuko take the Quattroporte down Storrow Drive in the early evening. Zuko is relegated to the back, but he leans so far forward he might as well be in the front. The Charles River sparkles against the lights of the sibling cities, Boston and Cambridge. Siblings yes, but different. Bostonians quip that you need a passport to traverse the river into the People's Republic of Cambridge.

The ride is the smooth journey of an upscale car commercial. Traffic is light, and the views of downtown are spectacular. Neither the views nor the traffic will last, but as of now, it's driving Nirvana. They exit Boston city limits and sail through the overpass into Cambridge.

Gabriel has just brought up Akinola's Instagram feed when horns erupt and almost-impossible-to-replace Maserati tires squeal in protest. Zuko yelps and tumbles forward into the front seat. Gabriel looks up in alarm.

Sellers sheepishly averts his eyes. "Sorry. I was looking at your phone and not the road. That dude literally stops traffic."

"I'm scrolling through the Insta feed of one Akinola Adeoye," Gabriel says.

"Why, Gabe? Aren't we on more urgent business than desperately photoshopped social media posts?"

"He's Joe's personal trainer and our destination."

"Again, I ask, why?"

"I think he's Joe's *very* personal, personal trainer."

"Oh," Sellers replies. "Typical. Although I can't fault his taste."

"I think Joe left the data with him."

"Really? What is he? How did you figure that out?"

"He's dall or passing himself off that way. He's not a Salem adept, and there's no registered adept in our territory with that name. I found him on Joe's carefully—but not carefully enough—scrubbed social media."

"Ah," Sellers says, taking a deep breath. "He's either dall or a spy."

"Exactly. If he's a witch, I want you to tell me right away."

"I'll read him at a glance."

They drive on into Somerville. The formerly working-class city is now a hybrid of million-dollar condos and modest homes. Gabriel studies a building that wasn't there last year. That's ten million. The numbers go off in his head as they drive, a displaced buzz, block after rehabilitated block.

"Look at this," Gabriel says, showing Sellers an Instagram photo at a red light. "He's complaining that he's thick."

Akinola is resplendent in his tight-fitting shorts and nothing else while posing for a shirtless selfie in the gym mirror. His smile explodes, a supernova across the screen.

"Thick?" Sellers asks. "He has abs."

"Yes, but his abs have been reduced from six to four. That counts as thick in his world. Apparently, he suffered an accident that involved an extra serving of guacamole."

"Oh, Sweet Hecate," Sellers exclaims. "I bet he can feel my hate from here."

"Here's a video of him doing pullups in slow, perfect form. I'd show you, but it's just too irritating. Even his muscles have muscles. He has four hundred thousand followers. How is that possible?"

"He's polished and working on his brand. Sculpted pecs and washboard abs at twenty-three make all things possible. If he were white, he'd have a million followers."

"How many do you have?"

Sellers makes a show of giving this question careful consideration. "Ninety. Why does his face have to be so perfect?"

"Life isn't fair," Gabriel says.

"What if he's not home? He's gorgeous and twenty-something, and those types are never home."

"I booked an appointment and paid extra for a workout at his house. You can do it online. Look, here are pictures of his roommates. One is a blond guy with dreads and no body fat. He probably gets cold in the Sahara."

"Birds of a feather," Sellers replies.

They park outside a brownstone. Next to it on the corner, a small storefront has a sign that says, "Personal Training By Appointment Only." The small type reads, somervillemuscle.com. The neighborhood is in the middle of full-on gentrification. Dumpsters full of detritus sit in front of two buildings undergoing a gut renovation. BMWs cavort with Hyundais for the time being.

Before Sellers and Gabriel can knock, Akinola appears at the door in a loose-fitting tank top and shorts. He doesn't appear surprised to see Gabriel and Sellers are unprepared to work out; his surprise is covered up by his confidence.

"Collinsworth?" he asks, looking at Gabriel because he's standing in front. "You bring your dog to work out?"

"You used my name?" Sellers says to Gabriel.

"Akinola, my name is Gabriel Kelly. I used my friend's name because I thought you might know me, and I didn't want to put you off."

Gabriel peers inside the room. The small well-equipped gym smells of testosterone and cleaning products. Posters of beach scenes in almost every region of the world line the walls: Brazil, Lebanon, Thailand, Cape Town, Spain, California, and Australia. Gabriel gets it; no matter where you go, if you train with me, you'll look good on any beach.

Taking in Akinola's annoyingly innocent eyes and disarming demeanor, he can tell the guy never met a beach he didn't like. Gabriel reaches out mentally to the young man and gets tequila shots, an upcoming trip to Puerto Vallarta, and grief. Not a huge amount of grief, but it's there, a sincere sense of loss.

He doesn't know about Joe yet. And why would he? Who would tell him? But he knows something is seriously wrong. What is grief, if not love persevering?

"I don't know you," Akinola says, looking them up and down.

"I was a friend of Joe Martin."

"Joey?"

Joey? Joe was many things, but "Joey" wasn't one of them.

"May we come in, please?" Gabriel asks. "We won't be long, and I paid for the hour."

"Okay, sure," Akinola replies, but he hesitates and lets Gabriel push the door open. There's no offer to sit. Gabriel gets a flash of biking in the Arboretum and Joe saying something to Aki. He called him Aki.

"He called you Aki, didn't he?" Gabriel asks.

"My friends call me Aki. Don't your friends call you Gabe?"

"No," Sellers volunteers. "Just me. I'm his only friend."

"He said something else." Gabriel massages his forehead with one hand, hearing Joe in Aki's mind. His stomach writhes over Joe's words to Aki. *Your kisses taste like coffee-flavored whiskey.* But what comes out of Gabriel's mouth is "He said he trusted you."

"Do you know what happened to him?" Aki asks.

"Ah, yes. Someone poisoned him. He was murdered."

"Murdered? Oh my God." Aki takes an involuntary step back and looks away. "When I didn't hear from him, I called his office, and they said he'd died. It's been almost a week, and there's been nothing in the paper." Akinola bites his lip as if to stop the quaver in his voice. It doesn't work. His voice betrays him, and the room is awash in his pain. Gabriel drinks it in and wonders if Aki's pain is worse than his and feels a pang of guilt.

Of course, there would be little news. The Houses pay PR firms a great deal of money to kill stories about anything that comes even peripherally close to their business. Kill fees are their stock and trade.

"I'm trying to find who killed him," Gabriel says, "and to do that, I need to find something very valuable to him—his work. Do you know where he kept it? Did he give you anything? Can you help me find his killer?"

"Is that why he was killed?"

"Yes, it was for his data."

Aki takes a calming breath and regards Gabriel with solemn eyes. "He never gave me anything, but he used my laptop a lot. Which is weird, right? His was a rocket, and mine is a piece of junk. I told him he could use my PC, where I play video games. It's amped up with RAM, but he never did."

Gabriel meets Aki's eyes and scans his wide-open mind and finds no hint of a lie, not even evasion. Gabriel pushes a suggestion into Aki's mind to trust him. He dampens Aki's natural suspicions, suppressing them all.

"Come on." Aki nods his head to a door that leads into his adjoining apartment. Zuko is the first to follow him. Gabriel and Sellers follow into an older but well-kept kitchen. A few dishes and three blenders sit in the sink. Gabriel imagines all three going at once to fortify the roommates with kale and banana smoothies at 6:00 a.m. Do they fight over the last beet to make juice?

Aki wordlessly walks by a white boy with dreadlocks and grabs a laptop from a table.

"Here it is," he says and hands it to Gabriel.

That's when it explodes.

*

"DID YOU HEAR the clanging and the banging?" Herrera asks.

Rizzo checks her watch. It's already 8:00 p.m. Despite staying late and going over the facts, again and again, something is eluding her. "Clanging and banging?"

"Yeah, in the men's room. We heard this loud bang and what sounded like screaming. And before you start saying we're hallucinating, there's a hole in the lavatory ceiling. No one can explain what happened. Everyone is talking about it."

"Not everyone," Rizzo says dryly.

"Point taken," Herrera says.

Rizzo shoots Herrera a quizzical look. "A dozen police detectives and no one knows what happened? We should keep that out of the recruiting brochures."

Herrera utters a wry laugh. "No, that's nothing to brag about, but what's a police HQ without some ghosts?"

"I don't believe in the supernatural, Officer Herrera," Rizzo says in a bored monotone.

"No, of course not. What did you find out about Peter Brandon?"

"Mr. Brandon worked summers at his father's waste disposal company, and none of that is particularly exciting until you dig into his duties. One of them was animal pest control around dumpsites. Can you guess what they used to control coyotes, foxes, and wild dogs?"

"I'll go out on a limb and say sodium fluoroacetate."

"Your limb would not break, Officer Herrera."

"That's damning evidence," Herrera exclaims. "Peter Brandon knows all about the poison, and he had access to it."

"Yes, but it's circumstantial. We can't link him to the poison. We can't prove how Martin was poisoned. Do you have the forensics report?" Rizzo outstretches her hand, and Herrera drops the file in it.

"Give me the cliff notes," Rizzo says without looking up from her desk.

"You were right to test Kelly's coffee grounds. The lab found salt in them."

Rizzo's eyes flash up and meet Herrera's. "Do continue, Officer Herrera."

"Check your phone," Herrera says.

"If you did something right, can you do it without the self-satisfied tone?"

Rizzo checks the text that Herrera sent her. It's a Google search:

Salt in coffee grounds. The addition of salt in coffee dampens bitterness without using other additives. Salt brings out the natural sweetness of coffee and maintains pleasant aromas. If people are sensitive to bitterness, even in specialty coffee, adding salt is a good alternative to milk and sugar.

"Herrera!" Rizzo exclaims, standing up.

"Yeah, salt looks and tastes just like the poison sodium fluoroacetate. If Martin's habit was to put salt in his coffee grounds, how easy would it be to put poison in the salt container? I took the liberty of sending a forensics team to the apartment, paying careful attention to any and all salt containers. I have a car waiting."

Rizzo smiles. "Tone aside, Junior Detective Herrera, I'm beginning to like you."

"Junior Detective!"

Chapter Thirty-Two

THE SUPERNATURAL

Although Homo sapiens psychica divide themselves into two warring factions with different ability manifestations, there is no evidence that witches possess anything not grounded in our knowledge of quantum psychics.

—National Intelligence Strategy White Paper: Top Secret (TS): Release of this document will cause severe damage to the security of the United States—Adept Assets

"WHAT WAS THAT?" Sellers cries.

"My laptop," Aki protests. "What happened to my laptop?"

The blond with dreadlocks, Aki's roommate, joins them in staring at what was once a computer but is now a thousand shattered shards of plastic. "Dude, that was radical," he says. "Did we lose electricity?"

"That," Sellers says. "That was something I've never experienced. Was it a Regna?"

"Maybe, or a powerful well-trained Provectus," Gabriel replies. "We didn't sense a thing. And clever. They avoided overtly attacking us, so they didn't draw Anisa's attention.

"Yes," Sellers agrees. "They obeyed the letter, if not the spirit of the law."

"What's going on?" Aki asks, his voice soft and his look uneasy.

"Nothing. We came and worked out and your laptop broke. It's our fault, and we're paying for it. Remember?"

Gabriel locks eyes with Aki and the blond dreaded roommate. They have a silent one-sided conversation where Gabriel tells them how the evening went, how they worked out, and there was an accident with the laptop.

"Oh," Aki says. "That's right. You owe me another set of squats." His roommate turns wordlessly and walks away, presumably to snack on celery.

"Until next time," Gabriel says. "It was great meeting you. Have fun in Puerto Vallarta."

"How did you know about—"

"Good night, Aki."

When Gabriel and Sellers get in the Quattroporte, Gabriel says, "Seal it."

Sellers nods and concentrates.

Seal the room,

Quiet as a tomb.

See no more,

We ignore.

A frisson of energy wraps around car. Then, Gabriel focuses like he never has before and builds the strongest psychic defense he can. He imagines an impenetrable wall with landmines leading up to it.

Sellers starts the car, and they pull away.

"I need you to go to the Elite Sports gym on Dartmouth."

"What for?"

"I know where Joe hid the data."

"You know we're being followed. Whoever destroyed that laptop is going to destroy the data or take it for themselves."

Gabriel looks at Sellers and smiles.

"Oh," Sellers says. "You want them to follow me while you—let me guess. Are you going to teleport out of my car?"

"Yes, I can teleport where I want to go because I've been there before, so I plan on being in and out before they know I'm there. The car is sealed from adept and witch senses, so that should give me a head start. Park outside for a while and take your time getting out of the car. I hope they'll think I'm still in it. Then, walk inside. It's closed, so do your witchy stuff. That should intrigue them."

"All right. I'll say hi to Ankit for you, and good luck."

"And, Sell, you work out. You look great without a shirt."

Gabriel winks at Sellers, then focuses on his task. He grips Zuko's paw, and everything becomes easier. He pictures his destination in his mind and centers himself. It's almost as though he can feel the planet spinning on its axis, so many swirling atoms. Slowly, he sees it and grabs hold of it. Gabriel also sees what it looks like to Sellers—he and Zuko floating backward out of his car. Gabriel and Zuko appear in the locker room of Elite Sports, but it's the Elite Sports in Harvard Square, Cambridge, not Dartmouth Street in Boston. This location is closest to Joe's work. Gabriel saw something in the corner of Aki's mind that Aki didn't think was important. Joe insisted on using his overnight locker when they trained together.

Zuko sits, panting. Teleporting is exhausting, and Zuko used most of his energy. Gabriel breathes in and out to gather himself, his heart pounding. He goes to Aki's locker and, still a bit weak in the knees, opens the lock with a flick of his hand. He moves a towel, three bottles of hair gel, soap, a bottle of creatine, and cocoa butter out of the way, and there it is, a flash drive in the back. It's the same type Gabriel saw in Joe's office. He grabs the drive and keeps the walls around his mind as tight as he can.

"Come on, Zuko. Let's go home."

Thankfully, the gym is closed, so Gabriel and Zuko take their time making their way through the gym, regaining some energy. The urban bustle of Harvard Square is a welcome sight until Gabriel comes face-to-face with General Aung.

*

OFFICER ESTEBAN HERRERA stands in the reception area of Peter Brandon's condominium building. It's a long way from his "just above the poverty line" roots in Long Island. Still, while studying criminal justice and eventually law at Boston College, Herrera met many students from wealthy families. What strikes him most, standing here, is seeing so much wealth in one place. It's such a large building, with so few apartments. "McMansions in the sky" would be a more suitable name.

Herrera glances over at Rizzo, recalling that she's grown up in buildings like this. He considers making a crack about it, but knowing she's sensitive about any mention of her father, he lets the barb die on his lips.

Leaning in close to the receptionist, he speaks sotto voce to prevent anyone from overhearing. After all, what would the neighbors think? "Tell Peter Brandon that Detective Esteban Herrera and Detective Rizzo from the Boston Police Department are here."

The receptionist nods and picks up the phone. He holds it to his ear for so long that Herrera believes Brandon won't answer, and he fears he'll have to go up anyway. Then the neighbors really would talk. Finally, the receptionist says, "Mr. Brandon, a Detective Herrera is here to see you. May I send them up?"

Herrera imagines Peter in front of that giant Keith Haring painting. Brandon's mother paid 3,545,000 dollars for the piece. That's the listing price of the apartment. Herrera can't afford to insure it, and even if he did, where would it fit in his house?

The receptionist nods and Herrera goes to the elevator. Standing outside Peter Brandon's door, Herrera and Rizzo glance at each other. Herrera gulps while Rizzo suppresses a smile.

"Herrera," Peter says, opening the door. "It's a little late in the day. Oh, I didn't know you were here, too, Detective Rizzo. Come in." Peter smiles a genuine smile, seeming happy to see them. And maybe he is. The survivors of murder victims are often subconsciously shunned after the initial shock of a murder subsides. No one thinks to invite them to the usual events after a violent death.

"I decided to finish up a love song I was writing for Joe before he was killed," Peter says, his smile morphing into benign resignation. "I had put it away, but today, I needed to finish it. For him."

"Thank you, Mr. Brandon," Rizzo says. "But we must ask you to come with us to headquarters."

"To headquarters?" Peter asks, his expression turning serious.

"Well, this is the stage of the investigation where we start to handle things more formally. We have to ensure that every "t" is crossed and every "i" is dotted. You understand."

Peter looks at Rizzo for a long time, his eyes unblinking. His expression fades to a blank nothing. Then he gazes at Herrera pleadingly, but all he gets in reply is an impassive stare. Finally, Peter's expression takes on a sweetness.

He's getting it, Herrera thinks.

"Okay, but come on in. As you can see, I should put on better clothes."

Peter opens the door wider, and the police officers enter. Their footsteps echo on the marble floor.

"I see you have a concert scheduled in Inman Square later in the week," Rizzo says. "Do you think your new song might be ready by then?" Rizzo asks, her voice as light as spring rain. Herrera makes a mental note.

"I didn't take you for a jazz fan, Detective Rizzo," Peters says. "If you'd like to come, I'll arrange for comp tickets. The best seats in the house."

"You're not attempting to bribe an officer of the law, are you, Mr. Brandon?" Rizzo asks with a smile.

Peter stops on his way to his bedroom and turns. "Not at all, Detective. Tell you what, I'll arrange for tickets when this is all over."

"Yes, that would be most appreciated."

"Are you a jazz fan, Detective Herrera?" Peter asks.

"Me?" Herrera says, pointing at himself. "No, not really."

"I'll still arrange for tickets for you, too, and we'll make a fan out of you yet." The levity has returned to Peter's voice. "Have you had a breakthrough in the case? Is that why you're bringing me in? To wrap this up?"

Herrera turns to Rizzo, his eyes beseeching, and holds her gaze.

Rizzo turns to Peter. "Yes, I think that's fair to say."

"Are you able to tell me, or is that part of the formality?"

Rizzo doesn't hesitate. "We concluded that Dr. Martin was murdered and that the murder weapon was poison, staged to look like salt. The poison was deliberately placed in your salt container, knowing that Dr. Martin used salt in his coffee to remove the bitterness. No one thought to examine the salt in the house when we arrived here at the scene."

"Someone poisoned the salt in his coffee?" Peter says, looking at the wall, speaking slowly as if the thought siphons all his energy.

"Yes," Rizzo says.

"I hope you don't think I had anything to do with that? It was Gabriel Kelly. They were having an affair. He had access to the house." Peter's voice goes up an octave, and his eyes widen.

"Where is your car, Mr. Brandon?" Rizzo asks.

"My car?" Peter says in surprise, his face flushing with color. "It's in the shop."

"Yes, it's in the shop," Rizzo agrees, withdrawing her notebook. "It's at American Motor Works having some minor bodywork done. Now, why is that exactly?"

Peter Brandon's red face twitches at the mention of bodywork. "And what does that have to do with anything?"

"Every indication in our investigation leads us to believe that Dr. Martin was in control of his life and looking forward to the future. He would not take the trouble of putting the poison used to end his life in the salt container. Someone else did that."

"It wasn't me," Peter says, crossing his arms.

"Murder, Mr. Brandon, is an angry act. No matter how calm and controlled a murderer is, the anger always seeps out. I always look for the angriest person in the murderer's circle. It's almost impossible for a murderer to control. We have a search warrant for your car because the same color paint as your Tesla was scraped off a fire hydrant on Charles Street moments after someone tried to run down Mr. Kelly. I haven't heard from forensics yet, but I have a feeling we'll have a match."

Rizzo waits for a reaction, but Peter stands there and says nothing. "Do you have any comments or anything to add, Mr. Brandon?"

"To what? Your fairytale? I think I'll remain silent."

"I see," Rizzo says. She gazes at Herrera, who removes some papers from the breast pocket of his coat. "Detective Herrera has your search history, which you assiduously tried to delete. But computers these days, Mr. Brandon, don't forget a thing; this is no time to be a teenager. There's nothing in your search history leading us to the poison used to kill Dr. Martin, but you did look up an old coworker at your father's company. A man you knew would have the poison, sodium fluoroacetate."

"So? I'm not saying anything. I want a lawyer."

"You're not under arrest yet, Mr. Brandon," Detective Herrera says.

"There's something else in your search history," Rizzo says. "You found information on Mr. Kelly's family, and that's not easy. You found an obscure article in the *Economist* called 'Boston's Silent Billionaires.'"

"Yes," Peter says. His face loses the veneer of innocence he painstakingly cultivates. "They pay lots of money to keep their names out of all media. They even paid *Forbes* to keep them off the billionaire's list. Money is mother's milk to Joe. Gabriel stole him from me. He was my friend, and he betrayed me. Did you know his family, through their investment firm, is a top ten holder of Covian stock? As rich as I am, he found someone even richer and tossed me aside."

"What makes you think they were having an affair? They met, yes, but only at Dr. Martin's office, and they spoke on the phone and texted, but only briefly and always during the day. Hardly a recipe for a steamy affair."

Peter rubs his forehead, and his eyes become glassy. "Before we go to the station," he says, barely above a whisper. "I'd like to hear how Joe's song sounds in front of an audience. Would you mind listening to it?"

"Mr. Brandon," Detective Herrera says.

"I, for one, would like to hear it," Rizzo says, staring down her partner.

"Thank you." Peter approaches the piano and takes his seat. "This piece is called 'Forever Mine.'"

The melody flows out of him. The music comes to life at the skillful touch of his long, deft fingers. The out-of-time meditation calms all of them, and Herrera is left hoping they have time for one more. He feels he has to bear witness to the last performance of Peter Brandon in front of an audience.

"Mr. Peter Brandon," Detective Herrera says. "You have the right to remain silent."

Chapter Thirty-Three

TRAUMA

Does emotional trauma increase adept abilities? We suspect this is true. We are studying the interplay between trauma and adept genes.

—National Intelligence Strategy White Paper: Top Secret (TS): Release of this document will cause severe damage to the security of the United States—Adept Assets

"YOU WERE RIGHT. The dog teleported with us," Aung exclaims.

"It's the *Lupus vinculum.* Their brainwaves are connected. That's another theory Martin stole from me, and I told you we need that dog."

Gabriel's clothes are made of lead. It takes all his strength to move his arm. He ignores Aung and turns to Barbara. Why is she talking about the *Lupus vinculum*? He quickly glances around and tries to shake his head out of the fog of being teleported. He's in Barbara's Cambridge triple decker. The telekinetic power of two Provectus-level adepts holds him immobile. He can't turn to see, but he senses a familiar mind when he reaches out.

Someone puts a needle in his neck.

"What did you do to me?" His words are beginning to slur.

"I gave you a potent dose of Jubilee," Barbara says. "You do know the history of the drug? It's a superb antidepressant for *Homo sapiens*, but for *Homo sapiens psychica*—that's you—it diminishes psychic abilities to almost nil and imparts a sense of euphoria and invincibility. You probably won't notice the invincibility part. In your mind, that's your normal state. I also gave you an indecent dose of Ambien. Sorry if the dose is too high. It's tough to tell. There aren't many double-blind studies of adepts, and by not many, I mean none."

"How can you do this?" Gabriel asks. His eyes feel as though they have leaden weights on them.

Barbara smiles, and it isn't the mocking one he expects. It's the smile he grew to love, a glimpse into the women he shared jokes with and for whom he gave up weekends, sanding and painting her porch. This Barbara briefly appears as if she's peeking out from behind a mask. This smile hid a monster, even from him. Barbara laughs and tilts her head back.

"How cliché. How can the kindly old woman usher in a better world? Or why isn't the kindly old woman not a doormat? Not invisible? You're so like my first husband."

"Did you kill him too?" Gabriel asks groggily, straining to stay awake.

"No, that was myocardial infarction, but your question deserves an answer. Isn't it obvious? The world will herald me for the greatest medical discovery in history. I'll lead teams that will cure diseases and extend quality of life. From what little I know about adept politics, General Aung here—I understand you're acquainted—will become patriarch of Southeast Asia. I hope that clears things up. You were always a bit naive, Gabriel, despite being a world-traveling telepathic polyglot. I always wondered how you managed it."

"It's quite an accomplishment," Gabriel retorts sardonically.

"Your life is accomplishment-free."

"Maybe." Gabriel tries to yell his defiance, but he can't get enough breath. "But you're a fool. Shreyas Anand made a deal with me—the data for a degenerate killer. You're nothing to the Anands except a witless tool, and Aung will get rid of you. You're expendable the second he gets the data."

"He's desperate," Aung says, staring into Barbara's eyes. "He's thinking about Joe being poisoned. He's despondent." Aung turns his gaze to Gabriel. "Martin's death was unnecessary."

"Yes, well, I lost my temper," Barbara says, pushing back her hair. "I thought I had the data. When he told me that day you were coming, I knew immediately why he did it. He called you for adept protection because if the Angeles refuse to go public, there is no glory for Joe, no Nobel Prize. But I didn't kill that pompous glory hound."

She pauses, obviously gathering herself, and takes two steps toward Gabriel. She locks her gaze on him.

"He stole my life's work, so you can take him off that pedestal you've put him on because he's a common thief. You interrupted Ankit and me, but you already know that, or you should. I realize now it wasn't you who was the key, it was your dog. It was the *Lupus vinculum*. How could I have been so blind? That's why Joe mapped the genome first. It was because he mapped your dog and found a similar sequence. If he had shared that with me, I could have protected him."

"How could you know that? You're a liar, and you're betraying the Koli. You're playing a dangerous game." Gabriel wants to scream it from the rooftops, but all that comes out is a raspy squeak. "You killed Joe."

"I'm not lying. The bastard boasted about it to me. I had access to plenty of adept DNA, but the *Lupus vinculum* was the clue in plain sight."

Aung frowns at Gabriel. "He did steal from the Koli and forged an alliance with the Angeles. Since you're bringing up dangerous games."

"Peter or Meyer killed Joe for betrayal," Barbara says. "Or a House or government we don't know about did it. Not that I care, but I did make an anonymous 911 call after you bumbled into the apartment. I know your family love the police. I called the NIS too. They're very interested in you. Thank me later. We barely got out of the apartment in time when Martin dropped dead. And I didn't know you could teleport. We underestimated you, which was a mistake. Well played, hiding your rank. Whose idea was that? Russell's?"

"Who cares?" Aung protests. "We have the flash drive. We need to leave. We're not safe in Salem territory."

"I know these flash drives," Barbara says, holding it in her hand. "There's no getting to what's inside without the password. Too many failures and the drive will erase itself. We're not leaving without it."

"The walls around his mind are coming down. You were right to drug him," Aung says. "Gabriel, what is the password? I'm with three powerful Pyu adepts. They're Provectus, like me. One of us will see it in your mind."

Gabriel looks past Aung, into the living room, and sees the same female lieutenant who fantasized about killing him back in the Burmese jungle. She smiles at him.

"I'm sorry you saw that," she says. "It was just a thought. I'm not bloodthirsty. We were told you were a secret Regna spy sent to steal information and kill us. You scared me. You still do."

"I scare you?" Gabriel says.

"She should be scared," the voice inside him says. *"They'll kill us once they have the password. You do understand that?"*

The voice rings in his mind in painful ricochets. It isn't the voice of the bullies who mocked him or the pitiless Shreyas Anand. It's a familiar voice. It's his own.

"I see it." Aung stands and walks over to Barbara. "The password is the serial number imprinted on a diamond that Martin gave him. It can be read with a loupe."

"Finally," Barbara exclaims. "We have it."

"There's a problem," Aung says. "The diamond is in Gabriel's store, and his witch friend warded it against theft. There is no walking in there and taking it."

The reality of what the ward means contorts Barbara's face. "What do you mean warded!" she bellows, her hands bunched into fists.

The Jubilee must be fading. Gabriel feels Barbara's pain as her nails dig into the flesh of her palms.

"Some alarm system? Who cares?" Barbara shrieks. "Pop in there and get it."

Aung huffs in frustration. "It's a ward of protection put in place by a powerful witch. It's potent magic."

Good thing Sellers isn't here to hear that.

"You're going to let that stop you? And you want to succeed the matriarch?" Barbara scoffs.

"At the risk of sounding boorish," Gabriel says in a low controlled tone. "You'll never get away with this."

Aung glares at him for a long moment. "Get away with what? You stole the data yourself an hour ago. The Angeles paid Martin for it. It belongs to Meyer despite what Martin may have thought. Perhaps I should give it to Meyer, extract a reward for it, and give you up to the tender mercies of his chief inquisitor?"

"How did you know I had the drive?" Gabriel asks. "How did you follow me there so quickly?"

"The Pyu House runs several governments. We're military. You never guessed we'd triangulate your phone? When your cell popped up in that location, I knew you'd given us the slip. You young people and your phones. Now listen to me, we're going to teleport into your store, and you're going to give me the diamond of your own free will. That should circumvent the ward."

Gabriel laughs. "Barbara has lost it, but you have too if you think I am going to give you that diamond."

Aung tilts his head. Gabriel knows he's projecting to his followers, but the *J* dulls his talents. He can't tell what Aung is doing. He's Sightless. Everything is so quiet in this room and in his mind. How lonely it is with only his thoughts to keep him company. The dall are but tiny islands in a vast ocean. How do they cope with living in this isolation?

Aung's man produces a gun and, without hesitation or fanfare, shoots Zuko in the stomach.

A bright flash explodes in Gabriel's mind as anguish wracks his body until it blocks out all thought. Zuko's high-pitched yelps pierce Gabriel's heart worse than the pain in his gut.

"Block his pain receptors," Aung says dryly. "And keep his thoughts contained. If Regna Anisa feels anything, we'll be dead before we hit the floor."

"That's not how the *Lupus vinculum* works," Barbara says. "Only Gabriel can feel the dog's pain."

"If you know so much, why did Joe beat you?" Gabriel rasps.

Aung walks slowly toward Gabriel until they're eye-to-eye, and his warm breath ruffles Gabriel's hair.

The voice screams, *"Let me out."*

A thought from Zuko enters Gabriel. Zuko's fear is thick bile in his throat, but Zuko masters it. *"Run, brother,"* he says.

"Aren't you tired of running?" the all too familiar voice asks.

"When I have the diamond in my hand, your gift to me, free and clear, you can take the dog to the best vet money can buy and get back the part of your soul I'm ripping away. Does this not motivate your generosity?"

Gabriel growls at Aung.

Barbara laughs. "The *Lupus vinculum.* Joe seduced you to study you. And to think I said you weren't worth the bother."

Gabriel's heart sinks at the sight of Zuko's snow-white coat, now stained red. He struggles to stand and glares at Aung with unblinking eyes.

"That's our cue to leave," Aung says, and grabbing Gabriel by the arm, they disappear.

*

WITH A BURST of energy, the front door shatters and tumbles into the hall. Barbara and the Pyu adepts cringe and cover their heads. As one, they look upward as if the ceiling will collapse around them. Sellers strides into the room, holding the athame high above his head. He points the tip of the blade at the fireplace, and the sapphire in the hilt burns a deep cobalt blue.

Sellers centers his gaze on the oldest adept, the one who put Zuko to sleep. Sellers's eyes glow the same cobalt blue as the gleaming jewel in the athame. His three brothers follow, all chanting in unison. Each brother assumes a corner, representing the cardinal directions. Fire bursts to life in the fireplace as smoke billows up the chimney, but the chute is closed for the coming summer, and smoke fills the room. Undeterred, the brothers continue chanting—a lullaby coaxing the adepts to sleep. Barbara chokes on the smoke and runs for the back door.

"Help us," one of Aung's men yells at Barbara, but she makes a mad dash.

"Enough." A Pyu adept screams, and then, just as suddenly, his lined face relaxes. His lips become a resolute horizontal line. His attack centers on Sellers, who stumbles backward from the psychic barrage but doesn't lose concentration.

Sellers counters with a flurry of his own. Still, the brief respite allows Aung's team of adepts to recover their footing. One of them tackles Connor, Sellers's oldest brother. The wind goes out of his chest in a whoosh when their bodies hit the floor. Both men grunt in pain.

The spell is interrupted, but Sellers and his two remaining brothers continue the chant. Smoke from the fire churns and whirls until it surrounds the adepts and enters their mouths, flooding their lungs. They begin to choke all at once, their throats convulsing in unison. Connor rises and rejoins his brothers in the chant.

"Where is Gabriel?" Sellers's question ricochets across the room.

The adepts frantically join hands and stand together in a line. Every window in the house shatters in a torrent of broken glass, wood, and splinters. The adepts throw the brothers off their feet, and the chant abruptly stops.

That is when Ankit Anand of the Koli House arrives.

Chapter Thirty-Four

ADEPT MARRIAGE

The ruling families strictly control adept marriages to maintain powerful bloodlines. Adept culture is akin to a modern feudal state.

—National Intelligence Strategy White Paper: Top Secret (TS): Release of this document will cause severe damage to the security of the United States—Adept Assets

DESPITE THE PAIN in his side from Zuko's bullet wound and the drugs that Barbara gave him, Gabriel manages to keep it together because now all he can hear is the voice. It's no longer a whisper. It's a frantic plea. *"Let me kill him."*

Aung nods. "It's sad, and I'm sorry, Gabriel, but I need that diamond. The world needs to change. You and your bonded dog live, and I'm overdue in Rangoon. You don't lose anything. The Salem have no claim on the data."

Gabriel turns to begin the sad journey to his office when a hard rap sounds on the door. *Bang, bang, bang, bang, bang!* It's an awful panic-inducing sound, the pounding incessant and unrelenting. There is never anything good on the other side when the shaking of your front door rattles the foundation. Gabriel's breath catches in his throat when Aung beckons to him, and his brows furrow into a single line.

"Ah," Aung says. "The dall police officer. Get rid of her."

On his way to answer the door, Aung grabs Gabriel's arm and pulls him in close he can feel Aung's breath. "That's good. I can read in your mind you don't want her hurt. Do what I tell you, and she won't be." His voice is low, and he releases Gabriel's arm.

I have to make this quick, Gabriel thinks. The spark of Zuko's life is waning. He's slowly bleeding out.

"You'd let Zuko die?" the voice accuses.

Gabriel walks away from Aung, making his way to the front of the store. The door withers under the insistent knocking. Finally, he unlocks it with a forced smile.

"Detective Rizzo," Gabriel says, opening the door only a few inches. "What a surprise. I'm swamped right now. Do you mind if we do this tomorrow?"

She pushes past Gabriel and strides inside. Typical, he thinks. Out of the corner of his eye, he sees Detective Herrera jog up the stairs of the brownstone storefront.

"Detective Herrera. I don't have time for this." Despite his protestations, part of Gabriel wishes this conversation would last forever because when it ends, so does life as he's known it.

"No, we can't do this tomorrow," Rizzo says. "We've arrested Peter Brandon for the murder of Dr. Joseph Martin."

"Interesting," Aung says. "He couldn't help himself."

"What is that supposed to mean?" Herrera asks.

"Yes," Gabriel echoes. "Tell us." With the drug's effects ebbing, if he's going to die, he'll die knowing the truth. He gathers his strength and looks Aung in the eye.

If you know who killed Joe
Confess it now, or be my foe
In this room, truth will prevail
All your plans sure to fail.

Here in his shop, every plank of wood and speck of paint put there by his sweat, Gabriel feels the spell ignite. The power wells up inside him, fills him with confidence.

Aung glares back at Gabriel, and his eyes are murder. "I'm a military-trained Provectus of the Pyu House. You can't—" Aung's words abruptly end, and he staggers back.

"I don't know, and I don't care," Aung says. "Our goal was the data, and we have it."

He doesn't know. He doesn't care.

Both Herrera and Rizzo pull their firearms and aim them at Aung. With a wave of his hand, Rizzo and Herrera slam against the wall and remain pinned.

"What?" Aung screams. "You threaten me with the dall and witches?"

"It wasn't me," Gabriel says, holding up his hands. "I didn't compel them. It wasn't me."

"It was me," Keira says, her lithe frame dressed in pink with lipstick to match.

She appears in the room with two men, likely twins, both muscular with short black hair. One has a two-inch scar above his right eye.

"It's me, and I brought backup this time." Although she's at least seventy-five, Keira's voice is young and tinged with excitement. There's a gleam in her eye. "Boys, boys, boys, don't waste my time."

"Every minute I don't have that diamond," Aung says, "your bonded dog gets closer to death. Can you feel his life slipping away? I bet you can. Give me the diamond. Fight the Angeles with me, and he lives." Aung releases Rizzo and Herrera, and they drop to the floor.

Adepts, when they speak, are like anyone else. Some are good liars and others can intimidate with a turn of a phrase. But when time is at a premium and the stakes are high, they open their consciousness to erase all doubt. Many adepts only do this for close family members or intimate partners. Some never do it in their lives, but Keira D'Cruz does it now. She drops the walls around her thoughts with a slow cold smile that never reaches her eyes.

Gabriel and Aung are free to read her thoughts, turning over the rock to what lies beneath. As Gabriel learns her intent, the twins tap a line, and he understands. He's going to die, and so is Aung. Keira will risk war and Regna Anisa's wrath. Aung's face betrays that he understands the better part of valor, and he teleports.

"Don't hurt the dall," Gabriel says, his voice tight and low. "They're just doing their job."

Keira turns to the stunned detectives and orders, "Leave." Zombielike, they shuffle out, the singsong door chime echoing in the store.

"Now then," Keira says. "Where were we?"

"*Matarlo ahora*," the twin with the scar says.

Not that Gabriel needed to hear that to understand. Aung read Keira's thoughts and fled for a reason, and now, with the combined power of the twins, Gabriel fears that he'll never leave.

"Give me the diamond," Keira says. "I'm open to you. You know I speak the truth. Give it to me, and I'll kill you quickly, and Zuko lives. Refuse, and you'll be a long time dying."

Keep her talking, Gabriel thinks. Convince her you're not a threat. Be small. Be the Media the world knows you to be.

"But we are a threat. Stop lying," the voice says.

"You used Peter to run me down?" Gabriel says. "I recognized his car, and I knew he was being compelled." Anger boils deep inside him, and he begins to rage out of control.

"She killed Joe for trying to be the favorite of the Angeles patriarch. She tried to kill us," the voice says.

Gabriel points a finger at Keira. "You had no right to use him like that."

"If you had the courage, you could kill the Angeles," the voice says.

All Gabriel can respond is, "That's against adept law."

He believes Keira. She can ill afford to let him live now. The Jubilee still plays havoc with Gabriel's thoughts, but some things become clear under her pitiless gaze. Where is Anisa? Why can't she feel him? Is it the Jubilee?

Gabriel remembers when both sides of the family gathered for a July fourth celebration when he was seven. Gabriel kissed Anisa's cheek and exclaimed how much he loved her, and Uncle Russell said something strange: "Regnas are alligators, Gabriel." And before Gabriel could ask him what he meant, an ice cream appeared, and the thought shuffled to the back of his mind.

Alligators. What did Russell mean by alligators? But Gabriel did know. He always knew on some level, and now, when he no longer has the luxury of not knowing, this memory pushes to the front. Older alligators will eat younger ones to survive or to ensure they remain the apex predator. Isn't that what a Regna is at the end of the day? An apex predator? Why are Regnas only born to suitable families?

Gabriel is aware of all the stored ley energy in the twins, and he remembers that long-ago visit to Mount Rushmore when his body hummed so violently with ley energy he thought he would explode. On that hot August night, his great-great-grandmother visited him, unbeknownst to his parents. Anisa took his burgeoning power and locked it away in his head, bottled it up, and buried it. But when she did, she left behind an imprint of her misgiving and guilt. Gabriel inherited that, a maelstrom whirling around him in a million bits of splintered fear and pain, all too willing to cut him down.

The coppery taste of blood fills his mouth, and he wonders when he bit the inside of his cheek. He thinks of Zuko, alone and bleeding for the crime of being his. He reaches out to Zuko's and finds him alive and in pain.

"I'm sorry, Zuko. Hold on." Gabriel sends the thought with all his strength. He remembers saying it to Joe. Will he fail again?

Two emotions rule the universe—fear and greed—or at least this tiny corner of it. What was it that Sellers said about his pain and his power? *Stop fighting the voice, and let it become part of you because it is.*

And then, there is the thought Russell inadvertently pushed into him, or was it inadvertent? *Five hundred. There are five hundred of these brutal baby Regna nuclear reactors walking around in the world, ready to explode.*

Is that what Gabriel is? A nuclear reactor? His parents always said it's fine to be a Media. Oh, how they smothered him with low expectations. Anisa damaged him to make her life convenient. She diverted the true path of his soul. She dammed up his power and created the voice, this splintered part of his personality. So now, with little time in his life remaining, Gabriel lets all that anger, sharpened over time to a razor's edge, cut into him and draw blood. He listens to the voice and opens the cage Anisa built for it. For him. He lets it all crash down. The pain and the power so intimately intertwined, wash over him until they seep into his cells. He accepts a poisoned ocean of it, and he forgives Anisa. Gabriel forgives his parents, and he forgives Joe for never loving him. Gabriel is happy that Joe found happiness, however briefly, with Aki.

Gears click into place in his mind like a bicycle chain that gets back in the groove. He embraces the waterfall and allows the deluge to crash down on him. Maybe it will kill him. Would that be such a bad thing? No one should have this kind of power. Not even him.

He sees something in his heart and finds Sellers there. He half expects it to surprise him, but it doesn't. Deciding to accept himself for what he is and scared of what he might find, Gabriel lets himself be what he always has been. He's frightened, but that's okay. Isn't it? He's complicated. He's a man of many things. Too many of them are faults. Most importantly, he's a man in love, but not with Joe, and that is a surprise.

Adept power moves exponentially through the ranks. An Incepto has the power of two and a Media the power of four. Most adepts are Inceptos or Medias. Gabriel's mother is a Provectus, and his father is Periti. A Periti has a power of sixteen. Peritis are proud and respected adepts capable of amazing feats. Then comes a Provectus, 256 on the adept scale. Powerful and fearsome, they are the adept elite, recruited for law enforcement and to defend the clan. And lastly comes the Regna, 65,536 on the adept scale.

This is what clicks into place now in Gabriel. The voice merges with him, and Regna power surges within him. He can sense every heartbeat and touch every consciousness for miles. Looking into Keira's, he sees an oil slick cloud. Patriarch Meyer ordered her to kill Gabriel, and she relishes the order. Gabriel notices something missing in her, but not so with the twins. They're here to do their duty to the clan.

Gabriel reaches out and embraces their power, which is nothing to him now. He can break every bone in their bodies and drop them unceremoniously. The bruising memory of Anisa burns in him—that day when she ascended to Regna and experienced the same thing he is now. All those dead witches and she carries the weight of those souls to this day. That's the thing with adepts when they pass down a memory. They learn from the mistakes of others.

"Have it your way," Keira says, but her smile slips when she says it, and a flicker of fear so unfamiliar to her crosses her face.

"You're right, Keira," Gabriel says. "We don't have time for this."

Gabriel cuts off the oxygen to Keira and the twins until they squirm and lose consciousness on the floor. Next, he opens a portal and calmly walks through.

When Gabriel teleports into Barbara's living room, he's surprised to see Sellers and his brothers. At least, he assumes they're Sellers's brothers. They share the same haughty look and spiky black hair.

Every molecule in the room comes into focus—the blood of Gabriel's brother Connor, and Zuko's searing agony because the Mumbai adepts no longer block his pain. The panic flop sweat of Ankit's team hits Gabriel in the nose, and he welcomes it.

"What are you doing here?" Sellers exclaims. "Can't you see I'm rescuing you?"

"Ankit," Gabriel says. "And Sellers. Having a party without me?"

"I have Barbara," Ankit says. "She's Koli and has diplomatic immunity. I'm taking her and the data. Tell the Pyu and your crows to let us go before this turns into an international incident."

"'Crows,'" Sellers exclaims. "Just because I detained you is no reason to use slurs."

Gabriel spares Sellers a quick smile and turns on Aung's adepts. "Go home. This stalemate is over."

They say nothing in reply and, instead, attack in well-trained unison—two of them with telekinetic energy and two with a psychic attack.

Gabriel laughs and projects a roar into them: *I am Regna Gabriel Francis Kelly. I'm sending you to a mine in the Mogok Stone Track. Don't come back. You don't want me in Rangoon.*" Gabriel opens his consciousness as Keira did, and one of the Pyu adepts soaks his pants.

"Sell, will you kindly drop the containment spell?"

"Certainly, dear sir." Using the athame, Sellers scrapes the wooden floor and a surge of energy is released.

Gabriel nods and, with a wave of his hand, opens a portal to where he bought the rubies. He pushes the Pyu through. Via Zuko, Gabriel briefly catches the sweet scent of the dense Burmese jungle.

"We're here to rescue him?" one of the Sellers's brothers asks.

"Zuko," Gabriel exclaims. The dog's ragged breathing echoes in the room, but he manages to open one soulful brown eye at Gabriel. "I'm here," he says and holds the dog in a gentle embrace.

"You're a Regna of the Salem House?" Ankit says. "You have no right to hold us. I'm a designate of the Koli government."

"Give me the drive," Gabriel says.

"No. It's ours, and so is Barbara."

"That's right," Barbara says. "I'll have that data yet."

Gabriel considers his choices and it's like peering over a cliff. Ankit is right. The Koli have a case to be made, and he has no right to seize it.

The Koli must have some sharing agreement with the Angeles. Gabriel can force Ankit to stay while he summons Russell and Anisa, but all they'll do is punt it to the Regna Assembly and some kind of political settlement. Let the Koli and the Angeles fight it out. *I have the password, but I need Barbara. She's in this up to her neck.*

"Leave with the data, but not with Barbara. Sever her ties to the Koli government and leave with the drive."

"No," Barbara cries. "I'm a Koli asset."

"Not anymore," Ankit says. "As special envoy of the Koli House, I release you, Barbara Bates, from our service."

Gabriel nods to Sellers, and he drops the containment spell around Ankit.

Ankit nods in return. He opens a portal, and for a brief second, Gabriel sees the plants in Shreyas Anand's office before Ankit steps through.

The brothers stand there, soaked in sweat and blood, looking at one another.

Connor, Sellers's oldest brother, approaches him and places a hand on his shoulder. "Mom just bought you that shirt. She's gonna be pissed."

"We'll bill House Salem."

Gabriel faces the Collinsworth brothers. "Thank you, I owe you." He then points at Barbara. "Don't let her out of your sight. I'll be back for her. I'm taking Zuko to the hospital." And he teleports away.

Chapter Thirty-Five

BURNING

The first historical burning we can find in adept records was in 1287. From the patriarch's description, the burned adept suffered from what today would be best described as schizophrenia.

—National Intelligence Strategy White Paper: Top Secret (TS): Release of this document will cause severe damage to the security of the United States—Adept Assets

THE BAR IN the Seaport district has oversized windows and an upscale clientele. Some enjoy a drink only until their table is ready in the upstairs Michelin-star restaurant, but most are here to socialize and imbibe. Detective Herrera loves the bar because there's no menu. This encourages talking with the mixologist and agreeing on an appropriate tipple, or the bartender will create one. When Herrera chose the place, he said, "We're gonna need a special drink."

Through the window, Herrera spots Rizzo striding down the street, her coat whipping behind her. She opens the door and immediately spots him in his discrete corner.

"Sorry I'm late," she says, taking a seat.

"I don't think two minutes counts as late," Herrera replies with a wink.

"The woman behind me with the purple jacket and pearls. She's taken quite an interest in you."

"Who can blame her?" Herrera says.

"She took your photo."

"She what?"

"Did you notice the man she's with? Don't look." Rizzo's face becomes an emotionless mask. "What did I say about knowing your surroundings, Detective Herrera? If I were to ask you to describe everyone in this bar, could you do it?"

"Ah."

"They look so much alike," Rizzo says. "I'd guess they're related, not a couple. They're probably brother and sister. The girl looks like a young Elizabeth Taylor."

"Who's that?" Herrera asks.

When the bartender comes to take their order, Rizzo gestures for her to lean in close and says, "I'm a police officer," and discretely shows her badge. "I'm going to ask you to look as if you're taking our photo, but I want a photo of the couple three tables behind us to my right. The man is dressed in a white linen shirt, gold cufflinks, a Rolex watch, and a blue suit jacket. His companion—"

"I see them." The bartender takes Rizzo's phone in hand. "Smile," she says with enthusiasm and makes a good show of taking the photo, then deftly returns the phone.

"Thank you. Let me know if you ever want to consider police work. And may I have a glass of champagne?"

Herrera lets out a breath. "That was smooth."

"I'm sending the photo in now. Shirley in forensics will run it." Rizzo studies the image. "Who are you? Are you adepts, or have I met my first witch?" Rizzo hits send. "In other news," she says in a light tone, "it's all good. The paint on the fire hydrant and the paint from Peter Brandon's car is an exact match."

"That is good news. Are you going to close the case?"

"That's why I'm here. I'm going to write two reports. One for you and me, and one for the official police record. Have you read Martin's work? In particular, his PhD dissertation, like I asked?"

"Yes. I read it twice. I've been up all night."

"Me too," Rizzo agrees, her eyes taking on a faraway look. "In one of my first interviews with Peter Brandon, he mentioned Martin's theories. I thought they were all theoretical...well, more hypothetical than theoretical. I chalked it up to ivy tower navel gazing. I couldn't believe it was real, but I had to follow the evidence."

"I couldn't believe it until last night," Herrera says, staring into the abyss of his drink. "Remember the banging in the police bathroom? The state of the ceiling? The same day Kelly dropped off his passport with no record of his entry."

"Yes," Rizzo says. "We know Brandon drove to Manchester, New Hampshire, twelve hours after Martin asked for a divorce, then drove back with poison and used it to kill his husband. Yet, he passes every lie detector test when he says he has no memory of it."

She adjusts a pin in her hair and sighs.

"It stands to reason he contacted the Anands of Jeebom immediately," Herrera says. "In fact, it's likely, but wouldn't Martin have guessed that?"

"We have no record of that either. No text, phone call, or e-mail."

"He knew Gabriel Kelly, and we saw what Kelly can do. Maybe he thought Gabriel would protect him?"

"Maybe," Rizzo says. "Gabriel Kelly and his entire family are our special project from here on out."

They raise their glasses and toast.

"I have one last piece of news," Rizzo says. "Gabriel Kelly wants to see Peter Brandon."

*

THE BLARING BUZZER alerts the guard that the visitors have arrived. It's a brutal sound, as if from the depths of hell. Gabriel looks at the guard, and he's tempted to probe him for signs of insanity because he must be insane, listening to that all day. The guard rises from his chair with a heavy sigh and begins the bureaucratic kabuki dance necessary to admit visitors to see a capital murder suspect.

Finally, Peter is led into the waiting area and an empty chair. The clanking of his shackles makes Gabriel wince.

Rizzo asks, "How are you getting along? Your attorney will arrange bail soon."

"Are you the good cop today?" Peter quips, looking between her and Herrera. Without waiting for a reply, he turns to Gabriel. "And why are you here? What do you want? Angry because you can't have Joe?"

"I'm here because you're innocent." Gabriel delivers the words as plainly as he can. He remembers when Uncle Russell uttered them when he was in jail. He needs Peter to believe him as he believed his uncle. Herrera gasps at Gabriel's statement, but Rizzo's face is tawny stone.

The anger emanating from Peter leaves his body, and he relaxes as his expression takes on a wistful look. "Do they have to be here?" Peter asks, gesturing at the detectives.

Rizzo nods a subtle yes and attempts a disarming smile. She fails.

"Just look at me," Gabriel says. "Imagine you're pouring a glass of wine on your deck, and we're about to chat."

"That's a nice thought," Peter replies. "But I don't see that happening. Not ever again."

"Do you remember when we met?"

Peter studies him, centering his gaze. "Yes. I remember. You were my first fan. You walked up to me after my first solo concert at Berkely. I thought you were trying to ask me out. I'm glad you didn't. You don't have a chance, even now. Sorry. Not my type."

Peter pauses, expecting a reaction, but when Gabriel doesn't, he says, "You loved the music but didn't know why, and I liked that."

"That's right. You answered all my questions. Remember when you gave me a list of albums to listen to in order, so I could see how jazz evolved? We have to do the same thing now for Joe. We have to arrange everything in order."

In unison, Gabriel and Peter rub the palms of their hands on their thighs to dry them. Gabriel isn't sure if he's picking up on Peter's anxiety or projecting his into Peter.

"In order? Okay, well, I liked Joe, so I thought I'd throw a dinner party and introduce him to my friends," Peters says. "Do you remember that first dinner? I had no idea he'd date you and not me, but I got him in the end, for all the good it did me."

"The dinner when I first met Joe?" Gabriel asks.

"Yes, do you remember his reaction?"

"He was warm and sweet. He had a way of making me feel that I was fascinating and eloquent."

Peter tilts his head at Gabriel and doesn't respond.

"Ah," Gabriel says. "That's not Joe, is it?"

"No. One of his many faults was that he thought he was better than everyone else. And I thought he was. Barbara, he respected as an equal. If you don't mind me saying, you're not someone he'd normally treat with such respect."

"He knew who I was. He knew what I was, didn't he?"

"You're just figuring that out? Yeah, he understood what you were, right from the beginning. Whatever that is. I think he expected to meet you at the dinner. I suspected something was off, and it bothered me. So, a year later when we were together, after you guys broke up, I snooped. Despite all of Joe's intellectual gifts, cyber security wasn't one of them. Barbara traced your family tree. Did you know that? He had it diagrammed on his computer. There you were, on the side of the family that descended from a white man, not from the Black man your ancestor married later. The side with little political clout. Am I right?"

Gabriel stares at him. Peter *is* right. An adept-less dall human is right. *Barbara was the first to have my family tree though.* "Yes, you are." Gabriel darts his gaze away. He expects Peter to press his advantage, but Peter only half nods in response. "I remember that night. Joe fell in love with my dog Zuko. I just thought he loved dogs."

Peter laughs, one that says, *You and me both.* The smile slowly fades from Peter's face. "Zuko was the key. The dog gave Joe the advantage over Barbara and everyone else. Don't ask me how."

"I know how. Zuko is adept like me. Dogs and humans evolved in this way together. I'm one of the few adepts who can bond with a dog psychically. Joe took Zuko's blood. He said he was going to do a detailed DNA test. Maybe Zuko was a mix of something more than poodle and Bernese Mountain dog, Joe said. What an idiot I was." Gabriel puts his face in his hands and chokes back a sob.

When Gabriel looks up, there's pity in Peter's eyes. It twists Gabriel's stomach that a man wearing shackles and facing life imprisonment pities him. *I may be slow, but I learn.*

"You loved him, but you didn't know him. We have that in common," Peter says. "And since we're doing things in order, it wasn't long after that dinner he left Jeebom and switched to Covian. Joe wasn't the sharing credit type. I remember asking him, 'Will you get Gabriel to help you with the switch?' By then, I figured out your family ran an investment firm. He said, 'I need Gabriel's family, but not Gabriel.'"

"Have you, ah...have you met my uncle Russell? He's shorter than me but comes across as tall. He's dark-skinned and bald, always well dressed. He's a straight bow-tie-wearing Tim Gunn."

Peter pauses, then says, "No, I've never met anyone in your family."

"Did Joe ever talk about his theories with you?"

"Yes. We were married, you know."

"What did he say—" Gabriel leans forward. "—about me?"

"Why?" Peter exclaims.

"Because I think someone—someone like me—tampered with your mind. Compelled you to kill Joe with the poisoned salt. Someone made you want to run me down."

"Compelled me? Someone like you?" Peter hesitates again and stares at the wall. "I thought the abilities he theorized about were something like being aware of someone's thoughts subconsciously. Something that might explain why some people are good at gambling or negotiations, but it's much more than that, isn't it?"

"It's much more than that. Peter, I want to look inside your mind. I want you to speak aloud so Rizzo and Herrera can hear you. I'm asking for your consent to search for evidence of psychic trauma, if there are things you can't tell me. Is there a part of you that believes you did it unwillingly?"

"You're crazy," Peter says.

"Was Joe?" Gabriel retorts.

In one smooth motion, Peter puts his face in his hands. A sound, unearthly and unfamiliar to Gabriel, comes out of his mouth. The monotonous drone, a helpless dirge, draws all matter into it. Gabriel places his hand on Peter's cheek, who grasps it and raises his head to gaze into Gabriel's eyes. Peter nods a solemn *yes*, and Gabriel nods back.

For the first time as a Regna, Gabriel enters another person's consciousness. Entering one can be like hoping to find a particular sentence in a book by randomly opening it. To read one well, you must read it like a book. Search for symbols—just as a page number is a symbol—and follow them.

Gabriel thinks of Joe and focuses on his virtues. He remembers his wit and consuming passion for giving something to the world. He remembers why he loved Joe, why Joe loved Peter, and the joy his talent gave him. That thought takes Gabriel inside a memory of Peter's home. This memory of the two of them together is what Peter wants to last forever. The two of them together in that room is the key.

"Did Covian have a fire drill?" Peter asks Joe with a chuckle.

"No, not today," Joe replies, but in a thick low tone. His eyes meet Peter's, only for a moment.

Peter's heart stops, and he remembers that look in Joe's eyes. Peter figures out Joe wants to end it and struggles to find the words. He recalls that moment before Joe starts talking, and Peter's body turns to stone.

"I haven't been happy for a while," Joe says. "Haven't you noticed? This isn't working. Not for me."

Peter says nothing, and his pain is a dagger in Gabriel's heart. Peter knows there is no working on it, but he asks anyway. And then the anger comes that, to Joe, he was a means to an end. Then the bitterness fades to sad resignation.

"Are you okay?" Joe asks.

Peter raises his eyes to meet Joe's. "No. No, I'm not."

And then Peter starts the car to drive to Provincetown. After one night, he goes north to buy sodium fluoroacetate. It's all too fast and too sudden, too adept. Whoever did this tried to cover their tracks. Someone erased Peter's memory, but there are places in our minds that forget nothing. Anyone who's experienced their life flash before them knows we retain every moment and conversation. Gabriel wades into the ocean of Peter's memory and focuses on Ankit because Ankit has to be the killer. Gabriel imagines his accent and cadence. There's nothing.

Next, he imagines Keira. At a first meeting, she wouldn't be threatening. He searches for a young woman in need, or maybe a jazz fan, and finds nothing. For Keira, he searches for flashes of gyms and ambition, but those hooks reveal nothing.

Gabriel sucks in a breath, and his heart races. *The murder weapon. Focus on that.* And then Gabriel is inside a memory of Barbara having dinner with Joe and Peter.

"You worked for your father's waste management company?" she asks.

"Yes," Peter replies. We used sodium fluoroacetate to kill rodents and other pests around the sites. I hated that."

"Sodium fluoroacetate," Barbara replies. "We have that in the lab. So many chemicals have so many uses."

In Peter's memory, Barbara stands as if in bright sunshine.

The memory morphs into another excellent day. The summer season on Cape Cod is still a month away, and the seasonal employees haven't arrived in town yet. It's still possible to get a table without booking a week in advance. Peter loves the spring in Provincetown, and his joy shoots through Gabriel's body, making him smile. Maybe this spring, Peters thinks, he'll landscape the front of the house himself since he'll have time. Why not stay here the entire summer? He doesn't need to be in Boston to sell the ostentatious apartment that Joe insisted on buying with his money. This summer, he decides he'll be the lead in his own rom-com.

Peter just sits down on his Adirondack chair with a cup of tea—because he threw all the coffee away—when Barbara appears out of nowhere. What is Joe's ex-boss doing in Provincetown? Peter takes in her dark-blue suit and pearl necklace. "What a surprise," he exclaims. "You look dressed for work." Why, oh, why did I say that? he admonishes himself. It's not my business if that's how she wants to dress. He tells her, "For a second, I was gonna ask how you knew I was here, but I told you this morning."

"Life is full of surprises," she says. Her voice is young and clear, but it rings in his mind, not in his ears. Everything makes sense when she talks to him. He wants to please her.

"You were right about Joe," Barbara says.

And then an idea comes to Peter. He forgets about Joe's ex-boss and drives to New Hampshire and from there to Boston, where he puts poison in a salt container already filled with poison by Barbara, stores the rest on his side of the closet, and drives back to Provincetown. It all seems like a dream.

Barbara is an adept.

Gabriel lets go of Peter's face and lets himself experience the odd mixture of his own pain intermingled with Peter's. He gives in to the avalanche of loss and lowers his head. It's sweeping over him when something stronger takes hold. Peter's love for Joe seeps into Gabriel, and for a moment, he doesn't know where his love for Joe begins and Peter's ends.

Chapter Thirty-Six

WITCHES

Adepts have divided themselves into factions, calling one faction "witches". Our witch assets initially believed their abilities to be supernatural, when in fact, their ancestors have found a way to pass down their memories and fire-dormant genes. So-called witches believe they're in possession of their ancestor's consciousness.

—National Intelligence Strategy White Paper: Top Secret (TS): Release of this document will cause severe damage to the security of the United States—Adept Assets

BENEATH THE FLATTERING light of the grand Louisburg Square library sits the diminutive Regna. To her right sits Russell, the patriarch of the original Salem-7 adept families. They're not really the seven founding families, but everyone loves a legend.

Gabriel catches a conversation on the grid where someone mentions the untimely death of Dr. Martin. He's described as the dall scientist who "unlocked our genetic code." He was that, but so much more. People have a hard time uttering the words "died" and "murdered," and Gabriel often wonders why. A person isn't less dead if they've passed on or gone to their great reward. As witches conjure spells, society conjures words to soften the blow, but still, it stings.

Gabriel's parents, Russell's wife, Priya, and the heads of the other families sit together. It's like an adept mafia, thinks Gabriel, chuckling to himself. The high priestess is vaping on Anisa's left, her black bouffant gleaming unnaturally. Patriarch Meyer of Southern California sits next to Russell. To Russell's other side sits the enigmatic General Aung. The smug Shreyas Anand and his wife, Deepa, sit at the end.

Gabriel wonders how often Anisa and Russell hold these meetings and realizes he never cared before today. The grid is abuzz, snippets of conversations include, "The families are having an emergency meeting. The Regna and the patriarch are presiding." The buzz must mean Russell wants the adept capitals to know he's assembling his people.

"It's not the Cuban Missile Crisis yet, but it's getting there," Russell says.

He tosses the remark off so casually that Gabriel Googles it. Well, he muses, Russell was an adult then.

The Jubilee has left behind a massive headache. That may explain Zuko's no-nonsense mood. The wary, wounded dog eyes the room suspiciously, disliking so many unfamiliar smells in his den. Zuko would not lie in his sick bed and limps beside Gabriel. Gabriel's anger at Barbara and Joe drills a hole in his heart. Maybe he was naive. If he was then; he isn't now.

Sellers leans into him. "Don't embarrass me in front of the high priestess."

"I'll try. By the way, avoid the coffee. My sister made it. It's terrible."

Regna Anisa levitates out of her chair and assumes the lotus position five feet above the Moroccan rug. At her age, sitting cross-legged is nothing short of amazing. Does his great-great-grandmother have a personal trainer? It isn't a ridiculous question as Gabriel watches her command the room. She's old and wizened but remarkably fit. Her display of power suggests her ability to fly. *A bold display of power is the whole point, though, isn't?*

A hush falls upon the room, an eerie silence as all eyes turn to Regna Anisa Aboud Walker.

Russell stands, taking center stage and says, "The keys to our genetic makeup have been recovered. Its ownership shall be decided at the Regna Assembly. The threat of our exposure has been averted. Perhaps only temporarily, but the immediate danger has passed. Our thanks go to Keira D'Cruz of the Angeles, who could not be here today as she suffered injuries at the hands of, as of yet, unknown assailants in the course of her duties. The Salem thank Patriarch Meyer for his efforts."

A smattering of applause erupts in the room, and Gabriel feels sick.

"Patriarch Meyer has alerted us to the dangers of a drug manufactured by his company that, when abused, deadens our sight and induces euphoria. It is highly addictive and has disrupted adept lives. Patriarch Meyer has pledged to cease production."

Russell pauses, and another tepid smattering of applause breaks out, notably not from Gabriel. He decides to project to the Angeles patriarch.

"*So close, Pat, you were so close. What will you do next?*"

"Hey, Gabriel," Sellers says, his brow furrowed. "What about the note that Rizzo found?"

"Oh, um, I don't know," Gabriel replies, his concentration broken. "I've thought about talking to her more about it, but maybe Joe did write it. He probably was afraid of me. Or Peter wrote it. I'm happy not knowing. Joe is dead. So many things aren't important now."

He keeps to himself that he suspects his uncle.

"How's Zuko?" Sellers asks.

"He'll be fine. No permanent injuries, and I've taken his memories of that night."

Sellers does his classic arched eyebrow look. "He's a noble canine, but that's redundant, isn't it?"

Gabriel tries to move, but he can't. Before fear takes hold, he hears Anisa's clear, young, vibrant voice. She's detaining him.

"*Your powers are maturing faster than you.*"

"*Regna Anisa, I—*" His thought trails off, and then Anisa speaks again.

"*You signed a blood pact with the witches.*" It isn't a question, but from the look on her face, Gabriel isn't sure if he should remain quiet or explain himself.

"*I did, Regna, by my friend Sellers's athame.*"

"*Again...*" Anisa pauses, and Gabriel finds himself dreading what comes next. "*You have freely given your blood, your genetic material.*"

"*Yes, but it was Sellers, and we were on the trail of a killer.*"

"*The ends justify the means?*" Anisa asks, and the image of General Aung flashes in Gabriel's head; he knows Anisa sees it too.

Gabriel's face warms with embarrassment. "*No, but what we did *was important."*

"Important, yes. I believe, you believe that. You have manipulated dall minds in contravention of our laws. You have given our blood to a dall scientist of a rival house. You conspired to share our genetic secrets."

Gabriel thinks about interrupting but decides he deserves this.

"All of this you have done without advice or counsel from those of us who govern this clan. We try to come to decisions that benefit all adept kind. Unlike me, you feel equipped to make decisions on your own."

Anisa's eyes are unblinking and sad. The sadness hurts even worse than not being able to speak.

"That will change. You are a Regna now, and Regnas serve." Anisa pauses and regards him with solemnity. *"You are a Regna woefully ill-prepared to handle your abilities. Our life is one of service, not blundering around the world with little understanding of what you leave in your wake. I forbid the use of your powers until we present you to the Assembly and you begin training. You will need that training if you wish to maintain your sanity and your position."*

"You toyed with my mind," Gabriel pushes into Anisa.

"I blocked your powers. Powers that would have overwhelmed you and your sanity, and they still might."

"You had no right to do that."

"It was that or your death. As a Regna of this House, you will learn adept law of which you are so ignorant. If you do not like our laws, then strive to change them. You did not grow into your powers like me and other Regnas. You are the most dangerous of adepts. You were born Regna. Your friend's death set you on the adaptation path because my circuit breakers left you a Media. The trauma broke the

chains around your power. Power such as that in a child drives com-munities insane. We often kill Regna Born because the risk is too great. Lecture me after you have been forced to kill an insane five-year-old raging Regna who has laid waste to half a town because, one day, you will have to do the same. Do you want those memories now? Do you want the memories of your mother begging me to contain your power?"

Gabriel says nothing and withdraws into himself.

"We must focus on the future and your role in the clan. I named you after Gabriel, the archangel who defends his people. Be the shield and become the sword only when necessary."

Of course, she named me Gabriel.

"Will you be able to protect and serve if you're bound to the witches?"

"What? I'm not bound." Gabriel tries to hide his shock, but it's futile.

"Aren't you? One last thing. Talk to your uncle only after your crow has sealed the room. You are not ready to handle the onslaught of thoughts at the full Regna level, and we are surrounded by spies. Leave it to Sellers to ensure your privacy. I am forbidding the use of your powers, and now you know my reasons."

"What do you know about—"

"That is part of the burden in being Regna. We know everything we care to know. Choose what you want to know wisely. Russell will adjourn for half an hour. I will send him to your room."

Gabriel blinks and sees Anisa across the room talking to Meyer. Their communication took place in less than a second. He reaches up to massage his burning head.

"Are you okay?" Sellers asks. "You look like you ate a bad oyster.

Remember your promise not to embarrass me in front of the high priestess."

"Heaven forbid." A million thoughts bear down on Gabriel as if the grid were an invading army. He marshals his defenses until he senses nothing and is practically one of the dall. Being an adept suddenly becomes a burden.

"That's better," Sellers says. "You're looking human again."

"Being Regna is no joke. I'm not sure I like it."

"Yes, well." Sellers smirks. "Some people are born to greatness and some have it thrust upon them. Although, in all seriousness, you are a bit of both."

Sellers moves to touch Gabriel on the shoulder but seems to reconsider and pulls back. Gabriel knows it's because he's a live wire with his newfound abilities, and Sellers doesn't want to risk touching him. He looks around the room and suddenly realizes no one has approached them. In fact, no one stands anywhere near them. Not a soul dares to risk even the briefest eye contact. Gabriel is in a room full of people and yet alone. He can taste their fear, and it's lonely. Gabriel huffs at the memory of being back in the ninth grade because Sellers is once again his only friend, but this time, his friend is afraid to touch him.

"Did you bind me?" Gabriel asks.

"Yes, but the spell, much to the HP's annoyance, is mutual. We are blood-bound to help each other. I found a way to betray her and keep my word. She said I'm a real witch now."

"But I didn't call for help."

"You didn't have to ask."

"What if the witches and adepts go to war?"

"It's up to us to make sure they don't."

"I felt your brothers' need to come to my aid," Gabriel says.

"Yes, they share my blood, much to my surprise."

"Sell." Gabriel touches his arm. "We'll have to discuss this more later. In the meantime, I need a favor."

Sellers sighs. "I'm in the Gabriel Kelly favor business. It's quite the cottage industry."

"Not exactly a favor," Gabriel says with a smirk. "I'll pay. I need you to seal my room. I need to talk to my uncle in private."

"Oh, really?" Sellers raises his hands in mock alarm. "Affairs-of-state Regna Gabriel." He bows ever so slightly.

"Can you spare me the dramatics and just send me a bill?"

"Yes, sir," Sellers says. "I'm obliged to tell you my rates have gone up. I'm friends with a Regna now."

"Thanks, Sell. When my uncle comes to my room, seal it."

Sellers nods, and they leave the library with every eye on them. Sellers doesn't follow Gabriel into his room; he waits outside. When Russell approaches, they nod wordlessly at each other. Gabriel shuts the door, and Sellers invokes the spell, nicking himself with the athame to form a blood seal. Its power tugs against Gabriel's mind.

Seal the room,

Quiet as a tomb.

See no more,

We ignore.

"A witch's blood seal," Russell says. "Impressive. You have a valuable ally in Sellers, who I'm sure gets you a good rate. What's so important? We're in the midst of a summit, in case you haven't noticed."

Gabriel stands by the bay windows on the far side of the room. There's a king-sized bed, a well-used desk, and a chair for guests. Russell reads the room and continues to stand. They are as far away from each other as possible.

"What's going to happen to Peter and Barbara?" Gabriel asks. "What's going to happen to Joe's data? I want Aki protected. He's a Salem asset from now on."

"Right to the point. I like that in a Regna. Of all the Regnas I've come to know, you would be the only one with that quality. Try not to lose it."

Russell takes a deep breath through his broad patrician nose. "All right, first, you are a Regna of the Salem House. You have a voice in its governance. Even a junior Regna has a right to know. Peter Brandon will go free. About now, the Boston Police Department is coming to grips with the fact they've permanently misplaced the physical evidence against him. Barbara Bates will confess to the murder of her colleague. We will align with the Houses Koli and Angeles and come to an agreement in a world where our genetic make-up is mapped as if it's on Google."

"Align?" Gabriel says. "The Koli and the Angeles tried to kill me."

"An unfortunate turn of events. I think we can all agree."

"Unfortunate turn of events?" Gabriel bellows.

"Quite. I don't have time to soothe your bruised ego or to assuage your hurt feelings. You serve this House and its interests. That is your function."

"Uncle," Gabriel says in a quiet tone. "Did you manipulate me during this?"

"Manipulate is a strong word. Steer is better."

"You were the one responsible for tipping me off to the mine in Burma. Did you know House Pyu thought I was a spy and would kill me? You told them I was a spy."

"Anisa is aging. Who knows how long she'll be with us?" Russell says. "This house needs a Regna."

"You wrote the note. You rolled the dice on my life, on my ascension."

Russell looks at Gabriel in the same way his father did when he failed to grasp physics. "You're why the Regnas are so dangerous. You have so much power and so little discernment. You still don't get it? You never ascended. Our powers are wrapped in our minds, and yours created an identity for your imprisoned power. You needed time to grow, Anisa said. I decided we were running out of time and couldn't afford to wait for your frustratingly slow maturation. I put you in circumstances that demanded you break out of Anisa's prison, and you successfully assimilated your Regna abilities as I knew you would."

"Knew?"

"Hoped," Russell retorts. "The Angeles were on the cusp of mapping our secret. I had to act."

"So, you sent me into Burma, into a dangerous situation, because you needed a Regna? The Pyu almost killed me."

"But they didn't, and I now have leverage over the data you foolishly gave away and a Regna heir."

Russell walks to the door. "If you'll excuse me"—he places his hand on the doorknob—"I have a summit to run."

Russell opens the door and breaks the blood seal with a subtle *pop* as Gabriel imagines every witch and adept in the house thrilled to know they can hear what Russell will say next.

"Your time, nephew, of moral certainty and being unfettered by the demands of leadership is over, and for that, I am indeed sorry."

Epilogue

GHOSTS

Adepts can share more than their thoughts. They can download complex memories and pass them to another adept. The adepts who agreed to speak to us describe it as another person living inside you.

—National Intelligence Strategy White Paper: Top Secret (TS): Release of this document will cause severe damage to the security of the United States—Adept Assets

GABRIEL'S SHOES BITE his ankles. Wearing this pair to go apartment hunting was a poor choice. A small price to pay, he thinks, for finally living on his own. If he's going to make some decisions and enforce others, he will decide for himself where to live.

Rain pummels the apartment's window, but through the cascading ribbons of water, he sees, of all things, a turkey. Living in his old neighborhoods with his parents or Anisa, he's never seen a wild turkey. This new place, with its diverse families and immigrant population, welcomes turkeys. Perhaps it will welcome him too?

"I'll take it," he says to the realtor, never averting his eyes from the water-battered window.

"Excellent!" she exclaims, her eyes lighting up. A young woman, no older than twenty-five, she sends her excitement humming through the air. "I'll put your application in, but I don't see a problem." She quickly gathers up her papers, shoves them in a folder and stands. "Need a lift back to the office?"

"No, thanks," Gabriel replies. "I'll stay and explore the new hood."

"Okay, but I have to lock up now. You don't have to go home, but you can't stay here, not yet anyway." She laughs, and Gabriel joins her.

Is this her first sale? Gabriel opens his mind to her but remembers his promise and shuts it down. He pledged not to use his abilities until he reports to the Regnas for training. He did briefly sense her disappointment in the stubbornly cold weather. *Spring in Boston is such a crapshoot.*

A dull ache takes up residence behind his left eye. Gabriel imagines it's the result of the cage door that imprisoned his Regna powers swinging open again and again battering some remnant of his bruised psyche.

If this were an old movie, Gabriel thinks, or a novel by Hammett or Chandler, he'd light a cigarette, and the scene would fade. Standing outside his new apartment building, he studies a bus idling at a stop sign. Its windshield wipers are a calming metronome on this raw day. He considers boarding it to see where it goes but instead continues to stand statue still, watching with dark and unfocused eyes as it pulls away. Today is Sunday, and on Sundays, he usually joins his parents and sister for a lavish midday meal. But not today. Gabriel zips up his jacket and pulls his hood over his head—his fingers as numb as the dull ache behind his left eye.

A black crow flutters over and perches on a wrought iron fence. It squawks and puffs out its chest. In its left talon is a small scroll.

What are you doing in Dorchester? the scroll says in Sellers's flowing script.

Gabriel smiles and glances around but sees no one. "What does it look like?" he says. "I'm finding a place to live."

Sellers appears on his right side, bearing an enormous umbrella and an open, wide-eyed expression.

"You grew out your hair," Sellers says.

"I knew you'd like it."

"You take great advice."

"Why the subterfuge? You could've asked to come along."

"Really?" Sellers responds with an arched eyebrow. "That would entail you returning my calls or texts."

"Point taken. I'm glad you chose now to manifest. I've been meaning to call."

"I heard about Barbara. Are you okay?"

"Yeah, I'm dealing. Is that umbrella big enough for both of us?"

"But of course, dear sir. I am nothing if not magnanimous."

Gabriel slides in next to Sellers, the only man in his life taller than he, and enjoys the respite from the cold drizzle.

"Barbara was an adept, Sell. I never picked up on it."

"She had good cover. The Indian coven warded her well, but what of her coven? Sorry, her House."

"Barbara's family died during the blitz when she was getting her doctorate at Oxford. Afterward, she came to America to live with distant dall relatives. The war helped her immigrate unnoticed, and the Stuart House lost track of her. She was perfect for the Koli. She was surrounded by dall and lost touch with her adept culture."

"I heard she confessed. But she's adept. Wow."

"She *was* adept. Anisa burned her," Gabriel says, hanging his head low.

"Enough of that. How did you lose so much weight?"

"I think the voice loved to eat. My appetite isn't what it used to be."

Sellers chuckles. "None of us are what we used to be. Part of me is sorry he's gone, and he *is* gone, right?"

"I think Joe didn't deserve the pedestal I put him on, and you were right about a few things."

"Just a few?"

"More than a few. I'm already thinking of Joe more as he was and not who I wanted him to be. And don't get me wrong; he was great—charming, extravagant, selfish, and vainglorious."

"Mostly vainglorious," Sellers says.

"Neither Barbara nor Joe were who I thought they were. For that matter, you're not who I thought you were. I was blind to that too."

"And you. What about you? Are you who you thought you were?"

"No, me most of all."

"What happens to the data?" Sellers asks.

"I don't know. The Regna Assembly meets next week. It'll be decided then. I don't see Uncle Russell giving up that diamond with the password. He's taken it, by the way." Gabriel doesn't mention the secret to infusing stones with ley energy. Did Russell seize that for himself? Or is it lost?

"Gabe, I need to ask you for a favor."

"Me? Of course, anything."

"You've heard of the Eternal Flame?"

"Oh, yes, it may be the most ley-rich jewel in the world. I hear some witches and adepts faint when they're near it. What about it?" Gabriel would give anything to see the gem. "Can you get me in to examine it? Will the high priestess let you?"

"Well, Gabe, that's the thing. The Eternal Flame has, well, it's gone missing."

"Missing? You mean stolen."

"The HP is angry and scared. Mostly scared. She's called in my ex—"

"Not Wally," Gabriel exclaims. "Was it Wally?"

"No. Not Wallace."

"Raul? I liked him."

"No. It was Bradford. Okay? The HP called on Bradford."

"Why him?" Gabriel asks. "He was the worst."

"He's powerful, and his family is well connected. He has a preternatural gift for...finding lost things."

"You mean stolen things."

"Yes, stolen. Please keep this to yourself. It's very delicate. The Eternal Flame is the symbol of our coven, a physical representation of our power. For it to disappear—"

"Okay. What's your favor?"

Sellers breathes in deeply, and despite the obfuscation spell, he pulls down the umbrella to more fully cloak their faces. He pitches his voice at a whisper. "The HP asked me to ask you to help us find it, but only if you can keep it quiet. I mean, the idea of adepts in our business—"

"She did, did she? She's a smart lady."

Sellers blinks in surprise. "She is, but why did you say that?"

"Because she knows you can trust me. She knows I think you walk on water."

"What?"

"Sell, I love you. And not in the way I thought I loved Joe by projecting what I wanted onto him. I love you because of who you are and who you proved to be. You stood by me through the lost data, the other Houses coming after me, through Joe and a bunch of other romantic train wrecks. It's always you I turn to, and it's always you who answers the call. You never said it, but I know how much you risked helping me, helping an adept. You put me first, and I want to spend the rest of my life putting you first. If you'll have me."

Gabriel leans up and kisses Sellers softly at first and then more and more urgently. Gabriel envisions this kiss being broadcast on the grid—Patriarch's Nephew Kisses Witch—and he doesn't care.

Sellers breaks the kiss, smiling broadly, his joy a battering ram into Gabriel's psyche.

"For the record, I can walk on water."

"I had no doubt."

"You're the only one that calls me Sell."

"And you're the only one who calls me Gabe—that isn't related to me."

"There's a cafe over there." Sellers points across the street. "Want to get out of the rain?"

"Yeah," Gabriel says.

Sellers takes Gabriel's hand, his long, elegant fingers lacing with Gabriel's shorter, thicker ones. Gabriel senses hair gel, the aroma of fresh scones, and way in the back of Sellers's mind, something else. He grips Sellers's hand, and Sellers's trepidation, alongside his love, is a shock. The emotions are as interwoven as their fingers. Gabriel is, after all, a Regna of the Salem House. Will their people reject them?

"What's next?" asks Sellers.

"I'm not sure," Gabriel replies. "But someone once said that every story starts in the middle, but this feels like the beginning."

Acknowledgements

I want to thank my acquiring editor, Elizabetta McKay, for her patience and keen eye.

I also want to thank Julie Hennrikus of Sisters In Crime for being the first to say, "You can do this."

A huge thank you to my beta readers, Dexter Sealy, Russell Willis, and Tom Favazza, especially Dexter, who must've read each draft ten times.

Thank you, Ric' Little, for being my sensitivity reader.

About the Author

Erick grew up in Lunenburg, Massachusetts, where it was impossible to find fantasy novels with diverse characters and points of view. Erick lives in Boston with his husband and their dog, a giant Bernadoodle named Niko, and writes the books he always wanted to read and the lyrics he always wanted to hear. When he's not writing, walking the dog, or making pasta, Erick is a vice president at an asset management firm.

Regna Born is Erick's debut novel with NineStar Publishing.

Email
erickinboston@hotmail.com

X
@erickinboston

Website
www.erickholmberg.com

BlueSky
Erickholmberg.bsky.social

TikTok
@erickholmbergwrites

Instagram
erickholmbergwrites

www.ninestarpress.com

www.facebook.com/ninestarpress

www.facebook.com/groups/NineStarNiche

www.twitter.com/ninestarpress

www.instagram.com/ninestarpress

bsky.app/profile/ninestarpress.bsky.social

www.threads.net/@ninestarpress